THE TABLE

THE TABLE

DENNIS LAMBERT

ENROUTE

En Route Books & Media
5705 Rhodes Avenue, St. Louis, MO 63109
Contact us at contactus@enroutebooksandmedia.com

Cover design by TJ Burdick
Cover photo image credit: Debbie Lambert

Paperback ISBN: 978-0-9988940-1-0
E-book ISBN: 978-0-9988940-7-2
LCCN: 2017943421

MORE PRAISE FOR *THE TABLE*

A fascinating Christian legend with a matching contemporary drama, *The Table* will capture your heart and inspire your soul.
　　　　　　　　　　　　　　　　　　　— Ronda Chervin, Ph.D.,
　　　　　　　　　　Professor of Philosophy and Catholic Writer

The Table is a gripping and beautiful story that displays the peculiarity of God's plan and how He can bring all things together for good. Lambert creatively weaves a narrative that follows what one might call a conspiracy of grace that spans over two thousand years. *The Table* serves as a reminder that our needs and God's interest in drawing close to His people are the same as when He set His saving plan into motion through a family in a small town all those year ago.
— Ryan Hanning Ph.D,Asst. Professor of Catholic & Theological Studies University of Mary – Tempe

To my parents, Art and Janet Lambert, to whom I owe the most important thing of all, the gift of my faith.
Thanks, Mom and Dad!

PART ONE

One

"Dad, do you believe in angels?" asked Joseph, distraught.

At the mention of angels, Jacob's mind was whisked back to the bedside of his beloved wife, Rebecca, so many years ago. He would never forget that night.

....

It was near the fourth watch of the night and Jacob hadn't slept in hours. It was unusually chilly outside, being the month of Tammuz. But inside the house it was a different story. The fever Rebecca had been experiencing over the last several days was at its blistering peak. It not only made her sweat as if she were at the well at noon during the summer month of Menachem Av, it made Jacob feel like he was in another place at another time. He began to question whether the heat he was experiencing was really from the radiating temperature of Rebecca's fever, or if it was more of an internal burning as he came to terms with the gravity of the moment unfolding before him.

Rebecca shifted on her sleeping mat, reached out, and brushed her fingers over the leg of the stool near her. Jacob had built the stool during their first month of marriage. He fondly remembered the request Rebecca made of him when he thought he had finished that stool so many years ago. At the time, the request seemed strange and he wondered what the other craftsmen would say if they ever found out. But being so young and so deeply in love, he happily complied with Rebecca's request. From that simple stool forward, everything Jacob built would contain the etching of her three-word request. If a man looked hard enough, he would find the inscription on the upper right-hand corner of the underside of the item. For a moment, Jacob felt a peace as the words filled his mind. He needed those words now more than ever.

The lamp next to the sleeping mat flickered high and low as its oil neared empty. Jacob knelt at his wife's side, fervently wiping her brow with a moist cloth and a tender touch. The washbasin between them also brought back the thought of better times. That very basin was there next to his son at his circumcision and aided in the cleansing of the delicate wounds that had entered him into the House of Israel.

What a good man Joseph has become, and I owe so much of that to you, Rebecca, thought Jacob as he continued to lovingly cool her forehead.

Though he was torn, confused, and near his breaking point, Jacob's face bore a smile of assurance, hoping to ease the pain of his beloved. Rebecca's eyes fluttered open and she smiled, despite her pain.

"Oh, my Jacob, how lucky we've been. So blessed, so filled with happiness! So much so that even now, in this very hour looking upon your sweet and lovely face, I remain happy and feel God's blessing upon us!"

Jacob did all he could to hold back his tears.

"My Becca, yes, we have been blessed. And God's greatest blessing has been our life shared together. You and I are truly one. Know that I love you, both now and forever." He clasped her right hand between his own calloused hands. She tried to squeeze his fingers, but she was too weak. All the same, Jacob felt it and his heart ached.

"Be still, my Becca, and let your hand become one with mine. I will fly with you this night. I will not let you go. I am never letting go."

Tears rolled down Jacob's face as he spoke. His love, his life, and the mother of his child had somewhere else to be. She had a journey ahead of her and he could not follow.

Rebecca's eyes glistened with tears and the steam of her unchecked fever. "And I will never truly leave you, my love. How can I, when I'm being held by a man as strong as you!"

They both began to laugh. As the laughs subsided, Jacob kissed Rebecca's hand and let his tears baptize her fingers with a love that was a gift from God.

Wiping his tears, Jacob replied, "Yes, my love. For certain, tonight I will fly with you as far as I am allowed to go. But promise me that when the Lord calls me, you will come back down to hold my hand and fly with me as well."

Rebecca smiled and said, "I will, indeed. And our flight at that time will be endless."

Just as it seemed that their words would lead to the dawn of a new life for Rebecca, she turned her head with a vitality and quickness of a woman in her prime.

Looking at Jacob she said with an authority that captured her husband's complete attention, "Before I turn in for this longest of nights, I must tell you something; something you must remember, something you must believe and carry in your heart for all times. You will know when to recall it and when to believe it. Do you trust me, Jacob?"

"With my life and the life of our son," he replied.

"Then do not write off what I am about to tell you as the delirium of a dying woman. Do you promise me that?" she demanded.

"Yes, Becca, I promise and trust in what you have to tell me," Jacob said, leaning into her and raising her hand to his heart as he spoke.

Rebecca looked through Jacob's eyes and into his soul, and spoke with total clarity and conviction, "Yesterday morning, when you went to get our water, I was visited by an angel."

"An angel?" Jacob exclaimed.

Her eyes, still fixed on his, convinced him more than any words could. An angel of the Lord did visit her; of this he was convinced.

"I believe you, Becca, please tell me what this angel said to you," he said.

With his heart open, Jacob listened to his wife's last words, the words spoken to her by angels. "Believe what Joseph tells you…"

Rebecca's final words fell from her lips as the oil in the lamp ran out and the flame ceased.

With his hand melted into hers, Jacob leaned forward and, kissing his beloved's forehead, whispered in her ear, "I will believe Joseph. And please know that I'm not letting go. I will fly with you, my love, and I will never let you go."

Two

Jacob had seen and experienced much during his sixty-eight years. He had known the great love of a woman, and had tasted the sweetness of life that only follows when one willfully abandons their soul to the soul of another. For over thirty years, Jacob had the joy of such a partnership with his wife, Rebecca. The half-smile he had given a pretty girl at the well near the town's gate when he was a young man of sixteen, was not only returned by the olive-skinned beauty of fourteen, but it set into motion a series of smiles, countless rounds of laughter, and a pure sense of joy that lasted until God took her from her walk on earth some twenty years ago.

Jacob never harbored any bitterness or resentment toward God for taking her. No, he understood that the Lord gives and that the Lord takes and he trusted God as to His motive in all things, even death.

He believed with certainty the words from the prophet Ezekiel, "Then you shall know that I am the Lord, when I open your graves and have you rise from them, oh my people!"

His belief in the resurrection of the body was further founded on the words of the prophet Isaiah who said, "But your dead will live; their bodies will rise." He not only believed in resurrection, he believed that someday he would once again be able to throw a smile at his beloved and a life of laughter, shared in love, would commence anew. This time, without end.

Even with the loss of Rebecca, Jacob counted himself among the most blessed of men to have been able to spend his life in the company of the best of all possible friends. Sixteen years before Rebecca left this world, she bore Jacob the gift of a son. The love of his son carried him through the loss of Rebecca. Jacob's every move in life was made, in large part, for the love of his boy. As Joseph grew, it was evident that he cared deeply about the people of his town and his honesty knew no bounds. Jacob took delight in his son's desire to know and follow the faith of his heritage. He became a well-respected young man at the synagogue and was known for his humility and thirst for all things spiritual.

Not only had Jacob's son grown to be a friend and respected man throughout the town, he also became a most capable business partner. Starting with an apprenticeship in his shop at the age of fifteen, Joseph showed a unique ability to calculate angles and plum surfaces with the expertise of a much more seasoned craftsman. More important than the manual skills he developed was his commitment to giving customers greater value for the money they spent than anyone would have expected. Though their focus on quality and customer value may have slowed production, and with it potential profits, both Jacob and his son were rewarded with a long list of clients that would never run empty. While other shops came and went as quickly as a dust storm out of the south, Jacob's shop was not only a staple to their town, but to neighboring villages as well.

Eventually, Jacob and Joseph's business partnership ended when the mildly progressive pain in Jacob's hands became daily and severe in nature, leading to significant deformity. The once sleek and powerful hands of a master craftsman now looked more like the fingers and knuckles of a begging leper. The two men consulted with several physicians to try to heal Jacob's hands, including the popular yet painful therapy of swatting Jacob's hands with the needles of the Utica plant. While this treatment had helped many other people, it just left Jacob's hands bloodied, itchy, and in worse pain than when he had begun the therapy. As a result, the full reins of the shop were given to his son.

For almost six months after his hands had failed him, Jacob would go to the shop nearly every day to see how he could help. His heart told him he could still pound nails and if he couldn't pound them any longer, he certainly could fashion them. His mind was sharp and full of desire, but given the state of his hands, any real assistance he could provide was extremely limited. The nails he dreamt of being able to pound, and the countless number of them he had pounded in the past, now only produced a treacherous heartache over his inability to do his life's work.

At the urging of Joseph, Jacob began to hang out with a group who his son affectionately called, "the other old men." At first, spending time with other widowers was difficult for Jacob. He was used to working, to creating, laughing with customers, and experiencing the satisfaction that comes from an earnest day's work. But in time, he and "the other old men" found joy in telling stories about their younger years and in helping those from their synagogue who were in need. In the spirit of giving and sharing joy, "the other old men," including Jacob, found satisfaction in the honest hours of each passing day.

Even though Jacob began to visit the shop less frequently over the last couple years, he would still stop by there on a regular basis to see his son. He would often bring Joseph lunch and they would both sit back and talk about what was happening in and around the village. But Jacob had other motives for visiting his son at the shop. Not only was there a son to visit, but also a brand new grandson and a most beautiful daughter-in-law. Conveniently, this family that owned Jacob's heart lived in the house adjacent to the shop.

"Family, nothing like it ever. Family is what God means when he says love," Jacob always said. It was a phrase repeated so often that when the verbal riff began to fall from Jacob's lips, his son would echo the phrase, word for word, right along with him.

And so, today was no different from other days when Jacob strolled over to see Joseph at the shop just before the noon hour. He carried with him a loaf of bread and some crushed olives. He almost seemed to be floating to the house as he could hardly wait to hold the family's newest addition in his arms.

Joseph's house and adjoining shop were located about a block behind the southern end of the Nazarene town center, where the markets and shops did a thriving business sustaining and catering to the needs of some five hundred people who called Nazareth home. Although Rome's occupation was not desired by any of the inhabitants of the town, which was comprised mainly of Jews with a smattering of Syrians and Greeks, life went on. For those with a strong work ethic and an entrepreneurial spirit, money and a decent way of life could be had.

Joseph's house was of typical Nazarene fare and design, with the exception of having an extra room within the square confines of the house, and a small but separate shop located just behind the homestead. While not extravagant by Nazarene standards, Joseph and his family were doing all right. This was, of course, due to Jacob, who gave over the house to Joseph when his physical condition reduced the idea of work to the vapors of a passing dream. How Joseph had argued with him to stay and live with the family! After all, they had the extra room that Jacob had built himself many years before. They also had one of the best flat roofs in the city, which made sleeping on it during the hot summer nights one of the most comfortable experiences possible.

Joseph always ended his arguments by saying, "How can my father say no to both the love of family and a fine flat roof?"

But no, Jacob wanted his son and new family to grow and discover the joys of love and life for themselves and within their family proper. Besides, at the time when his hands began to cripple, his good friend Ephraim had recently lost his wife and was in a bad and lonely way. The only thing that made Ephraim smile after the death of his beloved was Jacob's offer to move in with him.

And so it was: the house with two rooms, a shop in the backyard, and one of the best flat roofs in all of Nazareth became the property and nest for Joseph, his wife, Mary, and their newly born son, Jesus.

Jacob circled around the north end of Joseph's house and made his way to the backyard and to the shop. Joseph and his family had just returned from Bethlehem the day before and Jacob was anxious to catch up with his son. He was even more excited to smother his new grandson with a rain of kisses. The eight or so chickens owned by Joseph's neighbor parted in equal shares in the wake of Jacob's stride. Half of the birds moved to the right of Jacob's path and half to his left, clucking at him the whole time.

Jacob smiled and chuckled to himself, "Oh, so it's the parting of the Red Sea again?"

When he approached the shop he saw that the wooden door hung open. Its openness prevented him from delivering his customary greeting involving two long knocks followed by four quicker pulsed knocks. Jacob was a creature of habit and terrible humor, and that's what his family truly loved about him, or so he hoped. As he stepped through the doorway of the shop, he spotted his son sitting on a stool, his back to him, with his face resting in the crux of his two hands. His work tunic, normally turned an off beige color by this time of the day due to the perspiration of his work and by the countless shavings of cedar and pine that would work their way into the fabric of his garments, was still white from a recent washing by his wife. It was clear to Jacob that his son had done no work that morning.

Jacob, moved with concern, placed his hand on Joseph's right shoulder. "My son, are you all right?"

Joseph turned slowly and tried to force a smile on his face. "Hello, Father, good to see you," he said.

The tone in Joseph's voice confirmed that something was not right. Jacob wasted no time in trying to determine what was wrong.

"Son, I know you better than the few hairs remaining on my head! Share with me, what's troubling you, my boy?"

Joseph shook his head. "I don't know where to start. If you were anyone else, you would have a hard time believing me."

"You're welcome to try me, and I hope you will," replied Jacob.

Joseph, his face dark and serious, leaned in and asked, "Do you believe in angels?"

Three

Michael's cell phone rang with the standard pre-loaded T-Mobile ring tone. Though he was the creative type, Michael was never one to venture deep into any option offered by technology. He didn't need a phone with a hundred apps on it, or a large screened one on which he could watch a baseball game. And he certainly didn't need his phone to play "A Hard Day's Night" when someone was trying to get ahold of him. All he needed was a simple ringer and a button to push to connect the call.

"Hello, Michael here."

"Yo, Michael! You sitting down?"

He recognized the voice immediately. If he hadn't, the "yo" would have been sufficient enough for him to know that it was Jim Thane. Michael never really knew how to address his relationship with Jim. Should he be introduced to others as Michael's friend or as his agent? Agent always seemed a bit pretentious and perhaps a little off from being completely accurate. Certainly, there was a time when Michael would have relished labeling Jim as his "agent," and during that time the title would have been far more appropriate. But both time and circumstance had moved Michael on to bigger and better places. Jim, at this juncture, was definitely more friend than agent.

"Hey, Jim! And yes, I am technically sitting down. I'm on my way home and am just about to exit onto Pecos Road. So what has you so excited?" asked Michael.

"Two words, my friend, just two words," Jim replied.

Michael sensed a smile in his voice.

"Am I supposed to guess?" asked Michael. "Because if I am, I'm going to loft up a half-court shot and guess that Led Zeppelin is getting back together and that Jimmy Page wants me to tour with them as their new rhythm guitarist! Am I anywhere close?"

"Close! It does have something to do with joining a rock and roll tour, already in progress," answered Jim.

Jim's response caused an abrupt pause in the conversation.

"Okay, Jim, you have my full attention. What's up?" asked Michael, suddenly serious.

"Let me cut to the chase, my friend," said Jim. "I have you and the Lil' frigging Debbie Band booked to open for Robert Grey on October twenty-ninth at Celebrity Theater!"

Michael reached for his turn signal, plunked it down, and slowly made his way to the north shoulder of Pecos Road, his mind reeling.

"Yo, Michael? Are you there?" Jim asked.

After putting his car in park and brushing off the initial shock, he pressed Jim for more details. "So you mean to tell me that in less than three weeks, instead of playing at Mullins & Follensbee's Bar and Grill, the Lil' Debbie Band is going to play at the Celebrity? How, Jim? How did you manage that?"

"Oh, ye of little faith!" exclaimed Jim, with more than a little pride filtering through his upbeat voice. "My connections run very deep, my friend. Have you forgotten, I actually worked with Robert back when he was getting his start? So, I gave him a call when I saw that he was coming to town and asked him if he wanted an opening act. And boom, you're in!"

"Simple as that?" asked Michael, with a mild tone of skepticism.

"Pretty much. He said that while he trusted me and my judgment, he did want to check you out before saying yes. To make a short story as short as it should be, I sent him a link to your website and he checked it out. Not only did he like it, he noticed your dedication section to your dad. It turns out your dad once sat in with him when he played in Phoenix back in the day! How's that for some cosmic weirdness?"

"That is pretty darn cool. Debbie is not going to believe this. Heck, I don't even believe it! She is going to freak!"

"Oh, and I saved the best part for last. Brace yourself... You get paid a whopping sum of twelve hundred dollars for the gig! Don't spend it all at once!" Jim laughed.

"Well I guess it's time to quit my day job!" Michael quipped.

With a more somber tone in his voice, Jim said, "Well, maybe not quite yet. But Michael, I still believe in you. I always have. And my door to you remains open. You should see how this goes and possibly reconsider giving the industry an earnest shot. Besides—"

Michael politely cut him off mid-stream. "Jim, I appreciate your confidence and the belief you have in me, and for getting us this incredible gig. It is way cool and will certainly be a night to remember. But things have changed since back then and I'm happy where I am in life now. Besides, what are the chances?"

"Trust me, Michael; I have seen stranger things happen to people who had less talent than what you have in your right earlobe. All's I know is that I remain ready to take on the task if you ever decide to go for it. And one other thing..." Jim seemed to pause for effect and then continued, "With regards to your 'what are the chances' comment, Mr. Gray mentioned that he is looking for an opening act to finish his tour. That could be you and Debbie! And that, my friend, could open up a lot of doors."

For a moment the idea of making it in the music world swirled once again in Michael's mind. It was a dream he had had since he was a child playing air guitar to his parents' Kiss albums. But that dream had long since been retired and exchanged for a better, long-term proposition. Or so he thought.

"I appreciate that, Jim, all of it. But, things have changed. Let's just take this one step at a time. Let's play the Celebrity, have our moment living our rock and roll fantasy, and evaluate from there. But please, don't get your hopes up."

"Understood, my friend," replied Jim.

"Okay, I've got to go now. I'm just about home and can't wait to tell Debbie about this. Oh, and while I'm thinking about it, can you please call Donald at Mullins & Follensbee's and explain why we need to cancel? I don't think he'd believe me!"

"Will do, sport. Take care, and again, congratulations!" Jim said, ending the call.

Michael hung up his phone, put his hands at the ten and two positions on the wheel, and stared blindly out his windshield. He wasn't thinking about the excitement of going home and telling Debbie about the gig. Nor was he thinking about standing on stage in front of two thousand people laying down a heavy lead in his favorite key of E. Instead, he thought of his father and how proud he would be. He couldn't wait to call him and tell him the news after he shared it first with Debbie.

Four

Jacob pulled up a stool opposite Joseph and set aside the bread and jar of crushed olives he brought. There was no doubt about it, this son of his was now a man, a very good man. At the age of twenty-three, Joseph carried with him the wisdom of a much older and seasoned man. People saw this in the son of Jacob and it was one of the main reasons that the steady flow of customers continued to make orders at the shop even after the master craftsman had retired. Not only did Joseph have the kind of wisdom a father would hope for in a son, he was also remarkably handsome. He stood nearly six-feet-tall, and while not muscled liked a chiseled Goliath, his frame was supported by great strength and tone. His rich brown hair fell to just above his neckline. Though it wasn't what one would call curly, his hair had enough wave to it that it accented the well-defined features of his face. Out of respect for the law, Joseph, like all the other adult males in Nazareth, wore a beard which he kept trimmed close to his face. His dark eyes were deep, both in how they were set within the structure of his face, as well as in the compassion and understanding they held for others.

Jacob looked into the depth of those eyes and said, "As a matter of fact, son, I do believe in angels." With a slight pause, which afforded him enough time to think of Rebecca's final words, he added slowly, "And so did your mother."

At the mention of his mother, Joseph looked up and managed a slight smile and asked, "She did?"

"She most certainly did, my son. So now that we all agree that angels are real, please tell me what's on your mind."

Joseph placed both of his hands on top of his head and combed his fingers through his hair as he leaned forward on the table. "Oh dear God, where do I begin?" he asked himself out loud.

"The beginning is always a good place to start," Jacob said, trying to assure his son.

Joseph removed his hands from his hair, straightened his posture, and looked directly at his father and said, "Dad, I know that you are a smart man, a very smart man. You are more insightful and wiser than any man in town. Given that I know that, you must have known the obvious regarding Mary and me."

"You mean the fact that she was pregnant before you were formally betrothed?"

Joseph nodded. "If you knew this, why didn't you ever say anything about it?"

Jacob paused, leaned into the table, folding his hands together he lifted his head and, placing his chin on top of his now pressed hands, he calmly answered his son, "The obvious is the obvious. It's the next step that one takes that can and will set a tone for a lifetime. You, Joseph, are a good man. You are the caliber of a son that any other father would crawl half naked in the worst of all hail storms to claim. Goodness like that never fades. Tested in any fire, it will not bend. Life's road is full of bumps and unaccounted forks, yet a man of your stature will always find his way safely home."

Joseph closed his eyes and allowed Jacob's words to settle over him. Opening his eyes, he met the stare of his father and smiled.

"Dad, correct me if I'm wrong, but was that not a long-winded way of saying that you were confident that it was all for the best?"

"Now why couldn't I have said it like that! You got it son!" Jacob said with enthusiasm. He continued, "Even when life throws us a crooked nail, a good man will find a way to make it straight, and you're such a man. Now enough of talking about what we already both know, what about all this angel stuff?"

Joseph took a deep breath, held it, and slowly and audibly exhaled. Would it be easier to let him believe the lie about Mary's pre-betrothal pregnancy than to tell him the truth? *He was proud of me, he believes in me, he loves me,* thought Joseph. *If I tell him anything further, if I tell him the truth, do I put that love and trust in permanent jeopardy?* As the last bit of his deeply held breath left his chest, something inside him said, *Believe in what you believe and place all your trust in its center.*

With that, Joseph turned to Jacob and said, "Dad, I did not have relations with Mary nor did any man."

A long pause hung over the shop and its two inhabitants. Joseph found the strength to tell the truth and his inner resolve did not allow him to drop his eyes from his father's face. Jacob was momentarily stunned. He felt the same unexplainable feeling some thirty years ago when, during a storm, an arch of lightning struck the ground inches in front of his feet. While the effects of that lightning strike lasted several hours, the sudden recall of Rebecca's words let this garment of shock dissipate faster than a spoonful of cooking fat being introduced to the hottest of frying pans. *Believe what Joseph tells you.*

Jacob looked at his son with sudden calmness. He reached across the table and let his two workman's hands encompass the now folded ones of his son. "I believe you, son, and I also believe that you have more to tell me. I am ready to listen. Put away any doubt, I will believe all you have to tell me."

With the thought of what he was about to reveal to his father, literal chills ran through Joseph's body. These chills were accompanied by tear ducts, full and overflowing. Jacob saw in his son pure truth and he knew that no matter what he was about to say, he was going to believe him.

"Isaiah's promise is now. It is here, Dad." Trying to gain his composure, Joseph wiped the steady flow of tears with the sleeve of his tunic. With his face sufficiently dry, he raised his eyes to once again meet his father's. "And don't ask me how or why, but God has given Mary and me a role in all this."

Joseph paused and tried to gauge his father's reaction. To his surprise, he saw his father grin, which planted itself in the center of his beard. Jacob's eyes, the eyes of wisdom, also gleamed and appeared to be sending a message of belief to Joseph.

"Nothing is beyond God, not even this. So, Jesus your new son...?"

"Yes, Father, He is I Am."

Looking upward, Jacob extended both of his arms, opened and raised them. He held his arms in this position for minutes while he gazed upward. His mouth opened, but words did not follow. Tears of happiness and of awe were all he could communicate. After a few moments the words of his heart were finally able to be made audible. In deep praise Jacob said aloud, "Oh hear, oh Israel, the Lord your God is One. Have mercy on me and my family. All praise to You who knows no boundaries and who has chosen my family in the fulfillment of Your promise. Your will be done!"

He brought both of his hands down to the table, reached over and took each of Joseph's hands into his and said, "Not only do I believe, but I have never been so honored and proud to call you my son."

Joseph's problems evaporated, at least momentarily, as he heard the words of his father. Joseph was relieved that Jacob so readily believed him. But time did not allow him the option of running from or escaping his problems for very long. He must pack up his family and leave before nightfall.

As for Jacob, he closed his eyes and thought of Rebeca and her final words to him. He smiled, knowing that she too was a wonderful part of

God's greatest plan. He whispered to her, "I do believe him. Thank you, my angel!"

Five

After hanging up with Jim, Michael put his old 1998 Crystal Parchment colored Lexus E300 in drive and got back onto Pecos Road, heading west toward Fortieth Street. His house was located about two blocks east of Fortieth Street in the heart of the south Phoenix suburb of Ahwatukee. His car, like his house, was older but clean and meticulously maintained. His house was a typical 1,700 square feet, three bedroom, two bath, stucco home complete with desert landscaping located in a moderate upper-middle class neighborhood. He and his wife, Debbie, had purchased it three years ago before the real estate bubble totally busted. While they hadn't lost major bucks like others in the Phoenix real estate market, it was clear they wouldn't be pulling a Jefferson's and moving on up to the west side of Ahwatukee any time soon. It was down in the west side of Ahwatukee where many of the Arizona Cardinals and Diamondbacks lived and, as Ahwatukee urban legend had it, Rod Stewart was reported to own a home as well.

All that was well and good for Michael. He wasn't big on craving more. Bigger and better and battling the Joneses for bragging rights and justification of self-worth was never an obsession of his. Being happy, giving back to others, making music, and his life with Debbie was the keeper of his aspirations and the source of his daily joy.

Michael and Debbie had met thirteen years previous in high school when they were both in their junior year. Debbie liked to brag that they had met on a blind date, set up by their mutual friend Cindy Thompson, but Michael would always be quick to quip back with the truth.

"No, it was technically a one-sided blind date because you didn't know who the beans I was, while I certainly knew who you were!"

And it was true. Debbie had caught Michael's eye sometime back in their freshman year. Being a large Catholic school, Seton High had a uniform policy that required the girls to wear either the patented Catholic pleated skirt or khaki shorts. Michael didn't have a preference between the two, just as long as Debbie's tanned and flawless legs were in plain view.

Even though Michael first fell for the legs, after their first date all of Debbie's additional qualities began to find equal favor in Michael's heart, especially her mind and soul. At five feet three, Debbie defined cute. Other girls attempted to invoke beauty with heavy investments in makeup, Scottsdale-ish fashion, and excessive hair products, but Debbie had to do very little to outright own the category of cute. Simply put, had Meg Ryan been born twenty years later, she would have had to settle for runner up to Debbie in the Miss Cute Universe pageant. Like Meg Ryan in her heyday, Debbie wore her blond and brown highlighted hair short. Though she owned contacts, she was always more confident and comfortable wearing glasses. Her perpetually dark tan didn't begin and end with her legs. A blessing from her father was the inheritance of a deep olive complexion that could just think of the word sun and turn itself into a tan as if she had just returned from a Hawaiian vacation. The funny thing about this gift of skin was that it did not come from an expected Italian or Middle Eastern heritage, but rather from a family that Debbie very affectionately called "The Pollacks" for obvious ethnic reasons.

Yes, Debbie Retzke was everything Michael could want in a girl. She was not only cute, but like himself she was someone who realized that there was a world outside of the self, and that by giving back a person received so much more in return. In sum, Debbie was beautiful, both on the inside and on the outside.

Michael Fortunato had an Italian heritage, but his own external hue was more in line with what someone might expect from a Polish background. Still, his skin could color up to a point where, if he was out of town, someone seeing him might think he was from some place sunny like Phoenix. Though his skin tone was outside stereotypical Italian bounds, his crop of very thick and wavy black hair was right in line with his Fortunato and Italian heritage. If it was Debbie's legs that first caught Michael's eye, it was Michael's hair that caught the whim of Debbie's heart. Matching his hair for thickness and filling out his five feet, eleven-inch frame, Michael's body was muscular, featuring broad shoulders, defined pecs, and a fine posture. He looked all the part of a football captain and most certainly might have been had he had the time to commit to the practice that organized sports required. Instead, his free time was spent between working after school as an assistant coordinator in his church's music department and practicing hour after hour in his bedroom on perfecting his own musical talent on guitar.

In addition to having a true, shared desire to help others, Michael and Debbie both shared a deep love and talent for music. Michael's musical voice came at the aid of six metal strings; Debbie's musical voice was, in fact, her voice. Ever since she was a child she would sing in whatever choir that was available to her. While her voice was superior to most other members of whatever choir group she joined, Debbie preferred to be a part of the larger choir rather than take a solo or lead. Despite the encouragement and hopes of many a choir director who recognized her talent and craved for it to be heard, Debbie's shy demeanor and insecurities prevented her from ever being a choir's main attraction.

Michael, on the other hand, was neither shy nor an egomaniac. Michael grew up in a household of musical richness. His father, Phillip, was successfully employed for many years in the pharmaceutical industry. But, he was also a very accomplished bass player who had been in demand for many years in the Valley. Phillip's passion and forte was the blues, something Michael picked up from him at a very early age and never managed to shake. Michael began to take guitar lessons at the age of seven at a little music store called "B#, C" (pronounced as Be Sharp, See). The lessons provided a rich soil for an innate talent to blossom forth. Both his father and his guitar teacher, Lawrence Petross, recognized the talent that had lain within Michael from the moment he strummed his first chord. Lawrence was an accomplished musician in his own right. He even recorded several songs on guitar for Matt Mayer's latest CD. In all his years of teaching, he had never had a student with as much God-given talent as Michael.

Deserved and earned by his talent, Michael's father bought him his first real electric guitar, an American Stratocaster at the Guitar Center in Tempe, for his ninth birthday. White, with a white pick guard and a blond maple neck, this guitar would remain one of his dearest friends for the rest of his life. While other Strats, Teles, and an occasional Les Paul or two would make it into Michael's stable of guitars, Mr. White, as it had been named by the nine-year-old recipient, remained his number one ax of choice.

By age thirteen, Michael's talents were well known to the blues community of Phoenix. He began to gig with his dad's band, 3rd Degree, on select weekends at the two finest blues clubs the Phoenix Valley had to offer, the Blues Cellar and The Thrill Is Here. Though 3rd Degree had a talented front-man guitarist named John Walsh, who rightfully increased a club's butt-in-seat ratio well over expected averages, the crowds only grew bigger when it was announced that Michael Fortunato would be joining the band on stage. Part of the lure was the novelty of seeing a thirteen-year-old playing lead guitar in a well-established blues club with a well-established blues band. But for those who really knew music, they knew there was more to the magic being made on stage than the fact that it was coming out of a thirteen-year-old kid. There was no doubt that Michael Fortunato had a unique talent; a very, very unique talent.

The owner of the Blues Cellar, Pat Morris, was not only a successful club owner, but he was well known throughout the national blues scene. By booking some of the very best names in the blues world for his small club on Indian School Road, and often joining the acts on stage with his sick harmonica skills, Pat became ensconced in the broader American blues scene. He easily recognized Michael's talents. Pat saw Michael not just as a novel young teenager with talent, but as someone who had what he called the "licks that last." In many ways, Michael reminded Pat of Stevie Ray with a calming touch of Buddy Guy thrown in for good measure.

When Michael was sixteen, Pat introduced him and his father to Jim Thane, a successful studio owner and producer-promoter. Jim was well known and respected for recording and promoting some of the very best local blues talent in Chicago, including Veronica Scott and Jimmy B. Moore. After sitting in on just one of 3rd Degree's shows, Jim immediately recognized the talent that lay in Michael's fingertips. Up until that moment, Jim considered himself somewhat retired. Sure, he would record some local bands here and there in his home studio to make a little extra cash, but he felt certain that his time of full immersion into the music scene could be found squarely in the reflection of his personal rear-view mirror. But once he saw, or more appropriately heard, what Michael produced from Mr. White, what Jim thought he had posted in his past made a glorious return to his present reality. Michael Fortunato needed to be heard, and he was going to see to that. Or so he thought.

Six

After informing his father of the holy paternity of his son, Joseph broke the news that he and his family needed to leave not only Nazareth immediately, but leave all of Israel and Judah for an unspecified amount of time. This came as a crushing blow to Jacob.

"Leave? Why? And for how long?" asked Jacob.

"The angel told me that Herod wants to have Jesus killed and, based on Herod's recent behavior, I believe him. He said to leave by nightfall and that I would receive another visit when it is safe to return," explained a calmer, but still somewhat shaken Joseph.

"Where will you go?" asked Jacob.

Joseph was about to answer when Mary appeared in the doorway holding Jesus. To say Mary was beautiful would be like saying the sky is blue. In every way, Mary was beauty. What made her most spectacular was the fact that her beauty started from the inside and then worked its way out. She stood a slender five feet two with dark brown eyes surrounded by rich dark hair that fell to the middle of her back. Her skin was smooth and olive toned. Her hands, though beautiful, showed evidence that this woman was not afraid of work. The responsibilities of her daily life were reflected with pride in the toughness of her hands: gathering the water from the well every morning, pressing the oil from olives, cooking, spinning linen, creating the family's clothing, and tending to the needs of her now expanded family. All these things she did and she did them with great joy.

"He told Joseph that we are to go to Egypt, my Saba," answered Mary as she and Jesus made their way through the doorway.

Jacob's heart was warmed by the name Saba, which Mary had affectionately begun to call him just before she and Joseph left for Bethlehem. Saba is the Hebrew word for grandpa. She walked over to Jacob and, with Jesus still in her arms, received a most heart-felt hug.

"Oh, my darling Mary and baby Jesus! What a most happy and most sad day this is. I learned the greatest news possible, and then I learn that you must leave. I don't know if I should shout for joy or if I should cry my eyes out!" Jacob exclaimed.

"Always side on joy, Saba. God is good and, if he brought us this," Mary said, moving the blanket away from Jesus' face, "imagine the joy that is to follow. It will be difficult on all of us, Saba, but have faith. God is with us, always."

Looking at the baby Jacob felt a peace he never had experienced. Everything vanished from his mind. It was just him and the baby. Nothing else mattered and nothing else existed. The baby who was God looked into his Saba's eyes, communicating everything without saying anything. Jacob reached down and touched the little hand of God. Before meeting its mark, the baby reached out and grabbed Jacob's left thumb and gripped it. It was hard to say who smiled first, but in an instant smiles spread across both faces—the old man's and the baby God. The baby's message was received by Jacob. Trust.

What seemed like hours was but a moment between Jacob and Jesus. And learning a great deal from their exchange, Jacob leaned over and kissed his grandson's forehead. He understood the situation fully and was ready to help with the tactical needs that were before them.

"So if it is Egypt God wants, who am I to say Cana, Bethel, or otherwise!" Jacob said with his usual smile and bounce. "Do you know where you are supposed to settle in Egypt, or might you be looking for suggestions?"

"We haven't a clue, Dad. All I know is that it's at least one hundred miles from here and that's where God wants us to go. Why, do you have any suggestions?" asked Joseph.

"In fact, I do. Your mother's cousin, Shem, lives in a town on the northern coast called Sais. The area is rich with flax, which he makes fishing nets out of. The last I heard, he was doing very well and had a couple of guys working for him manufacturing nets for the fishermen in the area. I'm sure if you went there he could give you work," said Jacob, beaming.

"Work would be great," replied Joseph, "but knowing there's family there is even better." Joseph's nervousness and apprehension began to give way to hope. *God provides. He always provides,* thought Joseph.

"So, Mary, how does Sais sound to you?" asked Joseph.

"It sounds to me like we should begin packing. I'll start inside and perhaps you can review your work orders with Saba and—"

"Work orders!" cried Joseph. At the thought of work, a whole new set of anxieties set a course for Joseph's heart. Having to travel to Bethlehem had already put him significantly behind on his orders. He began to pace back and forth in the workshop, bringing his hand to scratch the top of his head as if solutions could be found through the act.

"Dad, what am I going to do! I am so far behind. Work has been too good lately!"

Joseph directed the question to Jacob, but Mary was the first to respond.

"Joseph, calm down. Look at your son." Again, she made the face of the baby visible by moving the blankets aside. Continuing with a true conviction, she said, "If He is with us, and He is, does anything else really matter?"

Joseph stared at Jesus and then again at Mary. Her simple wisdom penetrated him in an instant. She was right. Yes, there would be loose ends. And yes, it would be a long and grueling trip ahead to a land they didn't know. But above and beyond all of it, they had with them the very promise of God.

Joseph began to laugh at himself. "We were visited by angels and given the responsibility to raise the Messiah. Yet, here I am worried about work orders! What a fool I am!"

Joseph thought he was laughing on the inside, but real laughter emerged from his mouth in a hearty fashion. Mary was the first to join him, followed by Jacob, and then even the baby let out what sounded like a giggle. They all captured the absurdity of Joseph's worry in relationship to the favor God had shown them.

"Okay, okay, okay. I take it all back!" proclaimed a much more light-hearted Joseph. "All the same, Dad, you have to help me put these orders on hold."

Mary, along with the prized possession she still held in her arms, made a quick exit for the workshop's door. "I'll let you gentlemen handle those details. Jesus and I will be inside getting things packed for the journey."

With that, Mary made her way out of the shop. Watching her as she exited, Jacob took a moment to take in all that he had recently learned. He had always known that Mary was special. Very special. While other girls her age would be off playing games with each other, he would often see Mary around the village helping the elderly women do their chores, or playing with the children of widows. He remembered the great joy he felt when his son began to court her. Even though he felt, fatherly bias aside, that Joseph was the town's most eligible bachelor, Mary was still a jewel worth more than all the rubies in Israel.

Jacob often tried to find a word to sum up who Mary was, but the right descriptor always escaped him. Then one day when he was having dinner with his old friend Ephraim, thinking of the very topic, it came to him.

"Holiness!" he exclaimed.

Ephraim had slurped down another spoonful of soup and raised his eyebrows. "I thought we already said our prayers, Jacob?"

Yes, it came to Jacob then and it was solidified today. Mary had been and was currently the embodiment of holiness. He then began to think of his son, who was also called by God and had the mark of holiness. The reality of God's presence in his family hit Jacob like the waves of a storming sea.

Joseph was still talking about the orders that needed to be completed, but Jacob heard not a word. Instead, he got up off the stool he was perched on, walked to the other side of the table, and hugged his son with all his might. Joseph returned his father's hug with equal sincerity and they both began to cry. It couldn't be helped, nor did either want to prevent it.

"I love you, Abba," said Joseph.

"And I love you too, son," replied Jacob.

Seven

When Michael arrived home, his initial plan was to tiptoe his way into the house from the garage and to sneak up and surprise Debbie with a kiss to the top of her head. Goose, however, had other plans. Michael cracked open the laundry room door, and was met by a one and a half foot tall, solid but lean fifteen pounds of black and white Boston and Rat Terrier mix. Goose unleashed a series of welcome home barks, derailing Debbie's surprise. Had Goose owned a tail, it would have been in an up-tempo frenzy of a wag at the sight of Michael. But, Goose had no tail and no one knew why. When Michael and Debbie rescued Goose off the streets of downtown Phoenix, that was how he came equipped. He was a happy dog who was short one tail, but was never short of love. Michael would often tell Debbie that he thought dogs might be angels. While he didn't mean it literally, she understood what he meant.

"Oh, there's my good boy!" exclaimed Michael, opening his arms and letting Goose pour out all the love he had been waiting the whole day to lavish on Michael.

"Is that you, Michael?" came Debbie's voice from the kitchen.

"I certainly hope it is. If not, we got problems!" Michael said with a chuckle.

Michael turned the corner from the utility room and into the hall, which led into the Fortunatos' kitchen where he was met by his bride and best friend.

"Fancy meeting you here," said Michael in his typical cornball style.

"And what a strange occurrence it is seeing you here!" replied Debbie with a grin that couldn't be hidden.

Before any other volleys of nonsensical affection could be had, Michael reached out and grabbed Debbie by the hips, placing her squarely in front of him. In the split second that it took for him to kiss her, Debbie saw that he was much happier than usual. And that was saying a lot, since Michael was one of the most eternally happy people Debbie had ever met. His inward and consistent joyfulness was one of the qualities that most attracted her to him. Yet today, she could tell there was icing on his happiness cake, and she was just dying to get a taste of that frosting!

"So tell me—" Debbie began.

"You're not going to believe what happened today," Michael cut her off.

They both giggled at their impeccable sense of timing.

Debbie continued, "I could tell something good was up with you. So what's up, monkey man?"

Michael took her by the hand and, leading her to the music room, said, "I'll show you."

The music room was by far Michael's favorite room in the whole house. It was a room dedicated to a passion that he and Debbie both held most dear—making music. It was where they wrote songs, rehearsed with their band, and had the history of their musical lives on display. On the south wall of the room were mounted seven of Michael's guitars. Along with Mr. White, there hung a tobacco sunburst Fender Strat, a dark blue PRS, a candy-cola Telecaster, a flame red Gibson SG, a gold top Les Paul Custom, and in the very center of the wall hung his father's Olympic White 1962 Fender Precision bass. These guitars hung from the wall by u-shaped grips, which allowed each to be taken down and played with ease. Below the seven sources of Michael's joy laid his vintage Fender Twin Reverb amplifier, which was flanked by a fifteen-inch GK bass rig that his band's bass player, Bill Miller, used during practices. Next to the amps, and tucked in the adjoining corner, was a red speckled Tama drum kit flanked by a set of bronze Zildjian symbols. On the other side of the drum kit sat a twelve-inch Yamaha PA speaker, and its partner in vocal amplification sat parallel in the north-east corner of the room. A small portable Mackie mixer shared the same small table with that speaker.

The Lil' Debbie Band's history was depicted on this wall. Michael was forever thankful for a man named Carl who was friends with Dave Lara, the band's drummer. Carl hardly ever missed a gig and he would take the best dang photos of the Lil' Debbie Band in action. In the middle of the wall sat two large pictures Carl took of the band playing at the Tempe Town Lake's Fourth of July Festival they had headlined two years before. It was one of the best gigs in the Valley, playing to a crowd of over ten thousand people. The pictures were juxtaposed with several other photos of Debbie, Michael, and the band. Some of their favorites included Debbie belting it out on Beal Street in Memphis; a candid shot of Debbie holding and kissing the top of Cookie's (their rhythm guitarist) head as they were walking up the steps to take the stage at Ahwatukee's Concert in the Park; a close up of Debbie grinning at Michael as they played on the Great Lawn before a Cardinals' game; and perhaps the couple's absolute favorite picture was from a church festival when Fr. Charlie, their pastor, got up and played a song with the band. Yeah, this room was special to Michael. It integrated his favorite things in the whole world: Debbie, music, and friends.

"Okay, what do you want to tell me by way of showing me something in this room?" Debbie teasingly inquired while placing both her hands on her hips.

Michael grabbed Mr. White from the wall and plugged it into the Twin Reverb. Turning the amp on and looking directly into her eyes, he began to play the key lick to Robert Grey's hit, "Hot Smoking Lightning."

"Okay, so you learned a new song. Is that really what has you so giddy?"

Michael's smile grew even wider. "Do you know who that is?"

"Yeah, Robert Grey. And, I know he's coming to the Celebrity Theater. Did you get tickets to his show? The way you're acting, we better be in the front row or have backstage passes!"

"You have the second half right, Sweetness. We will be backstage for the Robert Grey concert, but we won't be sitting in the front row."

"Well that's pretty darn cool! I can't wait to meet him! So where are the seats?"

"Won't need them," Michael said, deliberately pausing, "since we are the opening act that night!"

Taking her right hand off her hip, she playfully pushed him in the chest. "Michael Fortunato, what are you talking about? Have you been drinking?"

Michael explained his phone conversation with Jim. In addition to telling Debbie that the band was going to get paid twelve hundred dollars, he informed her that they might be asked to continue as Robert Grey's opening act for the remainder of his national tour.

This hit Debbie, just as it did Michael, like a ton of bricks: half of which were happy bricks, the other half were bricks made of anxiety, held together by gobs of "what if" mortar. It was one thing if they were still twenty-two and didn't have a care in the world. If that were the case, then they would gladly go on tour. But they had long packed away the dream of making it in the music industry. They were both thirty-two and Michael had a good job selling pharmaceuticals, and Debbie loved being a kindergarten teacher. Making music in their little local band had been enough for her and Michael.

All the same, they both couldn't help but wonder, "What if?"

And so it was, they sat up half the night discussing the potential pros and cons over a bottle of Smoking Loon Cabernet. While no decision could be made that evening, they did agree on two things. First, that Debbie would bounce all this off her best friend and bandmate, Cookie, the next morning over coffee. Debbie had already texted her and arranged a meeting at the Daily Grind for 8:00 a.m. The second thing they agreed on, and the one that made the most sense, was the fact that they had not been asked to go on tour yet. The only thing they had been asked to do was to play the one gig at the Celebrity. They both agreed that they were getting ahead of themselves and that they both needed to back off a bit and stay in the moment. All the same, they both knew it was better to have this all thought out. If they were asked to go on tour, they would have to make a quick decision.

Eight

Joseph spent a half hour going over the orders that Jacob needed to either cancel or see to it that they were moved to another shop. Of course, Jacob would try to have most of the work sent to their dear friend and fellow artisan Simeon. Simeon was a very capable craftsman to whom Jacob and Joseph referred work when someone needed something fixed or constructed quicker than their shop could handle because of their workload. Though a very good carpenter and friend, Simeon lacked what Jacob called "the skill of human interaction." Preferring a more solitary life, Simeon fell short in the charisma department which so readily graced the character of both Jacob and his son Joseph. Due to this, Simeon's business never did, nor would it ever, reach the level of success experienced by Jacob and Joseph. Simeon rented a shop that was about two and a half furlongs from Joseph's shop. It was far enough that any work they passed on to him would require the use of a cart and an ass.

After assessing their current orders, they determined that about half of them were for various repairs of one sort or another. Those items included a stool needing a new leg, a chair requiring a new back, a table the owner wanted Joseph to add a drawer to, and a few other miscellaneous items.

Jacob and Joseph next looked at the orders they had for new construction. The first item was a very straightforward order for two table chairs; standard fare in every way possible. The second order, which Joseph had just recently started, was a bed frame. Unlike most bed frames that were made of common Cyprus wood, the man who ordered this bed frame was a well to do merchant named Ahaz who wanted his bed to not only be comfortable and look nice, but he wanted it to smell amazing as well. As such, he selected the much more expensive wood, cedar.

Nazareth bordered the southern hills of Lebanon, home to the best cedar wood in all the world, but the center of the cedar trade was still over four miles away from the shop. Securing the wood for any project meant not only the initial expense of the wood itself, but also the price associated with having it transported from Lebanon to Nazareth. These expenses required that Jacob and Joseph collect a deposit of fifty percent before the wood would be ordered. Ahaz had paid the deposit several weeks back and the wood had just arrived at the shop the day before yesterday.

"How do you think Ahaz is going to take the news that his order is either going to be shipped over to Simeon or needs to be canceled?" Joseph asked.

Jacob began to chuckle and said, "Don't worry about Ahaz, he and I go way back! I caught him with his thumb on his scale one day and, well, let's just say he owes me. I should have no problem selling him on the situation and the capabilities of Simeon." Jacob paused and then continued, "Speaking of which, what should we tell everyone regarding why you are leaving and can't fill these orders? You know they are going to ask."

Before Joseph had a chance to respond, Jacob exclaimed, "I know! We can tell them that Rebecca's cousin, Shem, suffered a grave illness that left him—"

Joseph interrupted Jacob before he could finish his thought. "No, Father. While the specific truth may not suffice, we will not lie. Just tell them that we had to leave and that we will be back. God will make it so that anyone who asks will accept that answer."

"Okay, Joseph, I may be an old mule, but I'm learning. I also believe that that will be the case." After a slight reflective pause Jacob added, "Your faith is inspiring, my son."

"Well I'm learning too, Dad. I'm learning, too," said Joseph.

Jacob stood up from his stool, raised his hands, joined them together behind his head, and began to stretch from side to side. There was little he could do to manage the ache of his aging body, but getting off his rear-side and stretching often helped take the edge off. After stretching his back, he began to pace the distance of the shop. Ten paces to the east wall, turn around, ten paces back to the west. It was a walk he was very familiar with.

As he walked the inside perimeter of the shop, the aroma of shaved wood, of which he never tired, produced within him a sense of joy and fulfillment. Though it was a smell he took in on a daily basis for over forty years, it was one that he never took for granted. God had given him a skill that he enjoyed and one that had treated him well financially throughout his years. Having worked amidst the backdrop fragrance of aged Cyprus, freshly cut pine, and the fine punch of cedar was an incredible blessing. It was like the time when one of his goats had twins, thought Jacob, laughing to himself.

Recalling a recent arrival of cedar, Jacob asked, "Aside from orders for construction, are you expecting any other shipments that I should be aware of?"

Joseph sprung up from his chair, knocking it to its side in one sharp movement. "Laban of Cana! I just ordered the cedar for his table when they dropped off the last load!"

Jacob froze. Laban, a very wealthy farmer from Cana, had been one of their longest and most loved customers. He was a man of fine culture whose appreciation for the arts and philosophy was second only to his love of acquiring wealth and his disdain for the Roman occupation of his homeland.

While not a handsome man, his refined tastes, his ability to lead, and his innate charm made him the desire of many women since the time of his adolescence. He was slightly shorter than most men, with dark, curly hair, the thickest of beards, and the densest eyebrows to match.

What he was missing in height he made up for in brawn. Laban was as thick and as solid as they came, earning him the nickname "The Stump" when he was a child. That nickname stuck until one day, when he had reached the age of twenty, the wrong person decided to sarcastically call him by that name. He took violent exception to it and, from that point forward, everyone respectfully referred to him as Laban.

Some twenty years ago he had come through Nazareth on his way back to Cana from a trading trip he had taken to Nain. He had stopped at the inn owned by Zachary of Sebaste. Though he had lived in Nazareth for over ten years, people still referred to Zachary based on his hometown. While eating at Zachary's inn, Laban took notice of the furniture in the room and was taken by the smooth lines of both the tables and the stools. He was impressed with the ornate cuts which helped to make the furniture stand out from the more common fare of the day. Most people would come and go from the inn without ever giving the furnishings a second thought, but Laban and his affluent nature were smitten by it.

"Zachary, was it?" inquired Laban.

"Yes, sir. Is everything all right with your stew?" asked Zachary apprehensively, knowing the lamb he had used was at the borderline of freshness.

"The stew's fine, Zachary. But let me ask you, where did you get this furniture? I have never seen anything quite like it."

Relieved, Zachary drew in close to the table and patted Laban on his right shoulder. "You are obviously a man with an eye for quality. This furniture was made for me by our local carpenter, Jacob. He is the best in Nazareth, no doubt, and you will never find a more honest man. His shop is just down the street," said Zachary, pointing Laban in the direction of the shop.

After finishing his meal, Laban paid his bill and left Zachary an extra drachma for his helpful assistance. Though it was about an hour after dark, and Jacob's shop had been closed for a couple hours, Laban was determined to meet this fine craftsman. Since he was set to leave for Cana at first light, Laban headed right over to Jacob's.

Laban and Jacob hit it off well. So overwhelmed by Laban's praise of his work, he wouldn't have cared if this man had come pounding at his door during the third watch at night! Jacob convinced Laban to spend the evening with both him and Rebecca as he brought out the best wine they had. Over multiple glasses of wine, Laban shared with them the story of how he and his wife Miriam had met in Jerusalem during the Passover and how his sons Seth and James had grown to be devout Jews and all around good men. And, of course, he pontificated for what seemed like hours on the evils of Rome and how someday Israel would stand up to them and their godless atrocities. Jacob and Rebecca shared their life stories as well, and tried to impress upon Laban the fact that God would take care of Rome in His time and that such things should be left to Him.

While they couldn't come to agreement on the issue of Rome, they had truly forged a lasting friendship in the matter of one evening. By the time morning came around it was as if they had known each other ten years versus the ten short hours that they had spent together. Upon leaving, Laban had left Jacob with an order for enough furniture to fill a house the size of Jacob's three times over!

Over the years, Laban continued to be one of Jacob's, and eventually Joseph's, best customers. Not only did he continue to purchase several items throughout the years, but the referrals that came out of Cana from him were very many and very uncustomary. After all, Cana was a good three miles north of Nazareth. It was nearly unheard of to make a purchase for commodities such as furniture outside of one's own town. But Laban was an influential man and Jacob and his son were highly skilled crafts-men, so such an exception was not only made, but enjoyed and appreciated by all those involved.

"Dad, you know there is no way Laban would accept anything made by Simeon. If I don't make it, he won't take it." As Joseph said this, he began to pace the length of the shop, scratching his beard as he strode.

A sudden look of realization appeared on Jacob's face.

Joseph caught it and asked, "What is it, Dad?"

Jacob brought his index finger up to his lips. "You are right, son. Laban would never accept anything created by Simeon. And as good as he is, Laban would know the difference. But I don't agree that, as you put it, if you don't make it that he won't take it." Jacob's tone was mocking yet friendly.

Joseph knew exactly what his father was getting at. "Dad, I appreciate it, but how can you? Your spirit is strong, but your body is a different matter. Take no offense, Abba, but you are in no shape to build this table."

Jacob couldn't help but grin. He said, "So you think you are the only one who is capable of giving lessons on faith today?"

"But Dad," Joseph tried to argue.

"Son, as you know, with man much is impossible, but with God all things are possible."

Joseph continued pacing the length of the shop, letting his father's wisdom sink in. When he hit the workshop's west wall, he did an about face and walked briskly until he found himself standing in front of the man he most loved. Reaching out, he grabbed his father in his arms and hugged him tightly. No words were necessary.

The next morning Joseph, Mary, and the baby Jesus, accompanied by two donkeys and ample supplies, left Nazareth and began their trek to Egypt.

Nine

Jacob wept bitterly after Joseph and his family left for Egypt. In his deep sorrow, he not only lost his happiness, but his appetite as well. If it were not for the encouragement of his friend Ephraim, Jacob might have gone days without eating. Despite how he was feeling, he saw to it that the delegation of work to Simeon went as planned. Simeon was grateful for the orders since business for him had been as scarce as rain in the desert.

Simeon had barely left Jacob's shop with his biggest order of the year when Laban's cedar order arrived from Lebanon. As the lumber was unloaded into the shop, Jacob reviewed the order in his mind. Cedar display table, a cubit and a half tall, three and a half cubits long, a cubit deep, a handbreadth by handbreadth square legs with uniformed ornamentation carved into each leg another handbreadth below the surface base of the table.

After running the dimensions in his head, Jacob looked at his hands. They were worse than ever. Not only had he lost most of his hands' mobility and dexterity, many of his fingers were now deformed. Bent at irregular angles, four of his eight fingers, not counting the thumbs, looked more like hooks than they did fingers. The remaining four, while not completely bent, were rapidly heading in that direction. On top of all this was the constant pain that welled from nearly every joint.

Placing his hands back at his sides, he walked into the shop and stood at the north end of the pile of cedar which needed to become both a work of art and function for his friend Laban. Though the prospects of his earlier promise to Joseph had filled him with fear, that fear was now replaced by large doses of hope and promise.

Kneeling in front of the cedar, Jacob bent and leaned his body into the boards. His hands spread over the smooth wood and, with his nose planted within the cedar, Jacob inhaled deeply the unmistakable scent of the most splendid of all woods. Very little in this world smelled as good as cedar to Jacob. In fact, he felt certain that heaven would be filled with the fragrant aromas of this freshly cut wood.

Jacob closed his eyes and began to pray. The only time he recalled praying anywhere near so hard was when he prayed by the side of his dying bride so many years before. While entreating the Lord for the safety of his family and requesting just a couple days of restored health to his hands, Jacob fell fast asleep on top of the pile of wood that was destined to become a table.

Ten

"I say if we're asked to tour with Robert Grey, then we go on tour with Robert Grey," said Cookie Reginald as she took a sip from her hot extra-large peppermint mocha. Wiping the coffee gathered on her upper lip, she continued, "I know that's easy for me to say, since I don't have much of a life, but—"

Debbie cut Cookie off mid-sentence. "Now that's simply not true!"

"Leave it to you, as always, to not let me cut myself down," said Cookie. "What I meant to say is that I haven't established myself, professionally, like you or Michael. So yes, it would be a lot easier for me to pack my Tele and hit the road. That's all I meant."

What Cookie said was true. At twenty-three, she was nearly ten years younger than Debbie and, to this point, had not found her place in the career world. Cookie's path in life had not been an easy one. She was born to Bobbie, a single mother in the somewhat famous town of Punxsutawney, Pennsylvania. Infamous for men in large hats and groundhogs every February second, the truth of the matter was that Punxsutawney was just a small town where most of its youth yearned to escape.

Bobbie, who had serious issues of her own, couldn't afford to take care of Cookie due to a lack of money and the ability to love anyone but herself. At least she had the sense to place Cookie in the care of her Aunt Linda, who lived in a shack of a house on Findley Street just off the Colonel Drake Highway. What the house lacked in amenities was more than made up for in the volume of love and faith that Cookie's Aunt Linda provided her. While Linda's job as a cashier at the Comet Market barely covered the bills, she always made sure that Cookie had what she needed and that she never looked poorer than any of the other kids in town. She even found a way to purchase the communion dress Cookie spotted in the front window of The Smart Shop as she walked home from school one spring before receiving her first communion. Cookie fell completely in love with that dress and Linda was full of joy to purchase it for her, even though she dipped into her emergency fund to obtain it. The day of her First Holy Communion, seven-year-old Cookie was the prettiest first communicant Saints Cosmas and Damien Parish had ever seen.

If faith and love were the two best things Linda gave to Cookie, the third was the gift and love of music. At age three, Linda began to teach Cookie how to play the old upright piano in her front room. By age six, Cookie could play songs by ear and became a bit of a novelty at both her school and in Aunt Linda's social circles. At age ten, inspired by seeing Rick Springfield on television, Cookie got it in her mind that she wanted to learn how to play the guitar. Though Aunt Linda was full of support, she did not have the money to buy her a guitar. She suggested that if Cookie wanted to take up guitar, then perhaps she should find a way to earn the money and purchase one.

And Cookie did just that. Taking any odd job she could find, be it cutting lawns, pulling weeds, washing cars, etc., Cookie was able to save up enough to buy herself a Fender Strat Pack in just a few short months. The Strat Pack was comprised of a beginner's electric guitar, amp, strap, and cord. The actual Squier Series Stratocaster came in a choice of three colors: white, black, or red. Cookie opted for the red for no particular reason other than she thought it looked better in combination with its white pick guard than the other two colors. Within a year, she could play just about any song by ear after listening to it just a couple times on her cassette player. Though impoverished by the world's standards, young Cookie Reginald was anything but poor. She had found her groove with life and, for the first time since being abandoned by her mother, she felt genuinely happy. Then, at age fifteen, all of that changed.

While working the late shift at the Comet Market, Aunt Linda suffered a heart attack and by the next morning she had left this world for the next. Cookie was crushed in every way imaginable. She loved her Aunt Linda more than most kids loved their actual parents. To say that a spiritual hole was shot through her heart that day was an understatement. Cookie was suddenly left without anyone she really cared for to take her in. Her mother, Bobbie, whom she had next to no contact with over the fourteen years of her life, had moved to Cleveland. And even if Bobbie had lived only a block away from Cookie, living with her natural mother was not a thought Cookie would entertain.

Out of necessity, Cookie moved in with her grandmother, Ida. Cookie had had very little contact with her grandmother over the years, even though they lived in the same small town. Ida, like her daughter Bobbie, had a myriad of issues that made for a dysfunctional life. Ida was a three-time divorcee and alcoholic who found her way in and out of one abusive relationship after another.

After a couple years of living within a loveless void, Cookie had enough. She contacted her cousin, Stephanie, who lived in Phoenix and asked if she and her parents would be kind enough to put her up for a while. So, right after high school graduation, Cookie hopped on a Greyhound bus headed for Phoenix with one suitcase, one guitar, and the beginnings of a drinking problem of her own.

"I understand what you mean, Cooks," Debbie said with a smile. "We haven't been offered anything yet, but Mike and I know that we have to be ready with a yes or a no if we are asked. Michael has a wonderful job making more money than we ever hoped for, and I love teaching so much. How can we just give that all up for a dream?"

Reaching over the table, Cookie took Debbie's hands in her own. "You once told me not only to have a dream, but to chase it. I think the actual words were 'embrace it and become it.' Yeah, I think those were the exact words you used if my recovering alcoholic brain is functioning correctly!"

And of course it was. Debbie remembered vividly that specific conversation. It wasn't all that long after they first met at a local neighborhood bar, Burba's, that Debbie had the first of many heart-to-hearts with Cookie.

Michael and Debbie had stopped by Burba's early that Thursday evening to talk to Dave, the manager, about securing some future gigs when they heard Cookie doing her acoustic act on the patio. Michael was tired, having just returned from a sales meeting in New York, and wanted to just go home and go to bed early. Debbie, however, was drawn to Cookie and her music. She convinced Michael to stay for a beer and to take in the performance. It didn't take but a song and a half before Michael forgot about his tiredness. Like Debbie, he felt drawn to the playing and singing of this pretty, petite, and captivating guitarist. Standing just under five feet two, Cookie weighed barely over a hundred pounds. Her fair Scottish skin was adorned with freckles and her deep blue eyes were framed by a mane of brownish-blond naturally curly hair that settled at the top of her shoulders. They both saw that she had talent and possessed the kind of stage presence that made people stay in their seats longer than they ever intended.

After Cookie ended her first set, Michael and Debbie struck up a conversation with her that led to them getting together for a jam session at the Fortunato music room. The jam session then led to an offer for Cookie to join their band, which led to Cookie and Debbie becoming the best of friends despite their age difference, which led to Debbie getting Cookie the help she needed to stop drinking, which was closely related to the conversation Debbie had with her about embracing her dreams and becoming them.

"Yes, Cookie, I remember." Debbie grinned and squeezed Cookie's hands.

"Okay then, question for you," Cookie said.

"Shoot," Debbie replied.

"I want you to forget everything we've talked about today and clear your mind about work and what you think your future will be." Cookie paused and then continued, "Now if you had a dream that you could do anything, anything at all, and you could achieve that dream, what would it be?"

Debbie chuckled. She knew exactly where Cookie was going with this. "I'd be a singer in a successful band and I'd spend the rest of my life singing and writing music with Michael, and you of course!"

Cookie stared into Debbie's eyes and firmly articulated, "Embrace it, and become it. Listen to me, sister, you spoke those very words when I doubted that I could amount to anything. And with your prodding and prayers, I started playing out, I finished ASU, and I gave up drinking. None of those things would have happened if you hadn't encouraged me and helped me to believe that dreams, when wished upon and held tight enough, can come true."

The sincere tone in Cookie's voice brought Debbie to the brink of tears. She was just about to concede and give way to the sentiment when a dose of what she thought was reality crept into her mind, "But what about—"

It was Cookie's turn to cut her off mid-sentence. "But what about Michael's job, what about my job? That's what you're about to say, right?"

Debbie nodded.

"Well, here is my objective response to those concerns. You are the most loved and well respected kindergarten teacher the Altadena School District has ever had. I've seen scores of kids in middle school, who you taught as five-year-olds, come up to you when we were out for dinner to ask you for a hug. Talk about making an impact on a child's life! If you left and wanted to come back, you would have no problem getting back in. As for Michael, didn't he just win Sales Rep of the Year?"

"He did," Debbie answered.

"I know this about the world of sales—show me a guy who is consistently a top performer like Michael and I'll show you a guy who will never have to worry about having a job. You see, Debbie, you really aren't risking a whole heck of a lot, now are you?"

What Cookie said made sense. It made more sense than it should, in fact. Cookie proved, once again, to Debbie that she was wise beyond her years. Looking up at Cookie she conceded, "You're right, Cooks."

"Embrace your dreams, become your dreams," Cookie threw out a final time.

Looking at her watch, Cookie realized she had to get moving. She had an appointment with Carol, a young homeless girl she had been mentoring for the last year and a half. "I have to run and meet Carol. Debbie, you asked me my opinion and I have given it to you. More importantly, I really feel that if given this opportunity and you don't give it a shot, you and Michael will always be thinking what if, and what ifs can eat people alive." As she got up from her chair Cookie reached down, hugged Debbie, and kissed her on the cheek. "Love you, Sis."

"Love you, too," said Debbie, returning the affection.

Debbie knew Cookie was right. With her heart racing and a swarm of butterflies flapping in her stomach, Debbie made the decision to tell Michael that they should go on tour with Robert Grey if the opportunity presented itself.

Eleven

When Jacob woke up it was twilight. By the amount of light that was left in the shop, he estimated that he had been asleep for about six hours. As he pushed himself up from the pile of lumber on which he had taken an extended nap, he was amazed that he woke without feeling any stiffness, aches, or pains. Once fully on his feet, Jacob raised his hands in astonishment. Gone were the twisted deformities of his fingers, gone was the pain his hands had experienced for so many years. In their place were the hands of a healthy, twenty-something carpenter. Looking upward in utter awe, he let out an almost inaudible thank you to God, so stunned was he by this miracle. He knew, instantly, that God had given him the gift of his hands so he could finish Laban's table for Joseph. He also knew in his heart that this would likely only be a temporary cure and that he would not be permanently healed. He held no regret or malice for that. This is exactly what he had asked God for and this was exactly what he received. How could he be anything but overjoyed?

Not knowing how long his fingers and hands would be able to function as the engine of his master craftsman's heart, Jacob lit the shop's two lanterns and immediately began construction of the table.

Twelve

When Michael got home from work that evening, Debbie had set the table with the one fancy white tablecloth they owned, their good china, complementary fine silverware, and a flowered centerpiece she had purchased at Safeway while picking up all the ingredients she needed to make her world-famous lasagna. It was the smell of Debbie's lasagna that first greeted Michael as he stepped into the house from the garage, followed by a welcome home pounce to the thigh from Goose. But it was the smile he saw on Debbie's face as she came out of the pantry with a bottle of Smoking Loon that made Michael feel the most at home.

Debbie's world famous, made-from-scratch lasagna, and the fancy table setting tipped Michael off that something significant was in play. For a split second he wondered if, by some miracle, she was going to tell him she was pregnant. But he quickly tucked that thought away. After countless years of prayers, numerous trips to specialists, and fertility tests, both Michael and Debbie were resigned to the fact that they could not have children of their own. They had recently been discussing the possibility of adoption, something they were both very much open to.

Holding up the bottle of wine, Debbie cheerfully said, "Nothing says welcome home like a glass of Smoking Loon!"

One of Michael's hobbies over the years, if it dared be called that, was to purchase inexpensive bottles of wine in the hope of finding one that tasted as if it should be priced ten times its actual cost. Drinking wine at the many dinner programs and award banquets he attended for work, Michael acquired a fine taste for good wine. But as much as he liked a Sliver Oak Cab or a St. Francis Magnificent blend, he could never justify the exorbitant costs of such fine wines. So his hunt went on to find that six to ten dollar bottle of wine that tasted like it should be served by a sommelier at a five-star restaurant. His search was rewarded about two years ago when he found it, the holy grail of inexpensive wine! It was none other than Smoking Loon Cabernet priced at eight dollars a bottle, or just $5.99 if you bought six at a time at Safeway. Since that time, he had joked that he was on a mission to convert the world to the joys and savings that a nice pour of Smoking Loon could provide!

"Well then, open that bad boy up and welcome me home!" Michael replied.

Debbie handed Michael the bottle of Loon. And, doing her best Marilyn Monroe impersonation, she said, "I hope you're in the mood for a fancy dinner."

Michael worked the corkscrew into the bottle. "I sure am, but you know what I'd like even more than a fancy dinner?"

"Down, tiger!" Debbie teased.

"You know, for once, I was not even going there," Michael said with a grin. Handing her a glass of wine he continued, "Something's up, Debs. The fancy table and the smell of your lasagna is giving it away I'm afraid. Care to let me in on it?"

"We have a little time until that lasagna is baked to perfection, why don't we sit in the living room with our Loon and I'll tell you exactly what's on my mind," Debbie said, moving into the living room as Michael followed right behind her.

Michael leaned back into the couch and listened intently as Debbie filled him in on her conversation with Cookie. She bottomed-lined it by telling him that if Robert Grey asked them to finish up the tour, they should embrace their dreams and do it.

"But what—" Michael began to argue, and Debbie cut him off.

"Any sales person who has accomplished what you have will never go unemployed." As she spoke those words, Debbie moved in very close and kissed his lips lightly. With her face just inches away and her eyes locked on his she continued, "Michael, if we don't go for it, we will spend the rest of our lives wondering, 'what if.'"

Debbie's words rang true. Michael had been thinking the very same thoughts over the last couple of days. He had a fantastic relationship with his boss, Brad Parker, and the company loved him. Both Brad and the majority of people in the organization knew of Michael's musical talents. Brad had been to a number of the Lil' Debbie Band's shows and the company had even commissioned Michael to write a song about one of their new products, which was played and distributed at last year's national sales meeting. *Perhaps they would grant him a leave of absence*, Michael wondered. *Well, it couldn't hurt to ask. No one has ever died from a no.*

"Okay, okay, baby," Michael said. "If you're in, then count me in as well."

"Really?" Debbie asked, the possibilities of a Robert Grey tour at her fingertips.

"Really. I'll try and take a leave of absence, but if they deny my request I'll hand them a resignation letter."

Debbie was ecstatic.

They continued talking late into the night which led to more smiles, more Loon, more kisses, more expressed dreams, and one very burnt tray of lasagna neither of them cared much about.

Thirteen

Carol Smith was a fifteen-year-old, technically homeless, girl whom Cookie had befriended. They came together through a program called New Pathways for Youth, which was a mentoring program set up to help homeless children in Phoenix overcome the obstacles they faced. Similar to the structure and principles of the Big Brothers, Big Sisters program, Cookie had become Carol's mentor about six months ago. As a mentor, Cookie would do different things with Carol, such as taking her to sporting events, shopping, going to the movies, and, of course, teaching her how to play guitar. But it wasn't necessarily the activity that mattered to Carol. What mattered was Cookie's friendship and support.

Like Cookie, Carol had a tough past. Her father walked out on his family when she was still a baby, leaving her mother, Veronica, to work multiple low-paying jobs, many at the same time. Despite Veronica's best efforts, she and Carol were evicted from their apartment nearly a year ago after Veronica was fired from one of her two jobs. The job she lost had her selling tickets at the Greyhound station off Interstate Ten and Seventh Street. She was let go for leaving a half an hour early to take Carol, who had been vomiting for two days straight, to the emergency room, even though it was a slow day and they had enough counter coverage to handle the day's flow. Her boss, Victor Hessling, was a sadist who seemed to enjoy creating misery in the lives of others. Despite having been fired, Veronica prayed daily for the softening of Mr. Hessling's heart. On one level, Carol had a hard time understanding why her mother would pray for such a man. On another level, Carol admired her for it.

Veronica's other, and now only, job had her folding sheets in the laundry room at the Downtown Sheraton Hotel. The bottom line was that she couldn't afford the six hundred and fifty dollars a month rent for the dump of an apartment they had lived in off of Fillmore Street. At least, not if she wanted to put enough food on the table. After losing their apartment, Carol and her mother moved in with one friend after another. But each time it led to strained friendships and hurt feelings. About six months ago, Veronica heard about the UMOM Shelter off of Van Buren and Thirty-Second Street. The shelter was designed for homeless families and offered Veronica and Carol the hope of saving enough money to get back on their feet and, once again, into an apartment of their own. Though it wasn't located in the best of neighborhoods, Carol could still attend Roosevelt High and Veronica was just a short bus ride from the Sheraton.

Cookie's heart was infused with a deep sense of love early on in life, thanks to the saintly nature of her Aunt Linda. Despite the bumps and turns in her life, she drew inspiration from the combination of her aunt's love and the kindness and encouragement given to her by Debbie in her time of need. For these reasons, Cookie wanted to pay it forward to Carol.

Before their first meeting, Cookie was very nervous. *Does this kid even want a mentor,* she wondered? Is she some tough street kid who would just push her away despite her needs? All those fears were shot to pieces when they finally met. They were introduced by one of the foundation's directors in the UMOM family room. Carol came to Cookie without any pretense. She bore only the longing to forge a meaningful friendship with an adult who had a desire to be her friend.

Carol was not the prettiest girl at Roosevelt High, nor was she the ugliest. She was average height for her age, with jet-black hair that she wore short above her shoulders. She was slightly overweight, but not so much that other people would tease her for it. Like most teenagers, she struggled with an acne problem. Suffice it to say, Carol's self-esteem was in need of a boost. Cookie's timing and warmth couldn't have been better. Carol sensed a legitimate interest in her from Cookie and in return, Carol gave Cookie her complete trust.

After meeting Debbie for coffee that morning, Cookie picked up Carol at the UMOM facility and together they headed to Chase Field in Cookie's white Jetta wagon to catch the Diamondbacks versus Pirates match-up. Dave, at Burba's, had given Cookie a pair of his season tickets after she told him about Carol and the work she was doing at New Pathways for Youth. While it was generous of Dave, there was no way he could attend over eighty home games a year, and he was glad to see them go to good use. Nonetheless, Cookie and Carol were grateful as they sat seven rows up from the infield, dead even with first base.

With a couple hot dogs consumed, and a bag of peanuts leaning halfway in that direction, the topic de jour switched to music.

"I almost forgot to tell you, I think I got 'Cinnamon Girl' all figured out!" Carol said with a wide grin of pride on her face.

"Cinnamon Girl," the Neil Young classic from the sixties, was a song that she and Cookie had been working on for several weeks. In addition to teaching Carol guitar, she also wanted her to have a good sense of rock and roll history. While Neil Young, circa the nineteen sixties, was well before her own time, Cookie had become an honor student of classic rock. Cookie took great pleasure introducing Carol to the Grandfather of Grunge and to a gritty rock and roll classic such as "Cinnamon Girl."

Holding one hand in the air, Cookie turned to Carol and yelled, "High five, sister, that is awesome!" As their hands met in a loud slap, Cookie asked, "Are you doing the pause at the end and then doing that little riff in C? A lot of people forget to tag that part and I hate it when they leave it out."

"Oh yeah, I got it down. When we get back to the shelter, maybe you can come up and hear it?" asked Carol.

"Sounds good to me. Speaking of music, have you ever heard of the Robert Grey Band?" Cookie asked, baiting her young friend.

"No, I haven't. But then again, I had never heard of Neil Young, The Talking Heads, or Deep Purple before I met you. I'm sure you're going to teach me about him. My guess is that he's a guitar player. Do I have that much right?" replied Carol.

"You do, indeed, my little girlfriend. But who he is and his stature in the world of rock and roll is only a little part of why I brought him up today."

With that, Cookie went on to tell Carol about Robert Grey's blues and rock history. She explained that while he was not a mega star in the world of rock and roll, like Jimmy Page or Stephen Tyler, he was one of the most respected guitarists in almost all musical circles.

"But the reason I brought him up is that he is coming to town next Friday night to play the Celebrity Theater. And guess who is going to be his opening act?" Cookie's smile was so large that Carol immediately understood what she was alluding to.

"Seriously? You and the Lil' Debbie Band are going to be doing a concert at the Celebrity?" Carol asked, genuinely impressed.

"Indeed, we are! Can you believe it? I can't even believe it! Carol, you're going to have to help me pick out something cool to wear. Promise me you'll help!" Cookie implored.

The fact that Cookie, a woman she highly respected and loved, was asking her for help with something as important as on-stage concert attire was certainly not lost on Carol. In fact, when she would go to bed later that night the request would come back to her mind and would help her achieve one of the happiest sleeps of her life.

"Of course, I would love to help you, Cookie," Carol replied, ecstatic.

DENNIS LAMBERT

"But you can only help me if you and your mother agree to come to the show. I've got front row tickets for you and I'm pretty sure I can get you backstage. What do you say, you in?"

"You bet, Cookie! I'm so happy for you. This is so awesome. I can't wait to tell my friends at school!" Carol said, leaning over to give Cookie a congratulatory hug.

After the Diamondbacks handled the Pirates four to two in nine innings, Cookie drove Carol back to the UMOM facility. As promised, Cookie went up to Carol's room to listen to her play "Cinnamon Girl." She was extremely impressed that Carol not only played the song correctly, but that she played it with genuine feel. Cookie also took the time to load up the iPod she had given Carol for her birthday with the set list Robert Grey was scheduled to play the night of their concert. She wanted Carol to enjoy the concert as much as possible and had always felt that knowing the songs really helped to make for a better overall concert experience, especially if you weren't familiar with the artist's body of work. Of course, Carol was very familiar with the Lil' Debbie Band catalog and even knew how to play a few of their songs. Cookie left Carol with two instructions: first to listen to Robert Grey's songs multiple times; second, to be ready at 3:00 p.m. on Monday so they could go to Cookie's apartment to pick out what she should wear to the show.

Of course, Cookie already had a good idea of what she wanted to wear that evening, but she knew that it would mean a lot to Carol to be involved in the process. And Cookie was right. For the first time in her life, Carol had begun to feel good about herself. Her confidence had increased and her sense of self-worth was at an all-time high. And the reason was simple, a legitimately caring person named Cookie had come into her life.

Fourteen

Debbie's blessing was all that Michael needed to trade out his dreams for reality. It was now settled—if asked, they would go on tour. If they toured, they would be exposed to multiple people in the music industry. Jim, who would undoubtedly travel with them as their manager, would be sure to leverage his relationships to help Michael and his band get a shot at a recording contract. While he certainly loved his job and the security that it brought, Debbie was right. If they didn't step into the batter's box and fully swing the bat, he would carry a bag full of what ifs with him the rest of his life. As long as Debbie, wise and wonderful, was next to him for the ride, all in the world would be right.

Bursting with excitement and energy, Michael called everyone in the band to tell them the good news and to see if they would be available to go on tour if called upon. He was thankful to learn that they were all available and biting at the bit for the opportunity. After obtaining each band member's approval, Michael scheduled a series of five consecutive practices.

For those who knew the band, and to the band members themselves, that many rehearsals were not really needed. The Lil' Debbie Band was tighter than tight and always had an excellent stage presence that was the envy of other musicians. But Michael didn't want to take any chances. He wanted to ensure that they were beyond tight.

Another reason he wanted to practice so intensely was to see if they could put a new song he had recently written on the set list. The song, "Be My Everything," was a ballad that put into words just how much Debbie meant to him. In fact, the only person he had ever played it for was Debbie. After hearing it, she broke out in uncontrollable tears. Thanking him, and ever proud to be his muse, she encouraged him to bring the song to the band. Michael sang very few songs as the lead vocalist, but with Debbie's encouragement and blessing, he couldn't wait to perform this one. And, he thought, what better place to debut it than at the Celebrity Theater the following week.

Fifteen

After four days of almost non-stop work, the table was completed. Running his hand across the surface a final time, Jacob took a couple of steps back to fully take in its magnificence. He stood speechless. His eyes roamed over the table's grain from end to end and from the bottom of each delicately carved leg to the table's top. A single tear said what Jacob could not. Then one tear led to another before he was finally able to speak.

"My Lord and my God!" cried Jacob.

Yes, there were tears and Jacob found himself weeping nearly as hard as when Rebecca passed away. But these tears were not wrought with sorrow, pain, or fear. No, they were tears of rejoicing, of gratitude, and of awe. His hands, over the past four days, felt no pain and were the picture of both proper structure and vigilant strength.

Jacob had been in the business of building things for over forty years. In that time, he had constructed thousands of pieces of furniture. But as he stared at the finished table, what would be the final work of his hands, he knew that this was the best work that he had ever done. It was a gift from God. He had witnessed a miracle; no, he had been part of a miracle! It was this realization, along with knowing that God was truly with both him and his family, which caused his parade of tears to continue.

The thought of God raining down his love on him drew him back to his masterpiece. Moving to its far right corner, Jacob got down on his knees and peered under the table. Slowly, and with a lover's touch, he ran his fingers across each carved letter of the phrase he had engraved an hour before. It was the same imprint that he had promised Rebecca he'd put on the underside of all his pieces of work after building her a stool when they were newlyweds. It was a promise he had kept faithfully and with great joy. They were the words Rebecca had given him, words that he didn't fully understand at first. But now he knew. He understood that they came through his own family, on loan from the great I Am. Rebecca's words were fully realized in their grandson, Jesus.

After tracing the words, he brought his fingers to his lips. Kissing them he moved them back to the carved words. He placed his fingertip kiss of a blessing on top of the Aramaic phrase, "Hahabia ahbato." Love has come.

Sixteen

The Celebrity Theater had been a staple in Phoenix for over forty years. It was unique as concert venues go, since it was set in the round. The theater contained a modest 2,650 seats, none of which could be considered a bad seat. A rotating stage ensured that no matter where someone sat, each and every concert goer would have an excellent view of the performance. Throughout its history, the Celebrity had hosted a countless number of great bands including Led Zeppelin, The Grateful Dead, Yes, and Heart to name a few. Later that evening the Lil' Debbie Band would be joining that list.

The Celebrity also held a very special place in Michael's and Debbie's hearts. Over the years, they had seen numerous shows there together, which always included Cookie once she became a member of their tribe. That's what Michael called the relationship of the band, but it most especially applied to the special bond that existed between Debbie, Cookie, and Michael. Cookie, for all practical purposes, had become family. In the last two years the mini tribe had seen over ten shows at the Celebrity, and a few of those shows included other members of the larger tribe.

In addition to the concerts themselves, the tribe made an event of those evenings by getting to the venue's parking lot two hours before the show and tailgating. The last show they had seen at the Celebrity was Heart about a month before. Bill Miller, the band's bassist, along with his young wife, Belva, came to that show and supplied the wine, providing both a Kendal Jackson Chardonnay and a Smoking Loon Cabernet. Bill loved his chardonnay but knew that Michael and Debbie favored the Loon. Cookie had made Swedish meatballs and her special hot brie cheese dip that Michael loved because she added raspberries to its center. Michael and Debbie brought homemade potato salad, chips, waters, soda, and the folding table to support the picnic fare. In between the munching, the sipping, and the laughter they talked about music. The usual gamut of that conversation included topics like what songs they were currently doing that they either loved or hated, what songs they should bring back to their set list, and ideas for new songs. It was that evening that Bill brought out his acoustic guitar to play a progression that he had been fooling around with. Not much of a wordsmith, Bill would often bring in some potential songs to the band which needed a lyrical tag. It was the four chords of the bridge that caught Michael's attention. He would later go home and build off that progression until finally "Be My Everything" came into being.

So there stood Debbie and Michael at the north entrance of the Celebrity, about to walk into the "Band Only" entrance. From where they tailgated in the past, they used to look over at the tour buses parked in front of this very entrance and dream about how cool it would be to walk off such a bus and into the backstage area. And now, here they stood with Robert Grey laminated band passes hanging from their necks, Michael with a guitar case in each hand, and Debbie with her gig bag strapped over her right shoulder. They were about to enter the very entrance they used to dream about. As Michael ascended the cement steps of the entrance he looked to his right and located the spot where they always tailgated. It was empty, and that made him smile.

The band had been asked to be at the theater three hours before the show to do a sound check. Robert Grey and his band had come in around noon for theirs and would be shortly heading from their hotel to the venue. For the most part, it was what Michael called a walk-in, walk-off gig. There was no PA for the band to bring in and set up, and the venue employed a sound company that would bring in virtually any amps, keyboards, sets of drums, and microphones they wanted. Despite having the option of having a drum kit there for him, Dave opted to bring in his own set of Pearls. Bill was more than happy for them to supply an Ampeg SVT bass amp with a matching set of eight ten-inch speakers. Erik Ogden, the band's keyboardist and trumpet player, was tickled to learn that the sound company had a Yamaha Motif Eight and opted for that. As long as Cookie had her Cherry Cola telecaster and her Nancy Wilson Signature Model Martin acoustic, she didn't care what kind of amp they provided. Michael, however, insisted on using his own vintage Twin Reverb. Not only did it sound incredible, but it once belonged to his father and he couldn't imagine doing this particular show without his amp or without Mr. White. Michael set down his guitars in the backstage area and was about to head out and get his amp from the car when a man, who he later learned was named Todd, offered to get it for him.

After handing Todd the keys to his car, he turned to Debbie and said, "You know you've made it when you have your own personal roadie!"

Taking Michael and leading him by the hand, Debbie walked him through the backstage area and then down the ramp which led directly to the stage.

"No, you know you've made it when you find yourself performing on a stage like this," Debbie said.

Both Debbie and Michael were blown away. It was a perfectly set stage, surrounded by nearly three thousand seats.

Debbie is right, thought Michael, *this is a much better sign that we've made it than having some guy named Todd lug in my amp.*

The whole tribe was already on the stage. Each of them was noodling with their instruments while waiting for the direction of the sound engineers. When Debbie and Michael walked onto the stage, Cookie put down her Martin and greeted them with arms wide open.

"Group hug!" Cookie proclaimed, wrapping her arms around Debbie and Michael, both of whom hugged her vigorously in return.

Cookie stepped back and grabbed each of their hands. With heavy sincerity, she said, "Thank you. Thank you so much for not only this, but for being there when I most needed a friend. I love you both and I couldn't be happier!"

Squeezing her hand extra tight, Debbie replied, "Cookie, it's a two-way street. I love you, too, and I don't think I'd be the same person if our paths hadn't crossed that night at Burba's."

"Ditto to that, Cookie. Thank you for everything," Michael added.

The sound engineer called for the band to ready their instruments for sound check. The process started with the drums. Dave methodically pounded each drum and cymbal separately until the engineer gave him a thumbs up for each.

Michael slung Mr. White over his right shoulder. His intent was to tune it and the Les Paul he brought for the show. But before he reached for Mr. White's tuning keys, he looked out into the theater. He spun himself slowly around looking at each of the sections that would soon be filled with people. As his turn brought him to the walkway that connected the stage from the green room area, he noticed Jim Thane standing at the top of the aisle. Michael knew that Jim must have been watching him soak in the atmosphere. Jim looked at Michael and gave him a grin and a thumbs up. Michael grinned back and slowly bobbed his head up and down. No words needed to be said, they knew exactly what each other was feeling.

Seventeen

Laban's men picked up the table, as planned, one day after Jacob had put his stamp on it. Given the importance of the client, Jacob was on hand to supervise all aspects of the delivery, especially getting the table secured safely in their wagon. Jacob took every precaution possible to ensure that not a single nick would blemish his work.

Since finishing the table, Jacobs's hands were once again filled with pain and his fingers twisted back into their previous deformities. Despite the pain, Jacob hadn't been this happy in a long time. He knew his life had been a blessed one and that it continued to get more and more hallowed with each passing day.

By the time Laban's men pulled out of Nazareth, Jacob was exhausted. Rather than starting the walk back to the home he shared with Ephraim, he turned and headed back to the workshop. He walked through the doorway of the shop, pulled up a stool, sat, and leaned his elbows on the top of the work bench.

He inhaled the rich aroma of cedar, holding it in for as long as possible. Yes, his life was blessed. Beyond blessed. He had just partaken in a miracle and lived to witness the miracle of miracles in his grandson. While he glowed and basked in these blessings, he could not help but think of

Rebecca. He missed her so very much. How he wished she could have been there to see the man Joseph had become, to have gotten to know Mary, and to have held in her arms the world's greatest miracle, their grandson, Jesus.

With these thoughts caught happily in the revolving door of his mind, Jacob laid his head on the work table and fell asleep. Soon, he began to dream. In the dream, Rebecca came to him looking as she did when she was twenty. Adorned in a blue dress complemented by a wreath of flowers in her hair, she took her beloved husband's hand in hers.

Looking at him with a love deeper than he had ever experienced before, she said, "As I hold you now, know that I am not letting go. Be still, my Jacob and let your hand become one with mine. I will fly with you this night."

Rebecca kissed the top of Jacob's head. With that kiss, he slipped from this life into eternal life. She had kept her promise to him. Lovingly, she led him home.

Eighteen

By the time the band was into their third song, any butterflies they had been feeling were replaced with confidence and smiles. The Lil' Debbie Band had never played better.

They opened the show with the powerfully grabbing "Contents May Shift," an up-tempo rocker custom fit to kick off a concert. They followed "Contents" up with their version of the Jimmy Hayes blues classic, "Neighbor, Neighbor," which Debbie dedicated to everyone in attendance.

"This one is for my Phoenix neighbors," she warmly declared.

The third song they performed that night was titled "Jeremy's Kingdom," and it was about a genius boy whose intellect was only surpassed by his ability to love others. The song was especially meaningful to Cookie since she co-wrote the song with Michael, the only song for which she had a writing credit. As they played it, Carol went crazy knowing that Cookie had penned most of the lyrics and a chunk of the chords. But what brought her fist in the air the most, was her cognizance of just how much the song meant to Cookie.

Carol was also elated that Cookie went with her wardrobe suggestion of a well-worn pair of jeans and a white, long sleeved shirt. Cookie had dubbed the top her "pirate shirt" due to its puffy sleeves and the fact that it laced up the front instead of using traditional buttons. Complementing the jeans and pirate shirt, Cookie wore a black leather vest that Carol thought made her look like a modern day Joan Jett. The crowning touch of her evening attire, and what made her look like a total rock star in Carol's humble opinion, were the black army boots Cookie wore with the bottom of her jeans tucked into them. Cookie couldn't help but grin through the entire song.

Michael and Debbie were especially in the zone that night. During those first three songs, the smiles they shot back and forth conveyed a deep love for what they were doing and for each other. Twice, Michael looked up the ramp leading to the backstage area and saw Robert Grey watching and nodding his head in approval. As the stage turned and rotated to the south end of the theater, Cookie saw Carol and Veronica in the front row wearing their backstage passes around their necks. Carol was beaming and both Cookie's and Veronica's hearts burned with happiness for her.

As the third song ended, Michael got onto the mic to introduce their new song. "Thank you, Phoenix! It's great to be here tonight with you all. But if I'm honest, I am thrilled to be sharing the stage here with my wife and best friend. Please give it up for Lil' Debbie!"

The crowd responded with a very respectable round of clapping and a few of those shrill whistles that some are gifted with the ability to do and the attitude to share.

After the applause died down, Michael continued, "This next song is a new one for the band. In fact, this is the first time we've played it out. It's a song I wrote with my little angel, Debbie, in mind. It's called 'Be My Everything.'"

As Michael finished speaking, Cookie started right in with the acoustic introduction. After a few measures, Michael began to sing.

"Love, you know, is a funny thing. It holds on tight to your richest dreams. We wish upon a star that they all come true…and then they do. Be my everything, be my everything."

With the crescendo on the second everything, the full band joined in with Cookie's guitar. Looking over at Debbie, Michael continued singing, keeping his eyes on hers for the next several lines.

"Whether the shadows of tomorrow become too dark, or our future days soak in radiant dreams, you are my everything, you are my everything."

The song went into the chorus and Debbie's voice joined Michael's as they gazed into each other's eyes.

"Be my everything, be my everything, my hope for glory, my muse in life's garden. Be my everything, you are my everything. My minutes, my seconds, and the hours in between. Be my everything, be my everything. You are my everything, be my everything."

When the song came to an end, two things were certain. First, that the world now knew just how in love Michael and Debbie actually were. Second, that they had a hit on their hands. The audience responded with an unprecedented standing ovation, which was totally unheard of for a local warm-up act. The response blew the band away, especially Michael who never expected that kind of response from a ballad, let alone a ballad he had written. The guy with a gritty rock-blues voice had now exposed a softer side of himself.

Their thirty-five-minute set began and ended in what seemed like thirty-five seconds. Nonetheless, it was a great thirty-five minutes and one that held the promise of additional opportunities. As great as the evening had been going, the Cinderella night was not quite over for Debbie and Michael. About halfway through Robert Grey's show, Jim got a message from the stage to ask Michael and Debbie if they both knew the blues classic, "Born Under a Bad Sign," in the key of E. Not only did they know it, they had performed it many times in that very key. Before they knew it, Debbie and Michael were back on stage, this time with Robert Grey. Debbie traded off vocals with Robert, and Michael traded him a series of menacing guitar licks. After a six minute all out jam, the song ended to thunderous applause.

Getting back onto his mic, Robert shouted with genuine enthusiasm, "Ladies and gentlemen, please give it up for Lil' Debbie and Michael Fortunato!"

Michael was sure he was dreaming as he exited the stage with Debbie.

Nineteen

After basking for well over an hour in the glow of their biggest show ever, it was time to disperse and head for home. Several band members said their goodbyes and made their way out the backstage door. Though she was still revved up emotionally from the show, Debbie was looking forward to going home and hitting the sheets. Michael, Debbie, and Cookie were about to leave when Jim Thane approached them.

"Guys, everyone is just about out of Robert's meet-and-greet and he wants to know if you can stick around to talk to him for a half hour or so. I've got a really good feeling and I think that we may want to hear what he has to say!"

Debbie was just too darn exhausted. "Michael, as much as I want to hear what he has to say, I think I am about to fall asleep here standing up."

"I can take you home," offered Cookie.

"Are you sure, honey? I understand, though, if you want to go," Michael said.

"Yep, mama has to go sleepy. Now give me a hug and a kiss, big fella," Debbie replied, placing her arms around his neck and planting a kiss square on his lips. As their lips separated, she added, "I love you very much. Thank you for this, and for everything."

Michael stared deeply into her eyes. "You are my everything, be my everything."

"I always will be." Debbie kissed him again, lingering a little longer than normal. When she pulled away, she looked at Cookie and asked, "You ready?"

Cookie nodded and the two women gathered up their things.

Michael watched Debbie and Cookie head out the very backstage door they once dreamed of being able to enter.

Twenty

Cookie swung a left out of the Celebrity and headed south onto Thirty-Second Street. About a block down and on the opposite corner of Thirty-Second Street and Washington, Debbie spotted a homeless man with a sign asking for food.

Helping the homeless was one of the things Michael and Debbie tried to do as often as they could. They went out about once a week to the park behind the library in downtown Phoenix to distribute twenty or so lunches to the homeless that they prepared beforehand. They also kept a constant supply of granola bars in their car to hand out to homeless people, like the man Debbie had just spotted. They never gave money, since they knew the sad fact that many homeless individuals had real problems with drugs and alcohol.

Debbie once heard a quote from Mother Teresa which she typed up, framed, and put on the desk they shared at home. It read, "Our ticket to heaven is a letter of recommendation from the poor." Between that and the scripture centering on the powerful and truthful, "Whatsoever you do for the least of my brothers, you do it for me," Michael and Debbie saw to it that they made a dedicated effort to help the homeless.

After spotting the man herself, Cookie knew what was coming.

Sure enough, Debbie asked, "Hey, Cooks, would you mind circling back around so I can give that guy some food I snagged from the green room?"

"You are such a wonderful person, Deb. Sure, no problem," replied Cookie.

Cookie circled her Jetta back across Washington and pulled over onto the gravel on the north side of the road, about three yards from the man holding the sign. As Cookie was pulling over, Debbie produced two protein bars from her purse along with a bottle of water.

"Be right back, Cookie."

"Be careful, Debbie," cautioned Cookie, rolling down her window.

Debbie approached the homeless man and asked, "Can you use something to eat?"

The man looked to be in his fifties, which likely meant that he was actually somewhere in his forties. His hair was long and unkempt, as was his beard. His skin was a dark tan and leathery. He was wearing an old Ocean Pacific t-shirt that had seen better days and a pair of jeans that likely hadn't been washed in months.

"Thank you kindly," the man said.

"You're welcome. I just wish I had more to give you," replied Debbie.

Just as she said that, she noticed a Burger King on the other side of the intersection. Debbie turned back to the man, who she thought could very well have been Jesus, and asked him, "How does a Whopper and fries sound? And I won't take no for an answer. With or without cheese?"

Before the man could answer, Debbie had started to cross the street so as not to give him the option to decline her offer.

Cookie watched everything and just grinned, thinking how incredibly kind her best friend was. Just as she heard the homeless man yell out, "with cheese," Cookie heard a sound that would change her life, and more so Michael's life, forever.

The delivery truck tried to brake but didn't have the time it needed.

In a matter of seconds, Debbie went from feeding a man who could have been Jesus, to actually meeting Him.

Twenty-One

The meeting between Michael, Jim, and Robert Grey couldn't have gone better. Robert loved everything about the band and commented especially on three things: the quality and energy of Debbie's voice; Michael's guitar playing, which he said he would put against anyone in the business; and lastly, just how great of a song "Be My Everything" was. Not only did Robert Grey offer the Lil' Debbie Band the opportunity to open for him the rest of his tour, but he also offered to put Michael and Jim in touch with his record label.

Everything Michael could have hoped for seemed to have come true. He literally felt like he was walking on clouds. Elated, Jim Thane offered to take Michael to Mullins & Follensbee's for a celebratory Guinness, but he politely declined citing that there was only one place and one person he needed to be with at the moment. Jim more than understood.

Michael headed down the cement steps from the Celebrity and made his way toward his car. As he reached for the door handle, he felt his phone vibrate in his front left pocket. Removing it, he glanced down and saw that it was Cookie.

Michael answered the phone and learned that his everything was no longer.

PART TWO

One

Mary and Jesus had known about Laban's granddaughter's wedding for a long time and both were excited to start the twenty-mile trip to Cana for this most sacred and joy-filled event. Throughout the years, well beyond the lives of both Jacob and Joseph, Laban continued to be a great customer and friend to Mary and Jesus. By this time, almost every piece of furniture in Laban's large and wealthy home came from the shop once owned by Jacob and Joseph, which had now passed into the capable hands of Jesus. But Laban's support of the family's craftsmanship didn't end there. Laban was the best salesman any professional carpentry shop could ever ask for, having sent more customers to Jacob's shop than could be counted. Even when Mary and Jesus moved their home and shop to Capernaum, business, in large part due to Laban, followed them in droves.

Through the years, Mary and Jesus got to know Laban's granddaughter, Rachel, very well. They had watched her grow from a sprout of a girl to the exceedingly beautiful woman that she had now become. Rachel was born about fifteen years after Jesus and was the youngest child of Laban's son, Seth. She was the only girl born to Laban's line, and was considered the jewel of Cana. She certainly was the crown jewel in Laban's eyes.

Though they had not yet met John, her husband to be, they had heard so many good things about him. John had inherited a lucrative family business in Jerusalem where he and his brothers produced some of the best clothing and fabrics in the area. In fact, John himself had created all the dresses the nuptial party would be wearing at the wedding. John was not only a successful business man, but he possessed a pure heart and was a man open to the ways of God.

In a similar way, Jesus had been working diligently in his carpentry shop for well over a decade. At age thirty, he stood a rugged seventy-one inches tall. His dedication and exceedingly high work ethic sculpted Jesus into one of the most physically in-shape men in the entire region of Galilee. His hands were strong from the years of gripping chisels, slamming hammers, and guiding planes. He wore his dark brown hair past his shoulders and, like his father and his father before him, he wore a beard that he kept well trimmed. Jesus was a truly handsome man. No one could exactly put their finger on it, but there was something special, something very special and peaceful about Jesus. He had an unexplainable magnetism about him. Though he was striking in appearance, this other, much harder to classify allure more accurately defined him and attracted so many to him.

Under Jesus' guidance, the carpentry business had been going well. But Mary, whose intuition was second to none, knew that its days were coming to a close. Being his mother, she knew Jesus better than anyone and recognized that his course in life was set for much deeper waters. Over the last several months she had a sense that he would soon be surrendering himself to wherever the Lord God was calling him. In fact, it was just a couple weeks ago that he brought two new friends to the house whom he had respectfully introduced to her, and then proceeded to talk with them for hours outside the workshop. Since that day, Andrew and Simon had become regular fixtures at the residence. When Jesus wasn't in the shop, he would take to meeting up with his two new friends on the shore where they had a thriving fishing business.

Just a couple days ago, Jesus' circle of friends expanded to include a man named Phillip. Jesus had invited Phillip over for dinner, along with Andrew and Simon. While they were eating, Phillip told Jesus that he had to meet his friend, Nathanael, who lived in Cana. Jesus took the opportunity to inform them that he and Mary were heading up to Cana for a wedding in a couple of days and asked if they would come along. All three gladly accepted the invite, eager to spend their days on the road listening to the captivating words of Jesus of Nazareth.

Mary knew that this gathering of new friends was the beginning; the seal had indeed been broken. Though she didn't know its exact course, she knew that this path would lead to much joy and to much sorrow, but most especially to God's plan for the world. When she would later think back to that dinner with Andrew, Simon, and Phillip, she would recall the looks in the eyes of those men as they listened to her son. That evening she saw in their eyes the same stares she observed in the women in town who would notice him. It was the same look that most people would have in every future encounter with him. It was the look of awe, of depth, of wanting, and of needing more than the world could ever offer. She understood those feelings more than anyone, as she experienced them each and every day of her life.

Two

That evening hung suspended. It seemed to have no beginning and no end. It just was. All elements of a standard evening, of a normal life that Michael had known and loved, were abruptly lost to a nothingness he never imagined existed. It wasn't pain, and yet it was pain in its severest form. He encountered numbness and a feeling of nonexistence, of no longer being associated or connected with life and all its previous beauty. He would have traded what came over him for any type of physical pain in a heartbeat. But he wasn't thinking about trades of that sort. He wasn't thinking at all.

Interrupting the nothingness, and at the same time adding to it, random thoughts came into Michael's head. These unsolicited thoughts bypassed the normal gateway and control of his conscious mind. They were able to slip their way into his brain as all other thoughts were slipping out. Among them were lines of songs, of movies, of poetry. Seemingly random, they carried a thread of connection: they were all associated with Debbie. As these untamed thoughts forced their way in his mind, each inflicted daggers of pain and added to Michael's feeling of nihility.

"Baby, baby falling in love, I'm falling in love again," by Hamilton, Joe Frank & Reynolds was the song he used to sing to Debbie when they first met. It was the first of the violent intruders.

"All I need is the air that I breathe and to love you," by The Hollies next stole into Michael's mind like a thief in the night. By itself it was one of the greatest love songs of all time, but it had a deeper meaning for Debbie and Michael. The song was featured in the film *Seeking a Friend for the End of the World*, a movie Michael and Debbie treasured since they both identified with the depth of the love its two main characters had for one another. Their love was so richly intimate that each could take on the reality of the world's end just as long as they were together, looking into each other's eyes.

This unsolicited movie reference led to movie lines from one of Michael and Debbie's absolute favorite movies of all time, *You've Got Mail*. The invading image came from the end of the movie when the character, Joe Fox, discloses that he is Meg Ryan's secret email beau.

Seeing her tear up at realizing that he was her secret internet pen-pal, Joe Fox offers her his handkerchief and says, "Don't cry, Shopgirl, don't cry."

To which Meg Ryan's character stammers out, "I wanted it to be you. I wanted it so badly to be you."

This scene had always caused Michael and Debbie to shed a couple tears whenever they watched it, and they were lines that they would often recite out of the blue as a way of expressing their love for one another.

Michael's favorite poem of all time was "Annabel Lee," by Edgar Allen Poe. Rather than the romantic beginning of the poem, what made its way to Michael's flowing consciousness that dark evening was the poem's painful ending.

> For the moon never beams without bringing me dreams,
> of the beautiful Annabel Lee;
> And the stars never rise, but I feel the bright eyes
> of the beautiful Annabel Lee;
> And so, all the night-tide, I lie down by the side

Of my darling—my darling—my life and my bride,
In her sepulcher there by the sea—
In her tomb by the sounding sea.

Unable to think, unable to process anything but grief, Michael was barely aware of Cookie being with him all that evening. It was Cookie who brought the news of Debbie's death to Michael. She knew that it would be better than having a cop show up at his door to break the news. Next to seeing her best friend die, telling Michael that his one and only, his everything, had passed away was by far the worst thing she ever had to do. Even though her hurt and sense of loss were immense, she had to be there for Michael. And so she sat with him in silence on the couch in his family room, hoping her presence substituted for the shallowness any words might have to offer.

At his innermost level Michael knew that Cookie was there. In the recess of his soul, whose ability to communicate with his conscious self had been currently muted, he was glad that she was there. While he felt nothing and was nothing, he was not alone.

Three

Jesus, Mary, and their three traveling companions made it to Cana on the second day of the week and one day before the wedding feast. As predicted, Laban and his wife, Miriam, warmly welcomed Mary and Jesus' new friends and gladly put them all up in their guesthouse.

Later that day, Phillip brought Nathanael to meet Jesus. Nathanael seriously doubted all that Phillip had told him about Jesus being someone special, perhaps him even being a prophet. Despite his initial skepticism, it took all of about two minutes and a single deep look into Jesus' eyes to convince Nathanael that this Jesus was no ordinary man. Even though he had previously received an invitation from Laban to attend the wedding, Nathanael readily accepted Jesus' invitation to join his mother and circle of friends at the event. Unbeknownst to him at the time, Nathanael had also internally accepted an unvoiced summons of Jesus to change his life and to change the world.

When Mary, Jesus, and their friends entered Laban's house the next day, the wedding feast was in full swing. What first greeted the entourage from Capernaum was a wall of music. The volume and vitality of the music took second place to the next greeting they received, which was the bear-like hug of their host and friend, Laban.

"Mary!" yelled Laban, with an enormous smile on his face. He nearly ran to her, giving her a warm and tight embrace. Turning toward Jesus, he said, "And Jesus, son of Joseph, son of Jacob! Welcome to my home and to this most festive and holy occasion!"

Miriam followed by greeting her friends with a less intense hug than the python-like squeeze they had received from her husband, but one which was packed with as much love. "Greetings, Mary and Jesus, how wonderful it is that you could make it here for this most holy day."

Unlike her solid stump of a husband, Miriam was a petite woman. To a stranger she might be described as frail, though she was anything but this. Since day one of their marriage she had worked hard alongside her husband and had helped to build their farm to make it as successful as it had become. That often meant doing the chores of men, including repairing fences, feeding the livestock, and tending the sheep. She was glad when their sons, Seth and James, were old enough to take on many of these chores. But even with them on board and helping out, she still would pitch in whenever she could. Laban loved this about his wife and was proud of her tough-as-nails work ethic. As proud as he was of his wife's work habits, he was even more proud of her greatness as a mother and of her beauty, comprised of both her physical appearance and her selfless heart.

When Laban first met her, Miriam had light brown hair that she had always worn shorter than most. Her eyes were set deep in her face and seemed to invite others to look directly into her soul. While her hair was now silver and her eyes surrounded by wrinkles, they never lost their soft texture and warmth. To Laban, she was as lovely as the day he married her.

On this most special day of Rachel's wedding feast, Miriam wore a brand new ankle length tunic which was a gift from John. It was made of the softest wool that she had ever seen or felt and was dyed a very beautiful and expensive light purple. She wore with it a matching veil that covered her head and fell eloquently down her back, nearly the length of the tunic.

"It is an honor to be here with you and with your family on what is a most holy and, as I see it, festive occasion!" Jesus said with a grin, casting a glance at the celebration that was already in full motion.

"Yes, indeed, my friend. You might know a thing or two about building furniture, but I am a master when it comes to throwing a great feast!" proclaimed Laban with a hearty chuckle. He next turned and greeted Jesus' accompanying entourage with fully extended arms. "Welcome everybody! Good to see all of you good men of Galilee as well."

Seeing Nathanael as he entered the house, Laban continued, "I see you have met up with this fine band of nomads from Capernaum! How are you doing, Nathanael?"

Nathanael replied, "I have never been happier. Much peace to you, Laban, to Miriam, Seth, Rachel, John, and to your family."

Laban embraced Nathanael. Then, turning to the other guests from Capernaum he said, "Years ago I would have bet a few drachmas that Nathanael here might have been the groom tonight!"

Nathanael was just a few years older than Rachel and the two of them had developed a lasting bond of friendship as children, which had been maintained over the years. But the blooms of romantic love had never developed between them.

"She's much better off with John than a perpetual student and dreamer such as myself!" exclaimed Nathanael, gripping Laban's shoulder.

"Well, come in everyone, come in! If anyone needs to wash up, please help yourselves to the basins," Laban said, as he pointed to the table at the end of the hall.

On the table sat two porcelain basins along with a large pitcher and several towels. At its side was an attendant whose job it was to pour water from the pitchers onto the hands and feet of the guests. Jesus looked at the table and grinned.

Laban, following Jesus' gaze, said, "Yes, that is Jacob's Miracle Table! Of all the furniture that I have purchased from your shop, this is my most prized piece."

"It means a great deal to me as well, Laban. It is more than just a table, is it not?" inquired Jesus.

Putting his arm around the shoulder of Jesus, Laban nodded, "It is, indeed, more than just a table."

The two men stared at the table for what seemed like several minutes but in reality was a few passing seconds. Joseph had shared with Jesus, on more than one occasion, the story of this miraculous table. The story told of how, when his family fled to Egypt, God provided momentary healing to Jacob's deformities and pain in order for him to build the table.

The table was so much more than a surface to set things or a place for people to eat their meals. At its core, the table represented the power and glory that is love, that is God.

As the day progressed the festivities continued to grow in their magnificence. The over three hundred guests were having a wonderful time laughing, well wishing, toasting, and feasting on the most tender beef and lamb they had ever had. Laban had demonstrated once again that no one knew how to throw a celebration as well as he.

As the sun was beginning to set, the uninterrupted merriment appeared to take a slight detour. Simon nudged Jesus and pointed to a slight commotion across the room. Mary caught the nudge and, with Jesus, followed Simon's finger. They saw Laban expressing himself rather passionately to the head waiter. Mary thought, at first, that perhaps Laban was getting complaints about the noise level from the Romans. Laban did a very poor job of hiding his feelings about the evils of Rome to just about anyone. It was because of this that the Romans kept a keen eye on Laban and did everything they legally could to make his life miserable.

Upon seeing the commotion, Mary said to Jesus, "Perhaps I should go over and see what's concerning Laban."

Mary rose from their dining table and went across the room to where Laban stood. She could see that Laban was upset. He had both of his hands on top of his head with his fingers weaving in and out of his thick hair.

Placing one hand on his shoulder and the other on the elbow that was nearest to her, Mary asked, "What is it, Laban? You look troubled. Are the Romans complaining about the feast?"

"Mary, for once it has nothing to do with those pagan Romans. This is…this is quite embarrassing," Laban said, running his fingers through his hair again. Continuing he said, "Either the guests are having far too much fun or I didn't order enough wine. Cletus, my head waiter, just informed me that we are about out of wine!"

Mary knew the pride that Laban took in hosting any occasion, let alone this most important celebration. She also knew that he wanted to make every last detail of Rachel's wedding day the best it could possibly be. She felt compassion for Laban and squeezed his shoulder more firmly.

"Do you have any way of securing more wine?" asked Mary.

"I'm afraid not. Before coming to me with this news, Cletus had his people check what other options there might be in town to get more wine here, but there's none to be had. And there is certainly not enough to suffice this crowd," replied Laban in a tone of defeat.

In an instant Mary's compassion turned to action. Looking at Laban she said, "Please send Cletus to me."

Laban, stunned by the authority in her voice, gaped at her.

"Send him now. Please," Mary said in response to Laban's blank stare.

There was something in her voice and her look that Laban could not explain. All he knew for certain was that he was suddenly convinced to follow her direction. His worry was replaced with a calmness he had never felt before. Without speaking a word, he nodded and went back to the kitchen area to find Cletus.

As soon as Laban left for the kitchen, Mary whirled around and looked to where Jesus and his friends were sitting. They had witnessed, from a distance, what had occurred. While they couldn't hear a word spoken over the jollity of the feast, they saw that Mary had somehow taken control of the situation. Looking at Jesus, Mary extended her arm and, opening her right hand, she moved her index finger back and forth, giving Jesus the universal sign for "come to your mother right away." Jesus immediately got up from the table with Andrew, Simon, Phillip, and Nathanael in tow. He and his friends made their way across the room to where Mary was standing.

"Mother, what is it that has Laban upset?" asked Jesus.

Before he could answer, Cletus and Laban appeared from the kitchen. Mary nodded to them and held up her index finger in their direction, indicating that she needed a minute to talk to Jesus. With that simple action, Laban, Cletus, and Jesus' friends all backed up to the nearest wall to provide Mary and Jesus the privacy requested by her very authoritative finger.

Moving closer to Jesus, Mary spoke in a low voice, "They've run out of wine and can't find any reserves to bring in."

Jesus felt the same pangs of compassion that Mary did when she first heard of the situation. Jesus knew that this wedding was very important to Laban and how such a thing as not having enough wine could bring embarrassment to him, the host of all hosts. All the same, it seemed like his mother was looking at him for a solution, a solution he did not have.

"Why are you looking at me this way, Mother? Your eyes seem to be insinuating that I can fix the problem," Jesus said.

Calmly, but with the assertiveness of Joshua commanding a battle, she looked directly into her son's eyes and said, "I know you can help. So please, help them now."

Jesus knew what she was saying. But now was not the time. It was too early for him to step out in this manner. *Soon, but not yet,* thought Jesus.

"Woman, whom I love and adore, it's not yet time. Please understand that."

Before Jesus could finish his sentence Mary turned to Cletus and said, "This is my son, Jesus. Whatever he tells you to do, you do. Trust me. No, trust him and everything will be fine."

Cletus glanced at his boss. Laban nodded in agreement.

"Yes, my lady," answered Cletus with a slight bow of his head. After bowing in respect to Mary, Cletus' head raised and turned toward Jesus as he waited for his direction.

Jesus inhaled deeply and conceded internally that his mother was right. In thinking about it for a mere second, he couldn't think of a time when she wasn't right. Little did she know the cascade of events that she had now set into motion.

Looking at Cletus, Jesus said, "Have your staff fill six stone containers with water and cart them over to that table." He pointed to the table with the basins for handwashing, the same table Laban had named the Miracle Table. "I will meet you over there when you have them ready."

Cletus had a very puzzled look on his face, which Laban picked up on immediately.

Laban said to Cletus, "Just do it."

And with that, the look of puzzlement was erased from Cletus' face and he left to secure the water containers for which Jesus had asked.

Jesus turned to his mother who was smiling. No words were needed. Jesus smiled back as he thought to himself, *Mother, Mother, so wise has the Father made you!*

As they walked back to the dining table to wait for the containers to arrive, the look of puzzlement that had appeared upon Cletus' face had now transplanted itself onto the faces of Andrew, Simon, Phillip, and Nathanael. Nathanael began to revert to his previous thoughts that this Jesus of Nazareth, whom his friend Phillip was hailing as the next great prophet, might be a little off the mark. The other three companions, though perplexed at the request, felt a burning in their hearts that they might witness something remarkable. In the short time they had known Jesus, they had often felt that same burning by just hearing the words he spoke. None of them had ever considered themselves as followers; they had all in fact been leaders, especially Simon. But to this man, to his authority, to his kindness, and to his words that resonated like no other's, they would forego leadership and gratefully follow him.

After about twenty minutes, the six stone containers, each holding thirty gallons of water, were carted in and set in front of the table made by Jacob. Jesus had asked for the containers to be set in front of the table for two reasons: first, so they and his actions would not be visible to the guests who were in the other room; and second, because he wanted what was about to happen to be near the love and legacy of his family here on earth, of which he considered the table to be a part.

Cletus sent one of his staff to Jesus to tell him the water containers were ready. Hearing that all the preparations had been made, Jesus got up from his table in the dining area and motioned for Mary and his friends to accompany him. When they arrived at Jacob's table, they found Cletus and Laban waiting alongside the six filled water containers lined up in perfect symmetry across the front of the table.

Jesus approached each container and pressed his hands to the top of the sides of each. At the touch of the first vessel, Jesus was overcome by the simple sensation of its coolness and its texture. It felt less like fired clay and more like the soil of Eden. He inwardly thanked God for his creation and moved to the next stone jar. Placing his hands on its sides, he thanked the Lord God for his earthly mother and for the wisdom and grace He had granted her. Touching the third, he prayed for all those he encountered today. Laying his hands on the fourth, he asked God to strengthen the four good men who themselves were now watching him as his hour had now begun. He also prayed for the other eight who would soon follow. As he touched the fifth earthen vessel, he prayed for the fortitude that he would need to follow the path which was carved out for him since the beginning of time. And as he gripped the sixth and final container, he thanked God for his entire earthly line, and most especially for the love and guidance of his mother, for Joseph, and for his grandfather Jacob, the builder of the Miracle Table.

Jesus stepped away from the table and faced the select group with tears in his eyes. Intimacy with the Father often produced such tears of connection. Looking into the faces of those he loved, he noticed tears in the eyes of his mother, Laban, and his disciples. The sacredness of his silent prayers pierced the souls of those who stood with him. Without it being revealed, all felt that something of a miracle had just taken place. This miracle was not what was about to be made known to Cletus and others, but it was the more precious miracle of God's real presence among them.

Looking to Cletus, Jesus asked, "Do you have a cup?"

Cletus motioned to one of his workers to bring him a cup from the utensils table. When the cup arrived, Cletus offered it to Jesus.

Rather than accepting the cup from Cletus he instructed him, "Immerse it in one of the containers and drink from it."

Cletus dipped the cup into the vessel nearest to him. As he brought the cup to his lips, his nose was filled with an aroma that spoke of a fine vintage rather than the nothingness of water he had expected to encounter. He drank from the cup and realized that his nose was not deceived. He tasted the best wine he had ever experienced. At the first sensation of its taste, Cletus' hand opened and the clay cup containing the remarkable wine fell to the floor. The cup shattered into several pieces and Cletus dropped to his knees, wrapping his arms around Jesus' legs and began to weep. Jesus placed a hand on his shoulder and asked Cletus to get up.

When he stood up straight Jesus whispered to him, "Please give the orders to serve the wine and tell no one what you saw. And Cletus, never stop believing, ever."

Holding back any further tears, Cletus replied, "Yes, my Lord." And with that, he gave the orders to his staff to begin serving the wine.

All those left standing there, members of a small yet elite group who had just witnessed a moment of heaven touching earth, were left without the capacity to speak. What could be said? What needed to be said?

Jesus approached each and hugged them, whispering in their ears,

"Know and believe." After he had hugged the last, he spoke to the small group which had witnessed God's glory, "There is more to come, a love that you cannot yet comprehend. As for the rest of the night please stay and enjoy Laban's generosity and join him in this most sacred celebration. I need to go now and pray to my Father. I will see you all in the morning."

He took a few steps toward the main entrance of Laban's house and suddenly stopped and went back to the table of Jacob. Jesus ran his hands gently and with a reverent tenderness over the top of the table. Placing both hands on the center of the table he bowed his head, closed his eyes, and said a prayer to his Father. After he finished the short prayer, he lifted his hands from the table's center and took a step and a half to the right end of the table. At its corner, he reached his hand under the table and found the engraving his grandfather had etched so many years ago. His fingers felt the contour of the letters, which spelled out the words of Rebecca.

"Love has come," Jesus said softly, but loud enough for both Mary and Simon to hear. "It has indeed. It has indeed."

Four

Unbeknownst to Laban, the Romans were keeping a closer eye on him than he would have ever thought. Word of his anti-Roman rants had been reported to various ranking Roman officials all the way up to Quintus Octavius, the Legion Legate of the area that encompassed Cana and several nearby towns. Quintus was an ambitious man who had worked his way up the ranks quickly by most standards. However, he felt he was long overdue for the promotion to the even higher rank of Imperial Legate.

Quintus had been appointed to his current position three years prior by the emperor himself. Most Legion Legates would serve at that rank for four to six years before receiving additional advancement. But Quintus was keenly aware of some who had risen to the rank of Imperial Legate after only three years. If it was possible for anyone to ascend to that position so quickly, then Quintus most certainly could as well. In order to achieve this advancement within his self-designated time, Quintus needed to ensure that order was completely maintained within his area of control.

Insurrection, on the part of an emerging group of the Judean population, had been increasing steadily over the past couple of years. These so called Zealots, who despised everything Roman, had been responsible for inciting riots and murdering numerous Roman soldiers throughout Judea.

As such, the current tolerance for this group was at absolute zero. So much so that if a Judean citizen was heard speaking anything against Rome, they were immediately suspected of being a Zealot and were then watched very closely. Given Quintus' desire for promotion and increasing power, this kind of profiling and investigation was taken to an even higher level within his jurisdiction than in most other areas.

So it came to be that Laban, while certainly not a Zealot, had come under the watchful eye of the local Roman authorities. In fact, on the night of his granddaughter's wedding feast, a low ranking Roman Centurion and an even lower ranking foot soldier had been assigned to watch over the wedding festivities to listen for any anti-Roman verbiage expressed by Laban.

Though they were given orders not to be obviously present at the event, as in standing in the middle of the dining room while dinner was being served, they were not to remain invisible to those gathered either. Their orders were to be seen but not to be obtrusive. As such, they walked the perimeter of the house or stood near its entrance. To the guests, it was not surprising that a couple of Roman soldiers would be posted nearby. Any time a large gathering was occurring in Cana, especially at weddings, a Roman presence was not an uncommon sight.

So neither Laban nor his guests took much notice of the freshly commissioned Centurion and his minion who were assigned to watch them that night. What they didn't know was that these soldiers were not sent to simply ensure order to a large gathering as much as they were sent to observe the suspected Zealot, Laban.

And so it was that this Centurion took a keener interest in what was going on inside the party than most men who would have been assigned to observe a typical wedding. He and his companion spent much of their time looking and listening through the open windows and standing in the doorways with their ears wide open. Even though the target for the evening was Laban, the young Centurion took notice of the man he heard everyone refer to as Jesus. There was something about this man, something about his command and presence that caused the Centurion to pay more attention to him than to Laban. He was so focused on this man called Jesus that, at one point in the evening, Laban, on his way to relieve himself, had walked right past the Centurion unnoticed. The foot soldier, however, observed that his commander's focus had deviated and that their principle target was now outside and in prime proximity for them to eavesdrop on.

Giving the Centurion a slight tap on the shoulder, he said, "Sir, would you like me to follow him?"

The Centurion heard the solider say something, but he was so distracted he had to ask him to repeat himself. "What was that, Jarinus?"

"Would you like me to follow Laban, sir?" replied Jarinus. Although he was annoyed that his superior officer had taken his eye off the target, he did his best to remain respectful.

"Yes. Just be sure to keep a proper distance," the Centurion ordered.

"Yes, sir." Jarinus turned and walked briskly toward the latrine that Laban had just entered.

As it turned out, relieving the feast's liquid intake was the only thing Laban had in mind upon leaving the house. Exiting the latrine, Laban strolled back inside the house without having a single conversation with the guests who were milling around on the grounds of the farm. Jarinus returned to the side of his superior somewhat disappointed that Laban didn't afford him the opportunity to eavesdrop on one of his conversations.

The Centurion resumed his gaze through the entryway windows and watched the crowd, most especially Jesus. As Laban returned through the main entrance of the house, he was met by the head wine steward. Laban appeared to get angry, to the point that he began to pull at the hair on his head.

Seeing this, the Centurion said to his underling in a low voice, "I'll stay here. You go by the front door and keep an eye on things there."

Jarinus nodded and quickly assumed his new post.

Jarinus' view of what happened next was somewhat obscured, but the Centurion saw everything. He saw the man Jesus and his mother come to the aid of Laban. He watched as the head steward brought Jesus six vessels. The Centurion was transfixed as this man placed his hands on the jars and looked upward, seemingly in prayer to his Jewish god. He saw the shock in the eyes of the steward when he sipped the liquid from those same vessels. And the Roman Centurion most certainly noticed the look in the eyes of everyone who was near Jesus, and in the behavior of the steward who threw himself at the feet of this oddly powerful man.

But what he remembered the most from that evening's interaction began shortly after simple water had been turned into gourmet wine. The Centurion watched as Jesus reverently ran a hand across the surface of the water vessel table. He observed how, after caressing the top surface of the table, Jesus briefly ran his hand underneath one of its corners. The Centurion saw him look upward and whisper something he couldn't hear. And what happened next was something that would impact him forever. Jesus looked through the open window and directly at him. As their eyes met, the Centurion was given a gift. Though he didn't know it then, this was a gift he would always treasure—Jesus smiled at him.

The Centurion went home that night feeling transformed. He felt as though a great change in himself was taking form. He couldn't explain it, he just fully experienced it. Before falling asleep, the man began to think about how some things seemed to happen for a reason. After all, he wasn't even supposed to have duty that evening. The truth was, reconnaissance work was a far cry from his skillset and current military assignment. His friend and fellow Centurion, Silvus, should have been there that evening. But Silvus' pregnant wife had gone into labor right before Silvus left for Laban's farm. Silvus happened to bump into the Centurion right after he received word of his wife's condition. Hearing this, the Centurion, who was always one to help out a friend, offered to take Silvus' post that evening.

Fate, thought the Centurion as he approached the grips of sleep. *It was truly fate. If not for being in the right place at the right time, I would not have encountered that man Jesus.*

Five

St. Philomena's Church in Mesa was a powerful pillar that supported the love Michael and Debbie had shared. While faith in Christ and in his church was what made their marriage noticeably special to others, it was the Holy Spirit, working through St. Philomena's, that continually strengthened and sanctified them both. It was their spiritual haven, their foundation of hope, and most certainly one of the greatest blessings in their lives.

Michael often heard his father talk about how it was divine intervention that had led them to becoming parishioners at St. Philomena's. Long before Michael was born, his father, Phil, and mother, Janet, had lived in the northern Chicago suburb of Gurnee where they were actively involved in their parish, St. Paul the Apostle. Janet was a member of the liturgy and environment committees, while Phil was active in the music ministry and served as a third degree knight on the parish's Knights of Columbus Council. The choir director was a devout young man in his mid-thirties named John Kane who was masterful at integrating both contemporary and sacred music into the Mass, which was both uplifting and liturgically correct. A fair percentage of the music John brought into the celebration of the Mass at St. Paul's was music written by Tim Booth or Tom Smith, both of whom were part of the music ministry at St. Philomena's in Phoenix. Through playing bass with the choir, Phil fell in love with the music they did from what he always would refer to as, "The guys at St. Philomena's." So when Phil and Janet made the move to Phoenix, the first place they decided to look for a church was at St. Philomena's. It took attending one Mass there for Phil and Janet to declare that they had found a new spiritual home. Divine intervention, indeed, seemed to have led the Fortunato family to St. Philomena's.

St. Philomena's was the church where Michael received all his sacraments and the place where he often encountered Christ in a very deep and real way. It was also there that he and Debbie were joined with Christ in the sacrament of marriage. And like his father, Michael, at the age of twelve and due to his immense ability, began sharing the musical talents God had given him and began to play at Mass. He felt blessed and amazed that he got the chance to play in the choir not only with his father, but with both Tim Booth and Tom Smith who were by then nationally and internationally acclaimed artists. A few years later, when Tom and Tim had left St. Philomena's for other opportunities, their replacement as music director was Matt Mayer whose musical talents only catapulted the music ministry legend of St. Philomena's to further heights. Matt's contributions included multiple contemporary Christian hits, Grammy nominations, and the chance to play in front of the Pope at a World Youth Day event.

Shortly after they were married, Debbie began to sing with the choir as well. Both she and Michael loved giving back to the Lord the gifts He had given them, and each felt blessed that they were a part of a choir so gifted with talent and yet so amazingly absent of ego. But as much as they loved the music of St. Philomena's, it was far from the thing they'd put at the top of their list of things they loved about the parish. Topping the list would actually be something not exclusive to St. Philomena's, and that was the true presence of Christ in the Eucharist. While common to all Catholic Churches, Michael and Debbie loved how St. Philomena's placed a great emphasis on bringing people deeper and deeper into the mystery of the Eucharist. The adoration chapel was a special place for Michael and Debbie. They went at least once every week, if not more, to pray and to be in the Lord's presence.

But of all things that St. Philomena's had to offer, one of the things the Fortunatos dearly loved was its Pastor, Fr. Charlie. It was Fr. Charlie who had married them and it was Fr. Charlie who put such an emphasis on the mysteries of the Eucharist at St. Philomena's. He had placed so much of an emphasis on the Eucharist that the parish's rich history of music had begun to be overshadowed by it becoming known throughout the Diocese of Phoenix as being a place of special devotion to the Blessed Sacrament.

So it wasn't surprising that the morning after Debbie's death, Michael wanted more than anything, needed more than anything, to get in his car and drive to his respite of respites: the adoration chapel at St. Philomena's.

Six

Cornelius Velius was born during the last year of the reign of Augustus Caesar and grew up in the town of Melfi in the Basilicata region of the Roman Empire. Melfi was a wonderful place for a child to be raised. It was far enough away from the city of Rome, about two hundred miles to the southeast, that the decadence and evils which often befall such large cities were at a sufficient distance so as not to have a detrimental effect on family life. Not that the Velius family had moved to Melfi to escape urban living. On the contrary, their family had called Melfi home for several centuries.

Cornelius' mother, Appia, was about as loving and nurturing as any mother could be. She was additionally blessed because she was as beautiful as she was kind. Cornelius was fortunate to have inherited her beauty. Her dark, thick hair, olive complexion, and unique eye color were gifts Cornelius received, which made him first an adorable child, and then later a very handsome man. Of all their shared features, the most remarkable one was the sky blue color of their eyes. In fact, no other family in Melfi had persons who possessed such blue eyes, or any shade of blue for that matter. Only Appia, a few relatives on her side of the family, Cornelius, and one of his four sisters, Zoe, had such unique colored eyes in all of Melfi. Zoe hated being different and if she could have been granted one wish, it would have been to have brown eyes like all the other kids. But having blue eyes never bothered Cornelius. In fact, he quite liked his rather inimitable eyes. He liked them not because they made him incredibly handsome, but rather because it created a unique bond that tied him even closer to the mother he deeply loved and admired.

Appia, likewise, loved Cornelius and his sisters. Though she loved all her children equally, if she favored any of them in the slightest, it was Cornelius. It wasn't because he was the only boy in the family, but because they shared similar dispositions. Like his mother, Cornelius had a poet's heart and their outlook on life reflected it. While so many people seemed to go through life without ever looking deeper, Cornelius and Appia were always searching beyond the obvious, always striving to find meaning and beauty in everything they encountered.

Appia noticed these tendencies in her boy at a very early age. She recalled how, at the age of five, Cornelius had been out one day playing war battles with his friends for several hours. Playing war was something the children often did since many of their fathers, most of whom served as their idols, were Roman soldiers. On this particular day, Cornelius came home and looked very sad. Sitting on a stool near the fireplace, the young boy sat with his eyes cast down on his sandals, his hands resting motionless on his knees, and bearing a pout that he didn't care to make obvious but that still made its presence known to his mother. Seeing this, Appia stopped cutting the vegetables she was preparing for dinner and went to her son. Getting down on her knees so she could be at his eye level, she took each of her hands and placed them on the sides of his face. She gently elevated his head so that their matched blue eyes met.

"Why so sad, my little soldier?" she inquired with a smile.

Rather than reply, Cornelius only began to look sadder and sadder.

Appia was about to say some words of comfort when she noticed a tear escape the corner of his left eye and roll down his ruddy and very pinchable cheek. Appia knew that Cornelius, like herself, was a very sensitive person. Instead of saying anything, she wrapped her arms around her boy and drew him to her. With his head buried in her shoulder, she began to pat his back in the hopes that she might be able to scour away any of the pains he was feeling. When his whimpering subsided, Appia released her tender grip and brought her eyes to meet his once again. She was just about to ask him what was wrong, but he spoke up instead.

Matching her stare, Cornelius very innocently and sincerely asked her, "What happens to us when we die, Mommy?"

Seven

It had been two years since Rachel's wedding and the only thing getting in the way of the prosperity of Laban and his sons was his inability to keep silent about his disdain for all things Roman. Rachel, by this time, was happily situated in Jerusalem with her husband, John. John's fabric business was doing well as orders kept hitting record levels month over month. During the same period of time, Seth and James helped their father build a farming empire in Cana. They easily had more head of sheep and cattle than the second and third most prosperous farms in the area combined. Like their father, Seth and James were as charming as they were good workers and businessmen. Like their father, and as a result of growing up in an anti-Rome environment, both the sons loathed the Roman occupation of Palestine. While both Seth and James shared their father's disgust for all things Roman, unlike their father, they didn't go around broadcasting their feelings. They knew that only harm followed those who opposed Rome, where even a simple statement of opposition could lead to the most serious of consequences. They often pleaded with their father to be careful with what he said and to whom he said it. But Laban was as stubborn as he was charming. Even Miriam begged him time and time again to keep his feelings for the Romans in-house. All the pleading of friends, sons, and spouse were to no avail.

One day a man came to Laban from the coastal city of Ptolemais to purchase thirty head of sheep. Ptolemais was a prosperous harbor city located about sixteen miles to the northwest of Cana. Ptolemais was known for its wealth and its higher level of sophistication than other neighboring towns. Laban had been there only once, but felt right at home with its well cultured citizens. The man introduced himself as Aryer of Ptolemais, a well to do farmer and businessman. Aryer was a middle-aged man who, like Laban in his younger days, had a muscular frame that told all who looked at him that he was a man who was not afraid of hard work. Unlike Laban, Aryer was tall by local standards, standing a little over six feet tall. He was dressed like any other Hebrew man and he wore a white, voluminous sleeved tunic to his feet that was complemented by a fine leather belt. Laban noticed the belt and was impressed since men with lesser means would not have been able to afford such crafted leather and would have had to make due with either a rope or a cloth sash with which to fasten their tunics. His complexion was that of a Middle Eastern native and everything about the man spelled elegant Hebrew to Laban. The only chink in his armor, from Laban's point of view, was that he walked with a noticeable limp in his right leg. Laban took an immediate liking to Aryer, not only due to his appearance, but also because of his name, Aryer, which meant lion in Hebrew. Growing up, Laban had a friend named Aryer and he always felt that he was lucky to have been named after such a strong, warrior-like creature. Although he had long gotten over it, Laban hated his own name when he was growing up because its meaning, white, was a long way from being as masculine of a name as the likes of lion!

Laban's comfort level with Aryer proved to be the vehicle of his demise. While working through the process of their transaction, Laban found an opportunity to verbally outline his hatred of the Romans. He told Aryer that because of his feelings and the way his people were treated, he looked for every opportunity to cheat the Romans out of their taxes.

"You take these thirty sheep that you're purchasing here today. I report to the tax collector that it was only twenty sheep I sold you and, just like that, I'm paying a rightful amount of tax versus the inflated rates the Romans want!" Laban declared with his standard bravado.

With his anti-Roman swagger now in full motion, he continued to brag to Aryer, "Just last week I sold a hundred sheep to a friend outside Nazareth and we kept the whole transaction under the table! I was able to give him a better price and, as for Rome..." Laban paused for effect and then continued, "well, Rome got squat!"

The smile on Laban's face exuded joy from cheating Rome any chance he got.

Aryer glanced back with wary eyes at Laban's declaration, but then caught himself tipping his hand a little too much. He quickly smiled in a way that indicated he was impressed with Laban's tactics. "Fair is fair and unfair is unfair," Aryer said.

"Darn right!" cried Laban, spitting on the ground as a sign of his repulsive attitude to the Romans. He continued, "And the very definition of unfair is everything Roman!"

Aryer paid Laban the agreed upon price for the sheep and told Laban that his herders would be by in a couple hours to take the sheep back to Ptolemais. Laban assured Aryer that the sheep would be fed and watered before his herdsmen's arrival and that the sheep would be ready for the journey. And with a handshake between two sophisticated and Hebrew men, the transaction was completed. Or so Laban thought.

What Laban did not know was that Aryer was not as he advertised. He was not from Ptolemais, he was not a well to do farmer, and he certainly wasn't Hebrew as Laban had presumed. He was in fact a Roman solider, or more accurately a spy for the Empire. Aryer's father had married an Aramaic woman while serving in Palestine. Such a mixed marriage was not a common occurrence, but it did occasionally happen. Because of this, Aryer, though fully Roman due to his father's lineage, received enough of his mother's looks that it was easy to mistake him as being Hebrew, especially when he was not wearing his Roman uniform. As for his name, it was only a nickname given to him by his fellow soldiers stationed in Palestine. He was the fiercest of warriors, the first to swing a sword in battle, and the guy everyone hoped was at their back when they went into a scrummage. Given his prowess as a combatant, his fellow soldiers in his legion gave him the fitting nickname of Aryer the lion! His real name was Marcus Sedonis and, due in part to having his right knee severely hammered in battle the year previous, the Romans put him to work as a spy.

His father often kidded him about his new career in the field of espionage saying, "That's what one bum knee, a combination of superior intelligence, and the ability to blend in with the locals will get you!"

About a week before his meeting with Laban, Marcus was briefed on the successful farmer in Cana. Numerous accounts by local citizens caused the authorities enough concern to consider Laban a threat to Roman peace. As a result, Marcus was pressed into service. His assignment was simple. Go pose as a man in need of sheep, meet with Laban, and see if he says anything against the Empire. One offhand comment against Rome would have been enough to get Laban in serious trouble and sufficient cause to get him sent to prison for at least a year. Cheating on Roman taxes put his offenses against the State at a significantly higher level, one which would cost Laban a great deal more than just time in prison.

Eight

After spending nearly two hours in the Adoration Chapel, Michael made his way into the church. He had an appointment with Rori Parmiter, the liturgy coordinator at St. Philomena's, to make arrangements for Debbie's funeral. Cookie was set to join him to try and help in any way she could, but more than that she wanted to be there to support her dear friend. Michael had some time before the appointment and he yearned to see the renowned mural that adorned the wall behind the altar of the church. It was Debbie's most favorite work of art. The thirty-by-thirty feet mural depicted thirty saints, along with possible future saints and religious people, against the backdrop of a lake at sunset with hues of orange, blue, and gold. In the center of the mural was the resurrected Christ coming down to earth and radiating light for all to see. The mural wasn't just beautiful, it was stunning. People from across the country would stop in at St. Philomena's just to experience this inspired work of art.

Michael knew how much Debbie loved the mural. They had both fallen in love with it the minute it was unveiled after a special Mass three years prior. He remembered Debbie once sharing with him the main thing that attracted her so dearly to the mural: its visual depiction of what was happening in reality. While the celebration of the Mass was occurring before them, it was also taking place in heaven with the very saints depicted on the mural at the very same moment.

Michael was thinking about that conversation as he entered the church. Walking down the center aisle, he kept his eyes forward on the mural. In the upper right hand corner was Michael the Archangel doing battle with the prince of evil and on the left was Gabriel blowing his trumpet, alerting the world of Christ's return. Lining the bottom of the wall were thirty saints and saintly people, which included St. John Paul II, St. Francis, St. Paul, St. Elizabeth Ann Seton, Blessed Mother Teresa, St. Vincent DePaul, St. Maximillian Kolbe, and St. John Vianney to name a few. At the center of the mural stood the church's tabernacle. As Michael genuflected at the outside of the second pew closest to the altar, he noticed for the first time that all those depicted superheroes of faith had their eyes focused on the tabernacle. Michael thought of how fitting that was. Once seated in the pew, Michael looked up at the center of the picture. Flanked by the angels Michael and Gabriel, Michael's eyes found the image of the risen Christ.

While the loss was overwhelming, Michael's faith held him together enough that he didn't completely succumb to the actual depths of his loss. His thoughts returned to Debbie's relation to the mural and again to how she loved the way it depicted the union of heaven and earth during the Holy Mass. He began to think about how she could now be joined within that very same unity which was so meaningful to her. It wasn't the same as having her in the pew next to him, but he knew that he would be joined to her in a way that was beyond the scope of human reason. It was that thought which caused the flood of tears to return. Michael's eyes filled and emptied, then filled again.

The mixture of loss and faith flooded Michael causing a rich depth of emotion and pain. As the tears and sorrow became more intense, Michael's head sank into his hands and he began to rock slowly back and forth in the pew. So lost was Michael in that combination of pain and the solace of his faith that he hadn't noticed Fr. Charlie had entered the pew and was sitting next to him. After about a minute, Fr. Charlie placed his hand gently on Michael's shoulder. Michael somehow knew without even looking up that it was Fr. Charlie. That simple feeling of pressure on his shoulder ministered more than any words ever could. Fr. Charlie knew that now was not the time for words. Both of them sat quietly next to each other until it was time to meet with Rori. Amidst his tremendous pain, Michael could never thank Fr. Charlie enough for being completely present to him, with him, and for having the wisdom to speak volumes of love without seeing the need to speak a single syllable.

Nine

When Cornelius was a few months shy of his eighteenth birthdate, his family had moved from Melfi to Caesarea as a result of a significant promotion his father received in the Roman army. His father, Decius Velius, a lifelong and ambitious soldier, had recently received the commission to serve as Primus Pilus in the Jewish land of Palestine. It was a huge advancement, one that would set up him and his family for life. In this position, he would serve as the senior-most Centurion in a legion of over fifty-six hundred men. Decius was a man who put, above all else, the virtues of discipline and honor to both country and family. Decius was broad shouldered and richly muscular due to his nearly twenty years as a best in class soldier of Rome. He was taller than most Romans of the time with dark black, curly hair and dark brown eyes. So deeply brown were his eyes that there was no doubt from which side of the family Cornelius had inherited his sky blue eyes.

Cornelius recalled hearing his father discussing the opportunity with his mother, Appia, in their home in Melfi when the first indication of Decius' potential promotion and transfer had surfaced. Appia had spent her entire life in Melfi. Melfi was the place where all her relatives lived, the place she played when she was a child, and the place where she was raising her family. Suffice it to say, the prospect of moving from Melfi to the Middle East was less than an exciting proposition to Appia.

"But Appia, this is an opportunity of a lifetime for me. For us!" Cornelius overheard his father say to his mother, both of whom were located in the front room of the house, unaware of Cornelius' presence just around the corner.

"Decius, but at what price? Our lives are blessed here in Melfi, are they not? So much joy we have had here. This is our place; this is where our family is. Now you want to take us to live amongst a culture we don't even know?" Appia spoke with more than a little emotion in her voice.

"My dear Appia, this promotion could be good all around. Think about it. My pay will go up to sixty times base pay. If I perform well, and I always do, I will be promoted to Praefectus Castrorum and then we will gain entry into the equestrian class!" pleaded an ambitious Decius.

As he said those last words, it dawned on Decius that ascending into the equestrian class of Roman society, to being in the social circles of those Roman citizens just under the rank of senators, while important to him, held no allure for Appia. He immediately wished that he could take those words back. His selling of the promotion was off to a poor start and he knew that he had better find a more salient benefit to the transfer than simply money and prestige. If he was to succeed in getting her to buy in, he would have to appeal to Appia's love of her children. And that's when a sure winner of a selling point came to his mind.

"Appia, the most important thing this move will do is greatly benefit Cornelius." Decius let those words hang and resonate in the air for a moment.

Appia, who had started to get perturbed by her husband's elitist reasoning, suddenly brought her head up from its dejected slump and directly met the gaze of her husband. Her blue eyes scrunched together and creases began to form on her forehead. Seeing her perplexed look, Decius knew he had gained her full attention. He felt a sudden confidence that he was about to land the knockout punch that would seal the deal.

Now very perturbed, Appia's voice increased in both its tone and bitterness. "How is moving the family to the ends of the earth, to live among people we don't know, leagues from Melfi going to benefit Cornelius?"

Now was his chance. Decius calmly responded, "As you know, dear, and as we have discussed on many, many occasions, I come from generations of soldiers who have served our country proudly."

Before he could say another word, Appia interrupted him and sarcastically said, "Yeah, yeah, and your grandfather served right next to Julius Caesar in the Gallic Wars, and a thousand years before that you had an uncle who served with Romulus and Remus. What does this have to do with our son?"

Decius decided to let Appia's sarcasm slide off him without rebuttal. Not that it was an easy thing for him to do. Decius' grandfather had indeed served right next to Julius Caesar during the Gallic Wars and received numerous commendations and battlefield promotions directly from the legendary leader. This was a source of great pride for the Velius family. He decided to let the highly unimaginative reference to Romulus and Remus pass right on by without comment.

"Precisely this, my dear Appia. Our son is fast approaching the age for him to enter into service. We both know that Cornelius is, well, is different from other young men his age. He is sensitive, attracted to the whims of writings and philosophy and, well, is bound to be of...let's say of a softer nature than the typical Roman soldier," Decius said, plotting out what he felt was now to be a winnable argument.

Appia, of course, knew these things about her son. Rather than ever considering them a weakness, she felt that his ability to look deeper into the complexities and beauty of life was an actual strength. These were the things she shared with and admired most about Cornelius. She was also very thankful that her extremely virile, man of men husband never looked down on their son for his soft heart and lack of Goliath strength. As tough of a man as Decius was, he accepted and greatly loved Cornelius and all his children for who they were.

Continuing his now well-formed argument, Decius added, "As Primus Pilus, I can have Cornelius assigned to any type of duty I care to have him assigned to. I would have that absolute authority. As it stands now, in my current commission, where and to what duty Cornelius would be assigned is out of my control. Appia, with this promotion I can keep our boy out of harm's way. I can keep him off the battlefield."

As he said those last words about keeping their son out of war, Decius placed his hand on Appia's arm and gave it a gentle squeeze. He knew that he had cinched the deal. Promising to keep Cornelius safe as a soldier would be the finer point that would get Appia and his family to make the move with him. Although he could have made the move on his own, given his love for his wife and family, there was no way he would leave them for several years for this or for any promotion.

As Decius squeezed Appia's arm, he suddenly felt a pang of guilt hit his gut. He had used his son's loving heart as a weapon. It dawned on him that the very reason he had just given his wife to accept the move should, in fact, be the only real reason why he should consider the promotion. Sure the prestige and money were all great prospects, but to keep his son, who while so different from himself he loved so much, out of situations that could harm him, should be the only reason to make the move.

"Decius, what you say is true. I will do anything, and I know you will as well, to protect our children. The children and I will go with you, providing that when you retire or have an opportunity to move back to Melfi, we will. Promise me that!" a suddenly more optimistic Appia said with a spring in her voice.

"Absolutely!" declared Decius. "And Appia," Decius lowered his voice, "I must come clean to you. I didn't just win an argument with you on this promotion, I won an argument with myself. I admit, at first this promotion was all about the power, the money, and the prestige. But as the words came out of my mouth on the ability to protect our son, that was when it really dawned on me that there is no other reason than that to take the promotion."

Appia wrapped her arms around her husband and buried her head into his chest. "How lucky I am to have a man like you. Cornelius is so different from you, yet you love him just the same. Thank you for accepting him as he is. I'm so lucky."

"I'm the lucky one. To have a wife like you, three lovely daughters, and such a wonderful and caring son like Cornelius. I, my dear, am blessed by the gods," Decius said as he affectionately squeezed the small of his wife's back.

A few tears rolled down Cornelius' cheeks. He knew that his father loved him, but always feared that his father didn't fully accept him because he was not the rough-and-tumble kind of guy. Hearing those words spoken by his father removed all such feelings. Cornelius' father truly loved him, accepted him for who he was, and would always be there for him.

Ten

Instead of seeing the two expected herdsmen who should have been coming down the road about that time to collect his sold sheep, Laban instead saw nine Roman soldiers marching in formation toward his farm. The soldiers consisted of eight men from the same Contubenium led by their Centurion, Gaius Illius. Under the command of Quintus Octavius, this Contubenium was one of three others whose sole job was to capture those found guilty of insurrection against the Roman Empire and to inflict whatever punishment the Legion Legate handed down.

Seeing the soldiers about a quarter of a mile from his farm, Laban quickly ran inside his house and began yelling, "Miriam! James!"

The tone in his voice sent shivers deep into Miriam who was in the kitchen and just beginning to prepare dinner. James also interpreted the timbre of his father's raised voice as an alarm and ran from the backyard where he had been working, through the house, and to its entrance where a very distressed Laban stood. Miriam joined James and saw the fear in her husband's eyes. Seth and his wife had left the day before for Nazareth to help a friend repair a house and were not present for what unfolded next.

"Father, what is it?" James inquired with more than a little concern in his voice. In all his forty-two years, he had never seen his father as distraught as he now was.

Miriam was equally concerned and suddenly very afraid. "Yes, dear, what is it?" she asked almost on top of James' words.

"Listen to me, we don't have much time. A small group of soldiers are coming up the road. Hopefully they are just paying me a courtesy visit, or maybe they want to buy an ox."

Before Laban could continue, James asked in a panicked tone, "Dad! How many times have we told you to keep your opinions on the Romans to yourself? What did you do now?"

"I have no idea, nothing that I can think of," replied Laban, who was sincere in his answer since he still had no clue that Ayrer was anything but a fellow Jew in need of some sheep.

Reminded of how close the soldiers were to the house, Laban spoke quickly, "We can talk about specifics later, but in the meantime I don't want to take any chances. James, take your mother out the back and head up to the top of the hill at the east end of the property. You can observe what happens from there. If they leave without destroying me or the farm, then return. If not..." he paused and continued looking directly into his son's eyes. "If not, then take yourself and your mother somewhere safe. I will stay here and see what it is they want."

While James wanted to stay and help his father in any way he could, he saw the concern in his father's eyes and did not argue. James knew that his father feared not only the worst for himself, but that he feared for James and his mother more.

James and Miriam each hugged and kissed Laban, and then left out the back of the house and made their way unnoticed up the forested hill.

With his wife and son on their way to a safe place, Laban returned to the front of his house and waited on the entrance path for the arrival of the Contubenium who were now less than fifty yards from him and his land. He tried to act calm, as if he got visited every day by a group of Roman soldiers. But he couldn't help his posture and body language that voiced his aching disapproval for the approaching men and all they represented. Standing with his arms folded in front of him and with his legs slightly spread apart, he made it known to his visitors that he was less than happy to see them on his property.

As the soldiers arrived at their destination, Gaius Illius commanded his men to assemble in a single line facing Laban. Gaius stepped to the front of that freshly-made line of soldiers. Looking at the man in front of him he inquired, "Are you Laban of Cana?"

"I am," answered Laban, who wanted to add more to that response but, for the first time, took the advice of his sons and bit his tongue.

Gaius took the scroll he had tucked under his left arm, opened it, and began to read, "Laban of Cana you have been found guilty of withholding from Rome its rightful taxes on the sale of livestock. You are also under suspicion of being a member of the Zealot party. By order of the Legion Legate, Quintus Octavius, we are to seize all your property, including home, livestock, and all personal material goods contained within the boundaries of your land. The accused is to be brought directly to the Praetor who will provide sentence for the crime of tax evasion. The Praetor will also determine, through rigorous inquiry, the charge of plotting attacks against the Roman Empire."

Gaius rolled up the scroll and made a forward motion with it pointing in the direction of Laban. Four of the eight soldiers, the two on each of the far ends of the line, advanced toward Laban. Three more soldiers formed a triangle of no escape around the prisoner, and the last went behind Laban and brought his arms behind his back.

Laban offered no resistance in fear that there could be repercussions for his family if he did. With his unopposed arms behind him, the soldier took the iron chain and cuffs he had been carrying on his belt and affixed them on Laban's wrists. Those same four soldiers, along with their superior, Gaius, led Laban away from his property and from those he most loved.

The other four soldiers had orders to guard the house until the Armicustos and his men arrived to strip away everything of worth from the house, barns, and property that was once owned by Laban.

Shocked by all they saw on top of the hill, Miriam and James kept a vigilant watch on the farm. They were deeply distressed at the sight of seeing their beloved husband and father being led away in chains. Had it not been for the four soldiers posted at their house, they would have immediately returned to it. But they decided instead that it was best to wait until they left. Less than an hour later, they saw another group of about twenty soldiers with five large wagons approaching the farm. The Armicustos, or quartermaster, had arrived along with several of his charges. Upon their arrival, four of the men were dispatched to tend to the livestock. They would remain at the property tending to the animals until it was decided where the herds were to be taken. The remaining soldiers began loading the wagons with everything once owned by Laban. Miriam and James watched from the top of the hill as all their possessions, all they loved, was taken from their house. Since everything Laban had owned was of top quality, nothing was left behind. They took almost every single item from the house and property that day, including the six miracle jars and a table that Laban loved almost as much as his family.

Eleven

If anyone could have a sense of the depths of dark emotion experienced by Michael, it was Debbie's parents, David and Dorothy Retzke, and Debbie's sister, Michelle. They had flown in a day before the funeral and had met with Michael at his house. Michael loved Debbie's family dearly and he was like a son to them as well. Michael's parents, Phillip and Janet, were also at the house when Debbie's parents arrived. Like the love the Retzkes had for Michael, the Fortunatos held Debbie in their hearts as a daughter.

Michael's disassociation with life, his feeling of nothingness, still hung over him like a prolonged Alaskan winter night which dared not end. He was there in the house with his extended family, a family that he loved, participating in round after round of shared memories and tears, and in the peppering of comments about Debbie being in the hands of our Savior. The vigil, held the evening before the funeral, occurred in a similar fog for Michael. A bit of clarity returned to him during Deacon Abe's homily when he spoke of the tender compassion of the Lord.

The tender compassion of the Lord.

The line played over and over in Michael's mind. Though he found himself deep in nihility, by a miracle of grace he was far from blaming God for Debbie's death. Tender compassion was one of the qualities Michael always associated with the Lord. And even in his darkness, in his current void, Michael felt that compassion draped warmly around him. Although it seemed very dim to him, the lamp of His love was lit for Michael and it was kindled by the very source of all tenderness.

Michael knew that Jesus was walking near him, yet the same dark night feelings followed him to the funeral Mass. Everyone was there. St. Philomena's was packed to near capacity. While funerals at the parish were typically better attended when the deceased was as young as Debbie, the large number of people who came out for hers was unprecedented. Those in attendance read like a veritable who's who of Debbie's life. There were the famous, there was family, there were friends, and there were the sweet children whom his angel, Debbie, had taught with such love and devotion. While a part of him was happy to see so many people come out to pay their deepest respects, Michael hoped he wouldn't have to talk to too many of them, if any. The Mass was important to him. He wanted to be there. He needed to be there, but anything beyond that he didn't feel he was capable of doing.

At Michael's request, Cookie sat with him in the first pew along with his parents and the Retzkes. Knowing just how much Debbie had loved her, and loving her as much as he did, he truly needed Cookie near him. And for the very same reason, Cookie needed to be in that pew as well. Michael recognized the pain and loss that Cookie was experiencing. It was Debbie who had calmed Cookie's turbulent world, and now that calm was seriously fragmented. Cookie viewed Michael as an extension of Debbie. Being close to him in the time of her own great need somehow brought her a remnant of Debbie's ever-calming peace.

The music for the funeral was chosen by Michael based on the songs that held special meaning to Debbie. They had played and sang together often at funerals and, due to that, they knew which songs meant the most to the other. In fact, during the meeting he and Cookie had had with Rori to plan the funeral liturgy, Michael recalled a conversation he had with

Debbie about a year before. It was right after they had done a funeral Mass at St. Philomena's where, over a breakfast for lunch at IHOP, they shared with each other the songs each would want to have played at their funeral. Of the list of about five songs Debbie mentioned, Michael recalled only two during their meeting with Rori. The first, by Matt Redman, served as the funeral's opening song.

When the music fades
All is stripped away
And I simply come
Longin' just to bring
Something that's of worth
That will bless Your heart.
I'll bring you more than a song
For a song in itself
Is not what You have required
You search much deeper within
Through the way things appear
You're looking into my heart
I'm coming back to the heart of worship
And it's all about You
It's all about You, Jesus
I'm sorry Lord for the thing I've made it
When it's all about You
It's all about you, Jesus

Michael recalled how, over a stack of pancakes, he asked his bride, "Now, Debs, you know I love the song, but how in a million years could 'The Heart of Worship' ever be considered a song for a funeral?"

"Just because the song doesn't talk about raising someone up on the likes of an eagle's wings doesn't mean it's not a good song to be sung at a funeral!" Debbie had feistily responded. "Besides, when I die I want to let people know the truth. I want them to know what really matters."

"And what truth is it that you hope this song communicates to others at your funeral?" Michael had inquired.

"That at the heart of worship, heck, at the heart of everything, stands Jesus." Debbie had put down her fork and her hands were now in full motion as she continued to passionately express herself.

"This relativistic world tries to make everything, including God and how to worship Him, based on their own notions and whims. And I hope that when I die and the choir sings this song, and you better remember to have them do this song, buddy or I'll be really pissed at you, that everyone will stop to think, 'What an odd song for a funeral' and that they take a few extra minutes to check out the words more closely. In doing so, I hope they receive the message. It's all about Him, Michael! It's always about Him! Love has come, come to us!"

Michael remembered wanting to ask her, "What if I die before you, who will tell the choir?" But her passionate soliloquy deeply pierced him. He knew she was right and he admired the depth of her response. Her ending word choice particularly stuck with him and caused him not to ask her anything more about her choice of song or about what to do if he were to precede her in death. Over the next year her closing words would return to him again and again.

"Love has come."

"What was that, Michael?" asked Cookie, who was surprised to hear anything come out of Michael's mouth, let alone during the consecration.

Michael wasn't aware that he had even said anything. He turned in response to hearing Cookie speak and simply nodded. Cookie decided to let it pass without any further inquiry.

The closing song was the other song Debbie had preselected for her own funeral. As Fr. Charlie kissed the altar, the choir began to sing.

Surely the presence of the Lord is in this place.

I can feel God's mighty power and God's grace.
I can hear the brush of angel wings,
I see glory on each face.
Surely the presence of the Lord is in this place.

At the phrase, "I can hear the brush of angel wings," Michael lost consciousness. Maybe it was for just a second, but during that time, which seemed to extend well beyond a second, Michael knew that he was no longer in church. He didn't know where he was, or how he got there, perhaps it was nowhere. But for that moment, and for just that moment, his pain had left him.

Cookie saw Michael slump forward during the closing song and caught him. Michael snapped out of it and began to straighten his body.

As he did, he turned his head toward Cookie and said to her for the second time, "Love has come."

Twelve

Three years had passed since the Velius family moved to Caesarea. Cornelius, now twenty-one, had been a member of the Roman army for all three of those years. His father, true to his word and for reasons of his own heart, kept Cornelius as far out of harm's way as possible. However, the one thing that Decius, despite being Primus Pilus, could not protect his son from was the intense rigors of initial military training. During this time Cornelius was expected to complete all the grueling aspects of training, which included finishing a twenty-mile march in full gear in under five hours. In addition to getting his body tuned and in optimal shape, during his training Cornelius learned the art of man-to-man combat, how to throw a javelin, and perfecting the numerous military formations needed to be a soldier for Rome.

To Decius' surprise, Cornelius had done quite well. Although he didn't finish with a top recruit award, Cornelius' ability to maintain an above average ranking came as a shock to his father. Decius had expected him to do poorly and to only be found fit for duty because he was the son of the Primus Pilus. But instead, those in charge of Cornelius' training gave Decius consistently good reviews on his son's progress throughout his entire training experience.

At first, being skeptical of the reviews he was hearing, Decius told these men to give it to him straight and not to sugarcoat anything about his son's performance or he'd have them assigned to the kind of duty that no man would ever want. Despite the ultimatum, the accolades on his son continued to pour in. He was so taken aback about the reports that Decius began to spy on his son during his exercises whenever he could. Sure enough, the boy was starting to look like a real Roman soldier!

While Decius was astounded and deeply proud of his son's emergence as a Roman soldier, Cornelius was not at all surprised by what he had accomplished. He knew how much being a soldier meant to his father and he was keenly aware of the rich Velius military lineage from which he came. He was so moved by his father's loving words, which he had overheard during that conversation between his mother and father three years prior, that he vowed then and there to make his father as proud of him as possible. And the one sure way to do that was to become the best soldier he could be.

During his training, Cornelius exceeded both his father's expectations and those imposed upon himself. He put on fifteen pounds of muscle and began to look a little less like an academic and a lot more like a soldier. His increased fitness, combined with his unique blue eyes, had also made him a person of interest to the Roman and Hebrew women of Caesarea.

Though Cornelius now had the look of a soldier ready for battle, Decius kept his promise to his wife to keep their son safe. Upon his graduation from military training, he had his son assigned to the Armicustos at the post just outside of the town of Cana. The principle role of the Armicustos, and those under his charge, was to handle all aspects of the acquiring, warehousing, and deployment of all weapons and supplies for the local legions. They were also responsible for the procurement and redistribution of all acquired property. Most of such property came from those found guilty of crimes against the state and from the spoils of battle.

The storehouse near Cana was the largest in Syria and provided supplies for two legions, including the one in Caesarea led by Decius. At the time of Cornelius' assignment to the Cana facility, the Armicustos there was an older and well respected Centurion named Celsus Balbinus.

Celsus was well organized and efficient, and the most reliable Armicustos any military leader dependent on provisions could ever want. He took great pride in always having the necessary amount of supplies and weapons on hand to support his Legions. In his thirty years of service as Armicustos, Celsus had received numerous commendations for his superior supply chain management. In fact, his agile methods of maintaining orderly inventory served as a model throughout Rome and he was often called to visit other legions to instruct them on how to implement his agile strategies. While most who serve Rome in the role of an Armicustos only rise to the lowest of Centurion ranks, Celsus' consistent efforts and excellence led him to the high Centurion rank of Princeps Posterior.

Almost immediately upon receiving Cornelius into his command, Celsus could see that his new recruit had a superior intellect and possessed the facilities to organize goods and calculate needs. Most of the sixty men under his charge were there for their muscle and not their brains, but Celsus noticed Cornelius' skills and quickly took him under his tutelage.

Due to his excellent contributions, Cornelius swiftly made his way up the soldier ranks. He advanced from the initial rank of Socii to Munifex in just three months. He next received his promotion to Deacanus, something that typically took a skilled solider two years to achieve, after only one year of service to Rome. After just two years of outstanding service, he not only became Celsus' right-hand man and second in command of the warehouse, he received the initial Centurion rank of Hastatus Posterior as well. Although it was the lowest rung of the Centurion rank, it was nearly unprecedented for a soldier of any assignment to achieve this within the span of just two years.

Despite knowing that Celsus was genuinely impressed and happy with his work, Cornelius couldn't help but worry that it was his father wielding his power as Primus Pilus that led to his quick accession to the Centurion ranks.

After formally receiving the promotion to Centurion, for which his father was in attendance, Cornelius pulled him aside and asked, "Father, I need to ask you something and I need an honest answer from you."

"If you're going to ask me if I had this promotion arranged and if you're getting it just because you're my son, the answer is a definitive no," said Decius before Cornelius had the chance to ask the question.

Decius continued, "Son, you have achieved all of this on your own. I said not one word on your behalf. If you are looking for someone to thank, well then thank two people. First, thank yourself for your exemplary efforts. Second, thank Celsus. He was the one, without any suggestion or input from me, who sent the request for promotion to the Legion Legate."

Looking into his father's eyes, Cornelius didn't need to make him promise that he was telling the truth. Decius was a man of truth who only spoke the truth. It was the virtue Cornelius most admired about his dad and was the characteristic he most wanted to emulate.

"Thank you, Father, for not interfering. I want to accomplish great things like this on my own. I may never be the battle tested warrior that you are—" Cornelius' voice caught in his throat. Gaining his composure, he continued, "but I still want you to be proud of me, Dad."

Hearing those words, the tough and hardened combatant was left momentarily speechless. The creases in his forehead deepened. He bit down on his lower lip in a desperate attempt to hold back the tide of emotion his son's words were now causing within him.

Placing both of his hands on the shoulders of his Centurion son, Decius tenderly looked down upon him and said, "Cornelius, I am very, very proud of you. And while I am proud that you made Centurion as quickly as you did, that is the least thing I am proud of when it comes to you."

Perplexed, Cornelius squinted his eyes and the creases that had been on his father's forehead appeared on his.

Decius clarified his thoughts. "Cornelius, I am proud of who you are, who you've become as a man. I admire you for having the courage to stand up for your convictions and for never compromising or hiding who you really are." Leaving his right hand on Cornelius' left shoulder, his left hand came and rested with its palm flush on the chest of his son. "Real men are those who follow their hearts, who are not anything but who they really are."

Removing his hand from Cornelius' chest Decius continued, "I completely understand that you had to become a soldier. But son, it's your intellect, your ability to learn, and your ability to take in and absorb the glory of life that are your true gifts. Be a soldier as long as you feel you need to, but also feel free to walk away once your service is fulfilled."

Decius drew his son close. After a short but meaningful pause, Decius added, "But whether as a soldier or not, always be yourself. Never stop asking. Never stop seeking. Never stop sharing the beauty you discover. And most especially, always be true to the truth. You are my son and I love you."

The blue-eyed Centurion went to bed that evening never being so at peace in his entire life. His hard work and intellect brought him recognition and promotion, the kind of which he thought would make his father proud of him. That was all well and good, but he discovered something that day which was far more important. His father, a man he most admired, was proud of Cornelius for who he was and not for what he accomplished.

Thirteen

While many individuals who lose a spouse blame God for their loss and often run far from Him, Michael did neither. He didn't blame God and he certainly didn't curse Him for taking Debbie from the world. He knew God was right there next to him. Even though Michael was aware that Jesus was with him in his darkness, wanting him to know that He loved him more than human comprehension could ever allow, wanting him to know that He felt the pains of his loss, Michael still could not shake off the numbness that had become his life these past three and a half months.

He tried to go back to his job selling pharmaceuticals two months after losing Debbie, but found out rather quickly that he couldn't handle the reception he received in every physician's office he visited. Well-meaning nurses, doctors, and staff inquiries about how he was doing and assurances that they were praying for him only served as a blistering reminder of his loss. After about a week of continual well intended consolation, he contacted his District Manager and good friend, Brad Parker, and requested extended time off. Brad, who considered Michael more of a friend than an employee, would do anything he could for Michael. He and his wife, Marlo, had been on several award trips and personal vacations with Michael and Debbie, and the four of them had become thick as thieves over the last five years. Upon Michael's request, Brad worked in expediential fashion with the human resources department and secured long-term disability at sixty percent of Michael's base pay for up to six months. Michael was thankful for Brad's help, but not surprised. He would have done the same for him and he knew that Brad always had his back.

Since receiving his disability a month and a half ago, Michael simply existed. He would sleep until mid-morning almost every day, something he hadn't done since high school, because sleep seemed to be the only remedy for his pain. He would pray and read the Bible in the morning. He would take Goose for long walks and had him constantly by his side during the day when he'd stare at the TV without hearing or comprehending much of anything that was coming out of it.

During this time of his numb existence, where he both was and wasn't, Michael found that he could only relate on any kind of real level to two individuals, as they were the only ones who experienced the profundity of loss close to the degree of his own. One was his four-legged walking buddy, Goose, who Michael knew greatly missed his other master. The other was Cookie, who lost not only a best friend, but the rock and creator of stability in her life. The numbness was still there when Cookie visited, but there was something about her truly understanding his loss that made him yearn for her company. And it was the same for Cookie and her immense pain. In mutual understanding comes not the relief of pain, but rather the ability to survive the moment.

Fourteen

Celsus the Armicustos gave Cornelius more than military opportunity; he ended up giving him two gifts that would turn out to be the greatest treasures of his life. The first was Celsus' granddaughter, whom he introduced at a dinner he hosted at his house shortly after Cornelius received the promotion to Centurion. Her name was Prisca and, as the story goes, it was love at first sight. Cornelius was instantly attracted to her profoundly black, curly hair. Though covered by a veil, Cornelius could see that her desirous hair reached down to the very small of her back. The hair that was visible seemed to reflect light in its abundance. He was amazed that while it was dry, it had an attractive sense of being wet. Complementing her intoxicating and rich hair were her deep brown eyes that seemed to invite the young Centurion to look deep within them. But the thing that most attracted Cornelius to Prisca was her smile and happy demeanor. Even before she noticed him in that room full of nearly twenty people, he observed how she so pleasantly interacted with others. She was a genuinely happy person whose smile was always present.

Observing her, Cornelius couldn't help but recall the wisdom of his mother, who had repeatedly said to him, "When the time comes for you to find a woman, find one who smiles. Where there's a smile, there's a happy life waiting within a happy wife."

The minute he laid eyes on Prisca he suddenly knew exactly what his mother had meant by those words. Thinking about it, he couldn't help but smile as well.

After observing them for some time, Celsus noticed the obvious attraction between the two young adults. He was overprotective of Prisca, having raised her from the age of twelve after her father was killed in battle. While he screened very carefully any man who showed interest in his granddaughter, he had no reservation regarding Cornelius as a potential suitor for his Prisca. In fact, truth be told, he had set up the dinner that evening in hopes that some sparks might fly between the two of them.

Celsus watched at a distance how Cornelius' eyes remained fixed on his granddaughter. He could tell that the young man was pierced by her beauty and impressed by her ability to own a room. His hunch proved correct; there was indeed a mutual attraction.

While Cornelius' fascination of Prisca was obvious to anyone in the room with a single working eye, Prisca was much harder to read. Sure enough, she felt Cornelius' gaze. She was genuinely moved by his interest in her, which he did such a poor job of hiding. Like Cornelius' attraction to her, she certainly found him to be a physically appealing man. However, any look she cast his way was swift and guised as a sweeping and casual look across the entire room. It was during one of those highly cloaked visual sweeps that his blue eyes and perfectly chiseled face began to take residency in that remote corner of her heart which she had been reserving for "the one." *There is something more than looks to this man*, thought Prisca. There was an innocence and sincerity. It appeared to her that, unlike most men she knew, this one held up no guard, no false pretense as to who he was. And she hoped that her initial gut feeling about him was right.

Prisca didn't have to wait long to find out. At that very moment, her grandfather was escorting the young man of interest her way. She could no longer play coy. As they walked toward Prisca their eyes met, and true to her nature, she couldn't help but smile.

Cornelius, now sufficiently melted by her seemingly positive reception of him, began to feel every type of young school-boy crush come over him.

Celsus began the introductions. "Cornelius, I would like you to meet my granddaughter, Prisca."

Extending his hand to her, the inwardly shaking Cornelius delivered a very firm and sincere, "It is an honor to meet you, Prisca. And, I must say, your name is almost as beautiful as you are."

Ugh! thought Cornelius. *Did I really just say that?*

Prisca took his hand and, maintaining her smile, looked directly into his eyes and replied, "Cornelius, why you just say anything that comes into your silly head, don't you?"

"Well, let me take my foot out of my mouth," Cornelius began, but then changed course. With a reinvigorated sense of confidence, he stated, "Actually, I'm going to stick to my initial silliness. You are very beautiful and your name is, again, almost as beautiful as you are."

Cornelius' sudden swell of confidence waned and he wanted to kick himself again. He still had her hand in his and he began to wonder if she could feel the profuse sweat now coming from his palm.

Instead of thinking he was silly or, on the other extreme, trying to manipulate her, Prisca sensed that he was being sincere, if not a little awkward. She liked that in a man, she liked it very much.

Still holding his hand, she responded, "You won't run off if I return the compliment, will you?"

Cornelius, sweating and with his chest palpitating as it never had before, had a hard time believing his ears. This beauty, this girl so out of his league, was going to compliment him in a similar manner?

Trying to remain cool and Centurion-like, he responded with a very unoriginal, "My feet are firmly planted, no matter what say you." He broke the overall silliness of his words with a revealing smile of his own.

"While I'm not yet crazy about the name Cornelius, I find you rather charming and, might I add, attractive in a blue-eyed and debonair kind of way."

Celsus took his cue, saying, "Well, I'm going to leave you two youngsters on your own. Please, Cornelius, make yourself at home and do try your best not to replant that foot of yours into your mouth!"

Cornelius and Prisca both laughed. As Celsus walked away their eyes met again, but for the first time in the privacy of their own intimate space. It was then that they realized their hands were still joined.

That initial handshake lasted far longer than most preliminary handshakes do and led to an even more gripping and loving relationship. They spent that night, and nearly every night for a couple weeks thereafter, learning about each other.

Prisca, like Cornelius, was a thinker and a seeker of true beauty. They shared their thoughts on the philosophy of the Greeks, in particular the teaching of Aristotle and Socrates, whom they both had studied. They found that they both liked the same poets and that each had written their own poetry.

Their initial reads on each other proved to be dead on. Prisca was indeed a happy and open book. She viewed the glass as always full, and if possible, constantly running over. And in Cornelius, whose name she eventually came to love as much as the man, Prisca found the most genuine and honest person she thought could ever exist.

And so it was that just four months after they met, they were married.

Fifteen

The first life changing gift that Celsus had given to Cornelius was the introduction to his future love and life, Prisca. The second gift came to him through Celsus' permission for Cornelius to help a friend out of a jam.

About a month after having met Prisca, one of Cornelius' dearest friends, Silvus, approached him with a huge favor. Silvus' wife had just gone into labor and he desperately wanted to be there for the arrival of their new child. The problem was that he had drawn duty that night and was assigned to keep an eye on a potential Zealot named Laban, whose granddaughter had just gotten married. Although it was out of his normal realm of duty and experience, Silvus turned to Cornelius because no one else was willing to help him out. Silvus' supervisor told him if he could find anyone of Centurion rank to replace him that night, then he would approve the shift of duty. And so he turned to his last resort, his friend, the quartermaster of Cana, Cornelius.

Of course, Cornelius wanted to help his friend, but like Silvus, he needed to obtain permission from his supervisor, Celsus. Celsus, fully trusting his favorite Centurion and future grandson-in-law, gladly gave the permission needed. More so, he was touched by Cornelius' willingness to help out a friend in such a way.

Unknown to Celsus, the permission he gave Cornelius that day would turn out to be an evening that would change the young Centurion forever. For it was that evening, at the house of Laban, he met the person of Jesus. Just as he had observed his future wife, Prisca, work the room at Celsus' dinner party and was drawn to her, he observed Jesus at that wedding feast and likewise felt drawn to him. He was immediately attracted to the man. His wonderment surrounding the man only grew deeper as he saw him pray over the clay jars of water and how he reverently addressed the table the jars were set before. But what really set into motion the desire for Cornelius to seek the man Jesus, was how his eyes met his own and with it, a smile. Cornelius knew that he had been invited to something great and significant, he just needed to figure out exactly what it was.

Sixteen

Reaching across the table, Carol placed her hand on top of Cookie's and said, "I wish there was something I could do for you, Cookie, after all you've done for me."

The comment seemed to come out of nowhere. They had stopped at the McDonald's on Seventh Street, just off Interstate 10, to grab an ice cream after spending some time shopping at the Arizona Mills mall. Cookie had barely dented her caramel sundae. Carol lost her appetite for her Oreo Blizzard once she sensed her friend's pain surfacing again.

"Don't you worry about me, sweetie. I'm fine," Cookie said as she squeezed Carol's hand in an attempt to be reassuring.

Carol knew that Cookie was anything but fine. While Cookie had never given Carol the full run down on the major valleys she had hit in her lifetime, Carol was astute enough, even at her young age, to know that Cookie had experienced significant ruts in her life, much like those that she was currently experiencing. Carol's intuition also told her that Debbie had been to Cookie what Cookie had been to her; the saving branch that pulled her out of the quicksand of a life that had been close to smothering her.

Carol often thought about all that Cookie meant to her, how she had literally saved her mental and physical wellbeing. How she did it was simple yet complex; Cookie loved Carol and became her friend. Carol used to wonder why Cookie was doing it. Why did she befriend her in the first place? Was it to make herself feel good? Was she trying to repay the fates for something that she had done in the past? Early on in their relationship, Carol would lament over these questions, but she began to care less and less about such things. The turning point came when Carol realized that Cookie was there for her because she truly cared for her. Cookie's authentic love had washed away all doubt concerning the legitimacy of their relationship.

If something ever happened to Cookie, Carol would be in unbearable anguish. Knowing this, Carol empathized with Cookie's grief over Debbie's death. She would do anything to help Cookie in her time of need.

In an unselfish way, Carol knew that what Cookie needed to move forward was to realize that Carol still needed her. Because of this realization, Carol unloaded a barrage of requests over the last couple of months to go to the movies, to go shopping, and to play guitar together. She wanted Cookie to know that she had a special calling and purpose in life, and that she was a significant part of her life. And so it was, they ended up shopping that day for nothing in particular.

Twenty seconds of awkward silence hung between Carol and Cookie. Carol didn't know exactly what to say, but she wanted to do something to reduce the amount of anguish Cookie was feeling.

In the last few seconds of that hanging silence, Carol floated up a quick inward prayer, *Holy Spirit, give me the right words!*

"I love you, Cookie. I love you so much and I would be lost without your friendship! Thank you, thank you for rescuing me!" Carol began to squeeze Cookie's hand and she didn't care that the emotion she felt brought tears and a raised voice that others in the restaurant could hear.

Carol's words came as a shot to Cookie's heart. In that moment, much of the pain over Debbie's loss was lifted. She would always have a hole in her core being over losing Debbie, but she could suddenly see clearly what was always there. Cookie had to move forward, and in doing so there were real ways to keep her friend alive in this world. Cookie realized that the best way to keep Debbie's spirit alive was by giving in the same manner in which her friend had given during her life.

With tears now filling her eyes and beginning to spill down the sides of both her cheeks, Cookie looked at Carol and in all sincerity told her, "I love you too, Carol, but know it wasn't I who rescued you. It was you who rescued me."

With both their hearts slightly lifted, they managed to finish their ice cream treats. As she finished the last of her Blizzard, it dawned on Carol that God had just answered her prayer.

"Thank you, Jesus, thank you," Carol said in the silence of her soul.

Seventeen

The front door to his new family home never looked as welcoming as it did when Cornelius approached it after finishing four straight days of doing the annual inventory. Cornelius was beyond exhausted as each of those days involved an average of fourteen hours of monotonous work. But it had to be done. Once a year, every Armicustos throughout Rome had to give their report of all property on hand, as well as have an accounting for everything that left the warehouse during the prior calendar year. The long days of physically counting the property contained in the immense Cana warehouse would have been enough of a burden by itself. But on top of it, Cornelius was responsible for ensuring that all documentation was in order for every out-shipment released during the inventory period. This involved reviewing every such document to certify that all was in order and that each "i" was dotted and every "t" crossed. Celsus prided himself on never having had an audit, and Cornelius, whom Celsus put in charge of this year's inventory, was going to make darn sure that it didn't happen on his watch either. All the documents would be in order, of this Cornelius made certain.

After one particularly grueling day of inventory madness, an exhausted and brain-fried Cornelius swung open his front door where he was greeted by a very loaded question from the prettiest girl he had ever met.

"Guess who just arrived in Capernaum?" shouted a busting at the seams Prisca. She jumped in the air right in front of Cornelius, forcing him to either catch her in his arms or let her drop butt-first onto the floor of their entryway. Landing secure in his arms, Prisca's arms locked around the neck of her Centurion husband and planted a firm kiss on his awaiting lips.

Cornelius' exhaustion was temporarily suspended by his wife's utter excitement. Seconds before, Cornelius was eager just to get inside his house and to crash on the bed in the hopes of recharging even just a little bit before dinner. But her high energy and bombastic state revitalized him. He couldn't help but smile.

"So, are you just going to stand there with that grin on your face, trying to bear my incredible weight, or are you going to take a guess on who I heard is in Capernaum right at this very moment?" Prisca asked as she took one of her fingers and tried to curl the hair on the right side of his head with it.

Cornelius hadn't a clue, but he knew that he had better take at least one guess or, based on previous experience, she would continue to ask the question over and over until he would finally venture at least one estimate.

"Before I do, Mrs. Velius, I must tell you that your load is either on the extreme light side or I'm the strongest man in the world!"

"Okay then, Mr. Goliath, what is your guess?" asked Prisca, continuing to twist her finger in his hair.

"My guess is that you received, on rather good authority, news that Augustus Caesar is visiting Capernaum."

He knew that his guess was ridiculous, but by this time he was extremely curious and was anxious to find out who was coming to Capernaum that had his wife so over the top excited. He also knew that to get the scoop, he would have to play her little game and at least give a single guess.

"Nope. I think that you'd like to meet this man even more than you would Augustus. Take another guess," Prisca playfully responded.

Her response only made Cornelius more curious, but all the same, he had no idea who it could be. Seeing that she was going to proceed with the "take another guess" tactic, he decided to derail that path as best he could.

"Give me a clue," Cornelius requested with his nose now just inches from hers.

Cornelius could only smile at Prisca's terrible acting. She put on a face that was an obvious ploy to communicate that she was looking into the deep recesses of her mind to try to determine a clue, while already having one handy. Finally, Prisca acted as though she just uncovered a gem of a clue. Lifting one finger in the air, she responded to Cornelius' request for a hint.

"Ah ha!" proclaimed the whimsical Prisca. Continuing, she delivered her clue. "You once spied on this man."

Immediately Cornelius knew who she was talking about. At that moment, he felt a temporary absence of being. His smiling face was replaced by a blank expression. It wasn't sadness or despair, it was more of a case of shock. Tingles filled his body with the sudden awareness of the man behind Prisca's guessing game. He slowly brought Prisca's feet back to the floor.

When she was firmly planted on the ground and looking directly at him he took his guess, which he already knew was correct. "Jesus?"

"Yes, Jesus! That's all anyone around here is talking about. Can we go and hear him, please?"

By that time, word of this man Jesus had spread throughout Judea. For a good couple of years, he had been teaching and healing the sick in the region. There were stories about him healing lepers, giving sight to the blind, and even one report that he had brought a dead girl back to life. While these things certainly piqued the interest of Cornelius and Prisca, what promulgated their interest the most about this man were the bits and pieces they would hear about his teachings. They were both intrigued by his views on how to treat others and about his instruction on social justice.

They had heard that he said, "Love they neighbor as thyself," and, "What good would it be for a man to gain the whole world yet lose his soul?" and of all things, that he "was the bread of life." While they understood and deeply appreciated the love of thy neighbor line, and both richly contemplated the wisdom of gaining the world but losing one's soul, they were eager to know what he meant by saying that he was the bread of life. Even though they loved its poetic ring, they had no clue as to what it meant. They often spent entire evenings throwing out ideas on what that line possibly meant, as well as others they heard which resonated in their hearts, yet which their minds could not comprehend.

Based on the things they had heard, both had begun to study as much as they could about the faith of the Jewish people. Through such study, each hoped that they could have a better context for understanding the actual meaning of his words. Among what they learned about the Jewish faith was their belief of a single God. Initially they found this very confusing and hard to process, having grown up in a culture that believed in the existence of many gods. But the more they studied about this particular belief, the more that they became open to its possibility. On top of all this study was Cornelius' personal encounter with Jesus that day at the farm of Laban of Cana. Combine all their study and Cornelius' brush with the man, and Jesus easily became the person Cornelius and Prisca most wanted to see and hear speak.

There was no question that Cornelius wanted to see and listen to Jesus firsthand. But at the same time, he knew that Jesus had recently caught the attention of Quintus Octavius, the Legion Legate. Quintus' tolerance for anything or anyone that caused his perfectly peaceful government any agitation was set at a level significantly lower than any other Legion Legate. While Jesus was not directly speaking against Rome, what he did have working against him was that the religious leaders of the Jews were all in a fury concerning his religious assertions. These ruffled feathers of the Jewish leaders resulted in complaint after complaint about this man to Quintus' reports. Cornelius knew that it was only a matter of time, or it was perhaps already underway, when a Roman reconnaissance group would start following and listening to Jesus.

"Yes, Prisca, we will go and see Jesus. How about we leave tomorrow very early?" Cornelius said.

Prisca, surprised but happy by the immediacy of Cornelius' plan, said, "But tomorrow is Friday, you have duty on Friday."

"Well, my dear, seeing how I spent the last four days working fourteen hour days and, in that time, completing the annual inventory, your grandfather was kind enough to give me tomorrow off!" Cornelius said, knowing that the news would delight her.

The fact was that the timing was perfect. Capernaum was a fifteen-mile trip from their home in Cana. By leaving early the next day, they could be there by midday which would then allow them to be able to spend two nights there before having to head back home and back to work.

Hearing this, Prisca's excitement caused her to jump right back into her husband's arms. Assuming their former nose-to-nose position, Prisca said in a soft voice, "I can't wait to meet Jesus."

"Me either," replied Cornelius. "Me either."

Eighteen

As planned, Cornelius and Prisca woke about a half hour before sunrise the following day. They packed most of the things they would need for their journey the night before and had them on the table ready to be secured to their donkeys. While Cornelius' position had made him wealthy enough to own a horse, he and Prisca decided that pulling into a poorer Hebrew town on a steed would draw unnecessary attention to themselves. Cornelius, in particular, wanted to remain as anonymous as possible on this trip. He knew that the Jews greatly disliked Rome and most held anything related to the Empire in disdain, especially Roman soldiers. Both Cornelius and Prisca understood how they felt. They could only imagine what it would be like to have some other country come in and tell them what they could and could not do. While most Roman citizens could care less about the people they forced into servitude of the Empire, Cornelius and Prisca's hearts went out to them instead.

Cornelius also wanted to be sure not to attract the attention of any Roman authority. Not that there was any law prohibiting him or any other soldier from taking a road trip to an occupied town, or for that matter, listening to the teachings of some itinerant preacher. All the same, he preferred not to attract the attention of either the Jews or of any Roman officials.

In addition to going by donkey, both Cornelius and Prisca dressed in simple tunics, the style of which would blend in well in a Capernaum crowd. Prisca also brought with her a scarf that would cover much of her Roman face. Cornelius' tunic contained a hood that he would put atop his head when they made it into Capernaum in the hopes of blending in as well as possible with the locals.

It was hard to say which of the two was more excited about going to hear Jesus teach. Ever since Cornelius had come home from his shift at Laban's wedding feast and shared with Prisca the magnetism of the man, she had become obsessed with learning as much about Jesus as she could. It was Prisca, in fact, who had been the one to initiate a means to learn more about the religion and culture of the Jews. She had turned to Sapphira, her grandfather's Jewish maid, to learn all she could about Judaism. Sapphira was more than happy to share everything she could with Prisca. She even went as far as letting Prisca know that outsiders of the faith, Gentiles she called them, could in fact convert to the faith if they so desired.

Most of these education sessions took place during the day at Celsus' house while Cornelius was at work. Every night after Prisca met with Sapphira, she would share with her husband all that she learned that day. By the time they left for this trip, both had a good knowledge base of the core tenets of the Jewish faith and culture; certainly a better one than most every Roman citizen in the area had. As a result of all this, the pair was extremely excited, perhaps even more excited than a young child preparing to open their birthday gifts, to see this man who held the interest of every deep thinker and lover of words in the region.

"So tell me again what you saw Jesus do at that wedding?" Prisca asked about an hour into their journey.

Prisca loved to hear stories. It didn't matter if she had heard a story a hundred times, she would be the person who would want to hear it again for the one hundred and first time. Of course, Cornelius didn't mind telling her this story yet again, especially now that they were going to see him.

"Well, I was just outside the open window of their front hallway when I noticed that the owner of the house, Laban—"

"The man who was later arrested for being a threat to Rome?" Prisca asked.

"Yes, one and the same. I noticed a commotion at the area by the front door. This Laban seemed in a panic. He was saying something to one of his servants that I couldn't make out when all of a sudden Jesus' mother—"

"Mary, right?" asked Prisca, who already knew the answer due to her own studies on the topic of all things Jesus.

Cornelius played along. "Yes, dear, you are correct. It was a woman named Mary."

Cornelius continued, "After a few words with Laban, this Mary gives a look toward her son who was sitting at a table across the room. Once he caught her gaze, she motioned him to come to her by wiggling her index finger. Jesus immediately got up and headed toward them."

"Ah! The power of a mother!" Prisca added with a chuckle.

"Ah! The power of a good wife!" Cornelius bantered back, also with a chuckle.

"That's right, and don't you ever forget it," said Prisca, amused.

"Anyway, Jesus comes over and it appeared to me that he was getting filled in on what the issue was that had Laban all upset. Moments later, I see Jesus giving direction to a guy who appeared to be the head servant. About five minutes later, I see this head servant guy leading other servants through the doorway, each carting in large water jars. Jesus pointed to a table on the far wall—"

"The same table that you later see him stroke with gentleness?" asked Prisca, although she already knew the answer.

"One in the same," replied a patient Cornelius.

Continuing with his story he said, "So the servants line up the six large jars filled with water in front of that very table. By this time, everyone who had been seated with Jesus has gathered around, including the local fella Nathanael we've seen around town. Jesus then goes up to each jar and places his hands on top of each, one at a time. He then turns his head upward with his eyes closed."

"When I told Sapphira about that she said that he was likely saying a prayer to their God, Yahweh," added Prisca.

"That's exactly what I thought was happening as well," said Cornelius. "But I tell you, Prisca, if you could have seen the reverence in this man as he did it, you would have felt as certain as I do that not only is he a wise and knowledgeable man, but a holy man of the gods as well."

"Well, if we want to blend in today, you might want to rephrase that last part to 'a holy man of God'!" Prisca wisely interjected.

"True. Good catch, my dear," Cornelius said, mentally filing that thought for later use.

Cornelius took up the story once again. "But what happened next really suspends belief. The head servant took a cup and dipped it into the first water jar. He lifted the cup to his mouth and took a drink. Almost immediately, he drops the cup on the floor and it shatters between the spot where the servant and Jesus were standing. By this time, I am right up to the window and I have a clear view of everything. I can actually hear the servant, who is now on his knees in front of Jesus, say, 'My Lord!' Jesus helps the servant up and, as he is beginning to stand, I notice that his tunic is stained red in the areas where his knees pressed the tunic to the floor."

"So you do believe what people have been saying, that he turned ordinary water into wine?" queried Prisca.

"I still don't know about that, Prisca. For all I know, the water jugs were already filled with wine before they were wheeled into the room," answered Cornelius.

"How do you explain the servant's behavior, then? Perhaps what they're saying is true. Jesus turned water into wine at that wedding."

"For now, let's table that idea and come back to it later," replied Cornelius, who was neither ready to say that's what happened nor deny that it could have happened.

"Now tell me about how he touched the table and looked at you!" This was Prisca's favorite part of the story.

"Okay. After all this happened, the jars that were in front of the table were carted off to the kitchen. Jesus was standing in front of that table we talked about. I watched as he ran his hand softly over the top of it. The way he did it was so tender, like a husband running his hands across his bride's hair on the night of their wedding. It was apparent to me that this table meant a great deal to him. His hands stopped at the center of the table and I saw him, once again, lift his head upward and his eyes close. After this, he went to the right corner of the table and reached his hand under it. He smiled and said some words that I couldn't make out. It was right after that, Prisca, that he looked up from the table and stared directly at me."

"And he smiled at you, right?" Prisca asked.

"Yes, Prisca. He smiled at me and such a strong feeling of love came over me. It's…it's so hard to explain the feeling." Cornelius did his best to try to convey what he felt during that smile, but failed miserably. How could what he felt be put into words, when the words to describe how he felt didn't exist?

"Oh, how your story makes me so excited to see him in person! To think, this very day we may be able to see and hear Jesus speak!" Prisca said in a state of unbridled joy.

"Oh! I almost forgot to tell you! I came across that table, the one Jesus touched, when I was doing inventory yesterday. And guess what?" Cornelius said, with a level of excitement that now matched Prisca's.

"My grandfather is going to give you the table as a gift?" inquired Prisca.

"No, he can't do that. He could be arrested for giving anything away. But, you're close! The table, along with the other property seized from

Laban of Cana, is going to be auctioned off next week!"

"I want that table, Cornelius!" shouted a pleased and determined Prisca.

"I want that table too, Prisca!" countered an even more determined Cornelius. "The real good news is this—Celsus and I have the right to purchase any item before it goes to auction. As such, I will be purchasing the table upon our return!"

Nineteen

Dave from Burba's had placed a call to Cookie about a week earlier and asked her if she would be willing to play his happy hour the following Saturday. Burba's was the neighborhood bar and grill that the Lil' Debbie Band often played at, and it was a place Debbie and Cookie had played even more times as the acoustic duo they called Violet. Whether it was the full Lil' Debbie Band or the scaled down Violet duo, each time they played Burba's was packed. Though Dave was appreciative of the revenue the band generated for him, the friendship he had developed with the band's core members meant a great deal more to him.

Dave's heart ached over the loss of Debbie and for the suffering he knew that Michael and Cookie were going through. His calls to Michael inviting him to go with Dave to both a Cardinals and a Suns game went unreturned. Dave didn't take it personally. He understood the grief and he gave Michael the space he needed.

Dave contemplated whether to invite Cookie to play the upcoming happy hour. His initial thought was that it might be good for her to get out and play. Perhaps the secret depths of music would help her to heal. Once these positive thoughts popped into Dave's mind, they were immediately at war with opposing viewpoints that began to fight for space inside Dave's head.

On the negative side of the battle, Dave thought that since Cookie and Debbie shared the gift of music, returning to it might open any wounds that may now just be starting to heal. He went back and forth on these thoughts and potential outcomes, cathartic healing versus worsening wounds, until he finally picked up the phone and made the call to Cookie.

When Cookie's phone rang and she saw it was Dave, she decided to let it go to her voicemail. She had been in the routine of letting most all her calls go to voicemail for many years. The only exceptions were if the calls were from Debbie, Michael, or Carol. Those calls she would always answer. She did this more out of habit than anything else, preferring to see first what someone wanted and then returning his or her call after. In this case, she hadn't spoken to Dave since the funeral and certainly needed the social buffer that voicemail provided her.

After her iPhone beeped to inform her that she had a voice message, Cookie retrieved the voicemail.

"Cookie! This is Dave from Burba's. I hope you are doing well. I just wanted to see if you would be interested in doing a happy hour for us next Saturday. You could play for as long or as little as you'd like. We would love to see and hear you. Hit me back when you can. We miss you!"

The message took Cookie off guard. She hadn't touched her guitar since the night at the Celebrity. Music had not been a priority for her over the last several months. Her mind began a similar mental debate, the likes of which Dave experienced in extending the invitation. At first, she thought that it would be too painful to be on stage without Debbie. How could she play music without her by her side? But on the other hand, Cookie thought that Debbie would want her to continue to play because she knew just how much music meant to her. As Cookie traveled down this path, she also began to think that getting back on stage would be a way of honoring Debbie and a way to keep the memory of her best friend alive. Like Dave, she went back and forth and back and forth between these feelings and options. And like Dave, while she was still right in the middle of the mental debate, she ended it by decisively picking up her phone and texting Dave.

"Will be there. Mind if it's only one set? And thank you."

Twenty

Capernaum was located on the coastline of Lake Gennesaret, also known to many as the Sea of Galilee. Capernaum itself laid right on top and in the middle of the great Via Maris highway, between the large metropolises of Damascus and Caesarea Maritima. As such, it served as a prime location for tax collectors to amass travel taxes from the countless sojourners who came through the town on their way to the many destinations that lied between the beginning and end of the highway. While the larger Gennesaret region was one of the most prosperous and crowded districts in all of Israel, Capernaum itself, while highly populated, was comprised for the most part of lower to middle class people, mainly fishermen and tradesmen.

Cornelius and Prisca made very good time that morning. They found themselves on the very outskirts of town around midday when they came upon a tax collector who was gathering tolls from travelers about to enter Capernaum from the south. A small line had formed and, when they were about four to five parties away from the collector's table, Cornelius could finally see the individual who was collecting the taxes. Once he spied a good look at the man, he saw that the collector was in fact a Jew. In his limited experience in the Cana region, it was typically a Roman soldier who gathered such taxes. He felt pity for the guy, knowing that it would be an incredibly tough job gathering taxes from his own people for an empire that the Jews universally despised.

Poor guy, thought Cornelius. *He must take a lot of guff from his people for taking on this job.*

Just as he was thinking this, the collector waved him and Prisca forward.

"Next!" the collector belted out. Without even looking up, the man asked, "Town of origin?"

"Cana, my good man," replied an always-respectful Cornelius.

The tax collector, not used to anyone using the word good in connection with himself or his chosen profession, peered at the couple in front of him. He immediately noticed Cornelius' blue eyes. It was the first time he had seen anyone with blue eyes. On top of that, he had never heard of any Jew or local nationality having such an eye color. He then looked upon Prisca and noted not only her beauty, but her lack of Jewish features as well. Although Cornelius had placed his hood over his head and Prisca a scarf over hers, neither could hide from this Jewish tax collector that they were neither Jewish, Syrian, Egyptian or any other group from which he typically collected taxes.

Cornelius knew that all this was going through the tax collector's mind. He also knew that Roman citizens were exempt from any and all travel taxes. Even though there would be no consequence for him to declare his Roman citizenship and to walk on by the table of the Jewish publican, Cornelius wanted to maintain his anonymity. So before the man could ask any questions about their citizenship, Cornelius reached into his purse and pulled out two coins.

"Two lepton, correct?" Cornelius said, offering the toll for a trip between Cana and Capernaum.

The tax collector, always willing to take money from anyone offering it, reached out his hand and took the two lepton from Cornelius without looking back up.

As he and Prisca walked by, they heard the man yell out, "Next!"

Having been to Capernaum on several prior occasions, Cornelius knew the quickest route into the town's center. Knowing that Jesus was gathering large crowds wherever he went, both Cornelius and Prisca would only have to ask a person or two before they would learn where Jesus was teaching.

When they arrived at the business hub of the town, they were greeted by the sounds and smells of the daily bazaar and open market. Cornelius and Prisca were about to approach one of the spice vendors to inquire on the whereabouts of Jesus, when Cornelius made eye contact with Nathanael of Cana who was heading in the opposite direction on the same street. The two men had never spoken a word to each other before, but Cana was a small enough town that if you called it home, your face and your name were recognizable to just about each and every inhabitant of the area. On top of that, Cornelius knew that Nathanael was a follower of Jesus since he saw him sitting at the teacher's table at Laban's wedding feast.

Nathanael, of course, recognized the highly memorable soldier with blue eyes. He had seen him around town on many occasions, but he most vividly remembered the Centurion as the minion Rome sent to spy on Rachel's wedding. When his eyes locked on Cornelius' passing glance, his whole body tensed up.

What is that soldier doing here, and dressed like an ordinary citizen? he wondered. In a split second, it occurred to Nathanael that the soldier must be here to spy on Jesus.

Cornelius could feel the contempt radiating from Nathanael. Fearful of becoming a distraction and wanting to diffuse any potential conflict, he made the quick decision to engage Nathanael rather than avoid him.

"Follow me and keep smiling," Cornelius whispered to Prisca.

With that, a broad smile spread across Cornelius' face. It was the kind of smile a man would give a dear friend he hadn't seen in years.

"Nathanael!" Cornelius shouted enthusiastically as he approached the young follower of Jesus.

The greeting and the smile stopped Nathanael in his tracks and raised his suspicions to an even higher level. He had been sent by the Rabbi to go to the home of a man named Zacchaeus and tell his wife that he had accepted their invitation to spend the evening with them. Nathanael typically handled all logistical elements of the travels of Jesus and his twelve closest followers. If it had to do with lodging, eating, or determining the best locations for the Rabbi to teach, Nathanael was the man who got the job done. At this moment, however, he was most concerned for the safety of the teacher. Rather than ignore the out-of-uniform soldier's greeting, he accepted the informal invitation and walked up to the smiling man and his wife in hopes of finding out why they were in Capernaum.

Extending his hand, Cornelius introduced himself to the follower of Jesus. "Nathanael, I am Cornelius and this is my wife, Prisca."

Nathanael looked at the extended hand of Cornelius and, rather than accepting it, looked up at Cornelius and said with disdain, "I know who you are and what you do."

"True, you may know what I do, but I doubt that you know who I am," replied Cornelius.

Nathanael was caught off guard by the man's intelligent response. He had thought that pretty much all Roman soldiers were a bunch of meatheads with the intellect of a wild boar during mating season. All the same, his love for the teacher had him suspicious of the man and woman before him.

"I know that you spied on Jesus at the wedding feast of Laban's daughter and that you later had him arrested," snapped a very on-guard Nathanael.

"Nathanael, I am a lowly quartermaster who helped a friend out that evening by taking his duty. Even though I was there and was, how you called it, spying, it wasn't on Jesus. I was watching Laban. My charge that evening was to keep my ears open and to hear if Laban said anything against the government of Rome. And for the record, he said nothing that evening and my report stated as much. I had nothing to do with his arrest, of this I assure you."

"Then why are you here and out of uniform? What is it that you have come here looking for?" asked Nathanael.

Simultaneously, both Cornelius and Prisca responded with the same answer, "Truth."

The synergy and timing of the mutual response caused Cornelius and Prisca to shoot a quick glance and smile each other's way.

"What my husband hasn't told you, Nathanael, is that while he most certainly wasn't spying on Jesus, we can't say the same thing about Jesus," said Prisca.

Nathanael's face began to squish up in confusion.

Before he could ask what she meant, Cornelius quickly stepped in and added, "What she means, and this is so hard to explain, but I felt... I felt that Jesus was spying on me that night. I saw what he did with the pitchers of water. I watched him as he prayed over them and how the servant reacted upon tasting the water. But more than anything, when that was all finished, he looked up at me." In speaking those last words, Cornelius' emotions began to get the better of him. He paused for a moment to compose himself.

Continuing, he said to Nathanael, "Jesus looked up at me and smiled. And I know that this is going to sound extremely strange, but from that moment on I felt an indiscernible yet deep connection with him. My life..." He paused again to gather himself. "My life has never been the same since that moment. If anything, Jesus was spying on me that night. And my wife, Prisca, and I are grateful for it."

What Cornelius had to say offered no degree of surprise to Nathanael. It was the same calling he felt ever since Phillip introduced Jesus to him before Rachel's wedding. He also understood the sustaining nature of that first encounter.

For the first time since recognizing Cornelius, the tension in Nathanael's body was gone.

Nathanael extended his hand to Cornelius. "What is it that I can do for you, my brother?" he asked, now welcoming and understanding.

Cornelius gladly accepted Nathanael's hand and inquired, "Will Jesus be teaching today? If so, could you tell us when and where that will be so we could hear him?"

"Yes, he will be speaking again this afternoon. He is now finishing up in the Synagogue just a few blocks east of here. He is scheduled to have lunch at Peter's, one of his followers, mother's house. After that he will be speaking on the side of that hill right over there," Nathanael said, pointing at a hill, the crest of which was directly down the road from where the bazaar was held.

"Thank you so much, Nathanael. Not only for the information, but for understanding and accepting us," replied a very sincere and grateful Cornelius.

"Truth, as you say, has an amazing way of understanding and accepting," said Nathanael, who felt somewhat blessed by being able to direct these individuals to another encounter with Jesus.

Twenty-One

After grabbing a couple of lamb kebabs from one of the market's vendors, Cornelius and Prisca headed toward the hill that Nathanael had pointed out earlier. Just a short distance up the hill, no more than twenty yards, was a large rock ledge that had become the place where teachers like Jesus, or possibly some small time entertainers, would address or perform to their audiences.

When they arrived at the hill there were easily a couple hundred people milling about in anticipation of Jesus' arrival. Cornelius and Prisca found a spot on a gentle slope of the hill near the right side of the stone platform. They picked the spot because of its proximity to where Jesus would speak, just ten yards away, and also because that area housed a jutting hunk of rock which was large enough for both of them to comfortably sit on. After spreading a thick wool blanket on the rock, they took their position and anxiously waited. From where they sat, they could see Lake Gennesaret on their right. They watched as numerous fishing boats sailed near the shore while others made their way toward the lake's deeper horizon. Together, Cornelius and Prisca watched the sea, both captivated by the ships' majestic white sails and seemingly effortless motion.

It didn't take long for Cornelius and Prisca to engage in one of their favorite public activities—people watching. What they noticed about this crowd was not only the fact that nearly everyone was Jewish, which they had expected, but how well-mannered and happy most seemed to be. About a half hour after their arrival, the crowd had easily doubled, perhaps even tripled.

Suddenly, the dull, murmuring conversations came to a stop when a man in the crowd shouted, "He's here! Jesus is here!"

The crowd began to applaud the arrival of the teacher.

Some called out, "Rabbi!"

Others cried, "Messiah!"

A few talented individuals used their fingers and thumbs to make very loud whistling sounds.

Cornelius' and Prisca's bodies began to tingle with excitement as the announcement and sudden cavalcade of noises preceded Jesus' entrance. They both stood up on top of their rock to see if they could spot the man they came to hear. Just below them they saw the middle of the crowd open up to allow Jesus and his entourage to make their way through to the rock ledge. The first thing they saw was a hand touching or grasping all the extended hands of those in the crowd who desperately wanted to make physical contact with him. As he made his way up the slope, the couple caught the first glimpse of Jesus' face. What they saw was a man beaming. He bore a smile that let everyone know that he appreciated their welcome and that he cared greatly for each of them.

Once he stepped onto the ledge, Prisca saw the man her husband had once seen and the man that she had heard so much about. She had expected to see a frail, intellectual type of a guy. But what stood in front of her was a man with broad shoulders and a rugged muscular frame. Outlining his smile was thick brown hair that was well cared for and that fell to his shoulders. His face was more beautiful than all the stories she had heard about him had described. No, it was not at all what she expected to see. All the same, his surprising appearance made perfect sense to her.

One of the several men who had accompanied Jesus onto the ledge extended his hands to the crowd and began moving them slowly up and down. In a matter of seconds, the crowd took the cue and sat as an impressive silence fell about those gathered. Jesus then stepped forward and surveyed the crowd from one side to the other. With his head centered and looking down on those gathered, he once again smiled.

After about ten long seconds he began to address the crowd. "I am often asked, how much does God the Father love us? Perhaps this story will help you to understand how deep the Father's love for you truly is."

For some unknown and certainly unanticipated reason, Prisca began to cry as Jesus started to speak. It wasn't an outburst and certainly no one around them noticed. But a steady drip of tears began to leave her eyes and start their journey down the slope of her cheeks.

Cornelius noticed and understood. He took her hand and squeezed it tightly. She looked at him and they shared a smile.

Continuing, Jesus said, "A man had two sons. The younger son said to his father, 'Father, give me the share of your estate that should come to me. I don't want you to be dead for me to begin to spend my inheritance.' His heart was broken by his son's request, but the father divided the property between his two sons and gave to his youngest half of the total value of his estate. After a few days, the younger son collected all his belongings and set off to a distant country where he squandered his inheritance on a life of drunkenness, carousing, and all things selfish. When he had spent his entire inheritance, which should have lasted him nearly a lifetime, a severe famine struck that country. Without a single lepton to his name, he found himself in dire need. So he hired himself out to one of the local citizens who sent him to his farm to tend the swine."

Hearing this, Prisca leaned over to Cornelius and whispered to him, "Sapphira told me that Jews don't eat pork or have anything to do with pigs. So what he's trying to show is just how utterly desperate the son was."

Cornelius nodded his head in acknowledgment of the information, which he didn't know and was appreciative to learn.

Jesus continued, "Now this so-called job paid next to nothing. So desperate had the son become that he began to eat the very slop he was feeding the pigs just to stay alive. Coming to his senses, he thought, 'How many of my father's hired workers have more than enough food to eat, but here I am dying from hunger. I shall get up and go to my father and I shall say to him, "Father, I have sinned against heaven and against you. I no longer deserve to be called your son; treat me as you would treat one of your hired workers."' So he got up and went back to his father. While he was still a long way off, his father suddenly caught sight of him coming up the road that led to his house. The father, seeing his son in the distance, was filled with compassion and love for his son. So happy was he to see his son that the father left his porch and began to run down the road to meet him. When he reached his son he embraced him, so much so that the momentum of the father's hug lifted the son off the ground. As the father held him in his arms, he kissed him and told him that he missed him and that he loved him greatly. His son said to him, 'Father, I have sinned against heaven and against you; I no longer deserve to be called your son.' But his father ordered his servants, 'Quickly, bring the finest robe and put it on him; put a ring on his finger and sandals on his feet. Take the fattened calf and slaughter it. Then let us celebrate with a feast, because this son of mine was dead and has come to life again; he was lost, and has been found.' Then the celebration began."

The crowd hung on every word. Cornelius could tell that what Jesus was trying to convey concerning God's love was not being lost on any of them. At this part of the story, Cornelius squeezed Prisca's hand tighter, sending the message to her that he was taken by the words he was hearing and that he was starting to believe in the possibility of a single, universal God who ruled not out of a base of fear and domination, but rather out of love.

"Now the older son had been out in the field and, on his way back, as he neared the house, he heard the sound of music and dancing. He called one of the servants and asked what was going on. The servant said to him, 'Your brother has returned and your father has slaughtered the fattened calf because he has him back safe and sound.' The older son became angry, and when he refused to enter the house, his father came out and pleaded with him. He said to his father in reply, 'All these years I served you and not once did I disobey your orders. Yet you never gave me even a young goat to feast on with my friends. But when your son returns, who swallowed up your property with prostitutes, for him you slaughter the fattened calf.' The father said to him, 'My son, you are here with me always; everything I have is yours. But now we must celebrate and rejoice, because your brother was dead and has come to life again; he was lost and has been found.'"

Jesus paused there and once again surveyed the crowd. After what seemed like a very long time but was only thirty seconds or so, his glance came and stopped at the couple sitting on the rock to his left.

As if he were speaking only to Prisca and Cornelius, he finished his story by saying, "That is how much the Father loves each and every one of you. There is no sin that is stronger than His love. You just have to believe."

Right after he finished, Jesus' eyes locked with Cornelius' eyes. Jesus nodded his head as if to recognize the Roman solider he knew and loved. Amazed, Cornelius nodded back.

Twenty-two

The evening went better than Cookie expected. While she originally only agreed to play for one set, the response was so wonderful and warming that she ended up playing two fuller than normal sets. She had not posted her appearance at Burba's on either her website or on her Facebook account. In fact, she had only told two people about her performance. Her first notification went out to Michael, albeit only by leaving a voicemail as he was either unable to pick up when she called or decided on his own not to answer. The second invite went, of course, to Carol. Carol was ecstatic to hear that Cookie was getting back on her performance horse and said that she and her mother would be there.

True to her word, Carol and Veronica were there at a table very close to the stage taking full advantage of the half-priced potato skins and wings. They had with them a young man who looked to be about eighteen or nineteen whom Cookie didn't recognize. He had dark black hair that was very thick and out of control. Cookie figured that either the untamed hair was a look he was going for, or the boy had obvious hygiene issues. He kept his head down as if he were detached from everything around him. The mixture of his thick hair, which covered much of his face, combined with his penchant for keeping his head down and focused on the top of the table, prevented Cookie from getting a good look at his face. After sizing up the appearance of this new friend of Carol's and Veronica's, Cookie noticed that on the floor next to him was a brown backpack. She also noticed that one of the backpack straps was looped around the right leg of the boy. Surely if Carol had a boyfriend she would know about it, thought Cookie. Since they had arrived just as Cookie began her first song, one that she wrote titled "Butterflies and Minor Keys," her opportunity to meet this boy would have to wait until after her set.

The first song went off easier than Cookie had expected. She knew, however, that from that point on she was heading out into deep emotional waters. She hoped she could successfully navigate them without encountering any serious musical or vocal errors and, most especially, without experiencing any significant pain.

After the applause from her first song dwindled down, Cookie took a moment to address the packed crowd and to let them know the direction of her song choices for the remainder of that evening.

"As many of you know, I lost a good friend not so long ago."

With that somber introduction, a pin could have been heard dropping on the cold cement floor of Burba's.

With everyone silent and looking at her, all except Carol's friend who continued eating wings with his face to the table, Cookie continued, "Normally she is sitting to my right here. I surely miss her." Cookie paused and she swallowed hard, trying to hold back the tears that had begun to line the corners of both her eyes.

Continuing she added, "And I know many of you do as well. To honor her, my plan tonight is to play for the rest of the evening only songs that we did together. Be patient with me as she was the one with the voice."

Without hesitation, Cookie went right into "Sister Golden Hair." She followed the America classic with "Wild Horses" by the Stones, two of Violet's most popular covers. During those first two songs she didn't look up. As Cookie hit the ending riff of the tender Stones ballad, her eyes rose and they were greeted not only by the wildly appreciative crowd, but most especially by Carol and Veronica whose applause was accompanied by an ample supply of tears.

From her perch on top of the stage, Cookie smiled down at Carol and mouthed, "Thank you" to her. Carol responded by blowing Cookie a kiss.

Cookie's eyes surveyed the applauding crowd searching for Michael. She didn't expect him to be there, so she wasn't disappointed when her quick scan of the house for him came up empty.

In her heart, she said a little prayer for him. "Be with him, Lord."

Before she began the next song, Cookie looked back at Carol's table. The young man still hadn't looked up. By this time, Cookie had surmised that perhaps the boy was autistic or had some type of special needs.

When her long set had finished, there were several people who wanted to talk with her, to give her a hug, to let her know they were there for her. She politely held them at bay until she made it down to Carol's table. Carol and Veronica were already standing with their arms extended, waiting to take Cookie firmly within their embrace.

After all were sufficiently hugged and feelings adequately expressed, Carol turned to Cookie and said, while at the same time tapping the young man on the shoulder, "Cookie, I'd like you to meet Anthony. Anthony, this is Cookie."

With that their young companion finally lifted his head from the table, and for the first time Cookie saw his face. The first thing she noticed, as did anyone who met Anthony, was his bright, baby blue eyes. *Very striking*, thought Cookie. She next noticed that Anthony was losing a minor battle with acne, but all the same his face had the structure that would soon make him a handsome man. At Carol's prodding, Anthony stood up. He was tall, slightly over six feet, and very slender.

Extending her hand to him Cookie said, "Nice to meet you, Anthony, I'm Cookie."

"Nice to meet you, too. What is your last name, Cookie?" Anthony asked, in a very gentle voice as his hand loosely gripped Cookie's.

"Reginald, Cookie Reginald," answered Cookie with a smile.

"Nice to meet you, Cookie Reginald," Anthony reiterated, now feeling a whole lot more comfortable having been able to greet Cookie in what he felt was the proper way.

Cookie asked, "What is your last name if you don't mind me asking?"

Anthony looked up for a split second. Once his eyes met Cookie's he quickly lowered his head.

"My name is Anthony Velario. Thanks for asking, Cookie Reginald. Your music is real good, Cookie Reginald. I really liked hearing your music," replied Anthony, whose eyes remained cast on the floor.

"Well thank you, Anthony, you are very kind," Cookie said in a warm and genuine manner.

Seconds later Anthony sat back down and diverted his attention once again to the table.

Cookie had known when she invited Carol to her gig that her mom was going to take her to see the Diamondbacks game that evening and that they would likely have to leave early. Veronica had received three tickets from her boss at the Sheraton in appreciation for the fine job she had been doing and she was looking forward to bringing her daughter to the baseball game.

"We hate to listen and run, but we have to get going," Veronica said apologetically.

"No worries!" said Cookie. "Is Anthony going with you guys?"

"He sure is!" Carol said, sounding upbeat as if to make Anthony feel more welcome.

Squatting down to meet Anthony at his seated level, Cookie was able to get his attention. When his eyes met hers she said, "It was nice meeting you, Anthony. I look forward to seeing you again."

Anthony gave a slight smile and said, "I hope to see you again too, Cookie Reginald."

Veronica interjected, "I'm sure you will see each other again. Anthony is staying at the UMOM shelter and, at least for the time being, we are kind of keeping an eye on him."

Curious as to what that might mean, Cookie let it go for the moment knowing that she would get filled in later by either Carol or Veronica.

As the three of them made their way out the door of Burba's, they ran right into Michael who was just reaching for the door as they exited. While he had hoped to be as unobtrusive as a pale shadow that evening, his plan quickly came apart when he bumped into Carol, Veronica, and a backpack wielding young man whom he had never met before.

Carol and Veronica were equally shocked to have run into Michael. Cookie had mentioned that she invited him to come out, but neither of them held out much hope that he would show.

"Michael!" exclaimed a surprised Carol. "How—" Carol caught herself about to ask him how he was and instantly stopped in her verbal tracks. She sorely wished she could take back her fumbled "How."

While far from true, Michael didn't want them to feel uncomfortable. So plastering a small smile on his face he responded, "I'm doing fine. How about you guys?"

"We're doing good, real good," answered Carol. Without knowing what else to say, an awkward silence began to hover between them.

Michael again made the move to break the uncomfortable tension. Noticing their male companion, he inquired, "And who is this?"

"Oh, my bad. This is my friend Anthony. Anthony, this is our friend Michael Fortunato," replied Carol.

Knowing that Anthony would ask for Michael's last name, she thought it best to introduce him by his full name from the start.

Michael extended his hand to the shaggy young friend of Carol's who seemed to have trouble making eye contact with him. "Nice to meet you, Anthony."

"And it's nice to meet you, Michael Fortunato. Are you here to hear Cookie Reginald sing? She sings very good," said Anthony while gripping Michael's hand.

"Yes and yes, Anthony. I'm here to hear Cookie, and yes she sings very well!" replied Michael, who for the first time since running into them sprouted a real smile on his face.

"Well, you enjoy it, Michael Fortunato cuz we got to go to the Diamondbacks game now," Anthony said, anxious to get a move on.

At that, the remainder of the group let out a laugh. With the tension relieved by Anthony's voiced desires, Michael put loving closure to their chance meeting by extending a hug to both Veronica and Carol.

"Nice to see you both," said Michael as he hugged each of the ladies.

"And you too, Michael. You remain in our prayers," replied a most sincere Veronica.

With their hellos and goodbyes behind them, Michael worked his way to the back of Burba's. He had hoped that Cookie would be playing as he entered and that he would just be able to enter unnoticed. But his poor timing found Cookie in between sets. Before he could even take a seat, he felt a tap on the back of his shoulder. Turning around he found Cookie looking up at him. At first she was smiling. But in a matter of seconds her smile quickly transformed into a quivering bottom lip.

The combination of seeing Michael and being with him in a place where they had played music together with Debbie brought upon her an uncontrollable rush of emotion. Before she had a chance to totally erupt, Michael reached out and placed his arms around her. He wanted to say, "It's okay" out of reflex, but both of them knew it wasn't. So instead they just stood and hugged each other for a good minute and a half. As their grip on each other subsided, the smile returned to Cookie's face.

"Do you have any requests, sir? And because you're so extra special, you don't even have to tip me!" Cookie said in an attempt to change the subject and to lighten the moment.

Playing along, Michael put his hand on his chin and made the universal, let me think about it pose. "How about 'Monkey Man' by the Stones?"

The minute he said it they both let out a burst of laughter. While they agreed on almost everything musical, "Monkey Man" had been the tune that they could never see eye to eye on. Michael hated it with a passion, while Cookie loved it. Cookie often would start playing it at practice when there was a lull, just to get a reaction out of Michael.

"I'll see what I can do!" Cookie said. "I have to tune up and start my next set now. Glad you came out. If you're up to it, maybe we can grab a coffee after the set?"

"Sounds good," Michael said without really committing.

Reaching forward, Cookie initiated their second hug and headed toward the stage.

Michael found a seat in the back and took in about half of Cookie's next set. His emotions were in a giant state of flux. Part of him felt good about being out and seeing his friend. But a larger part of him struggled with being in a music venue that he and Debbie had played at, along with Cookie, and just sitting there. Not playing. Without Debbie.

Rather than just slipping out unnoticed, he waved his hand at the stage and caught Cookie's attention. Once he had her attention, he blew her a kiss and gave her a thumbs up. Cookie totally understood and nodded affectionately in his direction.

Twenty-three

The day after Cornelius and Prisca returned to Cana was a workday for the young Centurion. It was hard to gauge who was more excited for Cornelius to go into work that day. Cornelius was just about out the front door when Prisca stopped him by grabbing the top of his collar.

Once he was facing her, she shot him a determined look and said, "You find that table and tell my grandfather that it goes nowhere but right there." Prisca pointed to a corner of the room where she had already visualized the table residing.

"Don't worry dear, no one wants that table more than me," replied her officer husband as he leaned over and gave her a kiss goodbye.

"Would it be possible to get some of your reports to bring it by today?" Prisca asked, looking like a sad puppy dog who knew how to draw out its master's affection.

"If we have enough men available, I surely will. Bye, dear, see you in a bit," Cornelius said as he breeched the doorway and headed to the warehouse.

"Bye, have a good day. And remember, no wood, no good!" yelled Prisca from the doorway.

Cornelius heard her and, laughing to himself, held up and waved his hand in acknowledgment as he continued to walk to work.

Twenty-four

Social services had originally wanted to bring Anthony Velario to Andre House, a homeless facility for men located in central Phoenix which was run by volunteers. But when his newly assigned caseworker, Nadia Arthur, found out that there were no rooms available there, she managed to successfully sweet talk the UMOM director, Sarah Gomez, a kind and compassionate woman whom Nadia had worked with on several cases, including Veronica and Carol's, to take him in temporarily at her facility. UMOM was, in many ways, the female counterpart of Andre House. While men were typically not a part of the composite UMOM landscape, Sarah Gomez made an exception for Anthony to receive temporary shelter due to his young age and innocent disposition.

Anthony had come to the attention of Nadia after she had received a call from Maricopa Hospital concerning a stroke patient who had been recently admitted there. His name was George Velario. George had been found lying on the corner of Adams and Seventh Street, unable to move the right side of his body. After being rushed to the hospital, it was determined that he had suffered a very serious stroke. For several days he was unable to speak and faded in and out of consciousness.

Finally, on the third day of his hospitalization George was able to relay to a nurse in a very slurred and barely understandable voice, "Boy... boy at place."

The nurse quickly notified the police who, along with social services, more specifically Nadia Arthur, went to the address listed on George Velario's ID: 435 E. Adams, Apt 3. As fate would have it, it was only a block from the spot where the stroke had unleashed its wrath against such a sweet man. When they arrived at the shambles of an apartment building, they found the manager whom they quickly commandeered, along with his set of master keys, and made their way through the dirty hallway to apartment three. After several volleys of unanswered knocks, the police motioned for the manager to open the apartment door. With an almost completely finished cigarette dangling from the corner of his mouth, the manager went through two wrong keys before he located the one that opened the door to the apartment. Once opened, the police and Nadia found what they had anticipated. Sitting on the sofa, oblivious to the noise and commotion coming from the other side of his door, sat Anthony with a brown cloth backpack in his lap, transfixed by the television that was playing an episode of *House Hunters International*.

The boy, whom she estimated to be in his late teens, didn't even move his head to acknowledge the parade of people who had now entered his domain. Nadia surmised very quickly that this boy might have some special needs. Realizing this, she moved slowly to the sofa and sat next to the boy.

"Hello, my name is Nadia, what's yours?" Nadia said, calmly and with a smile.

When she didn't get an immediate response she gently placed her hand on his shoulder nearest her and repeated the introduction. "Hello, my name is Nadia, Nadia Arthur. What's your name?"

Feeling a touch on his shoulder, the boy recoiled and twisted away from her.

"I'm sorry. I should have asked if it was all right to touch you. Again, my name is Nadia. Could you please look at me and tell me your name?"

At that, the boy turned and looked at Nadia. Her face greeted him with a warm smile that seemed to have its desired effect on the boy.

He finally replied to her introduction. "Hi, Nadia Arthur, my name is Anthony Velario. Nice to meet you."

Nadia was filled with a sense of relief not just for herself, but for the boy. The depth of his response, in its completeness and in his uncopied and unaided "nice to meet you," indicated to her that while Anthony may indeed have some special needs, he was far from being severely impaired.

Turning his head back to the television and still clutching his backpack, he continued their conversation by asking without the slightest tone of concern or fear, "Nadia Arthur, where is my Uncle George?"

"Anthony, please look at me." When he turned and made eye contact with her she continued in a most empathetic tone, "Anthony, your uncle is in the hospital. He had what's called a stroke."

"How much of his brain died?" Anthony quickly asked.

By the mere fact that Anthony knew a stroke was associated with brain damage and section death, Nadia realized that while Anthony might have significant inward tendencies, he likely had a very decent IQ.

"I don't think the doctors have determined that yet, but if you'd like I can take you there to see him. Would you like that, Anthony?" asked Nadia.

"Yes. Nadia Arthur, that would be nice," replied Anthony, who had turned his head and once again set his gaze on a couple trying to make a decision on what house to purchase in Tuscany.

"I will take you there now on one condition," bartered Nadia.

"What's that, Nadia Arthur?" asked Anthony, still glued to the couple in Tuscany.

"That you look at me when we talk and that you call me Nadia, just Nadia. Deal?"

Looking at her in full acknowledgment of her conditions Anthony replied, "Deal."

With that, Nadia rose from the couch and extended her hand to help

Anthony up. He reached out with one of his hands and accepted Nadia's assist while his other hand maintained a firm grip on his backpack.

Twenty-five

They say that time heals all wounds. Michael was finding this not to be the case. Nearly six months had passed since Debbie's death and his world had gone from shades of gray to a deep and deafening black. He still was unable to return to work. He rarely returned calls to those who cared about him the most and he spent nearly all his time in his house, alone. Most alarming to those who knew him the best was his loss of faith. Some would call it a case of the dark night of the soul that was encountered and written about by many saints. Michael didn't know what to call it, nor did he care to label it as anything at all. All he knew was that he didn't feel God's presence. What he felt was abandoned and alone. While he felt God's absence, it wasn't his abandonment that made him feel alone; it was the absence of his wife, his life, and his best friend that was the cause of his unshakeable and steadily increasing pain.

His absence at church over the last month had not escaped notice. Fr. Charlie had called him several times only to get Michael's voicemail. When his calls went unreturned he followed up with a couple of emails, which also went unanswered. After a week of failed attempts at communication, Fr. Charlie and Rori drove out to his house in hopes of being able to see him and to make sure that he was all right.

Michael had heard their car pull in the driveway. When the doorbell rang, Goose went nuts as he did any time the doorbell did its thing. When the shadows lingered at the front door longer than they should have, Michael got himself up off the sofa, and from the corner of the front window gently lifted the shades to see who it was.

The doorbell rang again and Goose barked even more obnoxiously than before. Michael saw that it was Fr. Charlie and Rori. Part of him wanted to answer the door, to invite them in, to hug and be hugged by them, and to let out a good and needed cry. But all the same, he couldn't. His emptiness remained. Unshaken and resolute to its mission of darkness and solitude, he carried the void back to the sofa where he curled up and placed a pillow to his head until Goose's barking became nearly inaudible.

Twenty-six

In the short couple of hours between the time when Nadia Arthur left the hospital and had returned with Anthony, the severity of George's condition had greatly increased. Though not common, his stroke was followed several hours later by a massive heart attack. Nadia and Anthony were fortunate that the doctor who was treating George Velario was at the counter of the nurses' station reviewing a chart when they arrived at the intensive care unit. After a brief introduction, the doctor reviewed what had happened with them.

"It appears that the same thrombosis, or clot, which originated in Mr. Velario's thigh and caused his stroke was also responsible for breaking free and causing a blockage in his coronary artery," explained the hospital's staff cardiologist Dr. Quinlan.

Anthony, who had been looking down the hall as Dr. Quinlan spoke, did not make eye contact when he inquired, "When that happens heart muscle dies. Did all of my Uncle George's heart muscle die?"

Dr. Quinlan, quick to notice that Anthony was somewhat autistic, shot Nadia a glance which conveyed that he was both impressed and touched by Anthony's question.

Before the doctor had a chance to reply, Nadia gently asked Anthony,

"Can you look at the doctor and ask him that question?"

Turning to face the doctor, the first thing Anthony noticed was the doctor's name tag. After registering its contents, Anthony's eyes zeroed in for the first time on his face.

"Dr. Kyran Quinlan, did all my Uncle George's heart muscle die due to the thrombosis?" Anthony asked for the second time.

"Well, Anthony, not all of your uncle's heart muscle died, but more of it died than I would have liked to see," replied Dr. Quinlan in a warm and caring voice.

"Dr. Kyran Quinlan, is my Uncle George going to die," asked Anthony in a tone that sounded matter of fact, but which was understandable given his special character. Anthony's eyes dropped from the doctor's face and focused, for no known reason, on the hospital's linoleum floor, near to where he had placed his backpack.

Dr. Quinlan placed a hand on Anthony's shoulder in an attempt to comfort him, but Anthony quickly recoiled. Understanding that many autistic individuals do not like to be touched, Dr. Quinlan took no offense.

He said instead, "Anthony, please look up at me."

Anthony began to lift his face toward the doctor.

Dr. Quinlan continued slowly and with a great deal of compassion, "I am not going to lie to you, Anthony. The clot was large and it did starve a very large part of his heart of oxygen. Not many people survive the kind of blow your uncle suffered today."

Anthony sucked in the bottom part of his lip and looked as though he was processing the news. After a few seconds had passed, Anthony asked, "Can I see him, Dr. Kyran Quinlan? Can me and Nadia Arthur, I mean Nadia, see him. I'd like to talk with him before he leaves."

"That would be fine. In fact, I think he would like that. Come with me and I will show you where he's at," said Dr. Quinlan as he led them down the hall and into ICU unit number three.

Twenty-seven

As he entered the warehouse that day, Cornelius' main mission was very clear—secure the table before it went up for auction later that week. Between the anticipation of owning the table and the high he was still experiencing from having just heard Jesus speak, Cornelius found himself feeling all sorts of giddy.

The entire lot of Laban's seized materials was being stored on the first floor of the two-level building in its northeast corner. Having just inventoried everything in the warehouse the week before, Cornelius knew not only where the lot was exactly located, but precisely where the table of Jesus had been stored within it. Without even stopping at the office for a cup of posca, which was typically his instinctive first stop each morning at work, Cornelius headed to that northeast corner of the building and to Laban's lot.

When he arrived at what should have been a neatly packed and arranged gathering of the property seized at Laban's farm, Cornelius found a disheveled mess. It was evident that things were not only out of the order they had been in the previous week, but it also appeared that several items from the lot were now missing.

"Please be here, oh please be here," Cornelius whispered to himself as he waded through the cluttered items. When he made it to the back wall where the table had been stored, to his dismay all that met his eye was an empty space where the table previously stood. With his heart sinking slowly to his sandals, Cornelius made his way rapidly out of the lot items seized from Laban. Once clear of that man's former wealth, Cornelius sprinted to the office.

"Celsus! Celsus!" he yelled.

Before Cornelius made it to the office, Celsus, hearing the desperate call of his top report and grandson-in-law, came bolting out of the office door. A look of real concern swept across Celsus' face, certain something terrible must have happened to his Prisca.

"Cornelius, what is it my boy?" Celsus asked, out of breath and somewhat panicked as Cornelius ran up to him.

"What happened to the Laban lot? Things are missing!" said a desperate Cornelius.

Thinking that Cornelius must have thought they had been robbed, and certainly not understanding why it was that Cornelius seemed so concerned over the matter, Celsus began to chuckle.

"Not to worry, my son. We have not been robbed, everything is accounted for," replied Celsus, who was glad that Cornelius' out-of-character display of panic had nothing to do with the wellbeing of his granddaughter.

"Accounted for? What do you mean? Where are the missing items?" asked Cornelius with a tone of sudden hope in his voice.

"A garrison in Jerusalem acquired them, the Tenth Legion I think it was. Word got out of the quality of Laban's property and they came in here like a swarm of ants on top of a fallen date over the weekend and took what they wanted. Not like we could tell them no as they had the proper paperwork," answered Celsus, who noticed the look of loss sweep over Cornelius' face again.

"I had promised Prisca the table. I had wanted the table," said Cornelius, his voice distant and his blue eyes glazed over.

Celsus noticed that other soldiers were starting to observe what was becoming a bit of a scene. Celsus motioned for Cornelius to come into the office. Once inside, Celsus shut the door and offered Cornelius a seat next to his desk.

Pulling up a chair beside him, Celsus asked, "So, my son, what has you so worked up about this particular table? There are plenty of other nice tables that are going to auction later this week, and you have the right, next to me, of first claim."

Both Prisca and Cornelius had shared their passion for philosophy and the arts with Celsus multiple times. In fact, Celsus himself was highly interested in these conversations and considered himself to be a fairly enlightened individual. Many evenings over dinner, they had even shared with him what they were hearing about the teachings of Jesus. Celsus was also fully aware that they had just went to Capernaum to hear him speak. But Cornelius had never told him about the table.

Over the next hour, Cornelius shared with Celsus not only the story of Jesus, the table, and himself, but of how Jesus had been affecting such a change in both Prisca and himself. It was hard to put into words, but Cornelius did the best he could to describe how it was that this itinerate preacher was making them look at life and faith in a new way that finally made sense. After trying and trying to express this, Cornelius finally found the words that best conveyed what was now written in his heart.

"Celsus, he is the answer to all my questions."

While Celsus found the words Cornelius expressed convincing on their own merit, it was the passion in his face that best conveyed the truth of what Cornelius was trying to communicate. Celsus deeply appreciated and respected their newfound passion for this man Jesus, but at the same time he felt concern for their safety.

"Cornelius, it's apparent that you and Prisca have found a song that you need to sing. I have no doubt that goodness is within you, and quite possibly in this Hebrew God and his apparent messenger. All the same, you have to be careful. While there has been tolerance for the Jews and their practices, that tolerance is quickly waning. I see a time, and perhaps very soon, where Roman citizens themselves will not be allowed to associate socially with the Jews, else they too will come under the wrath of Roman law and order."

Cornelius was wise enough to have seen the same signs of changing Roman sentiment. "I know, Celsus, I see it approaching like a storm. All the same, I cannot turn from the truth, and he is the truth."

"What I am saying is this, hang on to your truth, but hang on to it inwardly where it counts the most. Soon, expressing it on the outside could make you and Prisca an enemy of the Empire. Better for you to practice outward appropriateness now, and thus be prepared for the tide of intolerance that will likely sweep into Judea, than to not see the day of its arrival and the potential cost of disapproved behavior."

Cornelius knew that Celsus was right and that all of his wisdom came from his heart out of his love and concern for both Prisca and himself.

"Celsus, you have my promise, we will lay low. All the same, I still feel a burning need to have that table. It's hard to describe, but I feel as well that the table has a need for me," Cornelius tried to explain.

"Regarding the table, Cornelius, I am supposed to be in Jerusalem in two weeks to review with the Armicustos and his staff our system of inventory there. Suppose I catch ill and you go on that trip for me," Celsus said with a grin.

Cornelius knew exactly what angle Celsus was suggesting.

"I suppose I could do that. It would also be handy if I had in my possession a reverse order for that table. Perhaps, it would be even better if I brought a suitable replacement. Do you think I could get my boss to sign off on such a reverse order?" a suddenly happier Cornelius quipped.

"I think it can be arranged, yes. I believe that such a thing could definitely be arranged!" Celsus chuckled as he pulled at the end of his white beard.

Twenty-eight

As God's grace would have it, George Velario was conscious when Anthony and Nadia, led by Dr. Quinlan, entered his corner of ICU unit number three. He was hooked up to all sorts of monitors, IVs, and his ashen face bore a clear green oxygen mask. All the same, when he saw his nephew standing at the side of his bed he began to smile and raised his hand to Anthony. Anthony took his hand and smiled back at his uncle. It was the first time that Nadia had seen Anthony smile.

"The doctor said that too much of your heart muscle died. I love you, Uncle George," said Anthony with little emotion, yet for him, with a great deal of emotion.

This only made Uncle George smile wider since he knew that his nephew was actually telling him much more than just the simple words he stated. George tried to say something back to Anthony, but he couldn't be heard due to the combination of his weakened state and the confinement of the oxygen mask. Dr. Quinlan saw this and stepped in. He had a sense that this may be a goodbye and an even better sense to move to the side of the bed to remove the oxygen mask so that Mr. Velario could be heard. After removing the mask, Dr. Quinlan stepped back and hugged the wall behind Anthony and Nadia so he could monitor his patient's condition.

"Anthony!" George said in the loudest voice he could muster, which in reality was barely audible to those in the room. Happy that Anthony had gripped the hand that had not been affected by the stroke, George squeezed Anthony's hand as tight as he could. "I love you too, boy. Always have and always will." Noticing Nadia standing next to him he continued, "So I'm gone about a day and you go and find yourself a girlfriend!"

Nadia couldn't help but smile, but before she could respond Anthony quickly answered, "Nadia is not my girlfriend!"

"Well if she's not your girlfriend, then who is she?" asked George in a loving and teasing manner. He was hoping for the answer he next received.

"She's from social services, Uncle George. She's very nice. She came to the apartment and then brought me here. Her last name is Arthur but she wants me to just call her Nadia."

At that, George began to laugh as hard as his condition would allow. He, of course, knew of Anthony's propensity to call everyone by their first and last name. He was happy to hear that Nadia was not only there for him, but that she was assertive enough to correct Anthony's somewhat annoying idiosyncrasy. With his smile subsiding, the reality of the boy's future caught up to him. Moving his eyes from Anthony's, his attention now focused on Nadia.

Nadia knew what George was thinking and wanted to do her best to put him at ease. Before he had a chance to speak, Nadia leaned in and placed her hand on top of George and Anthony's joined hands and, with her eyes meeting his she said, "Mr. Velario, as Anthony accurately pointed out, I am from social services and I want you to know that I am taking good care of Anthony." Knowing the likelihood that George would not be pulling through she added, "No matter for how long, I assure you that he will be well cared for."

It was on the way to the hospital that Nadia had learned from Anthony that his Uncle George was not only his guardian, but his only living relative or family friend.

As for George, he understood exactly what she was saying. He knew that his time in this life was not long. His only concern was for the future care of Anthony. He saw in Nadia someone he could trust, someone that he had been praying for from the moment he entered the hospital.

After looking up to the ceiling and saying a quick thank you to God for his answered prayer, he turned to thank Nadia. "You are an answer to my prayers, Nadia. I can tell that you will ensure Anthony is cared for."

"Count on it, Mr. Velario," Nadia said reassuringly.

"Thank you, thank you, Nadia Arthur."

Hearing his uncle use his patented line made Anthony quickly respond, "Uncle George, she only wants to be called Nadia!"

Everyone in the room began to laugh. When the laughter subsided, George looked up at Nadia and the doctor standing behind her and made his request.

"Would it be possible if I can have a few minutes alone with the boy?"

"Of course, Mr. Velario, we'll be right outside if you need anything," replied Nadia.

"And Nadia, it's George. Please call me George."

"Okay, George, we'll be right outside," responded Nadia with affection. She and Dr. Quinlan exited the room, leaving Anthony at George's bedside still holding his uncle's hand in his.

"Anthony, you are right. Too much of my heart has died. My how smart of a lad you are!" began George.

"Are you going to die, Uncle George?" asked Anthony in the same tone someone might use to ask another person if they were going to the post office.

"Chances are yes, I may die very soon. But please don't worry about me, Anthony. I have had a good life, most of all because I have spent it with you," assured George.

"I'm not worried about you, Uncle George. If you die, God will take you to heaven and I will see you later in heaven when I die. That's the way it works," said Anthony.

"Yes, you are right as usual. That's how it works, Anthony," responded George. Continuing he said, "Now you listen to Nadia and trust her. An angel told me that she will help you when I'm gone. Do you promise me that you will listen to her and that you will do what she says?"

"I promise, Uncle George. I will listen to Nadia," Anthony assured him.

"Good. Now, for the other matter." He released Anthony's hand and pointed to the strap of Anthony's backpack, which was showing over his right shoulder. "Is it in there?" asked George.

"Yes, Uncle George, it's always in my backpack, unless I'm holding it," answered Anthony.

"Two things, Anthony. You must promise me two things. First, that you practice saying the story once a day. The story cannot be forgotten; do you understand?" George passionately inquired.

"Yes, I will practice the story every day. I promise you, Uncle George," replied an always compliant Anthony.

Of anyone whose responsibility it was to care for the story over the span of time, no one knew the story as well as Anthony. One of his special gifts was an uncanny ability to remember long sequences of things, particularly those spoken, like the story. Truth was, if he went ten years and never recited it, he could recite the story on demand and without leaving out a single word. All the same, upon his uncle's request, he would continue to recite the story once a day.

"Good," said George, who happily received Anthony's commitment. Continuing, George told him, "The second thing I need you to do is to share the story and its blessing with someone else at the right time. But, find someone who will continue to keep the story alive and the blessing safe for all time. You and I are the last of the Velarios I'm afraid. All the same, the story needs to be told to live on."

"How will I know who to share it with, Uncle George?" asked Anthony.

"I just prayed that an angel would send us Nadia, so too an angel will send you the right person. You will know when you meet them. Yes, you'll know when you meet them."

"Would you like to hold it, Uncle George?" a very intuitive Anthony asked.

After a pause of several seconds, tears began to well up in George's eyes as he realized that after sixty-eight years, this would be the last time for him to hold the blessing. The tears, fully submitting to the laws of gravity, began to slide down the dying man's cheeks.

Looking at the nephew he had raised and cared for about a million times more, he responded in a soft and receptive voice, "Yes I would, Anthony, very much so."

Anthony gently removed his backpack from his shoulder and set it on the hospital floor. After unzipping its top, he reached in and, taking the blessing with both hands, he gently placed it on his uncle's chest. George began to raise his right arm in order to hold on to the greatest gift in his life, aside from Anthony, but didn't have the strength. Seeing this, Anthony took ahold of his right arm and helped him to grasp the blessing for the last time.

As George's functioning arm came in contact with the blessing, all fear was replaced with an overcoming joy and calm. If he had ever doubted the validity of the story even one iota, those thoughts were now erased and replaced with utter belief and a peace that couldn't be measured or understood in human terms.

Placing his hand on one of his uncle's hands, Anthony closed his eyes and said, "Love has come, Uncle George, love has come."

George Velario, whose eyes were also closed as the rapture of holding the blessing for the last time embraced him, smiled and answered his nephew's declaration, "It certainly has, my boy. It most certainly has."

Twenty-nine

Cornelius was caught off guard by Prisca's easy acceptance of the table's loss. He had expected her to be very upset, if not somewhat skeptical that he would be able to reclaim it in Jerusalem. But as he explained the situation and his strategized solution, she uncharacteristically took it all in stride. At first, Cornelius thought that he must have done a good job assuring her that the plan concocted by her grandfather would work. As long as he could find where the table went within the Tenth Legion, his signed and sealed reverse order would be all that he would need to bring the table back to Cana. But he sensed that there was something else going on with Prisca.

On top of not seeming to be upset by the fact that he had come home without the table, she actually seemed to be a bit on the giddy side. When he finally pressed her on it, she said that she had some news of her own, but that she wanted to share it at the dinner that they had planned that evening over at Cornelius' parents' house. Nothing Cornelius could do during their hour of preparation before heading over to his parents' home could get her to leak even a fragment of her secret.

The more he would ask her to spill the beans, the more she would giggle and coyly say, "Wait and see!"

The home of the Primus Pilus was indeed one of the largest and nicest homes in the Cana District. The front entryway to the home was very large. The tiled pathway leading to the front door was seventeen cubits long and boasted a high covered ceiling supported by two massive marble columns on each of its sides. Just behind those columns, set about two feet back from them, sat two large round bowls which were three cubits in diameter, each containing a burning fire that not only lit the entryway of the house, but also set a tone of elegance for all who stood ready to enter. And of course, being the home of the Primus Pilus, the home was well guarded by an elite number of specially trained sentries, two of which stood stoically at either side of the front door.

As Cornelius stepped up to the entryway, he couldn't help but be impressed by what his father had accomplished. He was especially proud of the fact that his father had achieved his success while retaining the qualities that made him a very good man. Power often strips men of character, but not in Decius' case.

Before they made it to the front door, Decius, Appia, and Cornelius' younger sister Zoe, the only one of their four daughters still unmarried and living at home, greeted them with wide smiles and warm hugs.

"Welcome, son and daughter!" exclaimed a very happy Decius.

Though both Velius families lived in the same town and saw each other often, each time they met Decius and Appia greeted Cornelius and Prisca as if they hadn't seen them in years. They were very proud of their son and they were totally smitten by his choice in a wife.

"Yes, welcome my children!" Appia added, greeting them with a kiss on both cheeks.

Cornelius was very much a momma's boy, but over the years the bond between him and his father had greatly deepened. While Cornelius' own rise within the military certainly didn't hurt their growing affection for one another, it was not the main reason for their increasing levels of respect and admiration for one another. That was due, for the most part, to the acceptance of the recognized qualities of the other, although different, which made them both very good and moral men.

Zoe, as well, held a special place in Cornelius' heart. She was several years his junior and he had always been her protector and confidant, whom she could share anything with. The bond went beyond their unique matching blue eyes they had inherited from their mother. They also shared their mother's poetic outlook on life. Zoe had been hearing about the teachings of Jesus and, knowing that her brother and Prisca had just gone to hear him preach, she was anxious to get a full report.

"Please, everyone hurry inside and sit at the table. The venison cooked much faster than anticipated. I hate to greet and eat, but we must!" Appia said in a pleasant but directive way.

Once seated, the servants, another benefit of being Primus Pilus, began to pour wine and serve the bread. Two people at the table, Cornelius and Prisca to be precise, had been biting at the bit to initiate a path of conversation. Cornelius was about to kick off his desired course of dialogue by announcing that Prisca had something, a secret it seemed, that she wanted to reveal tonight. But before he was able to enunciate his first syllable, Zoe excitedly opened her desired lane of conversation.

"So tell us about Jesus! What did he say? What lessons did he teach? What does he look like?"

Before Cornelius had a chance to redirect the subject matter, Prisca stepped in and began to answer her, "Well, Zoe, he is a very handsome man, rugged looking, but more captivating than anything else about him is his command. When he spoke, it was with the voice of kindness, yet of extreme authority."

Zoe pressed on and asked, "What did he talk about? Did he share any stories?"

"He spoke on several topics, but the one thing that stuck with me the most was when he spoke about the one God of the Jews. He called Him God the Father and said that even when His people turn their backs on

Him and do evil things, He still loves them and will always take them back into His love," explained Prisca.

Chiming in Cornelius added, "Based on the story he told, however, it did seem to me that there was a condition to accepting such a person back into his good graces."

"And what's that?" asked Appia, intrigued.

"That the person is contrite about what they have done wrong. Once they legitimately show remorse and ask this Father God for forgiveness, then He forgives them. He holds no grudges, and loves them as much as I love you, you, you, and you," said Cornelius, pointing his eating utensil at everyone sitting around the table.

"Jupiter would never do that!" exclaimed Zoe.

"Well I doubt that Jupiter actually exists," commented Prisca. "But as strange as it may sound, when you listen to the words of Jesus it makes you feel that this God the Father could really be, and if that is true, then there would only be one God, not many."

"That would certainly make religion a lot easier to understand," Appia added just as one of the servants put a beautifully prepared piece of venison on her plate.

"I admire the searching and the exercising of the fullness of your minds. But need I remind you that we are subjects of Rome and, as such, subject to its religious practices?" Decius interjected.

"I don't see you bowing down to Jupiter, Apollo, or any of the pantheons of the twelve Roman gods," Cornelius said, hoping to draw conversation on the topic out of his father.

"True, but you don't see me going out of my way to recognize a god that is not part of the state religion either. All I'm saying is that these conversations are fine within these walls, but I wouldn't recommend them to be spoken out in the town square," replied Decius.

"I couldn't agree with you more, Dad. In fact, I had the same conversation with Celsus just the other day. What's inside will stay inside. We understand the times and we will not put ourselves or our families in any danger," assured Cornelius.

"Like I said before, I admire your passion and desire to understand deeper things. I just want to make sure that you fully know this. I'm very proud of all of you for your minds. You're thinkers and the world needs more of you!" Decius proudly declared. Continuing he added, "Just be sure to do it safely, since what is acceptable today with regards to religion, especially with this Jesus, could change with a drop of a hammer. The Jewish religious leaders are already starting to grumble to me and others about him. I don't see it escalating, but you never know."

Seeing his moment, Cornelius spoke before anyone else could, "Now if I may change the subject for a moment. It appears that my lovely wife, Prisca, is harboring a secret, one she would not tell me until I was here with all of you. So, I respectfully yield the floor to my wife and her bag of secrets."

"Not so fast! Tell them everything about the table, starting with your first encounter with it and then up to and including your plan to get it back," Prisca responded, enjoying keeping her husband waiting.

"That is not fair!" protested Cornelius. But he knew it was to no avail. Prisca had expertly baited the table hook and it was very apparent that everyone at the Velius table wanted to hear the story.

"Let's hear about this table first!" said Appia.

"Yeah, what table are you talking about? And how can a table have a story?" Zoe questioned.

Knowing that the only way he was going to learn Prisca's secret was to tell those assembled the full story of the table, Cornelius did not fight it. He told the story beginning with his short tenure as a Roman spy at the wedding feast of Laban's granddaughter, all the way up to learning of the table's escape from the warehouse. He concluded by telling them of his and Celsus' plan to bring it back to Cana. He told it all in great detail and left nothing out. When he had finished there was silence around the table as all were taken in by the story.

Even Decius seemed to ponder the significance as he broke the silence by saying, "Just to ensure that you get that table back, I will draft a command letter for you to take to the Legate of the Tenth Legion, not that Celsus' reverse order wouldn't be sufficient, but call it insurance. Now when you get this table, I wouldn't mind seeing what the fuss is all about."

Cornelius appreciated the support of his father's direct assistance in the matter, and what made him happier was Decius' apparent interest in the table and, perhaps, for what it represented.

"Thanks, Dad, it certainly can't hurt to have such a directive from you."

"And I want to see that table too, just as soon as it arrives in Cana. Understand, son?" Appia anxiously added.

"And me too!" Zoe chimed in.

"Of course, of course!" said Cornelius. "However, I am not even going to go to Jerusalem to get the table unless Prisca finally shares her secret with all of us."

Prisca began to smile as she slowly surveyed each and every face around the table. Starting with Decius, moving to Appia, to Zoe, and finally to Cornelius whose eyes she remained locked on as she revealed her secret.

"A new Velius is on the way! We are going to have a baby!"

Thirty

Nadia had learned a great deal about Anthony Velario over the couple weeks that followed the death of his Uncle George. She learned that George had been his legal guardian for the last ten of his eighteen years of life. George had assumed that responsibility with a receptive and loving heart after Anthony's father, Anthony Sr., was killed by a drunk driver on his way to work at a cabinet factory in South Phoenix. Adding to the pain of that sad story, Nadia had also learned that Anthony's mother had died while giving birth to him. George was the only remaining living relative that young Anthony had.

Anthony Sr. was George's younger brother, and he was just thirty-nine when he died. George loved his brother fiercely. He was a protector of Anthony Sr. as a child, and a best friend as they grew into adulthood together. It was not only out of responsibility that he took Anthony Jr. in; his decision ran much deeper than that. He had known Anthony since his birth and was both his godfather and confirmation sponsor. George loved young Anthony very much and didn't have to think for a fraction of a nanosecond to bring him into his apartment, into his life, and to care for him the best he could.

It came as no surprise for Nadia to also learn that Anthony had been diagnosed as being autistic. George did his best to see that Anthony received all the care possible. This proved difficult since George, who made only slightly more than what was considered the poverty level, could not afford any health insurance other than the state's Medicaid assistance coverage called Access. As a result, Anthony's care for his autism was far from optimum. But the combination of Anthony having a mild to moderate diagnosis of autism, along with George's self-study on the topic and his subsequent direct help in doing exercises to bring Anthony more into the world, truly helped Anthony to become an increasingly engaged individual who was nearing the stage of becoming self-sufficient.

George saw to it that Anthony graduated from high school through the special needs department at Roosevelt High. Through an amazing outplacement program at the high school, Anthony found a job working as a bagger at the Food City at McDowell and Forty-Third Avenue. The store was about three miles north of the apartment he shared with his uncle. Anthony had an annual bus pass and had no trouble navigating bus routes. He had been working at Food City for a little over two years now, starting out in a part-time position and then working his way to full time. The manager there told Nadia that he was doing an outstanding job.

After examining both Anthony's medical and school records, Nadia noticed that he had never had his IQ tested. Suspecting that he was much smarter than anyone would ever guess, she had him tested. As she predicted, Anthony's IQ was well above average. Given his high intelligence, his high functioning ability, his social withdrawal, and his unusual ritual preoccupations, such as always addressing people by both their first and last name, Nadia began to think his diagnosis was incorrect. Even though she was just a social worker, she had worked with many people who had Asperger's syndrome, and the behavior she saw in Anthony seemed to mirror the behaviors she saw in those individuals. While Asperger's is closely related to autism, a correct diagnosis could lead to a more specific treatment plan that could only help Anthony be more successful in interacting with and in the world around him. Now that he was on his own, Nadia felt that the more help given to him, the better off he would be going forward in his life without his uncle. So, she saw to it that Anthony was scheduled to see a well-respected psychiatrist who could evaluate and give her opinion on the accuracy of Anthony's current diagnosis.

The psychiatrist, Rachel Jeromy, had a very successful Paradise Valley practice. But unlike many of her colleagues who seemed to be just interested in making more and more money, Dr. Jeromy had always felt the need to give back to the greater community she served. Out of the kindness of her heart, she allotted twenty-five percent of her practice to seeing less financially fortunate individuals like Anthony, many times at zero cost to the patient. Due to her willingness to give so freely of her time, combined with the fact that she was one of the Valley's best psychiatrists, both she and Nadia developed a strong professional association as well as a meaningful friendship. While the appointment was not for a couple more weeks, Nadia felt very good about getting Anthony in to see her.

Nadia felt blessed, as well, with the synchronicity of life. When she first brought Anthony over to the UMOM facility, Carol was leaving the building at the same time. Nadia wasn't surprised that Carol recognized her, since she had been her and her mother's case worker going on two years, but what she didn't expect was for Carol to say hello to Anthony. It turned out that she was one of the tutors at Roosevelt High who would help the special needs students with homework and their studies. Carol had spent time helping Anthony in the past and had developed somewhat of a relationship with him. Hearing of this connection, Nadia couldn't help but think that God had just sent her and Anthony this angel. Nadia later followed up with Carol and Veronica and discussed with them Anthony's current lot in life, and asked if they wouldn't mind befriending him and keeping an eye on him while he was at the UMOM facility. Being the great people that they were, and seeing this as an opportunity for them to pay it forward, they happily agreed. Even after Nadia was able to secure Anthony a room at Andre House, a men-only shelter for the homeless or those in need like Anthony, Carol and Veronica often stopped in to see him or had him over for dinner. Nadia felt blessed and relieved that Anthony had this additional support. However, deep down she knew that this outpouring of feminine affection would be best if countered by the mentoring of a caring man as well.

PART THREE

One

L ike the morning sunrise defeating the shielding attempt of a fully drawn bedroom shade, light began to break through into the tiniest corner of Michael's life. Seeing Cookie perform certainly played a role in his slowly emerging rebound. Going into the show that night, he didn't know what to expect in terms of how he would feel. Would the music and its bond, which only a poet's soul truly knows, a bond that he and Debbie both understood and shared, bring him solace and some sort of unitive peace? Or would it revolt painfully against him? When Michael encountered neither extreme, he was surprised and happy that what he found was a neutral existence.

In addition to getting back out into the world, or at least to a single night at Burba's, the prayerful chipping away of both Fr. Charlie and Rori began to melt Michael's outer shield of spiritual numbness. Through their prayers, their emails, and voicemails of encouragement and love, Michael's need for God was once again being felt.

So it was fortuitous timing when Cookie called him the Saturday afternoon after her gig and asked him if he would be interested in going to Mass with her the following morning. Michael surprised himself when he said yes immediately. For months now, whenever he was asked a question or received an invitation to do anything, his instinctive system of defense would always default to, "Let me think about it," or, "I'll let you know." Cookie's timing could not have been better when she called a few minutes after Michael had picked up and began to pray his rosary for the first time since Debbie's death. It was, in fact, the first time he had prayed or called upon the Lord in months.

So together Cookie and Michael went to the 8:00 a.m. Mass on Sunday. Fr. Charlie was the celebrant, which warmed Michael's heart. As Fr. Charlie finished the words of the opening prayer he surveyed the congregation, and there from the altar he spotted Michael, third pew, center section. When their eyes met, Fr. Charlie smiled kindly at Michael.

None of this was lost on Michael. The simple acknowledgment by Fr. Charlie, together with the faith he felt from the congregation, worked in unison to help open Michael up to God's presence. As the first and second readings were proclaimed, Michael found himself in another place. Instead of listening to a single word of the readings, he began to think about God and his place in all that had happened over the last several months.

At that moment, he realized that God had never left him. Michael knew that God was always there at his side through every painful moment and through all of the tears that followed Debbie's death. Realizing this, what began to weigh on Michael was the only alternative reason for experiencing such a painful separation from his Savior; it was because he, Michael, had turned his back on Him. It was his pain that caused him to run away from God. Instead of running to the only one who could make him whole, he ran in the opposite direction.

A split second before guilt had the chance to inflict its venom on him, he heard a whisper deep within his heart, "We're together now, that's what matters, and that's all that matters."

The sudden wave of guilt was intercepted and crushed by a mightier love. Michael knew that he was still in need of a great deal of healing. But for the first time since the loss of Debbie, he began to feel that he was on his way back and that he was not alone.

Two

Loneliness had never been something that Anthony ever had really thought about, let alone experienced. His autism provided a physical barrier against it. And as an insurance policy against lonesomeness, he always had the buffer of being cared for by people who deeply loved him. While it was true that he could be quite content alone, the loss of his father and now his uncle, began to punch holes into the perception that he was somehow immune to the pain of seclusion.

He enjoyed going to work at Food City where he was well-liked. The store manager, Tom McCabe, was always there for him serving as a father figure of sorts at work. Tom was a good man who went out of his way to not only hire special needs individuals, but also to mentor them on the job and in larger matters of life when appropriate. Tom, as well as nearly every employee at Food City, went out of their way to share their condolences with Anthony after the loss of his uncle. Two of the other baggers took on his shifts the days after his uncle's death, and instead of taking the money for themselves, had it placed into Anthony's bi-weekly paycheck. If that wasn't enough, the whole store took up a collection for him, raising over eleven hundred dollars to help cover whatever extra expenses Anthony might have. Though he lived in his isolated world, he still felt and appreciated the love he had received from his coworkers.

When he wasn't working, however, strange and sad feelings began to permeate his being. These alien feelings not only began to affect his mood, they also made him feel not as hungry as he normally felt. He was glad that Nadia Arthur would visit him and that she seemed to care about him. But all the same, something was missing. For one, his Uncle George and his father had always taken him to Mass on Sunday. It was now several weeks since he had been to church.

As this thought suddenly occurred to him, he quickly found a pen and sticky note and wrote himself a note that read, "Go to church on Sunday." He placed it on his kitchen table to help him remember to do so. Thankfully, St. Matthew's was within walking distance from his apartment.

A few days later, on Sunday, Anthony went to church as planned. During Mass, and for several hours after, he found himself beginning to feel increasingly better and better. But that evening, after reciting the story and crawling into bed, the strange feelings came back. They were not as strong as before, but they still stood there confronting Anthony's heart. Reaching his hand to the floor by the side of his bed, he pulled his backpack on top of his bed.

Clutching it to his chest, he curled his body around it and began to pray, "Dear Jesus, I don't like how I feel. Please make me feel good again. I love you very, very much. Good night, Jesus."

Three

Cornelius, along with his two subordinates, Manius and Servius, left for Jerusalem on a Monday morning. Celsus' original plan involved Cornelius taking his place to lead an inventory seminar, but that seminar had been postponed by the Jerusalem legion for three months. Not wanting to wait that long to bring home the table, Celsus found some other documents that needed to be brought to the Jerusalem Armicustos. And so it was, he sent Cornelius and his reports forward with that smoke screen of a mission.

The plan was to leave early on Monday in order to make the table trade as quickly as possible so they could be back in Cana by the following Saturday. It was Prisca who overly impressed upon him the need for a speedy return. Her desire to touch the very table Jesus touched had her bubbling over in anticipation. For his part, Cornelius wanted to return home in rapid fashion not only to see Prisca's joy in physically connecting with the table, but to simply be with his pregnant wife.

It was sixty-seven miles from Cana to Jerusalem. The wagon containing the trade table was navigated by Manius and Servius and pulled by a single large quarter horse. With Cornelius riding a separate stallion, they estimated that their trip should get them to Jerusalem by Tuesday evening or Wednesday morning at the latest. It was Cornelius' hope to be back on the road no later than Thursday with the table in tow.

In addition to the replacement table, they traveled with the basic supplies for such a journey. They had enough food to last the three men a week, sufficient water, and swords. But of all the items they carried with them, none were more vital to Cornelius and his quest than Celsus' Reverse Order and his father's sealed Command Letter, both of which he kept safely under his breastplate. The trip would take them through three regions; beginning in their resident location of Galilee, through Samaria, and into Judea where the city of Jerusalem was located.

Early on in their trip, the table seekers noticed that traffic was heavier than usual and disproportionally in favor of the southern route. It was just about evening when they reached the town of Scythopolis, which was situated just north of Mt. Gilboa in Samaria. They had hoped to go about eight miles farther to spend the evening at a Roman outpost, but it became increasingly apparent that the horses were in need of a more immediate rest. So they found an inn in Scythopolis that had the capacity to board horses for the night. It was there that they inquired about the heavier than normal traffic heading south to Jerusalem.

"Why it's for the Passover, sir," the innkeeper said to the inquiring Cornelius. Adding, "If you think the roads are busy now, you should have seen them yesterday and the day before! If you had shown up yesterday, I wouldn't have been able to give you a room!"

Cornelius was somewhat aware of what the feast of Passover was and how important it was to the Jewish people. Part of his initial training involved learning the customs and practices of the Jewish community to which he had been assigned. It was during one of those training classes that he had learned that not only was Passover important to the Jewish people, but that as many Jews as possible would make a pilgrimage to their holy city of Jerusalem to celebrate it.

"On what day does your Passover actually take place, my good man?" asked Cornelius.

"It starts at sunset on Thursday," the innkeeper said in reply.

The information that Passover would be taking place while they were in Jerusalem completely fascinated Cornelius. Ever since his initial encounter with Jesus, he had experienced a growing interest in all things related to the man's religion. He also wondered if maybe, just maybe, Jesus would be there in Jerusalem to celebrate the Passover. How awesome would it be to have the opportunity to hear him speak again!

His travel partners, however, had no knowledge of Cornelius' interest in Jesus, nor did they care about the customs of the Jews. All they knew was that they were assigned the task of accompanying Cornelius, whom they both genuinely liked and respected, to the big city of Jerusalem to swap out a table. They thought that the assignment was rather silly. Why in Jupiter's name would they drive a table all the way to Jerusalem, swap it out for a nearly identical table, and then drive it back to Cana? When they asked Cornelius why the bother over a table, he simply told them that his wife wanted that particular table and he wanted to make his pregnant wife as happy as possible. While it didn't make complete sense to them, neither Manius nor Servius really cared. They were getting out of the monotony of the warehouse and had the opportunity to visit the big city of Jerusalem, to which neither of them had been before.

After a good evening meal and a solid night's sleep, the small company of Roman soldiers woke up early, ready to get a jump on the day. After squaring up with the innkeeper, the three men set out in hopes of reaching the city by that Tuesday evening. Had they made it to the Roman outpost the night before, they may have made it to Jerusalem that evening. However, the horses once again begged for a rest when they hit the town of Bethel in Judea, just eight miles north of the big city.

While they had enough funds to stay at another inn if necessary, Bethel did have a Roman outpost where Cornelius and his men were put up for the night. It was over dinner that he heard a soldier from the garrison sitting at the table just to his right saying something about some nut all the Jews were following around.

"I couldn't believe it when I saw it!" the soldier said in a tone of disgust. "This fanatic comes into Jerusalem the other day riding on a donkey, not even a horse, and Jews are lined up ten deep it seemed on each side of the road calling him a holy king. They even laid down their cloaks and palm branches before the donkey! And this guy is just smiling and waving to everyone. I tell you, these Jews are the strangest people I've ever encountered. If that's a king, then I must be Caesar himself!"

His friend sitting next to him chimed in, "And let me tell you, the religious authorities have it out for that man, Jesus, like you wouldn't believe. They've been nagging Pilate for weeks about how they'd like to see him banished from the city."

Part of Cornelius recoiled at the insensitive words spoken by the two ignorant soldiers, but at the same time a pronounced sense of joy and elation swept through him. Jesus was indeed in Jerusalem! Not only would he be securing the treasure of a table, he may have the opportunity to see him again. What a story that would be to tell Prisca!

"Sir, do you know this person they are talking about?" Manius asked Cornelius in a low voice, so as not to be overheard by anyone but his immediate party.

"I'll tell you this, don't believe everything you hear. Perhaps we'll bump into this Jesus and you can judge him for yourself," answered Cornelius.

After a good evening's rest, the trio from Cana rose early and saddled up for the final leg of their journey. It was about nine in the morning on Wednesday when they found themselves at the north gate of the city of Jerusalem.

Four

After picking up a text from Dr. Jeromy that she had finished her assessment of Anthony, Nadia agreed to meet her for a coffee the following morning at the Daily Grind on Bell Road just a few blocks east of Paradise Valley Hospital where she worked. The Daily Grind was a small independent start-up in the Valley which had steadily grown to ten stores due to their quality coffee and friendly service. Nadia also favored them for the lack of extreme political views for which a larger chain coffee store had become known.

When Nadia arrived, she saw her friend Rachel sitting at a far corner table with a chai tea already in her hand. Her red hair, long lean body, and her natural good looks always made her easy to spot in a crowd, and today was no exception. Since the place was packed, Nadia waved to Dr. Jeromy and held up one finger giving her the universal sign for, "I'll be there in a minute." With that, she stepped up to the counter and ordered her customary extra-large, non-fat, hot peppermint mocha, no whip. Within two minutes, her hot caffeine prize was in her hand.

"Don't you look wonderful!" exclaimed Dr. Jeromy as she rose up to give her friend a hug.

Nadia did indeed look good, as she always did. She stood just under five feet two, and weighed in at a petite ninety-eight pounds. She had long, thick, jet black hair that fell to just about the middle of her back. Her olive skin, combined with her rich hair and deep brown eyes, easily revealed to all who noticed her that she was of Persian descent.

Complimenting her physical beauty was her always stylish manner of dress. What caught Rachel's eye was Nadia's choice of a white cotton dress with black polka dots that hugged Nadia's body in a most flattering way from the top of her shoulders to the bottom of her thighs. She accessorized the dress with a large pearl necklace and a pair of high heel cork sandals.

"As do you, Rachel!" Nadia said in reply.

Rachel had forewarned Nadia that she had a hectic schedule that day and wasted no time as she moved right into her evaluation of Anthony.

"Well, Nadia, I think you were correct in your diagnosis. While I believe that Anthony's previous label of high functioning autism somewhat fits, I think that Asperger's is a more proper and definitive diagnosis."

"Due to his propensity for obsessive and repetitive routines, like always addressing others by their full names, combined with his display of social isolation and high intellectual and linguistic acumen?" inquired Nadia.

"Listen to you, girl! Those are exactly my reasons. You know, if you could spare about eight years of your life, I think you would make a wonderful shrink!" Rachel said with enthusiasm.

"Thank you, but spending eight more years in school just isn't in the cards!" Nadia said with a wide smile and flattered soul. Being conscious of Rachel's time limits, Nadia returned the conversation to Anthony.

"So, what recommendations do you have for Anthony?"

"Knowing you, Nadia, I don't think that I will be able to add anything that you haven't already thought of. I'm sure you're thinking about ongoing social skills training along with some social communication intervention. At this time, I don't see any need for medication, which surprises me since you'd figure his anxiety levels would be high given the recent loss of his only known relative. I am seriously astonished by how chill he is. I don't know how he is pulling that off, but it's a real gift."

"You don't think that his lack of grief is a sign of a more serious problem?" asked Nadia.

"Not in this case. You see, in my discussions with Anthony it's clear to me that he has been experiencing an expected level of grief. It is evident that he greatly loved his uncle and that he misses him. It's just that he has found a way to successfully deal with that grief," explained Rachel.

"Did you ask him how he was dealing with it?" asked Nadia.

"I did. Now, you have to understand that in dealing with Asperger's patients a response given by a patient may not always make sense to us. The key is if the response is meaningful to them. When I probed into his coping mechanisms, he responded to me by saying, 'Love has come, Dr. Rachel Jeromy, love has come.' When I asked him to expound on what that means to him he just smiled, picked up his backpack from the floor, and set it down next to him on the sofa," answered Rachel.

Nadia took a sip of her coffee. "Interesting. And regarding the backpack, it's always with him. I assumed that it's kind of a security blanket for him. Am I missing anything there?"

"No, I think you're spot on with that assessment," Rachel said. "In addition to the social skills training and social communication intervention, I highly recommend that he receives a good mentor, a big brother if you will. Though he's highly intelligent, he is at a very vulnerable point in his life and the guidance of a good man, and I do suggest a male mentor in his case, would certainly benefit him a great deal. Is that something you could set up relatively soon?"

"I couldn't agree with you more. I will work on it. I can't thank you enough, Rachel. What you do for others is such a wonderful gift," Nadia said as she reached over and squeezed Rachel's hands in sincere appreciation.

"Well, let the record show that for all you do, you are the real social hero," Rachel said, returning her squeeze.

Five

Cornelius and his men arrived in Jerusalem the morning before the Passover. He had learned in his studies of Jewish culture that the actual celebration of the feast would not take place until sundown the following day. Cornelius was, therefore, hopeful that Jesus would be teaching somewhere in the city that day. While he wanted to immediately investigate that possibility, he had to temper his desire so as not to let Manius and Servius on to his mounting attraction to a potential enemy of the state.

So rather than making his first order of business finding the whereabouts of Jesus, he and his men went to meet the Armicustos to inquire about the table.

The Armicustos assigned to the Tenth Legion, Marcus Calvius, was not at all like the majority of the men who comprised that particular legion. Cornelius had met Marcus on two other occasions while accompanying Celsus on quartermaster related business. He found the man to be gentle, intelligent, and very insightful, much like his own grandfather-in-law. This stood in sharp contrast to the men of the Tenth Legion who were comprised, for the most part, of soldiers who were not typically even Roman citizens. Most were mercenaries from the area of Thrace. They were known as the most brutal of all Roman Legions and served as the enforcers for the Roman governor, Pontius Pilate. It was Pilate's design to have such a feared force stationed in Jerusalem, the largest city in his area of rule, so as to keep the peace and the chances of revolt at a minimum. If Pilate was to remain in power, he had to ensure the armistice of the inhabitants of Jerusalem. Cornelius had often heard of their brutality and their apparent enjoyment when it came to carrying out punishments and executions given at the command of their governor.

They arrived at the station of the Armicustos about a half hour after breaching the north gate of the city. The Tenth Legion's warehouse was located about a half mile from the garrison where most men of that legion were lodged. They had barely stepped into the entrance of the warehouse when they were warmly greeted by Marcus himself, who happened to be looking over a current inventory list near the main door when Cornelius and his men arrived.

"Celsus' man!" Marcus declared, trying his best to remember the Centurion's name. Before Cornelius could assist him with his identity, Marcus rebounded and, placing his hand on Cornelius' shoulder said, "Cornelius! That's it! How are you, my friend? And how's Celsus?"

"You have a wonderful memory; I'm flattered that you would re-member my name," responded Cornelius, who was legitimately touched that he knew who he was.

Marcus, like his friend and colleague Celsus, was a well-respect-ed Armicustos who had been in his position just as long as his grandfa-ther-in-law had. He was an older man, standing about five feet ten inches tall with a thin frame, graying hair, and age appropriate creases in his face. He looked every part of an Armicustos whose success was dependent on a sharp intellect and not so much on a body made for battle.

"Celsus is well, as am I. In fact, my wife and I are expecting our first child." Cornelius beamed.

"Wonderful news, I am very happy for you, Cornelius!" Marcus said, legitimately happy to hear the news. Marcus continued by asking Cornelius the obvious question, "What brings you and your men to Jerusalem, especially at a crazy busy time such as the Jewish Passover?"

"First, let me introduce you to my men. Marcus, this is Servius and Manius."

Upon Cornelius' introduction, each man stepped forward and shook Marcus' hand. Reaching into the inside of his breastplate, Cornelius withdrew the Reverse Order and handed it to Marcus. He had a feeling that, given the reception he had received, his father's Command Letter would not be necessary.

While Marcus reviewed the order, Cornelius added, "It appears that a few weeks back some of your men came and took some seized property we had acquired from a local Zealot."

"Laban, wasn't it?" questioned Marcus.

"Yes, it was from the estate of Laban of Cana," confirmed Cornelius.

"Yes, that man had some wonderful furniture, never saw anything as good as it before. His loss, our gain!" exclaimed a cheery-sounding Marcus.

"Yes, his stuff was first rate," affirmed Cornelius. Continuing he explained their end goal, "Within the lot was a certain table that should have been pulled out of the inventory offering prior to your men's arrival. I apologize, but that was an oversight on our part. Celsus has sent us to procure the table and to replace it with another that we have carted with us."

"So you mean to tell me you and your men hiked all the way down here just to switch out a table? Either you Cana-stationed men are crazy or, for one reason or another, that table has some serious value, sentimental or otherwise to someone," quipped Marcus.

"The latter is true, Marcus. And on that note, I'm hoping that there won't be any other questions on the matter," said Cornelius in a way that was delivered as more of a hopeful plea versus a weighted demand.

"You're lucky that I like your boss so well, otherwise I'd have to tell you to pound sand! Better be a nice table you brought to replace it, that's all I have to say." Marcus grinned, letting Cornelius know that he was only pretending to sound like he really cared.

"Thank you for being so understanding, Marcus. If you'd point us to where it is in your warehouse, my men and I will switch it out with the one we brought with us and we'll be out of your way."

"I'd like to oblige you, but I'm afraid that the table has already been issued to somewhere in the garrison. But fear not, I am happy to inquire about its exact location and to give you my signed command for its switch out," Marcus assured.

Cornelius was relieved to hear this. "We really appreciate it, Marcus."

"But what's the rush! It's not often that soldiers from Cana get to come to the big city!" exclaimed Marcus.

At the sound of that, both Manius and Servius lit up. They had hoped that they would be able to take in some of the sights of Jerusalem. Unbeknownst to them, their commander was also very much hoping for a reason to stay in Jerusalem a bit longer.

Wanting to firm up their unofficial invitation as well as ensure their safety, Cornelius replied, "No offense, Marcus, but I'm sure you're aware of the reputation of the mercenaries of the Tenth Legion. As much as we'd like to spend the evening in this great city, staying at the garrison with those men doesn't sound all that appealing. Additionally, I'm sure that the Passover celebration has all the inns filled to capacity."

All too cognizant of the nasty and well-earned reputation of the very legion he served, Marcus let out a hardy laugh and said to the men in front of him, "I wouldn't even suggest a murderer stay one evening with those vermin! I know exactly what you mean as I am living that dream daily. Thankfully, I am the one who has everything they need, so they kind of do their best to show me some respect. Bottom line, we have bunks in the back of the warehouse and a kitchen as well. You can stay here as long as you need. In fact, let's go back to the kitchen and see what we can find you gentlemen to eat."

With that, the inventory specialists from Cana followed their host back to a very hospitable and early lunch.

Six

Nadia's very first stop in trying to find Anthony a suitable male mentor was to pay a visit to his two temporary female mentors, Veronica and Carol. As it turned out, when she went to their apartment to talk to them about it, Cookie was there giving Carol a guitar lesson. Since she was so close to Veronica and Carol, and because she had had the opportunity to previously meet Anthony, Cookie was invited into both the conversation as well as the potential search for a suitable mentor for him.

It didn't take Cookie more than a couple minutes into the request to suggest to Nadia that they tap the shoulder of Michael Fortunato. Cookie saw in this potential match up a real win-win for both of the men. Anthony would receive a fabulous male role model and Michael would receive a way back into the world through helping another human being.

After explaining everything that had transpired in Michael's life, and then relating to her his unbelievably high moral character, Nadia agreed that bringing these two people together could have untold benefits for the both of them. Nadia asked Cookie if she could talk to Michael about the opportunity and, if he seemed interested, to broker a future meeting between herself and Michael. Cookie said that she would be glad to accommodate.

After just a few minutes, Cookie began to think of the perfect way to bring Anthony and Michael together.

Seven

Shortly after eating the lunch so generously provided by Marcus, the three men headed out in different directions to see what the city of Jerusalem had to offer. While Manius and Servius very much liked and respected their commander, they did not necessarily share in his affection and interest for the Jewish culture. So after learning that Cornelius wanted to go and check out the famous Jewish Temple, both Manius and Servius politely asked if they could go their separate ways for the day. Of course, Cornelius didn't mind. In fact, he wanted to be on his own in the hopes of coming across Jesus. He felt his best shot at that happening would be at the Temple where prophets and teachers had a reputation of going to preach their various doctrines to the people.

Though Cornelius would have preferred to blend seamlessly into the crowd, he had no option other than to wear his uniform since he was technically on duty. As he made his way to the Temple, he couldn't help but feel the inhospitable stares of many of the Jews anchoring themselves onto his person. Cornelius didn't blame them in the least. What Rome represented to these fine people was oppression and hindrances on how they had lived for many years prior to the occupation. *And to top it all off*, thought Cornelius, *they had to put up with the merciless meatheads who made up the Tenth Legion.*

As the Temple began to emerge in the distance, Cornelius was amazed at the edifice he saw materialize above its walls. It was hard for him to fathom how such a wonderful structure had been constructed so long ago. Upon entering the Temple gate and working his way through the surrounding Temple wall, he was taken aback by the beauty and richness of the structure now fully in front of him.

Something this grand, thought Cornelius, *surely points to something grander still*. Though the sheer magnificence of the Temple captured his initial attention, the second thing he noticed was just how packed the courtyards of the Temple were. Marcus was right, the Passover festival was a most crazy time to be in Jerusalem!

After entering through the gate just a little before the noon hour, Cornelius turned right and found himself in what was known as the Court of the Gentiles. This area was a fairly open space between the surrounding walls of the temples, which housed the steps that led up to the Temple proper. As Cornelius began to walk the length of the court, he noticed a larger crowd gathered around the center steps that led up to the Temple. Cornelius instinctively headed over in that direction to see if he might have gotten lucky and found Jesus.

When he got within fifteen yards of the crowd, his heart began to pound. He had gotten very lucky, for there on top of the steps was Jesus teaching a crowd, which seemed to be numbered in the hundreds.

Even though Cornelius felt that he stood out in his Roman uniform, no one paid much attention to him as he moved his way closer to the base of the stairs. The people were used to the heavy presence of Roman soldiers within the Temple grounds, especially during Passover. On top of that, the people assembled around him were transfixed by the man preaching on the steps in front of them. As he settled into a position about five yards to the right side of Jesus, he noticed Nathanael standing next to him, along with several other of his followers Cornelius remembered seeing in Capernaum. Nathanael quickly noticed Cornelius and, rather than being bothered by the presence of a soldier, actually gave him a respectful nod of his head. Cornelius was flattered. He had once been approached with suspicion by Nathanael, but now he felt welcomed. Cornelius returned the nod and then listened attentively to what Jesus was teaching.

"Have you not read this scripture passage, 'the stone that the builders rejected has become the cornerstone; by the Lord has this been done, and it is wonderful in our eyes,'" Jesus said, apparently finishing a story that Cornelius wished he had heard all of.

Cornelius momentarily shifted his eyes from Jesus and began to survey the crowd around him. He noticed that while the majority of the gathering was in awe of the great teacher, there were some who may not have shared the same sense of admiration. Around him he noticed a scattering of men who bore faces full of grimaces, clenched teeth, and frowns. He could tell that this rather nicely dressed minority was, in fact, not pleased at all by the man and what he was teaching. Such a man stood to the very right of him. Suddenly that man's furrowed face turned pleasant as if to cloak his true feelings of contempt for the preacher.

Now looking agreeable and receptive, the man respectfully addressed the teacher, asking him in a loud voice, "Rabbi, we know that you are a truthful man and that you are not concerned with anyone's opinion. You do not regard a person's status but teach the way of God in accordance to the truth. Since next to me stands a soldier, I am reminded of our oppressed reality. Therefore I ask you, is it lawful to pay a census tax to Caesar or not? Should we pay or should we not pay?"

Cornelius cringed as unwanted attention was suddenly brought to his presence by the crafty and tactful man next to him. His initial urge was to slither his way out of the crowd and to leave the Temple grounds. Two things, however, kept his feet firmly affixed to the courtyard's pavement. First was his strong desire to hear and see Jesus; and second, he once again took notice that the crowd seemed too careless about his presence. They had turned their attention to the teacher and all eagerly awaited his reply.

The significance of the question was not lost on Cornelius. He knew that if Jesus talked against the Roman tax that he would be tossed in jail. He was also aware that if Jesus told the crowd to pay the tax that the crowd might reject him and all his other teachings. Thinking those things, Cornelius turned and looked at the man next to him and saw that he was now grinning. He had no doubt that this articulate, finely dressed, and manicured man had ulterior motives in being there and in asking his question. Cornelius' focus moved from the man next to him and returned to the top of the stairs where Jesus stood. When he refocused on Jesus, it was apparent to Cornelius that the teacher was unphased by the question. In fact, it seemed as though he himself was now grinning back at the man who asked the question. It was obvious to Cornelius that there was absolutely no buckle in this man Jesus.

"Why are *you* testing me?" asked Jesus, placing special emphasis and accent on the word "you."

Before the man had the chance to respond, Jesus' glance shifted to Cornelius. Directly addressing him, Jesus said, "Centurion, please step forward and know that you are among friends."

Cornelius couldn't believe that he was being called forward. Fear of a hostile, anti-Roman audience should have struck him to his core with dread, but he felt no anxiety, just peace. As he made his way through the crowd, Cornelius couldn't even feel the pavement beneath his feet. It was as though time and physical sensation had been suspended. He stopped at the base of the steps and looked up at Jesus. He couldn't help but notice Nathanael standing next to the teacher. When their eyes met, Nathanael waved Cornelius up the stairs. It wasn't the wave up Cornelius had so much noticed as much as it was the warm, inviting smile Nathanael gave to him.

"Please, come up here and stand next to me," instructed Jesus, motioning him forward.

Cornelius still didn't know exactly how he got there, or if in his capacity as a Roman soldier he even should have allowed himself to be directed, but as he mounted the top step and found himself in front of the teacher, he suddenly heard Jesus address him in a near whisper.

"Good to see you again, Cornelius. Do not be afraid about anything."

Before Cornelius had a chance to respond, before he could ask him how he knew his name, Jesus began to formally address him in front of the crowd. "Centurion, might I borrow a denarius from you?"

Cornelius reached into his pocket, pulled out the requested coin, and handed it to Jesus.

Jesus took the coin in his hand and glanced momentarily at it. Appearing satisfied, he tossed the coin underhand to the man who had asked the question. The man was less an athlete than he was an intellectual. The coin, which was perfectly thrown his way, bounced off his hand and onto the ground in front of him. Bending over, the man, now a little embarrassed by his miss of the coin, retrieved it.

Once it was in his hand, Jesus asked him, "Now look at the coin. Whose image do you see on it?"

"Caesar's," replied the man.

Turning his attention away from the man and focusing on the larger crowd, Jesus said, "Repay to Caesar what belongs to Caesar, and to God what belongs to God."

The wisdom of the teacher shook the crowd. All were in awe of his answer as it cut deep into the souls of those gathered, most especially that of the young Centurion. As he was about to leave Jesus' side and return to where he previously stood, Cornelius heard Jesus address him again in a low voice intended for just his ears.

"Cornelius, love has come. It is here, and it will be here always."

Cornelius nodded his head, finding that a verbal response was impossible. He walked back down the steps and saw the man who had asked the question turn and withdraw from the crowd. Cornelius saw the man place the denarius into his pocket. The young Centurion didn't mind at all, counting it the best spent denarius of his life.

Cornelius found himself back within the crowd when he heard Nathanael's voice addressing the crowd. "Good people of Jerusalem. The teacher must go now and prepare for the Passover. He will be praying for you all. Thank you for being here today."

Jesus and his entourage made their way to the bottom of the stairs and much of the crowd pressed in to try and touch him. His disciples did the best they could to keep their leader moving, but Jesus was making their job difficult. He reached and made physical contact with as many people as possible. Cornelius, still standing in the same place he stood upon his arrival, took this all in and watched as Jesus and the crowd made their way through the gate.

With the multitude now somewhat dispersed, Cornelius began to head toward the same gate Jesus had just exited. While the interaction with Jesus was brief, it was also endless in Cornelius' mind. As he walked out of the Temple area, he was both amazed and convinced. He was amazed at how Jesus knew him, not that he just knew his name, but that he actually knew who he was as a person. Of this, Cornelius was certain. In terms of his conviction, he knew without question that his military career must soon end and that he and Prisca were being called to follow this man.

Eight

It was 6:30 in the evening and Anthony had just returned to his room at the Andre House for Men after working an eleven hour shift at Food City. Wisely utilizing his forty percent employee discount, he placed the deli sub he had snagged for dinner in the small white Westinghouse fridge that came with the tiny one-room apartment. He was famished and couldn't wait to eat the sandwich, along with half a can of Pringles he had busted open the night before while watching reruns of *The Andy Griffith Show*. But the sandwich would have to wait until he fulfilled the promise he made to his uncle the day he had passed away.

Being regimented in his approach to everything, Anthony set a routine to verbalize the story of the blessing at the end of each working day. With Anthony, that time was variable since his schedule at the supermarket had him sometimes working days, sometimes nights. But if it was a work day, once he arrived home he recited the story before doing anything else. If it was a day off, Anthony's routine was to recite the story shortly after waking up and before he ate breakfast.

After placing his dinner in the refrigerator, Anthony took his backpack and set it next to him on the green vinyl couch that came with his room. He sat in the center of his couch, his designated place for reciting the story, and unzipped the top of his backpack. Reaching into the pack he lifted out its contents, placed it on his lap, and began to methodically recite the story word for word and without error, just as he had done for the last ten years. He was the keeper of the story, something he took very seriously and in which he took a great deal of pride.

Nine

It took Marcus longer to find the exact location of the table than he had anticipated. There was a break in communication between Marcus' office and the praetorium, and it delayed the whole exchange by a day. Cornelius was anxious to have the table in his possession and return home to Prisca, so he was relieved when Marcus gave him some good news on Friday morning.

Marcus made his guests a robust breakfast consisting of several eggs, ham, grapes, dates, and bread. Marcus knew that Cornelius would tell Celsus about the fine hospitality he and his men received from him and this pleased him greatly, since both of these older men prided themselves in extending the finest of hospitality to any and all welcomed guests.

Midway through his meal, Cornelius put down his fork and asked his host about the one thing that was most pressing on his mind. "Marcus, have you located the table?"

"I most certainly have," answered Marcus, who was happy to accommodate the young Centurion to whom he had taken a genuine liking. Putting down the ham bone he had been gnawing on, he continued to enlighten Cornelius and his men on the location of the table. "It is located in the north courtyard of Pilate's praetorium. It's the area that is adjacent to the jail. When you arrive at the praetorium, just ask someone where the guard house is and you'll find the courtyard and your table. I was told that it's there under a patio. I have sent word to the commander of the guardhouse that you'd be by today to trade out tables. I also told him not to hassle you, so you shouldn't run into any problems."

Cornelius found the idea of having to tell a fellow solider not to hassle another soldier he had never met a bit nauseating, but then again, they were talking about the composite makeup of the unruly Tenth Legion.

They had finished breakfast around 9:30 and Cornelius spent the next hour listening to Marcus talk about the old times he shared with Celsus. While Cornelius was taking in the stories of Marcus' good old days, his men readied the horses and wagon for the trip home. By this point, Cornelius was anxious and had several good reasons to want to secure the table and to start heading back to Cana. First, he had a pregnant wife at home whom he was beginning to miss dearly. Second, he couldn't wait to share with her his latest encounter with Jesus. And finally, and most impacting, he wanted to share with her the decision he had made, a decision he was certain she would embrace—to become a disciple of Jesus.

Just when he thought that they were finally ready to head out to retrieve the table, Cornelius discovered that Manius was nowhere to be found. More than a bit perturbed by this news, Cornelius began to grill Servius on his whereabouts. Seeing the mounting frustration in his normally calm leader, Servius quickly came clean with what he knew concerning Manius' whereabouts.

He relayed to Cornelius that Manius had met a girl the night before and, apparently, she was the woman of his dreams. Manius had asked Servius to cover him about a half hour earlier while they were readying the horses so he could go and say goodbye to her. He had promised to be back by now, but had failed miserably in keeping that promise. After determining that Servius knew where the girl lived, Cornelius sent him out to bring back the soldier. If not for his knowledge of the power and depth of love, Cornelius might have been tempted to write Manius up and to file for disciplinary action against him. But as a man who loved love, he instead caught himself at the peak of his frustration and, turning his emotions on a dime, began to chuckle.

Oh love, you are the pacifier of all! he thought to himself.

And so it was that the Cana team didn't end up leaving the warehouse of the Armicustos till shortly after 11:00 a.m. They found themselves at the praetorium fifteen minutes later.

Ten

Cookie, as it turned out, had become the master at chipping away. In this particular case, she had her chisel positioned on the barnacles of forfeiture, which had greedily affixed themselves to Michael. It was plain to see that these weights of sorrow and loss had Michael sinking lower and lower into a burrow of anguish, a place she knew that the further he plunged into, the harder it would be to find his way out. Loving her friend as she did, this was something that she could not stand by and idly watch. She also knew her friend well enough to know that any aid on her part had to move slowly, subtly, and cautiously. If she was too quick and obvious in her tactics, he would surely reject her assistance.

Cookie's plans had started with inviting Michael out to Burba's to see her play. This led to her inviting Michael to church and to his acceptance. Cookie felt that her prayers for Michael were starting to be answered. The weight of his despair seemed to have leveled off, and even slightly decreased. Where there had been only darkness, a faint hint of light could now be seen radiating from his core. Knowing that Michael was someone who derives happiness and a sense of purpose from helping others, Cookie was convinced that him helping Anthony would increase the light in his life. With all these things in mind, Cookie texted Michael and asked him if he would meet her at two that afternoon for a cup of coffee at the Daily Grind, which was located within the Fry's grocery store near Michael's house. In the text, she wrote that there was something she really needed his help with. Confident in his need to help others, Cookie was rewarded with a reply from Michael of a thumbs up emoji. Now, all Cookie needed to do was figure out how to present Anthony's case to Michael so he felt as though he were the one helping and not the one being helped.

Eleven

Cornelius didn't need to ask anyone where the guard house was. He figured that the north courtyard would be on the north end of the praetorium grounds and he headed there. Cornelius thought that rather than driving the wagon into the courtyard, it might be best to park it outside and first walk in to determine where exactly the table was located. Depending on its location, they might be able to just exchange the tables by walking them in and out of the area without the need to pull the wagon into the piazza.

As Cornelius and his men entered the courtyard area, the term courtyard suddenly seemed to be a cruel misnomer for what the young Centurion was seeing before him. Two long, one story buildings stood at a ninety-degree angle to each other with an archway gate separating them. In the crux of these two structures was a forty-yard square area of dirt. In the very center of the dirt yard stood a two-cubit high wooden post. The post was about a cubit and a half in diameter, the top of which contained an affixed short iron chain with wrist shackles at each of its ends.

Just like Marcus had described, the structure contained a thatched palm leaf patio under which Cornelius could see chairs and a table that was much smaller than the table he had come to accompany home. In three of the chairs sat soldiers of the Tenth Legion, or so Cornelius thought. It was hard to make them out because the area where they sat was heavily shaded by the patio's roof. The table he sought, his table, Jesus' table, had been placed in the dirt about five yards from the east side of the post with affixed shackles. On top of the table were some objects that Cornelius couldn't quite make out since they were still about twenty yards away from him.

As they neared the table, Cornelius saw the three soldiers rise up out of their chairs. At first, Cornelius thought that they were getting up to meet him and his men. They halted and stood at their position, waiting to be greeted as Roman protocol dictated. But instead of walking toward them, the Tenth Legion soldiers stood up and made their way toward the gateway that separated the two buildings, ignoring the three Roman soldiers who had just entered the center of their domain.

When the Tenth Legion soldiers stepped out of the shade of the patio, Cornelius saw men that looked far different from any Roman soldier they had seen before. To Cornelius, these soldiers resembled wild beasts more than they did men, let alone members of the Roman army. They were short, but as stocky as an ox and appeared to be near clones of each other. Their chests were covered with leather and their loins were girded with dirty wraps. Their arms were hairy, bare, and looked like they were created for the sole purpose of breaking things. Their hair was long, uncombed, and appeared as though washing it might be a bi-annual event. Cornelius had no doubt that if he were to make it closer to these men that the stench of uncleanliness and alcohol would be all encompassing. One thing was certain, Cornelius and his men had never seen Roman soldiers outfitted like the grime-laced, menacing men they saw heading toward the gateway. Suddenly, Cornelius heard a voice bellow out from just beyond the archway, which was intended for the three behemoths.

"Come and get it, dinner is served!"

From the gateway, Cornelius saw two more suitably dressed soldiers dragging a prisoner between the inside of each of their arms. The man sagged and staggered between the arms of the soldiers as he tried, unsuccessfully, to keep himself on his own feet. It was apparent that this man had suffered a recent beating, and Cornelius' guess was that it was at the hands of the Tenth Legion.

At about the same time that the prisoner was being dragged into the courtyard, Cornelius and his men cautiously walked toward the space between the patio and the table that he had come to retrieve. He was no longer sure if his primary motive was to regain the table for himself and his family, or if it was just to get the heck out of this armpit of a garrison as quickly as he possibly could.

One thing was for sure, he was glad to see these other soldiers dressed appropriately. He felt a lot more comfortable approaching them regarding the table than he would asking one of the three gargoyles for any level of assistance.

That level of comfort, however, quickly dissipated when he saw the soldiers thrust the prisoner forward onto the stone pathway instead of handing him off directly to the three beasts. Cornelius cringed as the left side of the prisoner's face smashed directly into the pavement.

"Here you go! Fresh meat! Bet you never got to scourge a king before!" bellowed one of the two soldiers.

"Yeah, bet you never got to scourge a king before!" the other soldier repeated, kicking the prisoner's side.

"A king?" inquired one of the two beasts who approached the beaten prisoner. The third beast stepped back taking in, with apparent amusement, the suffering of the bloodied man before them.

"Yep, look, we even made him a crown!" said the soldier to the prisoner's right, holding up a crown made of thorns. "It looks like we get to have ourselves a crowning ceremony later!"

Upon seeing this, Cornelius' mind went back to his boyhood days in Melfi. He remembered playing army with his friends one day when he stepped on a length of stray thistle. One thorn from that thistle branch breeched through the bottom of his saddle and pierced the heel of his foot. He recalled, in detail, just how excruciating the pain was and how he ran off in tears to the comfort of his mother. He couldn't even fathom the pain the man on the pavement would endure from those thorns if they were placed in his head.

Cornelius and his men watched as two of the monster soldiers each grabbed ahold of the man and dragged him into the courtyard.

"Whatever that guy did, it must have been pretty bad," whispered Servius to his two transfixed companions.

The prisoner shrugged both of his arms vigorously as they remained clutched in the hands of the two beasts. Within a few seconds, it became clear that the man's movements were not an attempt to escape, but rather to inform his captors that he wanted to walk forward on his own. Given the state that he was in just moments ago, Cornelius found it miraculous that this man somehow made it to his feet, let alone walk.

As the pair of beasts led the man toward the center of the courtyard, the third beast began to move his block frame toward Jesus' table. Cornelius suddenly knew what was about to happen to the prisoner.

Arriving at the center of the dirt square, one of the beasts kicked the man behind his right leg, forcing him to fall onto his knees. This positioned the prisoner directly in front of the wooden post Cornelius and his men had spotted upon their arrival. Two of the Tenth Legion soldiers took the hand of the prisoner nearest him and shackled his wrists to the wooden post. By this time the third beast was at the table, Cornelius' table, and was inspecting what appeared to be several tools that were displayed on top of it. He selected one item off the table. Seemingly pleased by his choice, he began to smile.

Cornelius and his men inched their way closer to the unfolding drama. They were now close enough to the table that they could see what the third beast was holding up. It was a Roman Scourge. This specific one was particularly menacing; its wooden handle was longer than most, appearing to be a cubit and a half in length versus the more customary half cubit. Attached to its end were three thin leather ropes, versus the more typical two, each of which were about two cubits in length. Each of these ropes contained an assortment of affixed pieces of metal, bone, wire, and hardened clay at intervals of a handbreadth in length. With the extra length in its shaft and extra leather tentacle, it was apparent that the scourging done with this instrument would be significantly more efficacious at inflicting pain than that of the typical Roman scourge.

As the beast with the scourge began to walk toward the now shackled prisoner, his two hideous companions moved to the side of the post opposite of where the table and Cornelius and his men were standing. They seemed to be giddy with anticipation at what was about to occur; they both stood wide-eyed and smiling. The prisoner's head turned and looked in the direction of the beast who was headed his way to administer his sentence. The prisoner caught the eye of his tormentor and nodded to him. The Tenth Legion soldier, now within striking range, cocked back his arm and then released the first forceful blow to the back of the shackled man. The blow hit its mark as the shards of metal, bone, wire, and hardened clay from the three leather ropes landed and implanted themselves deeply across the prisoner's back and sides. Giving the handle a slight tug, just enough to cause an extra jolt of pain but not enough to detach the hooks from the prisoner's flesh, the beast let out a laugh. He then relaxed his hold on the scourge and a second later flung his arm forcibly back causing the scourge's hooks to rip out chunks of flesh from the prisoner's body.

With the release of the first blow, the prisoner's head shot up as his whole body stiffened. Before the second blow struck, and for the first time, the prisoner's face turned in the direction of Cornelius and his men.

Cornelius had thought that he knew sadness, that he knew what pain was, but every feeling he ever had or ever would have was eclipsed by this moment. For a brief second, Cornelius didn't know if he was alive or dead. As that moment passed, real pain invaded his body and despair took charge of his mind. There before him was Jesus, the man he loved, the man he was about to give his life to. Questions of how and why this could be happening couldn't even make their way into his mind as emptiness, loss, and confusion took up every space of his consciousness.

After that, every instant of the scourging played out in slow and surreal motion to Cornelius. Multiple strikes to Jesus' flesh occurred. With each strike blood splattered in every direction. He saw blood hit the two other beasts as they continued to smile and they seemed to enjoy the sensation of having warm blood hit their chests and faces. Cornelius witnessed the blood splatter going in other directions as well. Time stood still as he saw Jesus' life blood land all over the very table he had come to claim.

So transfixed and displaced was he, that Cornelius didn't even notice one of the two properly dressed soldiers walk up to his side.

"I take it you're here for the table?" the soldier asked him.

After a long pause without a response, the soldier saw Cornelius mesmerized by the scourging and figured that he was enjoying it so much he didn't hear him.

"No worries, man, I understand. Awesome day for a whipping isn't it?" the soldier said, trying to get a chuckle of acknowledgment out of the Centurion next to him. After receiving none, the soldier added, "Well, suit yourself. Enjoy the show. When we're done here, go ahead and take the table and be sure to bring in its replacement."

With that, the soldier walked toward the beast who was currently inflicting the pain and called out to him, "Okay, Tug, one more is thirteen and you have to pass on the scourge to one of your buddies."

After the thirteenth blow, the troll named Tug traded positions with a different beast. During that momentary period of relief, Jesus again turned and looked at Cornelius. Their eyes met just as they did that evening at Laban's house. And just like that time, this man being tortured, this man near death, somehow managed to smile at him. After smiling at Cornelius, Jesus turned his eyes to the table and then back to Cornelius. When he was certain he had Cornelius' attention, Jesus nodded. Cornelius knew exactly what that nod meant and he would not let Jesus down. The table would be well cared for, well cared for forever.

The second beast and then the third began their turns trying to out-do the previous beast in his ability to inflict pain with the thirteen lashes granted to each of them. All the time, Cornelius stood motionless in a trance like state. After the final blow he saw Jesus, whose head was now slumped over the wooden post facing him, begin to speak to him. While he couldn't hear him, he easily recognized the three words mouthed from his lips. They were words that he had embraced, words that he often would say aloud, but he had never fully understood their meaning. As the beast unchained the prisoner and dragged him from the dirt yard and through the open gate, which separated the two one-story buildings and served as the berm of the courtyard, Cornelius found himself repeating those words just spoken by Jesus. While they stood in total contradiction to what he had just witnessed, he still knew that a deep truth lay within them, a truth that he prayed would later be revealed to him.

"Love has come. Love has come."

Twelve

Michael had experienced sudden glimmers of light that would some-times break through the darkness of his loss. But it seemed that as quickly as these moments came, they exited all the more rapidly, usually escorted by the strong arms of guilt. Michael would catch himself shortly after a happy thought or at the start of a smile and ask himself, "How can I be happy when my love is no longer here?"

It was these sharp barbs of guilt that made sustaining light and hap-piness seemingly impossible for Michael.

He found himself telling all this to Cookie in response to her question about how he was doing. As he promised, he had met Cookie at the coffee shop contained within his local Fry's grocery store. He met her because she said that she needed his help. At least, that is what his practical mind told him in order to have a plausible reason to get out of the house. While he was always willing to help someone in need, his subconscious knew that it would be just plain good to get out into the world, especially meeting up with a true friend.

"Michael, it is okay to be saddened by losing someone you loved so much. You have no reason to feel guilty for being alive and for being happy," Cookie said as she reached across their small table and took his right hand into hers.

"Cooks, I know you mean well and, truth be told, I would likely be giving the same advice to anyone else in my situation. But when you're in it, and it's happening to you, control and reason are two things that don't often make their presence known."

Cookie totally understood Michael's perspective. Mired in the grief of losing her best friend, she had experienced similar things. All the same, she thought about Debbie and what she would want for her, Michael, and all those she loved.

Still holding his hand, Cookie warmly extended this thought to him. "Michael, consider for a moment what Debbie would say to you about how you're feeling?" Letting that soak in for a few seconds, she continued, "Don't you think that she would want you to be happy?"

It took a couple seconds for the truth of what Cookie had said to take root in Michael's mind. When it did, Michael took in a deep breath in an attempt to hold in his emotions. He knew the absolute truth in the words Cookie had just spoken. There was no way that Debbie would want him to be anywhere near as miserable as he had become. As Cookie accurately queried, Debbie would most certainly want him to be happy. Pulling his hand away from Cookie's grip, Michael used it to brush back a tear from the corner of his left eye.

Cookie saw that what she said had made a needed impression upon Michael. Extending both of her hands upward, she laid them on the table on either side of Michael's latte. Raising her hands just slightly, her motion made the loving request for Michael to take hold of both of her open hands.

Michael grasped her hands as Cookie looked into his eyes. With all the empathy she could muster she said, "One of the greatest gifts you could ever give Debbie's memory is to live the rest of your life the way she would want you to live it. And while happy might sound like a trite and trivial term, there is a great deal of depth contained within it. Michael, she wants you to be happy."

Michael squeezed Cookie's hands as he bit down on his bottom lip again. Closing his eyes, he began to take deep and rapidly increasing breaths.

"It's okay, Michael. It's okay," Cookie whispered, returning the squeeze.

Michael's breathing slowed and he opened his eyes, nodding his head in agreement with her spoken wisdom. After feeling a bit more composed, he looked across their table for two at the person whose hands he was still holding.

"Yes, you are right, Cookie. But…but, it's so hard! Everywhere I go, everything I do, I see her. Heck, I swear I can even smell her at times! And I—I miss her so, so very much," he said with a grieving sense of pain.

Cookie gave both of Michael's hands a simultaneous shake and squeeze of recognition, letting him know that she understood. "When you feel like that, Michael, perhaps that's the time to ask her what it is that she wants from you. I'm convinced that when you do, you will hear her say, 'Be happy, Michael, be happy.'"

A smile spread across Michael's face, one of the few Cookie remembered seeing over the last several months.

"That's good advice, Cookie. I will try to do just that," Michael said as he gave Cookie's hands a final squeeze before he released his grip and went for a sip of his coffee.

Seeing an incredible segue way to her ulterior motive for their meeting, Cookie leaned in and asked Michael, "While I seem to be dispensing some good advice, do you mind if I try to hit the mark yet again?"

"Go for it," Michael said with his second smile of the day.

"Knowing you as well as I do, the one thing I can say unequivocally about what makes you happy is when you do things that help others."

"I'm not going to argue that point with you, but it sounds like you're trying to make me out to be a saint or something. And a saint for sure, I am not," responded Michael.

"But you don't argue the point that you enjoy helping others, right?" asked Cookie.

"True. But if anyone should be nominated for sainthood for helping others it's you. Just look at what you have done for both Carol and her mother. That's selflessness, that's beauty."

"And how do you think it makes me feel doing it?" queried Cookie.

"My guess is fulfilled and satisfied," answered Michael.

"And you know what I call it when I'm fulfilled and satisfied?" asked Cookie as she picked up her peppermint mocha, non-fat latte and took one of her last two remaining sips.

"What?"

"Happy. And that's what we both know Debbie wants you to be. So, in answer to the question of how to rebrand you a happy man, may I make a suggestion?" Cookie quirked an eyebrow at Michael.

"You're on a roll with the advice today. Go for it," Michael said with a grin.

"Find someone to help. Someone for whom you can make a difference in their life. True happiness comes from helping others, and I know that in saying that I'm stealing a page from your very playbook!" Cookie said with conviction.

"Let me guess, you already have someone in mind for me to help," stated Michael.

Raising a single finger in the air, a boisterous Cookie exclaimed, "As a matter of fact, I do!"

Cookie spent the next half hour telling Michael all about Anthony and his situation. As she told him his story, Michael recalled his brief meeting with the boy at Burba's. Everything he experienced in that meeting suddenly began to make more sense as he learned of Anthony's medical condition and his loss. Just as Cookie had expected, Michael's heart melted in hearing his story. Cookie also reviewed her meeting with Anthony's social worker and her recommendation that the best thing that could help Anthony at this moment was to have a good male role model in his life. Before Cookie even had the chance to formally ask Michael if he would consider being Anthony's mentor, Michael had willfully volunteered himself.

Thirteen

Three of the hardest days of Cornelius' life were experienced while traveling back from Jerusalem to his home in Cana. Though his mission was accomplished, he now had in his possession the table he sought, the actual significance of the table seemed to be in a state of flux. Jesus had been tortured and killed. While Cornelius and his men did not witness his horrific crucifixion, they had heard about it from the throngs of Passover participants who seemed to talk about nothing else as they exited the Jewish holy city.

On the first day of their journey back to Cana, hardly a single word was spoken between the three men. Manius and Servius, without knowing the exact nature of their commander's relationship to Jesus, saw how deeply their boss was affected by what they had witnessed and in what they heard had happened just an hour after. On top of that, both men were somewhat damaged by the brutality they saw imparted on Jesus. Like Cornelius, they had spent their time of military service solely in the department of supply allocation and had never been exposed to seeing such acts of torture. But as much as their sorrow may have stemmed from what they had witnessed, their larger sadness came at seeing their superior and friend so totally devastated by the events of the day before.

On the second day of their trip home, Manius grew brave enough to ask Cornelius what in particular had made him so saddened by the death of the man Jesus. While asking such a personal question of one's commander was technically an infraction of chain-of-command protocol, after what they had collectively been through, and knowing that their leader was less taxed with protocol and military formalities than other Roman leaders, Manius found it not the least bit difficult to ask him this question.

Cornelius' gut impulse was to tell his companions all that he knew about Jesus and to even relay to them the previous times he had met him. But almost as immediately as those thoughts had entered into his mind, the words of caution he received from both his father and grandfather-in-law regarding the potential ramifications of sharing his beliefs with anyone tied to Rome immediately presented themselves. Adding to his sudden turn toward caution was the fact that Cornelius was now uncertain about where his belief in Jesus stood. Utterly stunned by the death of this great teacher, someone he was about to pull up stakes and follow, all of that would have to be reevaluated. What happens now to this man's message? Was it just a flash in the pan? Were Cornelius and Prisca just taken up in a whirlwind of emotion, or was the man's message to be sustained, and if so, how? Given the parental cautions he had received, combined with his now swirling questions about who the man Jesus was, Cornelius put the question off by simply replying, "The cruelty of man devastates all men."

Manius felt certain that there was much more to Cornelius' feelings regarding Jesus, but he took from his leader's limited response that he didn't care to discuss it any further. Out of respect for Cornelius, Manius left it there and resisted the temptation to follow up with any additional questions. So much like the first day of travel, the second was marked by a sad silence.

That evening, while staying at a military outpost, the anguish of the last few days took their toll on Cornelius. He could not recall ever feeling as exhausted as he did on that particular evening. Yet, he had a difficult time getting to sleep. After an hour of tossing and turning and being bombarded with a string of random and disparaging thoughts, Cornelius rose up and exited the barracks. Making his way to the south end of the encampment, Cornelius found his wagon. Stepping on the rungs of the wheel, he swung his body over the wagon's side. He was greeted by the table, which was securely wrapped in canvas and tied down with rope. His hands smoothed over the top of the table. Even through the coarse canvas, touching the table gave him an immediate peace. With his hands still on top of the table, Cornelius dropped to his knees. Placing his head on the table in the space between each of his reverently placed hands, he found himself softly repeating the name of the man he'd come to love.

"Jesus."

He didn't understand how it was that his feelings of loss for this man seemed to be as painful to him as if he had lost one of his parents. At some level he knew that his feelings were totally irrational and not commiserate with the relationship he had had with the man. But the deeper person within himself prevailed and the sorrow he felt could neither be denied nor contained.

About a half hour after he had first placed his hands on the table, a great weariness came over him. The desire to sleep came in the wake of a true sense of peace, which had come upon him in being so near the table. Not wanting that sense of peace to end, Cornelius ducked under the table, curled up, and underneath its embrace he fell fast asleep on the floor of the wagon.

While Cornelius slept he began to dream. Though he saw nothing, he heard a familiar voice which he could not immediately place.

The voice told him, "Do not be afraid. Tell your two men what your heart first told you to tell them. Hold nothing back. And Cornelius, do not be afraid, ever."

And so it was that as the final leg of their journey home commenced, Cornelius circled backed on Manius' question. Being faithful to the voice, which he believed was somehow guiding him, he held nothing back from his two reports, his two friends. He told them all the stories he had heard about Jesus and the things he said, including those things Cornelius had heard firsthand. Cornelius told them of the miracles that were reported to have occurred at Jesus' hand, including one report of raising a man from the dead. He also shared with them his knowledge of the Jewish faith and how Jesus' followers connected him within that faith. Following the direction of the dream to not be afraid, Cornelius also shared with them his deepest secret when it came to his relationship with Jesus; that he had been planning to resign his commission and to become one of his disciples.

With each thing Cornelius revealed about Jesus, he fielded a minimum of two questions relating to it from Manius and Servius. Both men, while not sharing the same intellectual and philosophical bent as Cornelius, were nonetheless profoundly impacted by what their commander had to say about Jesus. As they entered the outskirts of Cana that late morning, Cornelius now felt certain of two things: first, that what he had shared with his men would not be shared any further; and second, that the voice in his dream had been the voice of Jesus.

Fourteen

Nadia Arthur was delighted by the phone call she received from Cookie informing her that Michael had happily agreed to serve as a mentor for Anthony. While she trusted Cookie's assessment of Michael's character, her job still required her to interview any volunteers who would be working with people placed in her charge. In preparation for their meeting, she had emailed Michael a form requesting information so that she could do a formal background check on him. As she expected, he had flawlessly passed the check.

And so it was that Michael met Nadia at the same Daily Grind at which he had recently met Cookie. At that meeting, just as she had anticipated, Michael passed her standard character questions in ace-like fashion. Because grief can be an obstacle when serving another, Nadia also tactfully and compassionately asked Michael questions relating to how he was doing since suffering the loss of Debbie. To these questions, Michael held nothing back. He spoke of the difficulty and the darkness he experienced since losing Debbie. He also relayed to Nadia the very things that Cookie had pointed out to him the other day regarding him having an innate need to help others. He took ownership for having that trait but did it in such a way as to not sound self-aggrandizing. Michael went on to tell Nadia that there may be some truth in Cookie's hypothesis that helping Anthony might, in turn, help him in his own struggle with grief.

"Michael, it's time for me to give you my professional opinion and recommendation on this matter, are you ready for it?" Nadia asked in such a way that Michael knew it would be an affirmative finding.

"I am ready to hear your professional opinion," said Michael, who in the short time he had spent with her had found her to be someone with a good heart and a real asset to have on the side of the community's self-interest.

"I think that your friendship with Anthony will do him a lot of good. As such, I suggest that you reach out to him through Cookie and Carol, and that you set up a first meeting as soon as you can. Moving forward, I recommend that you meet with him weekly for at least three months and then we can reassess if the frequency of your visits would need to change. How does this all sound to you, Michael?" asked Nadia.

"Sounds good to me. Now when you say visit, I'm envisioning taking him out somewhere fun, like to a ball game, bowling, you know things like that," Michael stated.

"Those are some great places to take him! But, don't feel that every time you meet with him that you have to take him to an event. The most important thing you can be doing for him is spending time with him. Let him see firsthand what being a good man is all about and help him to become increasingly more self-reliant," said Nadia.

Continuing, Nadia added, "Though Anthony is high functioning, he still has a disease called Asperger's Syndrome, which is very similar to autism, something I'm sure you noticed when you met him."

"I did," replied Michael.

"We have a class at social services being offered next Saturday morning on how to work with individuals with functional autism. I am not going to insist that you take it, but I do think that it would help you to connect with Anthony more quickly. How would you feel about attending it?"

"Well, it's not like I have a whole lot going on these days. I'd be glad to attend," Michael said with a smile.

"Fantastic! When I get back to the office I will email you the specifics. In the meantime, see about coordinating with Cookie and Carol about arranging an initial meeting with Anthony. It's probably a good idea to include them in your first meeting so that both of you can feel as comfortable as possible. How does that sound? Do you have any additional questions?" asked Nadia.

"Sounds like a plan and I think I'm good to go," answered an increasingly happier Michael.

After sharing a polite farewell and sharing his contact info, Michael hung back at their table as Nadia exited the store. Michael sat back down and, placing a hand on his coffee, he smiled yet again. Cookie was right, there was comfort in helping others.

Fifteen

Cornelius' home was located about a quarter mile off a sharp bend of the road on the northern end of Cana. As Cornelius rounded that particular crook in the road, Prisca, who had been ceaselessly staring in that direction in anticipation of her husband's arrival, quickly spotted him and his wagon as it made its final turn toward home. With total abandon, she dropped the broom she had been using to sweep the entryway to their house and ran toward her husband. While word of Jesus' death had not yet reached Cana, Prisca sensed that a change in the world had come, since she, like her husband, had a dream the night before of a comforting voice telling her not to be afraid, no matter what.

Seeing his wife running toward him, Cornelius gave his horse a snap of the reigns sending it and the wagon into a brisk gallop. Prisca was no match for the oncoming charging horse. She made it no farther than fifteen yards from the house by the time the wagon intercepted her.

Cornelius, who had thought every ounce of emotion had been drained out of him over the last three days, found that not to be the case as his eyes fell upon the love of his life. She had never looked more beautiful than she did at that moment. She was wearing her blue cotton ankle-length tunic joined by her white stola, which she chose to wear that day over both of her shoulders. It was by far Cornelius' favorite garment combination to see his wife in and he briefly wondered if she had chosen to wear it that day in anticipation of his return. The early afternoon sun seemed to caress each of her black shining curls and her brown eyes relayed not only how much she missed him, but also a mysterious knowledge that a paradigm shift had begun to set a course within their world. But in those first seconds of their reunion, nothing captured his sense of beauty and longing for his wife more than the now slightly visible bump which adorned her midsection.

Cornelius jumped off the wagon's front section and tears began to well up in the eyes of both he and his bride. At that moment, words seemed impossible. He gathered Prisca tightly into the warmth of his longing arms and he heard her give out a sob which she wanted to hold back, but couldn't. Seconds later, Prisca broke out in uncontrollable weeping. Cornelius held her tighter and he began to wonder if somehow the news of Jesus' death had made it to Cana before him.

Prisca couldn't exactly pinpoint why her emotions gave way. Sure, she missed her husband, but he was only gone for a week and that by itself wouldn't have the power to trigger such an emotional release. Its source came from a combination of three things: first, in seeing pain in her husband's eyes as he dropped from the wagon; next, from the peaceful dream she had the night before and the message it heralded; lastly, and most especially, from her intuition, which told her that something life-altering had occurred in the world.

"Shhhh, my Prisca, my love, my sweet love," whispered Cornelius as he stroked the back of her head.

Prisca still could not control her weeping. Cornelius held her tighter. He was very confused over his wife's condition. Did she hear about the death of Jesus? While he doubted that was possible, it would explain her emotional state. Was now the time to ask her if she knew what had happened in Jerusalem? Should he bring her to the rear of the wagon and present to her the table? Not knowing which direction to turn or what the right thing was to say, Cornelius spoke the words that suddenly and purposefully came into his mind at that very moment.

"Do not be afraid, Prisca. Never be afraid."

Cornelius felt Prisca's tense body relax as her weeping abruptly subsided. Prisca's arms dropped from her husband's shoulders which, moments ago, had provided her the security she most needed. Placing her hands now instead on his sides and stepping back, she lifted her face so that their eyes could meet. A sense of peace replaced the emotional chaos that had just gripped her.

With her eyes inquisitively fixed on his unique and captivating blue eyes, she inquired of her husband, "Did you hear that in a dream?"

Cornelius' eyes widened in surprise. Shocked he answered his wife, "Yes, last night. It was the voice of Jesus telling me not to be afraid, to never be afraid. In fact, he told me that very thing the day before in person. But how? How did you know? What made you ask me this?"

"I had the very same dream last night. I didn't know, however, that it was Jesus' voice until you just said it," responded Prisca as the truth of the ownership of the voice began to take root in her mind. As it did, she audibly affirmed, as much for herself as for Cornelius, "Yes, it was most certainly his voice."

As she said those words, all the factors that made up her intuitive nature now converged and helped her to begin to assemble the pieces of this puzzle before her. Yes, something had changed in the world, something that would impact it for all time. Of this, she felt certain. In her husband's eyes she saw something which hinted to her that he may have been a witness to it. But why would they both hear Jesus speak to them in a dream, and why would he tell them not to be afraid? And not be afraid of what? And did she hear her husband correctly when he said that Jesus spoke those same words to him the day before in person? What did this all mean? A dark and agonizing thought came to her.

"What has happened to Jesus?" Prisca bluntly asked her husband.

At his wife's question, every muscle in Cornelius' face twitched as they began to form deep creases of sorrow. Looking down at the ground for a brief moment, Cornelius breathed in very deeply. After slowly exhaling, his eyes once again locked lovingly on Prisca.

"Jesus is dead," were the only words Cornelius could say.

Sixteen

Michael had called Cookie shortly after his meeting with Nadia Arthur. He relayed to her Nadia's suggestion that his first meeting with Anthony might work out best if it included herself, Carol, and perhaps even Veronica. Cookie quickly latched onto the opportunity and asked Michael if next Saturday night would work for him, and if so, how dinner at Burba's sounded. Michael happily agreed and left all the arrangements to Cookie. All he had to do was show up at 6:00 on Saturday evening, and the simplicity of that suited him just fine.

As promised, Michael entered Burba's a few minutes before six. Before he even had a chance to scan the crowd to see where his group had congregated, the elevated stage directly across the restaurant's entryway caught his attention. On top of it were two stools, and two microphones affixed to their respective mic stands. To the right side of the stools, Michael spotted Cookie's favorite Takamine acoustic guitar, which was easy to identify by the butterfly decal she proudly displayed on the bottom rear section of her blond-colored instrument. It suddenly dawned on him that Cookie had raised the stakes for that evening when he spotted her waving in his direction from a table that was just to the right side of the stage area.

As Michael made his way to the table, Cookie, Carol, and Veronica turned toward him. They were all bearing smiles, except for Anthony whose head was down and fervently engaged in sipping his large Coke from a straw with his backpack by his side. Rather than feeling distant from their smiles, Michael, for the first time in a long time, appreciated these kind signs of welcome. He had once considered them facades and signs of sympathy, but now he saw them for what they really were—the welcoming of people who were simply happy to see him.

As he arrived at the table all the women stood up and gave him hugs, which Michael gladly returned. Anthony, who was still caught up in the joys of sucking down his carbonated beverage, looked up at Michael only after he first addressed him.

"Hello, Anthony. I'm Michael. We met briefly the other day as you and your friends were leaving this place," Michael said, extending his hand to Anthony.

In response to hearing his name, Anthony raised his head from his soda and looked at Michael's face. Remaining seated, Anthony took Michael's hand and, while shaking it, responded to his greeting. "I remember you. You're Michael Fortunato. You're Cookie Reginald's friend. Are you here to listen to Cookie Reginald sing tonight? She sings very good."

"I guess the answers to your questions are yes and, I guess, yes! I am a friend of Cookie's and while I didn't know it until now that she was performing tonight, I guess that I'm here to hear her sing!" Michael said with a smile as he took the open seat that was strategically placed in between Cookie and Anthony.

"So you're performing tonight, hey Cooks?" asked Michael in a way that indicated to her he wasn't upset by her obvious omission.

Before Cookie could respond, a suddenly engaged Anthony said in an excited voice, "Cookie Reginald said that you were going to play some songs with her tonight. That's why there are two guitars up there and two microphones. Cookie Reginald said that you play guitar better than anyone."

While he had noticed the two mics and the two seats, Michael did not initially notice the second guitar parked behind the Takamine. Looking back up on the stage he quickly noticed the second guitar positioned in the shadow of Cookie's acoustic. It was an old, beat-up Martin Cookie had found on Craigslist a few years before, which she used as a backup to her prized Takamine. Michael had played it several times during their past practice sessions and actually thought it played better than the Takamine. But Cookie's love and loyalty to her butterfly tatted Tak would cause her to respond with joking venom any time Michael brought up the topic of which of the two was a better guitar.

Michael quickly noticed the trap Cookie had so skillfully set. At the same time, he knew that her intentions were good. He knew that any argument he might make regarding his return to music would ultimately end up with Cookie pulling out the nuke of nukes from her arsenal.

"Don't you think that Debbie would want you to keep playing music?"

Of course, if it got to that question, Michael knew more than anyone that Debbie would indeed want him to continue to play. But was this the time? Was this the place?

With these questions looming, a tiny and unspecified voice spoke in his mind, "Why not?"

After all, it would serve as a nice ice breaker in his meeting with Anthony. He seemed to like music and it would be something they could build a conversation around. Even without trying to over analyze the situation, Michael couldn't come up with a convincing reason why he shouldn't sit in with Cookie. Even though he had decided to fall in line with Cookie's concocted scheme, he wasn't going to let her off all too easy.

"So, Cookie, are you planning to play the Martin tonight or is it there for any other particular purpose?" inquired Michael, trying to look perturbed.

Cookie's eyes expanded wide and, looking like a child who was just caught eating chocolate moments before dinner, tried to level a response. "Well I thought that—"

"You thought that if you had an extra guitar out, along with an extra mic and chair that I would somehow see my way to joining you for a song or two?" interjected Michael, who was still trying to act like he was upset by the mere thought of it.

As hard as Michael tried to act like there was no way in heck that he would consider the invitation, Cookie's intuition and knowledge of the man quickly saw through his poor acting abilities.

"Well actually, I wasn't even thinking or hoping that you would sit in on a song or two," Cookie coyly answered back.

By this time, all eyes at the table were focused on the banter between their two friends. In response to the suddenly puzzled look Michael's face had precipitously adopted, Cookie continued her verbal assault.

"What I was hoping for is that you would play an entire set with me. What do you say, Michael?"

Though the dark clouds that had ensconced themselves into his life had yet to drift out of the periphery of living, Michael recognized that light, as it always does, was fighting to find its way through. He had a lot of people to thank for that, most especially Cookie, whose ability to say the right things at the right time proved her to undeniably be a bearer of light.

"Do you already have a set list made up?" asked Michael.

"Sure do. You know all the songs like the back of your hand," replied Cookie.

"Is 'Monkey Man' on the list?" asked Michael as he cocked his head to the side in an inquisitive fashion.

"It is not," answered Cookie with a grin, which told Michael that she received and welcomed the good-natured ribbing he had intended.

"Then my answer is yes, I'd be delighted to play with you."

Everyone at the table was filled with a real sense of happiness, none more apparently happy than Carol, who let out a loud "Yes!" in response to Michael's answer.

Anthony had become so engaged in the verbal sparring match happening in front of him that he had momentarily forgone his pursuit of draining his third large Coke of the evening. Turning to the man seated to his left he stated and then inquired, "Michael Fortunato, 'Monkey Man' is a song written by Mick Jagger and Keith Richards of the Rolling Stones. The song appeared on their 1969 album, *Let It Bleed*. It is a great song. Why wouldn't you want to play that song?"

The entire table broke out in a hearty laugh. Everyone there, aside from Anthony, knew of the friendly disagreement Cookie and Michael had regarding the artistic validity of "Monkey Man."

After the laughter subsided, Michael turned toward Anthony and said, "You know what, Anthony, for you, *just for you…*" Michael quickly shot a look at Cookie that told her that what he was about to offer up was certainly not an admission of his fondness of the song. "I will be glad to play "Monkey Man." But Cookie is going to have to sing it. That, I refuse to do! How does that sound to you, Anthony?"

"Sounds good, Michael Fortunato," replied a satisfied Anthony.

"You know something, Anthony?" asked Michael.

"What's that, Michael Fortunato?" replied Anthony.

"I like your style. I think that we might just become good friends. How does that sound to you, Anthony?" asked Michael sincerely.

"Ask me that after you play 'Monkey Man,' Michael Fortunato," quipped back Anthony quickly and unexpectedly.

Anthony's fast and insightful wit took everyone at the table by complete surprise. In the time that any of them had spent with him, including Carol who had spent by far the most time with him, none of them had ever witnessed Anthony saying anything near that clever or funny. The entire table broke out in uncontrollable laughter, even Anthony who typically didn't laugh couldn't help but to smile. The people at the surrounding tables couldn't help but notice the outburst, nor could they help but smile at the apparent joy coming from the table next to them.

"And on that note, is anyone hungry? If so, what do you say we order up some appetizers stat!" declared a very happy Cookie.

As Cookie boisterously avowed open season on appetizers, she was desperately trying her best to hold back tears of joy. For the first time in a very long time, she saw that Michael was on his way back to the world.

Seventeen

After being dropped off by Carol and Veronica, Anthony made his way up the stairs to his second story room at Andre House. Even though it was not apparent to the outside world, Anthony had been experiencing a darkness similar to what Michael had been facing. While he certainly wasn't the type of person who needed a lot of people in his life, the loss of his Uncle George cost him not only the person he loved most in the world, but it also caused the perception of order in his life to rapidly dissipate. But for the moment, for that evening, happiness returned to Anthony's heart.

He had a very enjoyable evening and thoroughly appreciated seeing Cookie and Michael playing music together. He didn't need a whole lot of friends, but he had come to love all those who shared that evening with him in his own deep and sincere way. While he did not know Michael as well as the others, he saw within him someone he could trust and a person he could let into his life without the resistance he would normally put up when meeting someone new.

Anthony liked how Michael spoke to him directly and how he asserted himself in a manner that made him feel like he was being treated with respect and as an adult. Anthony felt patronized by most people, but with Michael he felt like he was being treated as a friend. For all these reasons,

Anthony happily accepted Michael's offer to grab some dinner and a movie the following Wednesday evening.

Anthony found himself sitting on his couch feeling happy. Without knowing why Anthony said aloud, "I love you, Uncle George. And I love you, too, Jesus."

Anthony couldn't recall the last time he cried. In fact, he didn't know at the time if he had ever cried. But as he sat there, in his small but warm room, a single tear formed in the corner of his left eye. He hardly noticed it as it freed itself from its place of origin and slowly trekked down the slope of his cheek.

People cry when they are sad, not when they are happy, he thought.

Reaching down to the floor, Anthony picked up his backpack. After setting it on his lap, he opened it and removed its contents. Once both hands had grasped the blessing, he began his daily ritual of reciting the story from start to finish.

Eighteen

The pain of Jesus' death could not be eliminated, but it was slightly reduced when Cornelius and Prisca lifted the table out of the wagon and carried it into their house. Prisca had previously cleared a space in their central room for the table. It was to this spot that the couple brought it in and set it. Even though the wood had begun to darken with age, Prisca noticed dark stains on the top and sides of the browning table. Her fingers instinctively touched the stains.

With her fingers still touching the dark marks on the table, she looked to Cornelius and inquired, "His?"

Cornelius knew exactly what Prisca was asking and was not shocked by her insight. Something greater than each of them was at work within them.

"Yes, it is Jesus' blood. It splattered on the table as those beasts scourged him."

"You saw this? You saw it all happen?" Prisca asked in a surprised yet reverent tone.

Cornelius was unwillingly brought back to the scourging by Prisca's question. He began to relive those excruciating moments. After a pause he replied in a near whisper, "There are things one cannot un-see. How I wish this was not one of them."

Cornelius sat with his legs crossed on the floor and his wife joined him. Once she was seated, Cornelius shared with Prisca all he had witnessed in Jerusalem. Tears could not be controlled by either the teller or receiver of the story. Through their tears, they joined hands and sought to comfort the other. Though he was dead, both of their hearts burned and spoke to their intellects. Their collective intuition informed them that somehow the authority of their friend Jesus, in death, had been elevated. While they did not know from where their certainty came, both knew that there was more to come and that Jesus' narrative had not ended with his death.

Throughout the day and into the evening, neither Cornelius nor Prisca left the vicinity of the table. Being near it brought each of them closer to Jesus. When exhaustion finally fell upon both of them, Cornelius left and went to their bedroom. Moments later, he returned to their central room carrying with him the blankets and pillows from their bed. Getting on his hands and knees, he caringly spread out the blankets next to the table. Once he had positioned their two bed pillows, he rose up and took Prisca's hand and guided her to their bed for the evening. As they laid next to the table, a great peace fell upon both of them. With both of them positioned on their sides facing one another, a smile formed on each of their faces.

"I am not afraid, are you?" asked Prisca, recalling the words from her dream the previous evening.

"Not at all, my Prisca, not at all," answered Cornelius with confidence and sincerity.

Before falling asleep, Cornelius looked up at the table. For the first time he noticed some etchings in one of its corners. Reaching up, he allowed his fingers to trace the outline of the words. He didn't know what they meant, but he felt a sense of comfort as his finger followed each indentation. In the comfort of the table's presence, Cornelius fell into a deep and peaceful sleep.

Nineteen

Michael arrived at Andre House shortly before 5:00 p.m. in his older, but very clean, 1998 Lexus ES300. It had originally been Michael's car, but once he received a company vehicle Debbie became its primary driver. Michael loved the car for many reasons, but chief among them was that it was also loved by Debbie.

Anthony was waiting for him at the curb dressed in jeans and a gray Ron Jon Surf Club t-shirt that didn't exactly flatter his lanky frame. Slung over his shoulder was the brown cloth backpack that Michael had yet to see Anthony without. Opening the passenger side door, Anthony slunk into the seat and positioned the backpack between his legs.

"Hey, Anthony! How goes it?" Michael inquired, trying to sound cheerful and welcoming.

Michael was very nervous about meeting with Anthony. His first cause for nervousness was just getting out in the world. While the scars of Debbie's death had just recently shown a desire to heal, the residual pain of her loss still made it difficult for him to go out of his house and to do anything that normal, happy people do. In addition to that, Michael found himself anxious about how he would interact with Anthony. Even though he had taken the class Nadia had suggested on how to interrelate with autistic individuals, taking a course and actually doing it were two distinct and separate things to Michael. Attempting to override his pain and fears, however, was the knowledge that this young man needed him. It was this motivation that sent Michael out that night, past his hurt and past his anxiety.

"Hello, Michael Fortunato. I am fine. How are you?" Before he allowed Michael to respond Anthony continued, "Your Lexus is a classic. A lot of people think that the color is green but it's not, it's Parchment Crystal."

Michael was astonished that Anthony knew the actual name Lexus gave the color of his car's paint. He also felt relieved that he may not have to be the one responsible for finding things to talk about during the course of their evening as Anthony was doing a fantastic job initiating conversation right out of the shoot.

"Anthony, how in the world did you know that?" Michael exclaimed.

"I just know, Michael Fortunato," replied Anthony without a hint of conceit.

"Well, for the record, most people think that the car is silver, not green, and certainly not Parchment Crystal," corrected Michael, trying to keep the conversation going as he pulled away from Andre House.

"Your Lexus three-fifty is not green or silver, it's Parchment Crystal, but most people say that it's green. No one would think it is silver," Anthony qualified, looking forward while he spoke.

Michael let out an unexpected laugh at Anthony's rather definitive thoughts on the color of his car's paint. He was surprised that the remarks resulted in laughter rather than in a bout of sadness.

"What's so funny, Michael Fortunato?" queried Anthony, still looking forward out of the front of the car.

"Well, Anthony, my wife and I used to have the same argument. She said the car was silver and I would tell her that it was green," explained Michael.

"Well, you were both wrong. The color is Parchment Crystal. But you were more right than your wife," said Anthony.

"Thank you, my friend, for that confirmation," Michael said, still smiling from the course of their conversation.

"Did your wife die, Michael Fortunato? My Uncle George just died," said Anthony in a monotone and matter of fact fashion.

Michael paused momentarily and made a decision right then to suck back any hurt he had in order to best help his new friend Anthony. Rather than dwell on his loss, he thought it more important to see how Anthony was doing with his. Perhaps having shared a similar loss might make him seem more approachable to the young man.

"Yes, Anthony, my wife, Debbie, was in an accident not too long ago and she passed away. I heard about your Uncle George; he sounded like a wonderful man," Michael said with sincere compassion.

"He was a wonderful man, Michael Fortunato. He loved me and took care of me," answered Anthony.

"Debbie loved me too, and she took real good care of me as well. I bet you miss your uncle," Michael stated.

"Yes, I miss him. But I still have the story and the blessing, and they both love me, they can't help but love me," Anthony replied.

Michael had no clue what Anthony meant by the story or about a blessing, especially about either loving him. He wondered if it was a product of his Asperger's or if he was speaking about something specific and real to him. He debated over the next several seconds whether or not to inquire about this story or just to let it gently find itself to the wayside of their conversation. Curiosity won this scrimmage.

"What do you mean by the story and blessing?" asked Michael.

Anthony seemed to process this question. After ten seconds had passed he responded to Michael's question. "I don't know if I can tell you the story yet, Michael Fortunato, or show you the blessing. My Uncle George said that I will know when to tell the story and to who. I need to wait until I know."

Still confused but not wanting to upset his new friend, Michael replied, "No worries, Anthony. If down the road you want to tell me about this story and the blessing, I'll be all ears. Speaking of being down the road, we're getting close to the theater. There are a lot of places to eat around here, what do you feel like eating?"

"Pizza is my favorite, do you like pizza, Michael Fortunato?" asked Anthony who, for the first time on the trip, turned and actually faced Michael as he gave his culinary declaration. Michael took that to mean that Anthony had a strong preference for pizza that night!

"Are you kidding me? I'm from Chicago, home of the greatest pizza on the earth! In fact, there is a place a block from the movie theater called Barro's that has pizza just like they make in Chicago. I'm in if you're in."

"I'm in," replied Anthony.

As he said it, Michael thought he saw Anthony smile for the first time ever. It was just for a split second, but Michael felt certain that Anthony had indeed smiled. This made Michael smile as well, both inside and out.

"Then let's do it!" said Michael enthusiastically as he turned off Interstate Ten on to Ray Road. Barro's was just a couple blocks west of the highway. In a matter of minutes, they found themselves entering the restaurant.

The evening went better than Michael had anticipated it could. All previous trepidation about having something to say to an autistic young man were wiped away. An almost instant bond took hold of both men.

After putting down an extra-large cheese and sausage thin crust pizza, washed down by four very large glasses of Coke by Anthony and two by Michael, the pair proceeded to the Ahwatukee 24 and saw *Transformers 3*. While it wasn't Michael's first choice, Anthony was quite excited to see it which, in turn, made Michael very happy.

While dropping Anthony off at the end of the evening, both men agreed to hook back up sometime over the weekend. As Michael drove home, thoughts of the evening came back to his mind. What was the story all about? And what did Anthony mean by the blessing? Both seemed very real to Anthony, so real that he claimed that they both loved him. *In due time*, Michael thought. *In due time, I will learn more.*

Arriving home, Michael parked the car in the garage. Just as he was about to push the button to close the garage door, he looked back over at his car.

As he stared at the car he heard Debbie in his ear. "Green? How can you say green? That car is silver, plain and simple!"

Staring at the car, the pain and the tears returned. How he missed his Debbie. He wondered if he could ever be truly happy again.

Half under his breath and through his pain, Michael softly said to no one, "It's neither silver or green, it's Parchment Crystal."

Twenty

For well over a month following Cornelius' return home, the most talk-ed about subject in the town of Cana was the news from Jerusalem that Jesus the Nazarene had allegedly risen from the dead. The Jews of the town were pretty much split on the topic. Half, fueled by the occasional eyewitness who came into their town saying that they themselves had seen Jesus alive and well, believed that such a miracle had occurred. The re-maining half, those who had typically thought Jesus a false prophet while alive, discounted and refuted every mention of his rising from death.

Cornelius and Prisca sided with the believers and went out of their way to accommodate at their home anyone who claimed to have seen the risen Jesus. They absorbed each story as it was told to them. In response to what they heard, Cornelius and Prisca would share with their visitors their encounters with Jesus as well as the story of the table. It never failed that once any of their guests would hear Cornelius' story of the blood stained table they would in turn reverence the table with heartfelt caress-es to its darkened spots. These witnesses to the resurrection would often leave Cana telling all who would listen not only what they themselves had seen, but they would also relay to their listeners the story of Cornelius, the Roman Centurion deployed in Cana, who possessed a table that had witnessed both the miracle of water being changed into wine as well as the obscene torture of their beloved Rabbi.

As word of Cornelius' role in the story of Jesus became better known to both the local and broader populous, concern for their safety became a major source of anxiety and sleepless nights for his parents. On the one hand, both Decius and Appia Velius had been drawn into the narrative of Jesus, which their son and his wife had shared in its entirety with their whole family. Prisca's grandfather, Celsus, had been intrigued by all he heard regarding Jesus from the pair as well. And like so many others, this parental triad felt a real sense of peace when they would come in proximity of the table.

Countering this sense of calm were mounting whispers and gossip that made their way to both Roman officer-parents, Decius the Primus Pilus, and Celsus the Armicustos. The talk in Roman circles was centering on how Cornelius was drifting from the state's pagan gods in favor of not only the Jewish faith, but that he had also become a believer in the radical idea that Jesus of Nazareth was himself a god.

The rumors of such a thing happening within his ranks, let alone from the son of the area's second-in-command, did not sit well with Quintus Octavius, the Legion Legate. Had it not been for the respect Quintus had for Decius and the exemplary job he had been doing, Cornelius would have immediately been stripped of his officer's rank, faced a court martial, and probable imprisonment. Instead, Quintus quietly met with Decius and asked him to have a word with his son regarding his behavior. The Legion Legate made it clear to Decius that what would make him the most happy was for his son to become highly visible in their public worship and sacrifices to the state deities, including Caesar, and that he would hear no more about his association with the lunatic followers of Jesus.

While word of Cornelius' ties to Jesus made it to the ears of the displeased Roman proletariat, word of him, his story, and of the table, quickly made its way to Jerusalem and to those who were closest to Jesus as well.

Twenty-one

Of all the topics that came up over pizza that previous Wednesday evening, the subject of God and religion had made its way onto the table of discussion shortly after each of the men had put down their first slice. Out of the blue, Anthony had asked Michael if he believed in God and if he went to church. After telling Anthony that he most certainly believed in God and that he did attend Mass, Anthony had reciprocated and informed Michael of his love for Jesus and that he used to go to Mass every Sunday with his Uncle George, but hadn't since his death. All of this led Michael into a monologue about God, specifically how important it is to have Jesus in your life and the importance of giving Him all His due by going to church every Sunday or Saturday evening. As he was trying to strengthen Anthony's faith with his words, an uncomfortable sting of guilt washed over him. He began to feel hypocritical since his own attendance at Sunday Mass had been intermittent at best since losing Debbie. And so it was, the two men decided that for their next get together they would attend 11:00 a.m. Mass the following Sunday at St. Stephen's, the church Anthony had attended with his Uncle George, and that they would follow it up by going to a Diamondbacks game.

....

As they got out of Michael's car and started walking toward the church, Anthony shared with Michael a little information about the pastor of St. Stephen's.

"Fr. Will is the pastor. I hope he is saying the Mass. He gives really good homilies and he has the longest beard I've ever seen."

"So what do you like more about Fr. Will, his homilies or his beard?" asked Michael as they neared the sidewalk that led to the entrance of the church.

"I can't decide, Michael Fortunato—one's fun to hear and one's fun to look at," replied Anthony in a serious tone, all of which caused Michael to laugh.

"Anthony, you really are a treasure. I'm very glad that our paths crossed," Michael said while putting a hand on Anthony's shoulder.

Instinctively, Anthony pulled away at his touch. One of the things Michael learned in his class on how to interact with autistic people was the issue many of them have with personal boundaries. Remembering that fact neutralized Michael's initial feeling of rejection. In reaching for his shoulder, Michael couldn't help but notice the brown backpack slung over the shoulder he had not touched.

"So the backpack goes everywhere with you, even to church?" asked Michael.

Stopping at the base of the stairs leading into the church, Anthony turned and looked directly at Michael, something that he rarely did with anyone. "Yes, Michael Fortunato, it comes with me everywhere. Mr. McCabe, my boss at Food City, won't let me wear it at work, though. When I'm at work I have to keep it in my locker."

"What's in it that's so important to you, Anthony?" asked Michael, who was trying to understand why he would be carrying this backpack, which was obviously containing something that had some weight to it, everywhere he went.

Looking down at the ground, Anthony responded in a tone that sounded to Michael like he was legitimately sad that he couldn't share that information with him. "I'm sorry, Michael Fortunato, but I can't tell you. Maybe someday, but not today."

"No worries. Just know that if there is ever anything you want to share with me, I'm a good listener and I'm great at keeping secrets," Michael said, just as he found himself an inch away from patting Anthony on the back before catching himself. Continuing, Michael said, "Well, let's go inside and see if we're lucky enough to get Fr. Will. I'm dying to see that beard!"

As it turned out, Fr. Will was out of town. The celebrant was Fr. John. As they walked to their car after Mass, Anthony informed Michael that Fr. John was really cool because he drove a big red Jeep Wrangler and that he liked to go hunting on quads. Michael quickly learned that Anthony was an expert when it came to knowledge of his parish priests.

The rest of the day went amazingly well as both men became increasingly more comfortable with each other. The Diamondbacks game they went to after Mass was exciting as well, the team having won in extra innings against the Pirates.

Once he was at home, Michael sat on his couch with Goose right next to him. Rather than turning on the news, which he always recorded and watched later, he just sat there, one arm on top of Goose and the other on the couch's armrest. He felt good about helping Anthony and about their emerging friendship. Michael also thought back to the beauty of the Mass he attended that day at St. Stephen's. The combination of everything that day felt right to him, as if his life, at least momentarily, was in proper alignment. Telling Goose to stay, Michael got up and went to his bedroom and opened the box he kept on top of his dresser and pulled out his rosary. Returning to the couch and to his waiting companion, Michael sat down and began to pray the mysteries of that day.

Twenty-two

Much had happened in the months since Cornelius and Prisca slept under the comfort of the table. The most incredible thing, in the eyes of both affected families, was the birth of Johan to the extremely proud parents of Cornelius and Prisca. His name was chosen by Prisca and enthusiastically endorsed by Cornelius due to what the name meant—God is gracious. He was as handsome as any baby could be. He was born with a full head of dark hair and the blue eyes of his father and his grandmother; Johan was a welcome joy to the Velius clan.

It was also during this time span that Decius visited his son and informed him that his excitement over the person of Jesus, who was put to death as an enemy of Rome, had made itself known high up the chain of command. Decius told Cornelius that his friendship and loyalty to Quintus Octavius was the only thing that had saved Cornelius from being immediately arrested and possibly court marshaled. Decius relayed to his son that as an officer in the Roman army, and for his very sake, he needed to refrain from showing any outward, verbal, or any other indicators of his interest in the legacy of Jesus. Most especially, Cornelius could not suggest to others that Jesus had risen from the dead.

Of course, Decius did this all in the loving way of a father. He respected and loved his son very much. Further, since the arrival of the table, his son's words regarding Jesus had both Decius and Appia thinking more and more about the possibility of the existence of only one God. Cornelius' sister Zoe was also consumed by the stories of her brother and of those who came through Cana claiming to have seen the risen Jesus. She would come over to her brother's house often to touch and be near the table, feeling total peace when she was near it. She began to hope and pray that she, like those who visited her town, would also see Jesus.

Two days after Decius had met with his son, Cornelius formally resigned his commission and walked away from the army. This decision did not come as a surprise to Decius, who half expected it. Cornelius' commitment to the Roman military had formally ended and Decius accepted that his son had become part of a greater yet unexplainable calling.

Celsus also understood and supported Cornelius' decision. He, too, felt a stirring in his heart toward seeking the truth that he had never felt so strongly before. Celsus even provided Cornelius with a job after he left the army, hauling supplies from one depot to another as needed.

As profound as all these events were in Cornelius' life, none were more profound than when Nathanael paid him and Prisca a visit.

Twenty-three

In keeping with his promise to meet with Anthony's social worker following his first few visits, Michael met Nadia Arthur at the Dutch Brothers coffee on Alma School Road and Southern Avenue. Their meeting was two days after Michael had taken Anthony to Mass and the ballgame. After they ordered and received their drinks—a medium, skinny vanilla latte for Nadia and a large, black coffee for Michael—they settled into a corner table.

Nadia opened the conversation with a general and casual, "So how goes it with Anthony?"

"I can honestly say it is much better than I had expected," said Michael as he took a cautious sip of his hot coffee.

After tasting her own latte, Nadia said, "Let's start with what you expected, and then you can tell me how your experiences differed from what you had expected."

"Well, I have to tell you that I was very nervous going into our first meeting. I'm a bit of an introvert as it is, and I thought that with Anthony being autistic I would have to be the one leading and generating conversation. But Anthony is actually a great talker," replied Michael.

"Believe it or not, Anthony is giving you a very high form of praise," boasted Nadia with a smile.

Gazing up from his coffee, Michael gave Nadia a perplexed look. He didn't need to say anything, his scrunched forehead informed Nadia that Michael needed her to add a qualification to her last statement.

Nadia obliged. "Most people with Asperger's don't go out of their way to initiate conversation. That is, unless they really like the person they are with and feel safe with that individual. Michael, it appears that Anthony has taken a shine to you."

"But Nadia, he started in with conversation right when he got into my car for the first time. How could he have made a judgement on me that quickly?" questioned Michael.

"Was that the very first time you met him? Didn't you meet him before with Cookie and Carol?" asked Nadia.

"I met him twice before, but I didn't have any real conversation with him during those meetings."

"Nonetheless, you evidently made a wonderful impression on him. I must say that it sounds like your relationship with him is off to a marvelous start!" exclaimed Nadia, who was pleased by this information.

In a very short period of time, Nadia had become very fond of Anthony and wanted the best possible future for him. She also had taken a liking to Michael and was especially sympathetic toward him. She had spent a lot of time helping people deal with grief and, based on all that Cookie had shared with her, it was obvious to see that the scourges of loss had yet to heal for Michael.

Before Michael had a chance to respond, Nadia asked him, "I understand that you are a musician. Did Anthony happen to see you perform?"

Michael began to chuckle remembering the night. "Yeah, Cookie more or less tricked me into playing with her one night when Anthony, Carol, her mother, and myself were all together at Burba's."

"Bet that has something to do with Anthony's initial comfort level with you. He absolutely loves music. In fact, he knows the history of rock and roll better than anyone I know," said Nadia.

"Not only that, but apparently he is also an expert on exterior paint colors of classic Lexus models," Michael added.

"What?" Nadia looked puzzled.

"Nevermind. Suffice it to say, while Anthony may relate to the world in ways different than you and I, that young man is extremely intelligent," stated Michael.

"Yes, he is. So tell me about the things that you guys did together," requested Nadia.

"Well, the first night out we went and got a pizza at Barro's—"

"I LOVE Barro's pizza!" interrupted Nadia, who lost all sense of objectivity at the mention of her favorite pizza place.

Her declarative outburst took Michael by surprise. First, it was unexpected; and second, because he couldn't agree more.

"It is the best, that's for sure," agreed Michael.

Leaning into the table with her latte clutched in between both of her hands, an even more bubbly Nadia added, "I love that the cheese is so prominent. I hate pizzas that go light on the cheese and then go heavy on sauce. One thing for sure, is that I am not a sauce girl!"

For a moment a couple of thoughts swam in Michael's mind. First, he couldn't agree more with her pizza assessment. He, too, despised pizzas that were too saucy and loved pizzas that laid their mozzarella on thick. The second thought exited quicker than it arrived. Not only did Nadia share his affinity for cheesy pizza, but as he looked at her leaning closer to the center of the table and closer to him, it suddenly occurred to him what a beautiful woman she was. She was wearing a pair of dark dress jeans and a white, cotton shirt that was complemented by a dark, suede, button down vest and a black scarf tied around her neck like women wore in the fifties. Her dark hair was tucked back in a ponytail making her deep brown eyes highly visible. Almost immediately, any thought of her beauty was replaced by a sense of guilt.

I'm sorry, Debbie, Michael thought to himself.

Not wanting to tip off his sudden change of mood, Michael quickly regrouped. Making sure he had a smile on his face, he responded to Nadia's last remark. "And I, for one, am not a saucy man."

As soon as he said it, Michael realized that those words could have a double meaning. He hoped that she didn't think that he was coming on to her. Trying to cover his tracks he quickly added, "I'm definitely more of a cheesy guy. Just ask any one of my jokes."

Immediately after he said it, Michael thought that what he said could be interpreted as him trying to be charming. *Just shut up, Michael!* he thought to himself. The smile that he had forced quickly evaporated.

Nadia suddenly became aware of how her personalizing of the conversation and leaning in could be misjudged. It was a reflexive response to her dietary Achilles' heel, pizza, especially from Barro's. Sure, Michael was a very handsome, creative, and caring man, all of which encompassed the character traits she looked for in the men she dated. But this was certainly not the time, and flirting of any kind was not what she had intended.

"So what did you guys do after getting pizza?" asked Nadia, hoping that it would help get them past what she felt was an awkward moment for them both.

"Movies, *Transformers* number whatever. While it wasn't a movie I'd go see alone, I was very glad I did," replied Michael.

"Because it made Anthony happy?" asked Nadia.

"Exactly. I kept looking over at him during the movie. He was so transfixed by the screen and he got so excited when those thing-a-ma-jigs started to fight," answered Michael.

"How could you tell that he was excited by those scenes? People with Asperger's are typically hard to read when it comes to excitement."

"It's hard to say. It would be difficult to give an objective answer that I know you scientists like. I mean, I can say that his eyes got wider when those things morphed or transformed, or whatever it is they do. But, well, just suffice it to say that I knew," said Michael in a voice in which the volume noticeably declined as he ended his verbal thought.

The reflective look on Nadia's face led Michael to believe that she was carefully processing what he had just said. The longer than usual pause in conversation began to make Michael feel uncomfortable.

Giving way to western man's inability to be still, Michael spoke. "What are you thinking about?"

Before she answered, a very real smile slid across her face. She momentarily looked down at her coffee and then met Michael's eyes. "Things couldn't be better. I mean, between you two. You are deeply clued into him and as mentioned, it's very apparent that he likes and trusts you a lot. You have no idea how rare it is for a mentor such as yourself to start out so strongly with a person with Asperger's. It's as though a divine intervention of some sort has brought you two together."

"Since I have no experience in this field, I defer to your divine assumption," answered Michael, who was glad to hear her affirmation that a bond had indeed been established between Anthony and himself.

"You seem to be a very smart guy, Michael, and I'm sure that you can tell that Anthony has become more than a client to me. I can't begin to tell you what a relief it is for me to see that he has made such a good friend in you. Thank you so much for agreeing to be his mentor. Hearing how things are going between you, and seeing what a great role model you are, well... It has taken a great weight off my shoulders," Nadia said.

"Well, it's a two-way street. Anthony seems to be just what I needed in my life. Now, if we haven't over used the phrase yet, that's what I call divine intervention," Michael said with a grin.

Over their remaining cups of coffee, Michael shared with Nadia what Anthony did on their second day out together. She was touched to learn that the men shared, among other things, a common faith and devotion to it. Nadia shared with Michael that while she had always believed in God, she had never been involved with any particular faith tradition.

After all the recapping was done on their first two visits, Nadia turned to some near term objectives for Michael to begin working on with Anthony. First on the list was assessing Anthony's ability to live independently. Nadia informed Michael that Anthony could not stay at Andre House indefinitely. She asked Michael if he could sit down with Anthony and obtain some basic income information from him. How often did he get paid? What was his monthly income? Was it based on a forty-hour work-week? In addition to gathering information on his income, Nadia asked Michael to find the right time to see how Anthony liked living alone. Was he doing okay? Could he live happily on his own? Things like that. She also informed Michael that Anthony's uncle had left him as the beneficiary of a hundred-thousand-dollar life insurance policy that would convert into a trust. Anthony would be entitled to that trust once everything cleared probate, something that was expected to take several months. She told Michael to tuck that info away for now and that the courts would likely ask for a trustee to be appointed over the trust. Nadia left Dutch Brothers with the parting shot that if he were open to it, she would be in favor of suggesting him to be that trustee.

Michael and his quarter cup of lukewarm coffee remained for a while at the table after Nadia left. As he sat there, feelings of happiness and sadness began to battle for control of his heart. The army of happiness was led by the thought that he may in fact be doing some good in befriending Anthony. The sadness assault was led by the thoughts of how he still missed Debbie and the guilt for having noticed how beautiful Nadia was.

Twenty-four

It was still early in the evening, certainly not past the first watch of the night, when a rather bold knock on the front door woke Cornelius and Prisca from their sleep. It was seven months since Cornelius returned to Cana with the table and about six months since initial reports of people claiming to see Jesus alive began to circulate. Since that time, word of the table had spread all throughout the region, to Jerusalem, and beyond. As a result, Cornelius and Prisca's home soon became a central gathering place for those who described themselves as followers of the risen Jesus. Cornelius and Prisca figured that the knock had to belong to one of these self-proclaimed followers who didn't feel like waiting until the morning to see and hear about the table.

"Ignore them, Cornelius. They'll figure out that the morning would be a better time to see the table," Prisca said in a whisper, hoping that neither the knocking nor her voice would wake Johan.

Cornelius was about to agree with her when another possible explanation for the knock came to him; perhaps it was the Roman authorities coming to arrest him for being friendly to these followers. He quickly dismissed the thought, knowing that the combination of his recent resignation from military service and his father's position in said military would make that an unlikely option. As he wrestled with these thoughts, another set of knocks sounded on the door. This time the pounding woke Johan, who began to cry.

Letting out a hefty and audible sigh, Cornelius directed Prisca to tend to Johan while he went to see who had been causing the commotion. Taking the lamp from the small table they kept near their sleeping mats, he lit it and made his way to the front of their house. Since he was just in his short sleeping tunic, he thought it wiser to inquire who was knocking on his door rather than just opening it to find out.

"Who is it?" His voice was a mix between sounding welcoming and imposing.

"It is Nathanael and Phillip, your brothers from Jerusalem," replied a voice from the other side of the door.

By that time, Prisca had put on her robe and was standing next to her husband with a now calmer Johan in her arms. Cornelius immediately recognized the voice of Nathanael from their previous encounters. He tried to place who Phillip was, but could not. All the same, both his and Prisca's hearts were racing with excitement. While they had heard many people they didn't know talk about seeing Jesus alive, on the other side of their door stood one of his closest disciples, someone they could trust and certainly someone who would have firsthand encounters not only with the person Jesus, but with the risen Jesus. At first, it didn't even register to Cornelius that Nathanael had called him his brother.

Opening the door, Cornelius warmly greeted his late evening guests. "Welcome! Welcome to you both!"

"We are so sorry to come to you this late, but we have just arrived from Jerusalem and had nowhere to go. We hope you understand," explained an apologetic Nathanael.

Cornelius extended his arm, which served as his guest's invitation to come inside the house. Once inside, Cornelius made them feel welcome no matter the late hour. "No need to be sorry, we are very glad to have you with us. As you may recall, this is my wife, Prisca, and this is our son, Johan. Prisca this is Nathanael and, and—"

"Phillip, I'm Phillip," said Phillip, warmly extending his hand to both Cornelius and Prisca.

As Phillip spoke, Cornelius began to recognize him. He recalled seeing him at the wedding of Laban's granddaughter as well as standing near Jesus when he heard him talk outside of the Temple.

"Your baby is beautiful!" exclaimed Nathanael.

"And what a beautiful name, 'God Is Gracious.' How true that is!" said Phillip, offering Johan a finger to squeeze.

"Where are you gentlemen heading? Please tell us that you have time to share everything that has happened in Jerusalem. We have so many questions and want to hear everything you know," inquired Prisca, whose excited tone let everyone know that she felt she was in the presence of very important people.

Looking over Cornelius' shoulder, Nathanael spotted the table in the dim shadows of Cornelius' lamp. Looking back at Cornelius and Prisca he said, "You are our destination. We have come to see you and to inquire about your table."

"Tell you what," Cornelius began to bargain. "We will tell you everything about the table if you promise to tell us all about Jesus, most especially if he in fact died and somehow came back to life."

A look of joy and astonishment, the likes of which Cornelius and Prisca had never seen, came over Nathanael and Phillip. They first looked at each other, and their smiles only widened and their joy intensified.

Nathanael turned toward the couple, his grin seeming to have grown even wider, and said to them, "It is true. It is remarkably and richly true. Jesus indeed lives."

Twenty-five

It was late morning, just a couple days after Michael had met with Nadia, when his cell phone began to vibrate. Looking at the screen, Michael saw that it was Cookie. Not too long ago he would have ignored the call, as he did with everyone else. For the first time in a long time, he not only felt ready to answer, but he also wanted to share with Cookie how it had been going with Anthony and to hear how she was doing.

"Hello, Cooks. What's up?"

"Not too much on my end. I'm more interested in hearing about how you're doing. And that, buddy, is the purpose of my call today," replied a cheerful-sounding Cookie.

"You mean you're not calling to try and trick me into playing another show with you like you did the other night?" answered a happier than usual sounding Michael.

"Oh no, I never do my trickery over the phone, that's always done live and in person," Cookie quipped back.

"I see, so I can stop looking over my shoulder then, at least during this phone conversation?"

"You're free not to be paranoid for the duration of this call," said

Cookie. She added, "So what's been happening with you, how are things going with Anthony?"

Taking Cookie's cue, Michael began telling her all about his first two meet ups with Anthony, sharing with her the same optimistic tales he had recently shared with Nadia. There was a step in Michael's voice that hadn't been there in a long time. For the first time since he could remember, he actually felt like talking with someone. After sharing with Cookie a full recap of his time with Anthony, there was a momentary silence in their conversation.

"You there, Cookie?" asked Michael.

"Oh yeah, I'm here. I'm just overcome with joy," responded Cookie, with a sniffle at the end of her sentence.

"I know, hearing about priests with really long beards driving tricked out Jeep Wranglers always gets me, too!" Michael said.

Michael's quick wit caused Cookie to pause the conversation once more. Before she resumed speaking, Michael was certain that he heard her sniffle again.

"Michael, it's incredibly good to hear you sounding like yourself. You know I pray for you every day, and I think my prayers may have just been answered in the form of an autistic young man."

"Well, I am starting to feel a little better, thank you. In terms of your prayers being answered, I believe that you, my friend, had a part in answering them," replied Michael.

"What do you mean?" asked Cookie.

"Nadia Arthur didn't pull my name out of a phone book. I'm smart enough to deduce that it was you who suggested my pairing with Anthony."

"And if that were true, would you be angry?" asked Cookie.

This time it was Michael who caused the momentary pause in their conversation. After reflecting for a few additional seconds, Michael responded, "Far from it. You're a wise and beautiful person, Cookie. Angry? No. Thankful? Tons. Thank you for your prayers and most especially for connecting me with Anthony."

"That's what band buddies are for, I'm just so glad to hear positive things are happening for you," said Cookie.

"Call it baby steps, but I'm taking them. I'd be lying to you if I told you that I'm whole yet, or anywhere near it. At least now, for the moment, I feel like I have a purpose," Michael said.

"At some point babies stop crawling and they take to walking, and then before you know it, they're running. Keep taking those baby steps, Michael. That's the important thing."

Shifting gears from the emotional to the more day-to-day Cookie added, "Oh, I almost forgot to tell you. Jim Thane called me a couple days ago and asked me how you were doing. He asked if I thought you'd be up to talking with him soon. It sounded like he really misses you. Would you be up to taking a call from him?"

Michael took a second to mull that over. He had been making progress toward reengaging in the world, but he was still nervous to return to it fully. Yet, Jim was a guy who had always been there for him. Perhaps Michael was ready to take another baby step.

"Sure, Cookie. If you talk to him, please tell him to give me a call."

After some additional small talk and a cordial goodbye, Michael remained sitting on his sofa looking blankly forward. He didn't even notice Goose on the floor to his right with a tennis ball in his mouth. Goose was staring up at Michael in hopes that a game of catch might result from his stalker-like gaze. Michael was happy to have people like Cookie legitimately caring for him, yet at the same time he couldn't shake the persistent hurt brought on by the absence of Debbie. This hurt was intensified as his mind brought back to him the thoughts he had momentarily experienced about Nadia. If loss was a dagger's stab, guilt was its forceful upward twist.

Twenty-six

It was early evening and Anthony had just completed his reciting of the story. After finishing, he remained motionless on his couch clutching the blessing that sat atop his lap. Telling the story, and most certainly holding the blessing, always made Anthony feel calm, reflective, and peaceful. It was in these moments that he often felt a special closeness with God. Feeling particularly moved this evening, Anthony began to talk to God from his spot on the couch.

"Jesus, I love you. Thank you for everything. I can't see you but I know that you are here because of how I feel when I tell the story and when I hold your blessing. Today I want to thank you for my friend Michael Fortunato. He makes me happy and is a very nice man. I think that he likes me too. Uncle George said that I would know who to share the story and the blessing with. Since I'm the last Velario, he said I'd have to find someone to share it with. I think Michael Fortunato is the person. Tell me, Jesus, if I'm right. If Uncle George is by you, ask him too. My heart will listen to your answer. Thank you, Jesus, for all the gifts of this day and I pray for a good day tomorrow. I love you, Jesus, goodnight."

Twenty-seven

Cornelius and Prisca were mesmerized by the men sitting across the table from them. While they hung on each and every word the men spoke regarding the very much alive Jesus, it was the appearance of the men that captivated them the most. These men looked like joy personified, like children at play on their happiest of days. Any ounce of fear, sorrow, anxiety, worry, or anger commonly seen in most men could not be detected in the expression of these two disciples of Jesus. Prisca and Cornelius didn't need to hear collaborating accounts from any other witnesses, nor did they even need Nathanael or Phillip to utter a single additional word to know that Jesus was indeed alive.

"So, would it be possible for us to visit with him too?" asked Prisca, hopeful.

"The answer to that is both yes and no. He is always with us and always wants us to be in communion with him," explained Phillip.

Seeing the confused looks on Cornelius' and Prisca's faces, Nathanael sought to clarify what Phillip had said. As he began to speak, his face radiated even more fully the joyful look of a child. "What Phillip is saying is true. What you need to know is that we saw, that is Phillip, myself and the other disciples—" He paused and his smile widened. "We saw Jesus leave to go to his Father in heaven just a short time ago. It was glorious and indescribable! The light, the love, it was so overwhelming and beyond understanding. But before he left us he gave us our mission and he told us that even if we could no longer see him, that he would be there alongside of us, beside everyone, just as I am sitting across from you in a very real and true way."

Dazed by this, Cornelius replied, "I'm sure that what he meant is that he would always be by you, and his twelve closest followers. Certainly, that doesn't include a Roman such as myself?"

"But it does! It most certainly does!" Phillip passionately declared. "In fact, one of the twelve asked Jesus the very same thing. It was Thomas, was it not, Nathanael?"

Nathanael answered, "Indeed it was. We jokingly call him Thomas the Clarifier, since he would always ask Jesus follow-up questions just to make sure he understood whatever it was that he was teaching. It would drive us crazy on most occasions, but other times his persistent inquiries, whether we would admit it or not, were things on which we all needed clarification. Anyway, when Jesus said that he would be with us always, just the same as seeing him in front of us, dear Thomas asked him, 'Lord, do you mean that you will be with us, meaning us your most intimate disciples, or do you mean everyone?'

"At that Jesus let out a laugh and said to him, 'Oh, Thomas, how I love you and your desire for clearness! Since I am going now to my Father, let me make it very clear: I am for everyone, Jew, Gentile, Roman, Greek, African, and for people you don't even know exist. I am present to all who desire my presence and always will be.'"

Phillip added, "He then reminded us all about our mission to make disciples out of everyone, literally everyone in the world. So indeed, Cornelius, his presence is for you just as it is for me or Nathanael."

Cornelius' hand slid across the table and found the soft hand of his wife. As their hands and eyes met, they both felt certain what their life was about to become. Over the last year, their hearts had been fashioned by a deeper purpose, by a divine source. Each day their hearts of love grew in size and desire. They realized at that very moment that their hearts could take on no more until they responded to the call now made clear to them.

Cornelius knew that his next words were spoken for the both of them. "Please, take us back to Jerusalem with you. We want to learn more about Jesus and your friends. We desire to join your mission, if you would allow us."

Nathanael's face lit up once again. "That's exactly why Phillip and I are here. We want you and your table to join us all in Jerusalem."

Cornelius couldn't believe what he was hearing. The look of elation that fell across Prisca's face told Cornelius that she was as equally jubilant with the invitation they had just received.

In his excitement, Cornelius' face began to radiate in a similar fashion to that of his two guests. He declared with exuberance, "If you will have us, we would be honored to become your disciples."

Cornelius suddenly realized that he had yet to uphold his end of the promise. "Speaking of the table, I still owe you all I know about it."

"Not to steal any thunder from you, Cornelius, but after the Rabbi saw the table at Laban's wedding, he told us a great deal about the table, including the miracle that it took to create it. He made it abundantly clear to all of us just how important the table was to him. That is why we desire you to share it with our brothers in faith. And by the way, you are invited to become his disciple, not ours," interjected Nathanael.

Cornelius' mind went back to the scourging of Jesus. He recalled how he tenderly looked at the table. It seemed to him, at the time, that Jesus focusing on the table somehow lessened the brutal pain that was being inflicted upon him.

"Oh, how I know that he loved this table," said Cornelius softly as his hands lightly ran across its surface. After pausing for a moment to reflect, he continued, "If it pleases you both, please share with Prisca and me what Jesus told you about this table, most importantly about the miracle of its creation. I will then be glad to add to its story by telling you everything I know that has happened to it since the wedding of Laban's daughter."

With that, Nathanael and Phillip relayed the stories of the table that Jesus had shared with them. They told Cornelius and Prisca how God healed his grandfather's withered hands in order to build the table. They shared stories of how Laban was Jesus' grandfather's and father's best customer, and how it was that he commissioned the table. They also told the couple about the times when Jesus was a child and his family visited Laban and his family in Cana, usually when they would be dropping off some more furniture his father, Joseph, had built for him, and Jesus would play underneath the table.

In return, Cornelius and Prisca shared all their stories regarding the table and the impact that it had on their lives. Cornelius had a very hard time telling his company about what he had witnessed in Pilate's courtyard. He was so moved that he couldn't hold back the tears that streamed down his face. Nathanael and Phillip, likewise, were emotionally touched by this story and similarly could not hold back their emotions. When Cornelius pointed to the spots on the table that had been stained by the blood of their savior, the two visitors dropped to their knees in front of the blood-marked corner. Placing their hands and then their heads upon the stained areas, both wept in sorrow for the agony Jesus went through on account of them and all mankind.

By the time all parties had finished sharing their stories of Jesus and of the table, it was late into the third watch of the night. Exhausted, Prisca showed their company to the roof of their house with Cornelius close behind her, dragging up the sleeping mats the men could use to get a restful night's sleep. They agreed to leave for Jerusalem the following day. In the morning, they would assemble the proper provisions for the trip, would load up the table on Cornelius' wagon, and take the time to tell their families where they were heading.

Before climbing down the ladder, Cornelius turned to his guests with a final inquiry. "One more question, this I must know. In the right corner of the table, on its underside, I noticed an inscription. Do you know what it means and how it got there?"

His two rooftop guests looked at each other and smiled yet again.

It was Nathanael who responded, "It was placed there by Jesus' grandfather, Jacob, the builder of the table. He put it under all his works. It reads, very prophetically, 'Love has come.' And indeed it has, my brother."

....

As Cornelius bedded down for the night, a sense of peace and purpose like he had never felt before overcame him. Love had indeed come he thought, and by some great mystery, it was calling to him.

As these thoughts raced in his mind, Prisca, whom he thought had been asleep, turned and faced him. She smiled at him and reached for his hand under their blanket.

As though she had been reading his mind, she said in a soft, sincere tone, "For the first time, Cornelius, the pieces of my life finally fit as though I have now been fully defined."

"I feel exactly the same way. I am not afraid to follow this path. I'm confident that Jesus or the God of the Jews will provide for us," answered Cornelius with his nose just inches away from his beloved Prisca.

Prisca closed her eyes and bit the bottom of her lip. Cornelius had seen this gesture many times before. It told him that there was something significant on her mind. Before he had the chance to inquire what she was thinking, Prisca spoke.

"You know how much I want to go with you to Jerusalem to meet Jesus' followers and to be a part of all of it. But as much as I want to hop on the wagon and ride out of Cana with you, Johan is too young for the trip and too young to be left here without his mother."

It pained Cornelius to think of not sharing this experience with Prisca. But as she voiced her concerns, he realized that she was right. He moved his hand to the side of her cheek and gently stroked it. His touch brought her lowered eyes back up to meet his own.

"As much as I want you with me, and as much as you want to go, I know what you say is for the best. But dear, know that this is just the beginning. Soon, Johan can accompany us both to wherever God calls us," Cornelius said in a most loving and consoling way.

Prisca grinned, which, based on past and frequent history, informed Cornelius that his wife had something to add to the discussion.

"What are you grinning about? Fess up, I know you're thinking something," Cornelius said, now also smiling.

"We are not the only ones in the family who have been touched by Jesus. I believe that your sister's heart has been touched as deeply as ours by Jesus. Zoe can't hear enough about him and she is always here just to be near the table. I think that it would mean the world to her if you asked her to go to Jerusalem with you," explained Prisca.

Cornelius was immediately taken by his wife's forethought. She was always thinking beyond herself and beyond any given situation.

"I think that's a great idea. Would you mind going to the house early in the morning and asking her while I get our supplies ready for the trip?" asked Cornelius.

"I will. She is going to be so happy!" Prisca said, placing her hand on the cheek of her husband. Looking into his eyes, seemingly into his very heart, she added, "Love really has come."

The synergy of hearing this phrase repeated was not lost on Cornelius. With a heart never as warm, he slept better that night than he had ever before.

Twenty-eight

A nthony slung his backpack into the booth and followed it in with his backside. He was dressed in his customary light-colored jeans and a light blue polo shirt. Michael slid in on the other side of the booth and like Anthony was wearing jeans and a polo shirt, although his jeans were dark and his polo was gray. The plan was to start their Saturday with breakfast at the IHOP right off Interstate Ten on Ray Road followed by bowling at Kyrene Lanes, which was just a few miles west on the same road. Bowling was Anthony's idea. Though he hadn't bowled in awhile, Michael and Debbie had been in a bowling league before they were married and Michael had held a very respectable one hundred and seventy average.

As Michael scanned the menu, he noticed that Anthony hadn't even picked up his.

"Do you know what you want to eat without looking at the menu?" asked Michael.

"Large stack of blueberry pancakes with extra whipped cream. That's what I always get at the IHOP. What are you going to order, Michael Fortunato?"

"Well, I think I'll get what I usually get: three eggs basted, hash browns, sausage, and wheat toast. And, of course, coffee," replied Michael, adding, "I guess I really didn't need to look at the menu either!"

"No, you didn't, Michael Fortunato. You didn't have to look at the menu," Anthony said, looking down at the table.

"Can I ask you a favor, Anthony?" asked Michael.

"Yes," responded Anthony.

"I know that you want to treat people with respect by addressing them by their full name. But when people become good friends, and I think we have, it's okay to just call them by their first name. Do you think you could just call me Michael?"

"I can try," replied Anthony.

"Well then, how about you give it a try right now? Ask me something and use my name within the question. It can be about anything you want, just as long as you only use my first name," instructed Michael.

Michael watched Anthony across the table. It appeared to Michael that Anthony was painstakingly trying to think of a good question to ask. After about thirty seconds of thinking, Anthony had his question.

"Michael, just Michael, can you keep secrets?"

Michael was not expecting such a question. He had thought that Anthony might ask him whether he liked blueberry pancakes or what his high bowling score was. All the same, he quickly responded, "First of all, just say 'Michael,' not 'Michael just Michael.' And yes, I can keep a secret. Do you have one to tell me?"

Again, Anthony looked down for almost as long as his previous pause. Without looking up at Michael he said, "I might have a secret to tell you. I think you might be the person Uncle George told me I would meet and who I should tell the story to."

Michael thought back on the exchange they had the previous Sunday before Mass regarding his backpack.

"Does the secret have to do with what's inside your backpack?" asked Michael.

Anthony looked up momentarily at Michael and then back down to his lap. With his eyes averted he answered in a soft voice, "Yes."

"As I told you before, I am very good at keeping secrets. Do you care to tell me now what's inside your backpack?" Michael empathetically asked.

Anthony's response came quickly, "Not today, Michael Fortunato. But soon, maybe. Uncle George said I'd really know when, and I think that maybe it will be soon that I can tell you," explained Anthony.

At that moment the waitress came to take their order. After ordering their blueberry pancakes and basted eggs, Michael redirected the line of questioning to the information Nadia had asked him to gather.

"So, Anthony, how do you like living alone? Are you doing okay by yourself?"

"It's okay with me, Michael Fort...Michael. I miss Uncle George, but I'm not afraid to be by myself. I get to watch anything I want on TV and can eat whatever I want," answered Anthony.

Michael filed away the dietary mention. He'd have Nadia follow-up and make sure someone explained to Anthony the importance of a good nutritional diet and what it looked like.

"I'm glad to hear that you are okay with living on your own. Speaking of which, I don't know if you know this or not, but you can't stay at Andre House forever. Andre House is for people to live in for a short period of time. Did you know this, Anthony?" asked Michael.

"No, I did not know that, Michael. Does this mean I have to move somewhere else?" Anthony asked without a change in tone or any indication of concern.

"Yes, eventually. And that's what I wanted to help you with today." Leaning into the table, Michael lifted his hands palms up as he continued to explain the basics of such a move. "The first part of moving to a new place involves finding out how much someone can spend on an apartment. How often do you get paid, Anthony?"

"Every two weeks," answered Anthony.

"How much is your check, usually? And how much do you make an hour?"

"I make fifteen dollars an hour and my check is nine hundred eighty-seven dollars and thirty-six cents if I don't work any extra hours. Sometimes I work extra hours, but sometimes I don't," replied Anthony.

"Well, a good rule of thumb is to use one fourth of what you take home, in your case that's five hundred dollars, to use toward your monthly rent. So when we start to look for apartments for you, we need to look for ones that are around five hundred dollars a month," said Michael.

"Michael, you said, 'So when we look for an apartment.' Does that mean you would help me look for an apartment?"

Michael was touched that of all the things he had just explained, what Anthony picked up on was his offer to help.

"Of course I would!" replied Michael enthusiastically. "Is that something you would like?"

"Yes," answered Anthony as the server arrived with their food. Feeling very hungry and desirous of his favorite breakfast food, Anthony immediately began to dig into his large stack.

Though it was a single word answer, Michael interpreted it to mean that Anthony would greatly appreciate his help. Touched, Michael added, "Then I look forward to helping you find a new place! If you're open to it, I can also help you develop a budget so you know how to save your money to pay your bills and food. And if you don't know how to do any of that yet, fear not! I will be glad to teach you," Michael offered.

Anthony looked directly at Michael, something he rarely did with anyone. "Thank you, Michael. I can use your help."

Anthony put down his fork and very cautiously moved his right hand across the table. Michael's hands were sitting flat on the table with his fingers curled inward. He watched as Anthony's right hand hovered over his left. It stayed there, suspended over his for several seconds. Then Anthony lowered it and patted the top of Michael's hand twice before it rapidly retreated back to his fork and stack of pancakes.

Anthony's touch hit its mark. While Michael's hand might have been Anthony's intended target, what he really hit with his gesture was the very center of Michael's heart.

Twenty-nine

To say that Zoe was excited to accompany her brother and the two disciples of Jesus to Jerusalem would have been the understatement of the century. When Prisca came that morning and asked her if she was interested in taking the trip, she let out a scream of exhilaration and began to jump up and down in front of Prisca saying, "Thank you! Thank you!"

Much like her brother, Zoe had a heart set on veracity. Words, experiences, and all evidences of truth which would escape the detection of the ordinary citizen were soaked in, nurtured, and thoroughly processed by Zoe. In studying Jesus, she could only draw one conclusion: that he was truth, or at least a bearer of it. It was one thing to hear the stories of her brother and sister-in-law and to touch the table that was somehow a part of the man, but it was an entirely different thing meeting with the very men who had spent several years at his side. It would be an experience that would fill both her mind and her heart with knowledge and truth.

On their two-and-a-half-day journey to Jerusalem, the sixteen-year-old, blue-eyed, and beautiful sister of Cornelius pelted Nathanael and Phillip with question after question about Jesus, the Jewish faith, and its belief in one God. Cornelius had initially worried that the two disciples would grow weary of her endless stream of questions. At the same time, part of him hoped they wouldn't since he was learning so much by listening to their responses to his sister's poignant questions.

As it turned out, the two disciples were anything but annoyed by Zoe's questions. To the contrary, the smiles on their faces never seemed to dissipate as they answered each and every question patiently and thoroughly. It was apparent to the Roman brother and sister that these two men very much enjoyed telling them all they had to offer. At one point, Cornelius interjected and asked them if he and Zoe needed to give the conversation a rest for a while.

Nathanael had replied, "This is our very mission, our purpose now in life, given to us by our friend Jesus. He has given us his Spirit to strengthen us so that we may never tire from telling others about him. This is a privilege, you see. May your questions and those of the entire world never cease!"

So it was that on the road to Jerusalem, Cornelius and his young sister learned about the Jewish prophecies relating to the Messiah. More importantly, the disciples explained to them how Jesus fulfilled those prophecies, most especially him being raised from the dead. While they spoke with knowledge and wisdom, what deepened Cornelius and Zoe's convictions that Jesus was indeed the Jews' long awaited Messiah, that he truly was the son of the one and only God, was the tone of love Nathanael and Phillip used when they spoke of him.

Thirty

It was approaching mid-day as they entered the city of Jerusalem through what was known to the Romans as the Lions' Gate, and to the Jews as the Gate of Sha'ar Ha-Arayot, which was located on the east side of the city. Both Cornelius and his sister Zoe had been to Jerusalem before. On those previous visits, Zoe had been drawn in to the city's attractions, markets, and history. Today, however, both she and her brother had a single focus.

When they entered the great city, it was as if they were wearing blinders like their horses. They hardly noticed the great crowds, the rich smells of food cooking, or even the magnificent sight of the Jewish Temple, which stood in absolute glory to their left. All they cared about was getting to the close friends of Jesus.

They rode east on the main road before turning left and heading for their destination in the area known as the Upper City. Their companions told Cornelius and Zoe that the place of the disciples was at the southern end of the Upper City, past the home of the High Priest who had manipulated both the Roman authorities and the Jewish citizens to have Jesus put to death. They also told them that it was the very same place where they had their last meal with Jesus, where Jesus first appeared to all of them after his death, and the very same place where they received God's Holy

Spirit. Having heard the details of all these events during their journey to the city, Cornelius was anxious to see and be in the very same house.

As they passed a well where women were collecting water Cornelius thoughts returned to the evening of Nathanael and Phillip's visit. Given his and Prisca's expressed desire to become followers of Jesus, Nathanael shared with them, during that long evening's conversations, the story of Jesus's baptism. He went on to share with them how his followers likewise shared in this same baptism. Desiring this same cleansing water, Prisca, Zoe, and himself were each baptized by Nathanael early the following morning.

After about half an hour, they arrived at their destination.

"There it is," said Phillip, pointing to a door that was located on the second level of a large home. A set of stairs led up to it and to its medium-sized patio.

As they dismounted from their horses and wagon, a man appeared from the door at the top of the stairs. He was a tall, middle-aged man, robust in stature. His black, wavy hair was accompanied by some intermittent streaks of gray, which brought about an appearance more of wisdom than of advancing age. His thick beard was due for a trim and was increasingly becoming more silver in color than its original black. Looking down on the new arrivals, he stood at the top of the stairs and raised both of his arms in welcome.

"So I finally meet the famous, blue-eyed Centurion who has the table of our Lord!" exclaimed the man in a loud and hospitable voice.

Coming down the stairs, he greeted his fellow disciples. "Welcome back, brothers, welcome back." The man vigorously hugged both Nathanael and Phillip. Then he moved on to Cornelius.

Extending his hand, the man introduced himself with an amiable smile. "Cornelius, I have heard so many good things about you. It's a pleasure to meet you. My name is Peter."

Gripping Peter's hand, Cornelius asserted, "No, sir, it is my honor and pleasure to meet you. We have heard so much about you on our way here. Again, the honor is all ours."

Noticing Zoe standing just behind Cornelius, Peter said, "Let me take a wild guess and say that this is your sister?"

"Yes it is, but how did you know that it wasn't my wife who was supposed to come with me? Are you a prophet as well as a leader?" inquired Cornelius.

All three of the disciples let out a hearty laugh, the loudest of which belonged to Peter.

"What a sense of humor you have, Cornelius!" roared Peter. He added, "Turn and look at your sister, what do you think was the first thing I noticed about her?"

Turning to look at Zoe, who began to bear a deep red blush from the sudden attention she had just received, it dawned on Cornelius how easy it was for Peter to make the connection to their sibling nature.

"Oh yes, her blue eyes and my blue eyes, of course," exclaimed Cornelius.

Putting one arm around Cornelius' shoulder and the other around Zoe, Peter said, "A prophet I am not. An observer of the obvious, I am."

Turning toward Zoe, Peter asked, "So what is your name, my other blue-eyed guest?"

"Zoe, sir. As my brother said, it is such an honor to meet you," said Zoe, in awe of the man whom she had learned Jesus had handpicked to lead his followers.

"Honor shmoner! We are all one with one Savior and one mission. Speaking of which..."

Peter made his way to the backside of the wagon, which held the table. The table was wrapped in several layers of soft blankets and then covered with a heavy tarp. The table and its covering were secured tightly to the wagon by several crisscrossing ropes.

"I assume this is it, the table Jesus told us about and of which recent travelers from Cana have been speaking incessantly about?" Peter asked.

"It is," answered Zoe as she watched Peter's hand extend over the wagon and then rest reverently on a corner of the covered table.

After a few seconds, Peter looked at the three men and directed them in a loud and happy voice, "Well let's get it upstairs!"

"Where is everyone else today, Peter? Is anyone in the room?" asked Nathaniel.

"Everyone's gone getting supplies or doing other things to prepare for the work ahead, save for Mary. She is upstairs making a stew," answered Peter.

Zoe, hearing the name Mary, wondered if it was the Mary that Nathanael and Phillip had just told the story of before they got to the city.

"Do you mean Mary the sister of Lazarus, whom you saw Jesus raise from the dead?" asked Zoe in a tone of awe.

The three disciples looked at one another and broadly smiled, as if asking one another who was going to answer her question. After several seconds had passed, Peter turned to Zoe who was now standing next to her brother. Looking at them both he said, "Wrong Mary. This is Mary, the mother of Jesus."

When Zoe heard that Jesus' mother was just a few steps from her, her mind momentarily shut down. She seemed impervious to everything around her. It was as if everything aside from the person of Jesus' mother no longer existed or mattered.

The four men watched as Zoe stoically walked past them like they were invisible, and slowly made her way up the stairs and through the doorway. As she breeched the entryway, Cornelius began to ascend the stairs more rapidly than his sister had. From the doorway, he watched Zoe walk toward a woman working over a stove on the far side of the room.

He saw the woman turn and notice Zoe. Mary was as beautiful as the first time Cornelius saw her over three years ago at Laban's wedding feast. She was striking in her middle age. She was wearing a medium-sized, blue-colored tunic tied at its center by a white rope. Her black hair, which fell well beyond her shoulders, was held back by a white ribbon. Looking into Zoe's approaching face, it appeared that Mary was reading deep into the younger woman's soul. It seemed Mary knew immediately that although Zoe had never met her son, she believed in him.

Cornelius watched as Mary held open her arms, inviting Zoe into her embrace. When Zoe saw Mary's extended arms, she ran into them and let out an audible sob.

"Welcome, my dear one. Our home is yours," Mary said, stroking the back of Zoe's head. As she did this, she looked up and smiled at Cornelius. "It's good to see you again, Cornelius."

"It is a privilege to be here with you, my lady," responded Cornelius, who, like his sister, was suspended in a moment of time that he hoped could be sustained indefinitely.

As quick as he wished for that time to stand still, a bellowing call from below brought it to a rapid end.

"Hey, Cornelius, how about a little help with this table!" came a shout from beyond the door.

Mary could sense Cornelius' hesitation and she reassured him with a smile. "You better go and help Peter before he gets out of sorts. I'll take care of this one. Besides, I'm anxious to see the table again as well," directed Mary as she continued to hug his sister Zoe.

With that, Cornelius bowed his head and stepped out of the room to help the other three men bring the table into the house.

Thirty-one

After meeting with Nadia and sharing with her Anthony's financial situation, Nadia encouraged Michael to begin the apartment hunting process with him. During that meeting, she asked him formally if he would be willing to serve as executor of the trust that was being set-up for Anthony with the hundred thousand dollars that was coming from his uncle's life insurance policy.

Michael was prepared for the question. He had been praying about it since Nadia first mentioned the possibility. Agreeing to the position of executor would initiate a very formal and long lasting relationship with Anthony. He questioned if he was the best person for the job. Was he ready at this point in his life, at this point of his loss, to obligate himself to such an important relationship? Each time Michael prayed on it, a vision of Debbie smiling would enter his mind. He took it as a strong sign that it was indeed the right course to take.

Aside from Debbie's seeming endorsement, Michael reflected on how much he had changed for the better since meeting Anthony. While he wasn't yet whole, Michael had begun to find not only meaning and a sense of purpose to his life, but he had also rediscovered his need to help others. The combination of all these factors resulted in Michael telling Nadia that he would help Anthony on all counts. He would help him find an apartment, would serve as his executor and, most importantly, that he would be there for Anthony for the long haul.

Michael was grateful coming out of his meeting with Nadia that none of the surprising, momentary feelings he had for her before surfaced while they were together. He was appreciative that, despite her attractiveness and caring personality, the only thing between them during the meeting was their mutual concern for Anthony.

The following week, after looking at about ten different apartments, Anthony and Michael found what they felt was the ideal place. It was located on Monroe and Twelfth Street just east of the Downtown area. The place was ideal for several reasons, but one of the most useful benefits of the location was that it was just four blocks from the light rail train, which could take Anthony to a station just two blocks from the Food City where he worked. This would save a great deal of travel time for Anthony when compared to taking the bus, as he had been doing. What sealed the deal for Anthony, however, was the view out of the picture window in the third story apartment where he could see the corner of Chase Field, home of the Diamondbacks.

A week later, with the help of Michael, Cookie, Carol, and Veronica, Anthony moved into his new one-bedroom home.

Thirty-two

Prior to bringing the table up the stairs, the men had to first move the larger table the group had been using for their meals several feet over in order to make space for the new arrival. After it was brought up the stairs and placed in the spot designated by Mary, Cornelius began to un-wrap the table from its several protective layers. Once its coverings were shed, Peter and Mary approached the table with reverent devotion. They placed their hands on it and allowed their palms to gently glide across its surface. There was no evidence of sadness on the faces of either Mary or Peter. What they displayed was a happy reverence. Mary maintained her composure even as she saw and touched the corner of table that held the largest bloodstains belonging to her son.

"Jesus' grandfather, Jacob, built this table. But truth be known, it was the Father of all who had it constructed," Mary said, her eyes fixed on the table.

"How's that?" asked Zoe, who once again showed no fear or awk-wardness in asking anyone any question.

Mary looked at Zoe and explained, "Jacob's hands were so crippled that he hardly could put on his own sandals, let alone build this or any other table. All the same, God used him to produce this very special table."

Mary's eyes moved back to the table's surface. After several seconds had passed, her gaze elevated and focused on both Zoe and Cornelius.

"It's amazing what God can do with the less than perfect, with the lame, and even with the sinful. We just have to listen and accept the miracles that He wants to give us. This table is indeed a miracle. I am so happy to see it once again."

Cornelius was amazed by her disposition. She had certainly heard the stories of what this table had witnessed. Nonetheless, she ran her hands across the wood stained by her son's very blood as he was viciously tortured, yet it seemed not to affect her. It was almost the opposite. She appeared to him to be, if anything, happy.

As though she sensed Cornelius' thoughts, she looked up at the former Roman soldier and said, "Having seen the scourging of my son, having seen his blood stain this very table, you might be wondering why it is that I am not saddened by its presence. Do you wonder this, Cornelius?"

Cornelius was about to tell Mary that he was in fact wondering that very same thing. But just as he was about to say it, another thought entered his mind.

"It's because he lives. That's why you're not saddened," Cornelius said, sharing his sudden thoughts with her and with everyone else in the room.

Mary flashed Cornelius a wide smile. "He does indeed live, and that is the reason I can smile in the presence of these stains. All the same, I wish no one the smallest measure of the pain that I had borne at the sight of my son's suffering and death. Nothing was worse, nothing could be worse. But as you said, because he lives my heart blooms with love."

Turning the conversation, she continued, "I remember you, Cornelius. I saw you looking in the window at the wedding. You witnessed my son's first sign right in front of this very table. I recall seeing your face as you watched. You looked very out of place in that uniform. Your eyes could not lie and it was clear that you were not a typical Roman soldier, nowhere near it. In fact, Jesus shared with me later that same night that you would become an integral part of his mission."

Cornelius' mind began to swim. He couldn't believe what he was hearing. Jesus had actually spoken about him to his mother that very night in Cana? And what did she mean about Jesus saying that he would become a part of his mission? Cornelius couldn't tell if he felt flattered or utterly terrified by these words.

"By the looks of you, I take it that Peter hasn't asked you yet?" Mary asked.

Mary's question only increased Cornelius' level of anxiety.

"He's only just arrived, Mary. I haven't had time to talk with him yet," said Peter.

At that moment, Cornelius heard several voices ascending the stairs.

Sensing that it was not the best time to go into detail about Mary's premature disclosure, Peter said to Cornelius, "Cornelius, don't worry one bit. We'll talk at dinner. Trust me, there is no reason to worry. Great things come to those whose faith is strong."

Thirty-three

It was about an hour after meeting the other eight male disciples of Jesus and three women, two more named Mary and the other named Martha, that the women asked everyone to wash up for dinner. During that hour before dinner, Cornelius and Zoe were received with incredible warmth and love by all. What seemed most unbelievable to Cornelius was that they all seemed to know a great deal about the table and were each so excited to see it and to touch it with their own hands. Several of them shared with Cornelius and Zoe stories that Jesus had told them about it. A young man who introduced himself as Thaddaeus told how the young Jesus would play beneath it, pretending it was his house, whenever his family had visited Laban's family in Cana. Simon, who Cornelius learned was a former Zealot, retold the story Mary briefly told of the table's creation by the crippled Jacob. While Mary's rendition of the story had lasted all of thirty seconds, Simon's version was told in broad and creative strokes, and it took over five minutes. With his hands waving and his voice fluctuating from whispers to shouts, Simon's love of the story was made evident. After hearing several similar stories from the others, it became clear to Cornelius that the table meant as much to each of them as it did to him. His table was no longer his table; it belonged to everyone.

As the women began to bring in the food, everyone took a seat on either side of the massively long table they had moved earlier. Lamb stew, legumes, bread, and an assortment of fruits, which included dates, pomegranates, and grapes, were brought to the large table. While the food was being brought out by the Marys, Martha and Zoe went around and filled everyone's cups with wine. When the women finished pouring the wine, they placed a newly filled reserve pitcher of it, along with extra loaves of bread, on the table Cornelius had once mistakenly considered his own.

During the meal there was a great deal of friendly conversation and joking. It reminded Cornelius of the larger family gatherings his own family would have to celebrate the major feriae, most particularly for Jupiter, when all sorts of aunts, uncles, and cousins would gather to celebrate the holiday.

The focus of most of the conversation was centered on the larger group learning all there was to know about Cornelius and Zoe. Cornelius felt as if he were in the presence of people more famous than the great actors and orators of Rome. And it was these great men and women, who served and were selected by Jesus himself, who now turned to him and asked him question after question about his family, his views on Rome, and about his own encounters with Jesus. He was overcome by the immediate bond he felt amongst this group. He couldn't help but feel that the bond was in some way being extended to him and to his sister Zoe. While excited by everything happening in front of him, a twinge of sadness entered his thoughts. How we wished Prisca could be there with him.

Dinner was still in full stride when Peter rose and asked for everyone's attention. Upon his request, the room acquiesced to a state of silence. From where he sat, he spoke a blessing in Hebrew, "Blessed are You, Lord our God, Ruler of the universe, who brings forth bread from the earth."

He followed this blessing with a second one, also said in Hebrew. "Blessed are You, Lord our God, Ruler of the universe, who creates the fruit of the tree."

After a short pause, Peter addressed everyone at the table. "My brothers and sisters, it was but a short time ago that our Lord Jesus, the Messiah, the Anointed One of God, sat at the very center of this table. He shared many things with us that we didn't understand at the time, but which have been made clearer to us since we received the Holy Spirit. And so it is that we do now what Jesus has asked us to do, that we continue to receive him as he himself so desires to be received."

Peter then leaned over to the center of the table and took a loaf of bread and brought it in front of himself. Raising it up so all in the room could see, he said, "This is the body of our Lord Jesus, broken for us and for the lives of many. Take and eat."

Peter then split the loaf in half and passed half of it to his left, and half to his right after taking a small piece for himself. When the bread was passed to Cornelius and Zoe, each took a piece and, like the others around the table, ate the bread offered to them. After the bread was passed and eaten, Peter motioned for Martha to bring him the pitcher of wine from the table of Jacob. After filling his cup, Peter once again stood so all could see. He raised his cup now filled with wine, and once again addressed the group.

"Jesus then filled his cup, this very cup. Holding it up, just as I am now, he said, 'this is my blood shed for each of you, the blood of a new and everlasting covenant.'"

After taking a sip, Peter passed the cup to his right. Each of the disciples took a sip and passed it to the next. After taking a drink and passing it to Zoe, Cornelius became overwhelmed with emotion. He didn't know exactly why, but as he looked around the table he saw that he wasn't alone. In the deep silence of the room, Cornelius saw tears on the cheeks of several of those at the table, including Zoe.

....

Cornelius anticipated that at some point in the evening Peter would pull him aside to discuss in detail what Mary had made reference to earlier in the day. That opportunity came almost immediately after dinner was finished. While Zoe helped the other women clear the table, Peter invited Cornelius to come out onto the patio with him. As they stepped out of the room, the stunning view welcomed them both to the beginning of that evening. The sun had begun to set and the sky was set in crimson strands. The second floor view gave Cornelius the opportunity to see the majestic southeastern wall of the city as the light of the sun highlighted it. The perfect tapestry of the approaching evening couldn't have complemented the day's events any better, thought Cornelius.

As they both looked out on the wall of Jerusalem, now glowing in an orange-red hue, Peter put his arm around Cornelius' shoulder. Still looking out at the wall, he asked him, "Do you now believe, Cornelius, without a shadow of a doubt that Jesus himself is the Messiah, not only the promised one of the Jews, but the very son of the one and only God that ever was?"

Turning to look at Peter, Cornelius affirmed, "Of this I have no doubt. But as I say this, there is so much I need to learn about him and about the Jewish faith."

Peter smiled. "You will learn what you desire because you have no doubt, because you believe. All of us, the disciples in the room and others, we believe because we saw with our own eyes." Peter paused as if he were reflecting on a past moment. The level of his voice dropped slightly and cracked just a bit as he continued, "We saw Jesus die a brutal death and then come back to life. We believe because we saw him leave the earth before our very eyes as he returned to heaven. I admire you, Cornelius. Your faith is amazing! Without having seen what we have witnessed, without even being Jewish, a Roman soldier at that, you believe! You are the first of many who haven't seen the risen Lord, but who are called to believe. You see, therein lies our mission."

Cornelius was flattered but didn't totally understand what Peter meant by this mission. He wondered what the mission he was speaking of entailed exactly and if he was to be a part of it.

"Tell me, Peter, what specifically do you mean by our mission?" Cornelius asked.

Peter squared his body with Cornelius'. As he placed his hands on each of Cornelius' shoulders, he answered, "The mission of the twelve is to set out to different lands and to share with the world the gift of life that Jesus has offered to all who believe. We are to tell the world about all we have witnessed and all we have learned from the Messiah. You, in your belief, demonstrate that believing without seeing is very achievable. Of course, I didn't need you to demonstrate it to believe it, as it is Jesus who is setting us out on this mission and he would never do so if there weren't an abundant harvest ready to be reaped."

"So when are you setting out for this mission, who will be going where?" asked Cornelius, whose own enthusiasm for this mission began to make his heart pump faster.

"We have been mapping all that out and are working on those details. We hope to all leave to different areas of the world next week," answered Peter, wrapping his arm around Cornelius' shoulders again.

Gazing at the Jerusalem Wall, Peter said, "Correct me if I'm wrong, Centurion, but my guess is that you're wondering about your role in all this."

Cornelius smiled. "Yeah, you might say that I am more than just a little curious on that."

Turning to face Cornelius once again, Peter began to explain to Cornelius the role they wished him to play in their mission. "I'm sure you recall over dinner the short break in the meal where I took the bread and wine and repeated the words that Jesus had said at that very table the last time we ate with him?"

"Of course. Those words spoke to me like no others have. But I must admit, I don't understand why they had the impact on me that they did," answered Cornelius.

"They truly are the words of life and we'll have plenty more time to discuss just what those words mean and the ramifications they have for the world. Suffice it to say for now, that of all the things Jesus wants us to share with the world, none is more life giving than believing in him and in the partaking of this breaking of the bread and sharing of the cup."

"So how does this involve me?" asked Cornelius.

"One of the things we learned from Jesus is that people respond well to that which they can see and touch. Thomas himself wouldn't believe that Jesus was alive until he put his fingers in his very wounds! We would love to purchase that enormous table from the landlord here and then use it when we share in the breaking of the bread and sharing of the cup. I mean, could you imagine being able to show the people—here sat Jesus and here he unwrapped this gift for the first time! Alas, the table is too big to bring anywhere…"

"But the table I carry also has a visual narrative that might be useful in your mission," interjected Cornelius.

"Precisely!" answered Peter. "Don't get me wrong, the story and his love is vastly enough. But as you saw in that room today, your table means a great deal to each and every person inside that room, as I'm sure it will for all who encounter it."

"So what, specifically, do you need me to do?" asked Cornelius, who was more than ready to serve the cause in whatever way he could.

"Once we leave and go to our separate assigned places to preach the words of Jesus, we would like you to visit each of us and our new communities with the table. Bring it to this city and to this disciple for a while, then bring it to the next, and so on and so on. Of course, we will be taking up collections wherever we are and we will be able to provide for you and your family. I know I'm asking a lot of you, Cornelius, and we would understand you saying no."

Placing both hands on Cornelius' shoulders again, Peter asked, "All the same, would you help us in this way with our mission?"

Cornelius didn't hesitate in his response, "It will be a privilege and an honor."

Peter smiled broadly and brought Cornelius in for a hug. As they embraced, Peter added, "In addition to becoming our table bearer, your own story about the conversion of a Roman Centurion will also be a powerful witness to those we hope to make the Lord's own. That is, if you are willing to share it."

"Again, Peter, it would be a true privilege to do so," answered Cornelius.

"You are a good man, Cornelius. We are honored by your willingness to serve our Lord Jesus."

As the men pulled back from the embrace, Cornelius asked, "Will it be okay if I bring my wife, Prisca, and or Zoe on these trips?"

"It most certainly would be okay. Zoe is a wonderful lady and I can't wait to meet Prisca."

"Prisca loves Jesus and will be ecstatic to learn what it is you would like us to do."

As they reentered the room, the rest of the disciples and Zoe had started to form a circle and were joining hands. Peter motioned Cornelius for them to join in.

Once all hands were joined, James, the son of Alpheus, began to speak, "Our Father who art in heaven…"

At which point everyone else joined in and said the following words in unison, "Hallowed be thy name. Thy kingdom come, thy will be done. On earth as it is in heaven. Give us this day our daily bread and forgive us our trespasses as we forgive those who trespass against us. Lead us not into temptation, but deliver us from evil. Amen."

For the second time that evening, both Cornelius and Zoe were moved to tears by words they had never heard before, but from which they were certain the heart of love resided.

Thirty-four

The Diamondbacks game finished up at about 9:15 p.m. They had just beaten the Cubs six to five in a game loaded with a lot of exciting back and forth offense. Michael was split by the game's ending. Since his family origins hailed from the Chicago area, he always held a place in his heart for the Cubbies. Anthony, on the other hand, was elated by the Diamondback's victory.

As they walked the six and a half blocks from the stadium to Anthony's new apartment, the conversation quickly shifted from the game-winning homer by Paul Goldschmidt to something that appeared to have been on Anthony's mind for some time.

"Michael Fortunato," began Anthony, before he was quickly interrupted and corrected.

"Michael. Remember, just call me Michael because we're friends."

"Michael, I have been thinking about a lot of things. Well, maybe not a lot of things like many, many things, but really only two things," said Anthony.

"If you care to share, I'm all ears," said Michael. When Anthony didn't immediately respond, Michael inquired, "Does one of those two things have to do with what's in your backpack and the story that you mentioned before?"

Michael had to admit, he had become increasingly curious about the contents of the backpack that Anthony always carried with him. He had even brought it with him to the game that night. Michael had thought it might not get past security, or at least they might open it up so he could finally get a peek at what was inside. He was greatly surprised that security didn't even look inside it. It just went through the metal detector and all that was said from the security man was, "Enjoy the game."

Anthony's previous mentions of the contents of his backpack and its alluded-to story, along with his uncle's cryptic message concerning finding the right person to share it with, worked together to increase Michael's level of interest.

"Yes, Michael, one of the two things is about the blessing and its story. I've been thinking about it and Uncle George was right. He said that I needed to share the story with someone since I am the last Velario and that I would know in my heart who that was. My heart has been talking with me, Michael, and it's telling me that you're the person I am supposed to tell," revealed Anthony.

Michael was both touched and intrigued. He truly had no idea what this blessing was or what kind of story Anthony had to tell. Anthony had built up a tremendous amount of suspense around the contents of his backpack without being aware that he had.

"Well, buddy, I feel honored, truly honored that you want to share this with me and believe me, I want to see what it is and to hear your story. But you said that you had been thinking about two things lately. What's the second thing that's been on your mind?"

They had arrived at the apartment building as Michael asked his question. Anthony turned and, in very rare fashion, looked Michael directly in the eye and said, "You never talk about Debbie. I heard from Cookie and Carol that you were married and that you loved each other very much and that Debbie died. Can you tell me about Debbie, Michael?"

Michael was stunned by the question. So unexpected yet so innocently presented, the query hit him like the combination of a prizefighter's punch to the gut, coupled with a child's request for a goodnight story. Anthony's mention of Debbie's name and departure from this earth almost caused him to become emotional. Michael tucked the bottom of his lip and took in a couple of very deep breaths through his nose, successfully keeping at bay any responsive outbursts. Anthony was about to open up and trust him. Michael thought there was no reason why he shouldn't return the favor.

"Have a seat there on the stairs, my friend. I will tell you about my darling, my life, and my bride." It was reflex that Michael quoted Poe's "Annabel Lee" at the moment. Since her death, that line played over and over in his head. Its truth resonated through his core since that was exactly what she was to him. As they took a seat on the apartment steps, both men looked straight out across the moderately busy street.

"So you want to know about Debbie? Well, my friend, let me tell you about my Debbie."

Michael took in another deep breath and then began to openly share with Anthony a little bit about the love of his life.

"I met her in high school. She didn't know me, but I knew who she was. We both attended Seton Catholic High School in Chandler. I first noticed Debbie during lunch one sweltering afternoon. She was beautiful. I tell you, Anthony, she almost stopped my heart when I looked at her. She had short, shiny brown hair with blonde highlights. Her skin always seemed so tan and incredibly smooth. And, dare I say, she had an incredible pair of legs! Why Catholic High Schools put their girls in skirts, I'll never know!" Michael paused to gauge his audience.

Anthony began to smile at his reference to legs and skirts.

Pausing a second longer he added, "But do you know what attracted me most to her, Anthony?"

"That she was so beautiful?" answered Anthony.

"Actually no, but yes, in a way also. Don't get me wrong, her stunning looks certainly were of high appeal to me! But what attracted me most to Debbie was who she was as a person. What I noticed before I even knew her was that although she was very beautiful, she hung out with girls who were not all that good looking, by the shallow world's standards, and who were not all that popular. She certainly could have hung out with the most popular and beautiful girls in the school if she had wanted. Instead, she hung out with the girls who were the most genuine and most real, not those who were popular just because they were beautiful. What attracted me most to Debbie, you might say, was her character. Does that make sense to you?"

"Yes, it does. My uncle always said to me, 'Be more concerned with your character than your reputation, because your character is what you really are, while your reputation is merely what others think you are.' He said that Coach John Wooden always said it, but I don't know who he is," answered Anthony.

"Wow! You have a fantastic memory! Do you know what that John Wooden quote means?" asked Michael.

Anthony didn't hesitate in his reply. "It means to be who you really are and not to be a phony."

"You are correct, young sir! Debbie was definitely herself. High character, honest, and a true friend," Michael said with enthusiasm.

Anxious to hear more about Debbie, Anthony asked, "So if you didn't know Debbie and she didn't know you, how did you ever meet?"

"We had a mutual friend named Cindy Thompson who thought that we would make a good couple. So she arranged for us to meet one Friday night at a school dance. Now mind you, I knew who Debbie was, but she didn't have a clue who I was! So that night I'm coming down a long hall, and walking in from the other direction, a ways down the hall, is Cindy and Debbie. As soon as Cindy points me out, Debbie turns and runs into the girl's bathroom!"

Once again, Michael looked over at Anthony. Instead of a smile, his face displayed the look of utter surprise.

"What, she didn't like you, Michael? Did she ever come out of the girl's bathroom?" asked Anthony, distraught.

Michael began to chuckle. "Yes, Anthony, after about five minutes she came out. Like you, I thought for a minute that she must not like me and that's why she ran. Turns out it was because she was very shy. Anyway, she emerges from the bathroom with Cindy leading her by the arm. I can't remember exactly what we first said to each other, and I know this is going to sound corny, but it was truly love at first sight. We hung out and talked the entire dance. After the dance, we went to a post-dance party at a friend's house and talked and talked some more. From that day on we were inseparable, like white on rice. We did everything together and always wanted to be together."

"Did you get married right after the dance?" Anthony asked innocently.

"Well, no. You see, we were just juniors in high school at the time. But I tell you this, buddy, I felt certain then and there that someday I would marry her," explained Michael in a reflective and pleasant manner.

"So when did you marry her?"

"Five years later. After high school we went off to college and right after we finished college we were married."

"Cookie said that Debbie could sing really pretty and that you were all in a band together. Can you tell me about that, Michael?" asked Anthony, eager to know more.

The thought of the band, their shared love of music, the countless gigs they did together, and most especially their last show, caused a sudden well of loneliness to burst within Michael's heart. A thousand shows, a thousand looks and smiles at each other as they performed all presented themselves before him. Oh, how she could sing. Oh, how beautiful she was. *My darling, my darling, my life and my bride, how I miss you!*

Michael stood up, tilted his head to the right, and swept his hand through his hair in hopes of composing himself. A single tear escaped and slipped down the side of his cheek. As the tear fell from his face, Michael felt a tug on his t-shirt. Looking down at Anthony's face, he saw the usual blank affect to which he had become accustomed. All the same, the tug on the shirt meant something significant, as reaching out in any physical way was highly unusual for Anthony.

"I'm sorry, Anthony. It's just—it's just that I loved her." Catching his use of past tense, he corrected himself as two more tears began their journey down his face. "I love her, I love her so much and—and now she's gone." Michael sat back down on the stairs next to Anthony.

"In answer to your question, my friend, Debbie sang as beautifully as she was."

Silence stood between the two men. One seemingly not knowing what to say, the other too inflicted to say any more. Anthony broke the silence first with a double tap on Michael's shoulder, intended to be strokes of comfort.

"She sounds wonderful, Michael. I can see that you really loved her. Let's not talk about her anymore because it makes you sad. Maybe some other time you can tell me more. How about I tell you something about love, something that will make you happy, Michael?"

Michael turned his head toward Anthony, his face still damp from the tears. He responded with a grin that showed his appreciation for the insight and tenderness of his friend.

"That sounds great, Anthony. Lord knows I could use it," answered Michael.

"Let's go up to my apartment then, and I will tell you the story and I will show you the blessing. Both are all about love," Anthony said with confidence and reassurance.

Thirty-five

After entering the apartment, Anthony pointed to the couch that had been in his family as long as he could remember. It was of a very worn, brown leather variety, the parchment of which had become soft and supple, like a worn-in baseball glove from its extensive use throughout the years.

"Sit there, Michael. I always tell the story on that couch," directed Anthony.

Michael was a little thrown off by Anthony's words. Seeking to clarify his confusion he asked, "I thought that I was the one, the only one you were going to tell the story to? What do mean when you say you always tell the story?"

"I tell the story every night. I promised my uncle and father that I would. The story has been told by a Velario for a very, very long time. Uncle George told me that the story is told in an oral tradition and that it has been told that way, word for word he said, since near the beginning of the story. I am the storyteller now and I say it every night, word for word, so the story will stay alive." Following his explanation, Anthony took a seat on the couch, placing the backpack between his feet as he did.

"So are you telling me that the words you say tonight are the same words that have been told since the story's beginning?" asked Michael, who was now more intrigued than ever.

"Yes, the story has been the same since the story was first told. But, Michael, this is not a pretend story, it is a true story. Every word in the story happened and is true. Uncle George said that lives have been changed and will continue to be changed, not so much by the story, but by the blessing." Anthony's usually blank face had been replaced by a more serious and direct demeanor.

Michael was further confused by Anthony's use of the word blessing. He had thought when he used the word before that it was in reference to the story. With his head beginning to swim, he asked his young friend, "I thought that the blessing was the story?"

Anthony began to laugh, something he rarely did. After a few moments of hearty and affectionate laughter, Anthony revealed the difference to Michael. "The blessing is what I carry with me in my backpack. It's what the story is about. It has been called the blessing for a long time because that's what it really is. Would you like to see it, Michael? Would you like to touch it, Michael Fortunato?"

As Anthony defined what the blessing was, for some unknown reason Michael felt his heart open up, as though it was waiting to be filled. Whatever this blessing was, Michael most certainly wanted it revealed to him.

"Yes, Anthony, I'd very much like to see it and to hold it if that's okay?"

"Of course it's okay. Uncle George told me that my heart would tell me when to share the blessing and the story, and who to share the blessing and the story with. My heart told me you're that person."

As the last word left his mouth, Anthony bent over and unzipped the backpack that he had placed between his legs on the floor. Michael leaned in, anxious to see what the blessing was. Anthony pulled out a piece of dark wood from the backpack. It appeared to be about fifteen by ten inches in width and length, and about three inches in thickness. The piece of wood seemed close to a square shape with the exception of one of its longer sides, which had a noticeable five-inch depression in it. It looked like it used to be a part of something larger, though all of its sides and edges were smooth.

So this is it? This is the blessing? Michael thought to himself. His momentary disappointment quickly subsided as Anthony handed Michael what he thought was just a piece of smoothed wood.

"This is the blessing, the miracle table of Jacob," said Anthony as he reverently transferred the blessing from his hands into Michael's hands.

Michael's mind didn't register Anthony's mention of the miracle table of Jacob. Once the blessing was in his hands, he became joyful nothingness. His eyes closed as his heart opened. He suddenly felt as though he was not there, and yet never so present. He felt himself breathe in deeply and slowly. With every inhalation, with every slight expansion of his chest, a deep sense of peace entered into his person. When he exhaled, none of that peace left him. It continued to fill him and was absorbed by every tissue of his body, by every sense of his soul. Just as he felt that peace, experienced its calm, it became trumped by another distinct feeling; no, by another distinct reality. He felt chills of unadulterated joy ripple through his body. The chills ebbed as the warmth of a thousand hugs began to encompass him. He felt as though every inch of him had become a single smile. What made no sense before, now did. Where he once felt alone, he now felt total connection. Peace was still there, but it had become overshadowed by something that he could only label as—what could only be—love.

Michael's transcendence was interrupted by words that never rang truer to him. They were words he had heard before, but only understood now.

"Love has come, Michael," whispered Anthony, yet it was heard with such forcefulness.

"Yes," was all that Michael could say in response.

The feelings of peace and love remained with Michael. While not as strong as they were moments before, Michael knew that his encounter with love, with the blessing, would have a lasting and immeasurable effect on his life going forward.

Anthony had known that Michael's encounter with the table would have a deep impact on Michael's well-being, just as it had for others for centuries. He knew that Michael was the person with whom he had to share his story and the blessing because he knew just how much he needed to see it, to hear it, and to touch it. The same love that had just entered into Michael spoke to Anthony's heart and told him Michael was the one.

"I want to tell you the story now, Michael, the story of the miracle table of Jacob. But I always hold it when I say it," said Anthony.

Michael didn't want to part with the blessing. But out of respect for its keeper, for the person who provided him the gift of amazing love, he extended his hands and the table fragment to Anthony.

Anthony suddenly understood the depths of love that had come upon Michael through the blessing. Even though he always held the table during his recital of the story, it occurred to him that Michael needed to hold it tonight much more than he did.

"Actually, I think you should hold it while I tell you the story, Michael, but sometimes I might reach over and touch it while I tell the story. Is that okay with you, Michael?"

If it were possible for a heart to visibly glow from one's chest, Michael's most certainly would have in hearing those words.

"Thank you, Anthony, that sounds wonderful," said Michael, returning the blessing to his lap. As he held the table on the sides of its shorter length, Anthony's hand came to rest on its top center. After pressing it there for a long fifteen seconds, he began the story.

"This is the story of the miracle table of Jacob, father of Joseph, grandfather of Jesus Christ, the Messiah.

"Jacob and his son, Joseph of Nazareth, ran a successful carpentry shop. A table of cedar had been ordered by their most loyal and wealthy customer, Laban of Cana. Upon the return of Joseph and his wife, Mary, the mother of our Lord, from the census in Bethlehem, Joseph informed his father of a dream he had. In this dream an angel warned him that Herod would be pursuing them, seeking to kill their infant son, Jesus. Jacob, whose wife Rebecca had shared with him on the evening of her death a similar account of an encounter with angels, immediately believed his son and sent them to a relative in Egypt where they would be safe.

"At this time, Jacob hadn't been able to construct any works of wood for several years due to the pain and twisted deformities of both his hands. Jacob prayed on the stacks of cedar that were to become Laban's table and fell asleep on top of them while still praying. When he woke, he found his hands healed. He built Laban's table and, as he always had, he etched the words Rebecca had requested to accompany all of Jacob's works on the underside of the table's corner: Love has come. Once completed, Jacob's hands became painful and deformed again."

At the story's introduction, Michael's heart rate increased. Chills of joy danced through his body as he realized the loving origins of the worn piece of wood, which after many centuries, now took its residency in his very hands. Michael correctly deduced that the blessing was a remnant of this historic and holy table Anthony had just revealed. Michael thought that this revelation certainly explained the unexplainable peace and connection with love's creation that came to him upon touching what he had thought was nothing more than a block of wood. With this revelation, Michael became even more attentive to each and every word of the story.

"Joseph and his family returned to Nazareth after spending more than three years in Egypt. Being a close friend with Laban and his family, Joseph, Mary, and the young boy Jesus often visited them in Cana. Young Jesus was drawn to the table built through a miracle of God by his grandfather. He would play at the table and often made a fortress out of it by covering it with blankets and hiding within it.

"Many years later, Laban held a wedding feast at his Cana farm for his granddaughter, Rachel. Mary and Jesus, along with some of his early disciples, Phillip and Nathanael, also known as Bartholomew, attended the celebration. Due to his vocal disdain for Rome, the authorities sent a Centurion named Cornelius Velius to the feast to spy on Laban and to listen for any words of subversion they could use to bring formal charges against him. While Cornelius witnessed no such words on the part of Laban, what he did witness led to his conversion to what became known as the Way. That evening the person of Jesus called to his heart. After being drawn to the Savior simply by being present to him, he watched as six large jars of water that were placed in front of the table were turned into wine by Jesus.

"After this encounter, Cornelius Velius and his wife, Prisca, went out of their way to hear Jesus preach. When Laban was arrested by the Romans under the charge of treason, all his property was confiscated and was to be sold at auction. Because Cornelius served as a quartermaster, he was able to purchase the miracle table of Jacob prior to auction. Before he claimed it, the Tenth Legion from Jerusalem took it from the warehouse where it had been stored, unware that it had been sold. Cornelius and two of his soldiers, one of whom was named Manus, went to Jerusalem to re-acquire the table. The table was located in the courtyard of Pilot. It stood just a few feet away from the pillar where Cornelius witnessed the brutal scourging of our Lord, Jesus Christ. Cornelius watched as our Savior's blood splattered on top of the table his grandfather and his Father in heaven had created."

Looking down at the table remnant, Michael noticed what he thought were darker areas of the wood. He was about to hold the fragment up closer to his eyes to determine if the darker spots might possibly be the stained blood of Jesus. But before he could, Anthony's hand came down on the wood. His fingers instinctively found their way and slowly traced the darker parts of the blessing.

Although he didn't need any additional confirmation, Anthony seemingly read Michael's mind and whispered, "Yes, it is his blood."

As Anthony lifted his hand from the table and continued his story, the fingers on Michael's hands quickly dropped to the table fragment and began to trace the salvific stains of the Lamb of God. Mesmerized, he was misplaced in a significantly expanded moment. A tear of adoration and complete surrender formed and fell from his eye. He watched as his tear splashed against one of the stained areas of the table. Michael was captured by the thought of his tears becoming entwined in the very majesty of the Lamb. In that instant, through the sweetly stained wood, Michael realized for the first time the totality of Christ's passion. In that moment of complete clarity, Michael offered up his own loss, his own suffering. As he did, Michael felt as if heaven itself rejoiced and embraced him.

Somehow, he could still hear Anthony speak while this other gracious reality played inside of him. Michael's outer person heard Anthony tell the part of the story of Cornelius and Zoe meeting with the Apostles and agreeing to serve in their mission as table bearers. While his ears took in the sounds, it was his heart that defined every sound and non-sound. *How beautiful,* he thought. *How pure, how true. Love as love can only be.*

His focus to the world around him slowly returned as Anthony began to tell about Cornelius and Prisca's first mission.

"Two months after the Apostles were dispatched to their missionary assignments, Zoe, Cornelius, Prisca, and their infant son, Johan, set out with the table to meet with Thomas in Medea. They spent a month with Thomas and those in the community who had come to know Jesus as the Messiah. They were warmly received and all were glad to hear their witness and to see the table that Jesus himself had loved. The table was used in the breaking of the bread and in the sharing of the cup over which Thomas presided in the place of Jesus.

"After returning to Cana, they rested. Cornelius and Zoe next set out to Lydia to the mission area of Matthew. Prisca and Johan stayed home since the previous trip proved to be too much for the infant. The table bearers were amazed when they arrived in Matthew's community. There were easily seven times the number of believers there than had been with Thomas. Time had allowed the seed to take root and the harvest was becoming ever bountiful. As it had been in Medea, the table was used for the breaking of the bread and sharing of the cup, with Matthew serving in the place of Jesus. While the table was in the community's midst, a man named Nariman, who had been blind at birth, regained his sight when he prayed, believed, and touched the table. Other healings took place, as well, through the people's belief in the blessing of Matthew and, some felt, from the stains embedded in the table."

Being true to his pre-story direction, Anthony reached out his hand nearest the table and placed it on top of it. It seemed to Michael as though Anthony needed to regain some type of fuel or energy through his contact with the table, which helped him to continue the story. After a few seconds, Anthony lifted his hand and continued.

"Cornelius and Zoe returned to Cana to spend time with their family. Both the communities they had visited were generous and made gracious donations to support Cornelius' family. After three months, Cornelius, Prisca, and the young Johan went to Pamphylia and to the community gathered by the Holy Spirit through Phillip. There, Phillip presided over the table on the Lord's Day, in the breaking of the bread and sharing of the cup. They spent three months with the people of Phillip and were met with many tears upon their departure. As had occurred in Lydia, many healings took place.

"In the year 48, Cornelius was summoned by Peter to Jerusalem for a great meeting that was held with the other Apostles and with Paul, the preacher to the Gentiles, along with his disciple Barnabas. Zoe accompanied Cornelius to Jerusalem since Prisca had just given birth to twins named Peter and Mary. Before the meeting began, the elders assembled first to read from scripture and to share together the Lord's meal. It was Peter, the chief amongst the elders, who on the Lord's Day stood in the place of Jesus and who gave the blessing, broke the bread, and shared the cup of the new covenant. After the table was used for the breaking of the bread, it was then used by Peter's scribe to record the events of the meeting. After a much heated argument and debate, it was decided that the Gentile faithful would not be required to undergo circumcision nor be required to adhere to the same dietary restrictions as their Jewish brethren.

"In addition to those Apostles and events already cited, the table bearers, in their various configurations, visited several other communities of believers including those led by Nathanael, Thaddeus, Matthias, and James, the leader in Jerusalem. Each community welcomed both the table and those bringing it with great love. As in all previous visits, the table was utilized on the Lord's Day in the breaking of the bread and sharing of the cup.

"In the year 64, Cornelius and Zoe came to visit Peter in Rome shortly after much of the city had burned. Peter was delighted by the visit of his friends and of the table. Fearing for their safety and the safety of the table, he cut their visit short due to Nero's venomous persecution of the followers of Jesus. It had become so intense that the reading of the scriptures and breaking of the bread had to be held underground. Two days after the table bearers left the city, Peter was captured and crucified for not surrendering his faith."

Once again, Anthony paused and placed his hands on the table fragment. This time it seemed to Michael that Anthony was reverencing the brave death and unfailing faith of the man Jesus had selected to lead his church. After a substantial pause, Anthony resumed the story.

"The very next year, Cornelius' advancing years prevented him from traveling with the table. Johan took Cornelius' place as the primary table bearer and the second keeper of the story. Along with his brother, Peter, his sister, Mary, and Aunt Zoe, they continued to bring the table to the followers of Jesus.

"Word made it to Johan and to Peter that the last remaining Apostle, John, requested the presence of the table. Together the brothers, along with the table, made the long journey to Greece and to the island of Patmos where John had been placed in exile on account of his professed faith in the resurrection of Jesus. When they arrived at the encampment where John had been provided a small house, they were met by an old Centurion whose job it was to screen any visitors wishing to see any of the exiled. When the old soldier stepped up to meet the brothers, his heart susurrated. Before him stood two Roman men, both with blue eyes, greatly resembling a man he once knew and deeply respected. He also noticed that in the wagon they drew was a large, covered object that was tightly tied down.

"*Could it be?* thought the Centurion.

"Before the men could introduce themselves to the old Centurion, the soldier queried them, almost certain of the answer he was about to receive.

"'Are you men from Cana and might your father be Cornelius Velius?'

"Johan and Peter were stunned. Before they could answer, the soldier made a follow-up prediction.

"'And my guess is that you're carting behind you a table.'

"Johan finally spoke, saying, 'How do you know these things, sir?'

"The Centurion introduced himself to the table bearers as Manus, a man who had not only served under their father's command, but who was one of the two men who had helped their father retrieve the table after witnessing the scourging of Jesus. Manus had become a believer in Christ and a secret disciple of John. Manus brought Johan and Peter to meet John.

"The sons of Cornelius stayed on Patmos for three months where the table served its communal function and also served as a desk where the Apostle John wrote a book he called a gift from heaven."

Michael looked down once again at the blessing. Instead of thoughts, for thoughts left room for doubts, certainties filled his mind. On this very piece of wood was the blood of Jesus, the fingerprints of Peter and the other Apostles, and impressions from the original pen of Revelations.

So in awe of these things, Michael only half heard Anthony's words of the table's travels during the second century. He recalled hearing something about the sons of Johan and Peter bringing the table to Ignatius, the Bishop in

Syria, and how they marched with him to Rome allowing him to use the table to write his final letters to the Churches he loved before he was put to death by the command of Trajan. Still in a state of awe, Michael only caught fragments of the story regarding the table's visits to Polycarp in Smyrna and to Clement in Alexandria by the table bearers and great grandchildren of Cornelius.

With Anthony well into the third century tales of the table, Michael's external focus returned and he listened once again to each word Anthony spoke.

"Though Christians had been greatly persecuted almost from their beginning, the year two hundred and fifty through the early years of the fourth century brought with them a torturous reign of imperial hatred. Led by the consecutive reigns of Trajen, Valerian, and Diocletian, Christians were martyred at alarming rates. Two table bearers, decedents of Cornelius, were brought to the Colosseum during the reign of Valerian and were killed for their testimony and for perpetuating what the Empire called fanciful lies regarding a so-called miracle table. Due to this intense persecution, the next eldest Velius, Lucius, brought the table back to the family town of Melfi, some three hundred miles outside of Rome. Due to Valerian's pursuit of the table, Lucius took the table and hid it in a cave within the Lattari Mountains and waited for the persecutions to subside. In order to protect the location of the table, he told no one where it had been hidden. In fear of the repercussion that torture might bring, he extended that silence even to his family. The persecution of the Christians, however, only intensified at the hands of Diocletian. So brutal and targeted was his hatred of Christians that Lucius and his siblings were forced on the run while the table remained in its cave. For decades, the closest anyone got to the table was hearing its story being told by Lucius and his brothers. Lucius was finally captured in Sicily. The evening before he was beheaded he sent word to his brother, John Mark, of a map he had drawn which revealed the location of the cave where the table was hidden. The map was concealed in the top of the internal doorframe at the house of their Aunt Joanna's in Melfi.

"John Mark and his brother James returned to Melfi and located the map. As they set out the next morning to find the cave, they were confronted by two Roman soldiers who had been looking for them and for other Christians in the area. The brothers had placed the map in a bag they had draped over their mule along with other supplies. Seeing the soldier's approach, John Mark slapped the flank of the mule sending it running in one direction while he fled in another, and James in yet another direction. While John Mark was captured and later brought to Rome for execution, James managed to escape. Without the map, James tried to recreate what his eyes had seen for only a short time. Drawing a map from memory, he set out to try to find the cave and the table.

"James searched for the cave, which he called the tabernacle of the table, his entire life. After his death, his son Decius and daughter Deborah both kept the story as well as the pursuit of the table. Using the map of their father, both searched for the cave nearly their entire lives. At the age of sixty, Deborah had a dream in which a young and beautiful girl, no more than fourteen years of age, appeared to her holding a white lily in her left hand and two arrows and a small ship's anchor in her right hand. The beautiful young girl told her that she would show her the location of the cave if she would first burn the map James had created. Deborah woke from the dream and immediately set the map on fire. The next day was overcast and rain seemed likely. Undeterred, she and Decius, along with his son Simon, headed toward the mountain the following morning. Through the overcast skies, a single ray of the sun pierced through the clouds and lit up a very tiny section of the mountain. Certain that it was a sign provided by the beautiful girl in her dream, Deborah persuaded her brother and his son to follow her to that spot of the mountain. When they arrived at the place of light, they were amazed when they found a cave they had never seen before. Entering it, they found the table. To ensure it was their table, Decius looked beneath each of its corners where he found the mark of Jacob. On top of the table they found a single, freshly cut, white lily. The year was 457."

Anthony once again paused to touch the table. Michael wondered if the finding of the white lily had produced in Anthony the same powerful emotion which he himself had just experienced after hearing of this miracle.

Anthony continued, "Over the next seventy years, the table stayed in the family home of its respective bearer. While the story of the table continued to be told as it had been since Cornelius' time, the outside world, due to its century-long absence, no longer sought out its presence as in previous times. Nonetheless, miracles, spiritual and physical, continued to occur within the table's vicinity.

"In the year 530, led by the Lord's calling, Cornelius Velius III joined the Brothers of Benedict at the abbey of Monte Cassino, which was located about halfway between Melfi and Rome. There he told Benedict the story of the blessing. After praying on what he had heard from Cornelius III, Benedict asked the young monk to return home and to bring the table back to the monastery. When Cornelius III returned with the table, Benedict placed his hand upon it and immediately felt overcome by its authority and authenticity. The following Sunday Mass at the monastery was said using the table of Jacob as its altar. During its time at Monte Cassino, word of its origins spread throughout Italy and many visitors came to see it. Many healings were reported by the faith of those who had come with reverence to the table.

"Word of the table's existence made its way to the Pope. In the year 590, during the time of a local plague, Pope Pelagius II requested that the table be brought to him in Rome so that he could venerate it and to celebrate Mass upon it. Mathias Velius, a monk and current table bearer at Monte Cassino, departed the monastery with the blessing and headed for Rome. When he arrived, he learned that Pope Pelagius II had just died as a result of the plague, which had decimated much of the surrounding lands. While there, Mathias met Gregory who had been installed by Pope Benedict I as one of the seven deacons of Rome. Seeing Brother Mathias in his monastic attire, Gregory introduced himself to him as a former monk from the Abbey of St. Andrews. During their meeting, Mathias shared with Gregory the nature of his visit, which led to Gregory's request to hear the story. After hearing the story of the Miracle Table, Gregory venerated it and asked if Mathias could stay with the table until the next Pope was chosen, as he was certain that the new Pontiff would also want to hear the story and to venerate the blessing. So Mathias and the table stayed in Rome for seven months until a new Pope was selected. The finally chosen Pope was Gregory himself. Pope Gregory requested that the table remain with him in Rome, along with Mathias as its caretaker. During its time in Rome, the table was made the altar of the Pope's personal chapel.

"In the year 594, Pope Gregory visited Monte Cassino and returned the table and its bearer to its former walls. Over the next three hundred years, the table remained at the abbey of Monte Cassino. During this entire period of time, a male member of the larger Velius family would take their vows and would enter the Order of Benedict at Monte Cassino. Each Brother Velius served at the monastery as the table's caretaker.

"In the year 801, the house of Velius was down to one direct male descendant of Cornelius. A pious man, Jason Velius, fell in love and married. Since marriage prevented him from becoming a monk in the order of Benedict, Jason retrieved the blessing from Monte Cassino once he became the official bearer of the table. Fluent in the story and possessing an absolute reverence for the table, Jason and his wife took great care of it and promulgated its story in the town of Naples where they had settled. In the year 850, the city of Naples was sacked by the Saracens from Arabia. Jason's children bravely rescued their parents and the table during the devastating raid and ended up settling in the coastal city of Fiumicino just east of Rome.

"Upon the death of Jason, his eldest son, Stephen, became the table bearer. Like their father, Stephen and his two brothers and two sisters held the blessing in sacred regard. Collectively they all knew the story word for word and openly told it to all interested parties. Word of the table spread again to Rome and many people came to see it. Some were said to have been healed through their faith in it and in its ultimate creator. In 865, Stephen and his family were visited by Fr. Pasquale, who was pastor of St. Cornelius Church in Rome. Being in the service of the patron whose church bore a similar name, Fr. Pasquale came to hear the story directly and to see the table for himself. Upon hearing the story and touching the blessing, Fr. Pasquale's heart was convinced that the patron of his church was indeed the very same Centurion who had served as the table's first bearer. Fr. Pasquale asked Stephen and his family if the table could be brought to St. Cornelius and once there, be consecrated by the Bishop and utilized for a period of time as its altar. The family agreed. So it was that Stephen, along with his wife and children, moved to Rome to serve as the table's caretaker as well as the caretaker of the St. Cornelius church.

"The table became the altar at St. Cornelius where many people came to reverence it and to hear its story. What once had intended to be a short visit by the table to the congregation of St. Cornelius, turned out to be a stay of nearly five hundred years. During this time, a Velius was always there by the table's side, caring for it, and sharing its story with anyone interested in listening to it.

"Following the death of Pope Benedict XI in the year 1304, a contested and long lasting conclave to elect a new Pontiff took place. Finally, in June of the following year, the Archbishop of Bordeaux, Cardinal Raymond Bertrand de Guoth, was elected and became Pope Clement V. During the conclave, the Archbishop de Guoth visited the Church of St. Cornelius where he developed a special devotion to the saint and the table whose protector he had become.

"When Pope Clement V moved the Papacy to Avignon France, he requested that the table and its bearer accompany him. So it was that Anthony Velius, along with his wife and seven children, brought the table to France where Clement V utilized it as the altar in his personal chapel.

"The table remained with each Pope whose reign took place in

France. When the Papacy returned to Rome in 1370, the table, seemingly forgotten about by papal officials, remained in France along with the current table bearer, Marcus Velius and his family.

"After the Papal Palace moved from Avignon, the people of the area remained upset for a long period of time. They had thought that the Papal Seat would remain in their town and in their country of France for all time. Because he was viewed as part of the Papal entourage, which the townspeople felt had rejected them, Marcus Velius and his family were shunned by many of the locals. So it was that Marcus and his family, including three brothers, two sisters, along with his wife and five children, all moved to the village of Lyon where the men were promised carpentry jobs by a loyal acquaintance.

"When Marcus passed away in 1399, his son Denis took on the role of table caretaker. He, along with his brothers and his remaining uncles and aunts, all knew the story word for word, and remained willing to tell it to all who had a desire to listen.

"In the year 1409, the town of Ars, twenty miles north of Lyon, was burned nearly to the ground by the troops of Viry."

Michael began to, once again, feel the charge of welcome curiosity surge through his body as he heard Anthony cite the name of the town Ars. As far as he knew, Ars, France was famous for one thing and one thing only, and that was being the town where one of his most favorite saints had served as pastor. While St. John Vianney's appearance in Ars was not until the eighteen hundreds, Michael began to focus even more intently on each word Anthony spoke, hoping that the table had indeed intersected with the Cure of Ars.

"When stability returned to Ars, a call for skilled carpenters was sent out to the surrounding areas. Denis and two of his brothers answered the call and did well financially in helping to rebuild the city. In 1411, Denis' family, along with the families of his two brothers, all moved to Ars where they ran both a carpentry and blacksmith shop. During the next four hundred years the table and its Velius caretakers remained in Ars. While the table's fame waned from the heights of its previous devotions, within the small town of Ars it remained highly revered and was thought to be responsible for several miracles.

"During the French Revolution, the Catholic Church once again faced persecution. Priests said Masses in secret at the risk of being killed. During this time, the Velius family offered their barn as a place to hold Mass. Once again, the table was called upon to serve as a holy altar of the Church.

"Due to the success of Napoleon Bonaparte, the rights of the Church to worship openly were once again restored in France in the year 1802. The table bearer at the time was Francis Velius. Once the Mass was allowed to be celebrated again in the Church, he and two of his brothers took charge of restoring the church in Ars, which had become severely neglected during the time of the revolution. Francis' other two brothers, along with their aging father and their families, left to join distant relatives in the United States in the colony of Maryland, who had sold them in a series of letters on the beauty and freedom of the emerging country.

"In 1818, the church of Ars received a new pastor, Fr. John Vianney."

In hearing those words, Michael began to slowly and reverently sweep his hand across the table remnant. As though he were rubbing the shoulder of a friend, he patted the table hoping to let it know the deep love and admiration he had for it. He smiled and shook his head, not in disbelief, but in awe that St. John Vianney, one of his patron saints, had been added to the long line of holy men and women who were a part of the table's story.

"After only a few days in town, Fr. Vianney heard from several of the townspeople about the miracle table the Velius family took care of. Shortly after hearing multiple reports on the table, Fr. Vianney paid a visit to Francis' home. After seeing the table and touching it himself, he was asked by Francis if he would like to hear its story. Before saying yes, Fr. Vianney asked if the story had any mention about a young girl holding a ship's anchor and two arrows in her right hand and a white lily in her left. All the Velius family members present, all knowing the story word for word, were in shock by the Father's reference to the girl. Francis asked him how it was that he knew about the girl who had shown his ancestors the way to the cave and to the table which had been hidden away so many years ago. Fr. Vianney shared with them that the same girl, who he said was the martyr St. Philomena, but to whom he referred more often as the Wonder Worker, had appeared in a dream to him telling him to seek out the table. With that, Francis told Fr. Vianney the story of the table."

Anthony once again took a moment to place his hand upon the remnant. Michael continued to be inspired by the total devotion Anthony had for the table and its story.

Sufficiently recharged, Anthony continued. "About a year after meeting Francis and his family, Fr. Vianney called Francis to the rectory where he shared with him his ever increasing devotion to St. Philomena. He told him of several cures that had occurred due to her intersession. The most spectacular of which was the healing of Pauline Jaricot in Mugnano. This woman experienced excruciating pains throughout her body and her condition caused her heart to beat at such a rapid rate that every physician she had seen gave her no chance to live. Her illness caused her to be in a state of constant exhaustion. Visiting the Shrine of St. Philomena at Mugnano, on the very feast day of the saint, Pauline Jaricot was completely healed. Fr. Vianney went on to tell Francis that Pauline had recently given him a relic of the saint to which they both shared a special devotion. He asked Francis for two things: the first was to build a side chapel to the church which would become a shrine to St. Philomena; the second was the request to have the sacred relic given to him by Ms. Jaricot displayed on the miracle table in the chapel. Francis said yes to both of Fr. Vianney's requests. There the table, bearing the relic, candles, and a statue of the Wonder Worker, stayed for the next seventy years, well beyond the death of Fr. Vianney.

"Francis died one year after the death of his dear friend and pastor,

Fr. John Vianney, in the year of 1860. His son Joseph assumed the job as table bearer and cared for the table during its time in the Church of Ars, telling all who were interested its story.

"From the time of Francis' death all the way through to the early 1890s, the Velius family received letter after letter from their family in America telling them of the wonders of the land and the amazing opportunities that awaited all who were willing to work hard. As the economic prospects in Ars steadily declined, Giorgio Velius, the son of Joseph who had become the table bearer after the death of his father, agreed, along with the other members of the larger Velius family, that the time had come for them to join their family in America.

"Giorgio and the other Velius family members arrived in New York harbor in 1893. They were processed with countless other immigrants at the recently opened Ellis Island. Shortly after receiving the papers that allowed them entry into America, Giorgio and his relatives noticed an error in the spelling of their last name. When they inquired about it, an overworked official offered them two options: accept the new name or take the next boat back to Europe. So it was, from that day forward, the sur name of the table bearer became Velario.

"Giorgio and the other Velarios who had just come to America moved to Baltimore to be near the relatives who had been pleading with them to come to the United States for so many years. When the larger family had finally been reunited, they celebrated with a feast that was served atop the table everyone in the family was deeply devoted to. At the end of the meal, Giorgio recited word for word the story of the blessing. Those who knew the story joyfully joined in forming a chorus of the blessed history.

"Giorgio quickly found a job as a tradesman where he specialized as a welder. He and his brother Peter worked together building the Bromo Tower, where Peter tragically lost his life in a horrific construction accident. To honor his brother, Giorgio named his first-born son after him.

"Giorgio and his family lived near the Baltimore Cathedral and made it their parish. The family invited the pastor, Fr. William Fletcher, to dinner one evening where they introduced him to the blessing and to its story. Fr. Fletcher was skeptical until his hand came to rest on the table. Upon setting his hand on the miracle table of Jacob, his heart became convinced of its authenticity. Fr. Fletcher began speaking openly about the table and sent people to the Velario house to see the table and to hear its story from the family. Since Giorgio worked during the day, his wife, Michele, who had come to know the blessing word for word, would tell the story to those who visited while Giorgio was at work.

"In 1906, the Basilica celebrated the one hundredth anniversary of the laying of its cornerstone by Archbishop John Carroll. For this celebration, Fr. Fletcher asked Giorgio if the table could be used as the credence table for the special anniversary Mass. Giorgio agreed and was very happy to see the sacred vessels of the Mass being placed upon it. He was also honored to have been asked by Father to wear a server's cassock and surplice and to stand next to the table during the entire Mass.

"In 1921, following an evening where he had told the story to a group of people who had gathered at his house, Giorgio was found dead the next morning with his hands and head resting peacefully on the table. His son Peter became the next table bearer and, like his father and generations of fathers before him, told the story to anyone who would listen and invited a great many people to venerate its blessing.

"In 1929 Peter Velario received a visit from a Fr. Floria, an Italian priest from the famous Monte Cassino monastery outside of Rome. Fr. Floria informed him that old writings regarding the table had been recently found in the monastery and that, after extensive research and investigation, they determined that Peter was the current keeper of the blessing. Upon Fr. Floria's request, Peter showed him the table. After both were seated in chairs next to it, Peter shared with the priest the entire story. Fr. Floria was greatly moved after seeing and hearing the story, which had only been alluded to in the writings at the monastery. He then requested that Peter and the table accompany him back to the monastery since it would add so much to the celebration planned for the fourteen hundredth anniversary of the famed abbey, which was to be held in just a few months. Peter felt privileged to once again serve in the true table bearer's capacity of his ancestors. Peter was free to go without anything holding him back. He was never married, nor did he have any children. Besides him, there was only one distant cousin left in the Velario family tree. And, he had only met him once when he was a young boy.

"Once at Monte Cassino, the table was prominently displayed, along with other famed artifacts from the history of the abbey, in the monastery's famed Modelli Gallery. Abbott Georgio Diamare allowed Peter to share the story of the Miracle Table with visitors two times a day during the monastery's fourteen hundredth anniversary year. The year was 1930.

"Like many of his ancestors before him, Peter found that the monastic life suited him well. In 1934, he took his vows and became a Benedictine monk there at the abbey of Monte Cassino.

"With the outbreak of World War II, the German army took great interest in the strategic location of the monastery. While they never occupied it, they amassed a great number of troops to guard all routes leading to it in order to keep the Allies from taking it. Believing that the Nazis had occupied and taken control of the monastery, in 1944 the Allied Forces sought to liberate it from Hitler's grasp. As a result, a total of four consecutive and brutal battles were fought at Monte Cassino.

"During the battle, the great monastery succumbed to harsh bombings and other vicious munitions. Entire walls, buildings, and priceless artifacts were destroyed. While many of the monks escaped in between the battles, twenty stayed to protect its belongings and its sacredness. Peter, refusing to abandon the table his family had protected for centuries, was one of only six monks who stayed at the monastery and who survived its devastation. The table, however, was largely destroyed with the exception of the fragment that remains to this day.

"After the battle, Peter took the remainder of the table and returned to America. He had come to realize in those moments of the battle, where death had been so near, the absolute importance of preserving the blessing and its story. Once in America, the now fifty-year-old Peter hired an investigator to locate his distant cousin and the only remaining Velario. After six months, the investigator found that his cousin had died during World War II, but had two sons. One of two brothers, Arthur Velario, was living in a small northern suburb of Chicago called Round Lake. The investigator also learned that Arthur's brother, Frank Velario, had been killed in a hunting accident two years earlier.

"Peter met with Arthur and, upon broaching the topic of the table, noticed Arthur's face light up at its mention. Arthur shared with his distant cousin about hearing stories of the table being told when he was young by older relatives, but how he never knew the complete story or that it was something other than a fable. With that, Peter showed Arthur the blessing. After holding it in his hands and hearing the complete story by Peter, Arthur was moved to tears. From that moment on, his life changed as he prepared himself to become the next caretaker in a long line of table bearers. Arthur was eighteen at the time.

"Peter spent the next ten years living close to Arthur as he grew into manhood and married. During this time, the story of the table was successfully transferred to Arthur. When Peter turned sixty, he returned to the restored Monte Cassino and to the vocation he deeply missed. With that, Arthur became the table bearer.

"After Peter returned to the abbey, Arthur's first child, Anthony, was born. Two years later, he and his wife had a second son they named George. When his children became old enough, Arthur in turn taught both of them the legacy and story of the blessing. Shortly after the brothers moved to Phoenix, Arthur passed the blessing to Anthony due to his advancing age and fading health. While Anthony had become the remnant's official caretaker, he and George often recited the story together. Both men came from modest backgrounds and any money they had saved was lost in the market crash of the 1980s.

"Anthony's wife, Cia, became pregnant. However, the happiness that had surrounded this miracle of life was short lived. She went into labor prematurely and, during the delivery, Cia's hemorrhaging could not be controlled. She—"

As Anthony told this part of the story, he paused. Michael understood the difficulty in saying the words. Anthony once again reached out to touch the table. This time Michael thought the touch was needed for the comfort of the storyteller.

Composing himself, Anthony continued, "She passed away. The baby was born so early that he was not expected to live since his lungs were not fully developed. While he was deeply saddened by the loss of his wife, Anthony Sr.'s attention moved quickly to his son who Cia had previously insisted on naming Anthony Jr. Anthony Sr. was told by the doctors that his baby had very little chance of surviving. Not wanting to leave the side of his beautiful baby son—"

Once again Anthony paused. After composing himself he continued, "...but feeling certain he could be saved, he left the room and called his brother George and asked him to bring the table to the hospital as quickly as he could. Once the remnant arrived, Anthony Sr. placed it on top of the incubator, which housed his tiny and dying infant son. Placing his hand on top of the blessing, Anthony Sr. began to pray to Jesus to spare his son. After an hour, doctors came in and were upset that a piece of wood had been placed on top of the hospital's expensive equipment. While upset, out of respect for the man who had just lost his wife and was about to lose his child, they asked Anthony Sr. in a kindly manner to remove the wood from the incubator so they could check the child. After checking the baby, the doctors were stunned. The very premature baby who could not and should not be able to breathe on its own, now was. The doctors in attendance had no explanation. But Anthony Sr. and his brother, George, did."

Anthony once again paused. Michael saw him bite down on his bottom lip. Taking in a deep breath, he continued, "Anthony Sr. died less than a year later as a result of a car accident. His brother, George, took in Anthony Jr. and became the table's next caretaker."

With that, Anthony stopped talking. At first, Michael thought he was taking another needed break due to the personal sadness the last line may have delivered. Then it dawned on him that that was where the story ended for Anthony; it was all that he was told and he hadn't yet found his voice and ability to add to it.

"That is all there is, Michael. Uncle George said I would know who to tell the story to. My heart told me it was you whom I should tell. Was my heart right, Michael?"

Michael tried to process the weightiness of those simple words. Anthony had no idea how right he was in choosing him to tell the story to. The table that heals, the blessing that rescues, found one of the world's neediest and delivered. Finally, the pain he had carried with him since Debbie's death had found a release. Sure, he would continue to miss her, miss her badly, but somehow he knew that the weight of the loss could be held up, could be supported by a blessing, a blessing named Anthony and the piece of wood he bore.

Looking over at Anthony, Michael lifted the remnant of life from his lap and placed it on the couch between him and his younger friend. As he placed his hand palm up on it, he motioned with a nod of his head for Anthony to take his hand.

As their hands joined on top of the table, Michael squeezed tightly and answered Anthony's question, "Yes, Anthony, I believe you told the right person the story. I needed to hear it, I needed to touch it and to be touched by it. It might sound strange to you, but because of you, because of the story, my life has changed. I felt lost and life's meaning seemed to have vanished. Now all that has changed. I thought that I had come to help you when in reality, it was you who came to help me. This is so, so difficult to explain."

As Michael tried to find the right words, Anthony began to laugh. Through his laughter he looked at Michael and said, "It's not hard to understand at all, Michael! It's so simple but people make it so hard to know. They think too much about things that don't need any thinking at all. No thoughts, just receive, receive everything. This is what the blessing is. It's not a story. It's not a table. It's a message; a simple message of everything."

Michael did his best to take in what Anthony was saying. While he didn't understand the words Anthony used, the peace and love he experienced while listening to the story seemed to echo the transcendent meaning of Anthony's words.

And just like the start of an avalanche, it suddenly came to Michael what the message was, what the simple message of everything could only be. He had heard the words before. He remembered Debbie saying them at, of all places, their local IHOP. He heard them again, whispered to him from heaven, during Debbie's funeral. And he had heard them no more than an hour ago from Anthony. But the deeper meaning and authentic application of these words didn't register with him until that very moment. With that realization, Michael smiled and began to laugh and cry at the very same time. Anthony laughed with him. Michael was certain that Anthony knew that he suddenly understood what the simple message of everything was.

Anthony took the initiative and squeezed Michael's hand tightly. Looking at him with a huge smile, two very uncommon things for Anthony, he affirmed his friend by saying, "That's right, Michael, love has come."

83617375R00214

Made in the USA
Columbia, SC
11 December 2017